ANCIENT DREAMS

JP ROTH

Black Rose Writing | Texas

©2020 by JP Roth
All rights reserved. No part of this book may be reproduced, stored in a retrieval system or transmitted in any form or by any means without the prior written permission of the publishers, except by a reviewer who may quote brief passages in a review to be printed in a newspaper, magazine or journal.

The author grants the final approval for this literary material.

First printing

This is a work of fiction. Names, characters, businesses, places, events, and incidents are either the products of the author's imagination or used in a fictitious manner. Any resemblance to actual persons, living or dead, or actual events is purely coincidental.

ISBN: 978-1-68433-472-8
PUBLISHED BY BLACK ROSE WRITING
www.blackrosewriting.com

Printed in the United States of America
Suggested Retail Price (SRP) $19.95

Ancient Dreams is printed in Baskerville

*As a planet-friendly publisher, Black Rose Writing does its best to eliminate unnecessary waste to reduce paper usage and energy costs, while never compromising the reading experience. As a result, the final word count vs. page count may not meet common expectations.

I dedicate this book to my brother Martin—
because I promised all this—
so long ago.

Special thanks to my incredible sister Clare, without whom, none of this would be possible!

Special thanks to my amazing husband Eric, for attending to reality, while I'm lost in all my worlds.

My most heartfelt thanks to my agent, Stephanie Hansen, for believing and dreaming with me.

Ancient Dreams

Πρόλογος
I have always hoped for luminous beauty, but ever feared the dark.
My story begins with a once upon a time—beings lived who could control the elements, immortality, and time. We called them gods and gave them our worship. They played us like toys, took our lives and sabotaged our love. Now, the gods are myths, legends of majesty that have no place in our civilized, modern world. I believed this until I opened a book and tumbled into a dream.
This dream takes me to another life, to a forgotten time in a bloody age. I dream of limitless power and revolving time—I dream a death and love that was mine.
My name is Cara Wynter, this is my story…

PROLOGUE

The flickering lights of a hundred torches bathe the room in a moving, golden hue. I jerk my arms. The pain in my wrists is sharp. Confusing. Deep in my dawning consciousness I realize chain manacles lock my wrists above my head. My breath is coming hard and fast, it echoes in a distant part of my mind. Around me, men in black robes sing or chant—in the dreams I am never sure. Their voices run together, merging into a single terrifying sound. Faces of death stare out at me from under black cowls, men wearing dark holes for eyes and skin peeling off their ancient cheeks in large chunks. They sing and their blackened lips pull back, revealing yellowed teeth, and rotted gums. The cloying air reeks of decay and death.

Abruptly, the chanting stops. To my right, I see the shadow of a blade poised eerily over my silhouette.

I struggle. Violent enough to tear the soft skin on my wrist. Still, I fight until the golden cuffs are slick, and coated in my blood. The echo of my scream bounces through the room, taunting me. Death is close. I can taste its cold, metallic tang on my tongue. Now, she is in front of me; her face swimming in and out of focus. She is beautiful beyond description. All of her is gold, save the lush red lips and violet, flashing eyes.

The dead creatures fall silent. The golden goddess lifts her head. Her voice—melodic as a sparrow's song—rises in an echoing chant.

"Asha avda, meshia envier
Karat me mortando,
Teresa dianda miyha Leisha encada."

I hear a voice in my mind. Thirteen days, it whispers.

The blade falls. It slices through my skin. I hear my ribs crack a second before it pierces my heart.

I scream his name.

I feel his hands on my body. He pulls me to his chest. "Don't leave me," he whispers. "I need you. Please don't leave me."

I have no choice, I want to say, but the blood filling my lungs cuts off my hopeless words. I gasp helplessly at my last taste of air. The world goes black as I die.

CHAPTER 1

WHAT YOU SEE HARDLY EVER TURNS OUT TO BE WHAT YOU GET.

It was crap is what it was. Every night for the last twelve, it was the same damn thing and I could not handle it anymore. The main reason recurring dreams suck is because after a while they become your reality. Then, the thing that used to pose as reality is reduced to nothing more than a collection of terrifying minutes, rapidly disappearing, counting down to the night. I planned to ignore that ticking clock to the best of my ability—I was going to get wasted.

Giant droplets of rain covered my car in a net of shimmering pearls. I put my Beamer in park and quieted the engine, cutting Taylor Swift off mid-verse. Most of the time I sat in the car and let her finish, but tonight even that modern goddess was doing nothing to lift my mood. Outside the wind bent the pines. A storm brewed on Mount Baker and soon it would wrap us in its fury. I opened the door and stepped out into a soft rain, painted with neon lights. *Larry's* sign flickered over my head, I looked up and I noticed the bulb in the *L* had died. I figured it would stay dead. He didn't need the sign, you either knew where this bar was or you didn't.

I pulled on a pair of soft leather gloves, making sure my sleeves covered my wrists. I took a breath for my nerves and stepped inside. The soul of this place mirrors its patrons. It smelled like sweaty flesh and raw leather, which fit quite well with the sticky linoleum floors, overpopulated fly paper, and fat couches full of their mysterious stains. Larry had his radio tuned to my favorite station and Taylor was just finishing her last, beautiful note of *Lover*.

I walked to the bar, hung my purse on the brass hook beneath it and took a seat. My twin sister, Lily and I came here all the time in high school. We would dress up as bikers, to match the Harleys parked outside, mess our hair, and wear leather jackets covered with patches that said stuff like: 'Reserved Parking In Rear', or 'Breaking Skulls 'Till We Die'. We'd strut in, flash our fake IDs, and choose a corner booth far away from everyone else, then drink and laugh until we could no longer stand.

No one cared at Larry's. That is why I liked it here, it is why I came—why we all did. In the dim lighting and copious cigar smoke I can be anyone. Here, I am not Cara Wynter—abandoned daughter and misfit extraordinaire. Here, I can blend into the swirls of smoke, and make up stories about the girl I wished I was. In the open spaces of my mind I can live in a sunny, kinder world where I was prom queen and the college sweetheart of a guy who likes the way my hair looks by candlelight. Perhaps I can be an actress with no boyfriend and a life that dazzles. Or, just an emotional girl who likes photography, sock dolls with buttons for eyes, and this is where I come to water my darker thoughts. Anything save the truth—that I am a strange, lonely girl, vividly dreaming her own death.

I have Lily, the best sister and friend a girl could ask for. We are, however, polar opposites. Sometimes that makes the loneliness worse.

Larry noticed me and waved. Dim bar lights bounded off his balding head, only to get tangled in his bushy beard and make it the color of Autumn. He wore a leather jacket that had cutoff sleeves. The bandana around his neck had seen better days, but his white t-shirt was spotless. I smiled and waved back. He sauntered over, hitching up his pants along the way.

"Cara, you're half drowned, can I get you something?"

"Hi, Larry. Whiskey, please." I shook the rain from my hair and took off my coat.

"Glad you stopped by Cara. Was meaning to drive over to the manor in the morning. Need a favor."

My stomach lurched. Inwardly I struggled to keep the smile on my lips. He took a step back, putting his hand up. "Nothing like last time I promise." He shook his big head. "No. Nothing like that at all."

"Whatever you need," I said. "You know that."

"My Ma died a few days ago, did you know?"

I nodded. "I'm so sorry Larry."

"Na, old gal wanted to go years ago. It was us that kept her here. Anyway…" He shoved his hand in his front pocket, and rooted around until he found what he was searching for, then struggled to pull his hand free. Larry's fist hovered over the bar top before it opened, and he set the item in front of me. "Now, I know you don't like to do this doll, and you can tell me to go straight to hell if you need to—"

"I would never tell you to do that." My hands made fists in my lap. "What do you have for me?"

"This was with some of her things. I thought of selling it, but not if it's an heirloom or keepsake. Then I would keep it, you know—like in memory of the old dear."

"I understand." Having grown up surrounded by tokens of memory, I did. Reading it, however, was the last thing in the world I wanted to do, tonight of all nights. It exhausted me. My soul already felt like it lay shredded at my feet. I feared the pain. I would do it, however, because Larry needed it, and because it was what I did. He had not lied, it was *nothing* like last time. Last time there had been sirens and guns, police, weeping parents, a missing poster and a little girl's shirt.

I pulled off one of my soft, leather gloves. Sighing, I closed my hand over the locket. Heat from Larry's touch still lingered. I tried not to move as the vibrations shot through my fingers and up my arm like tiny bolts of lightning. I did not press on the little latch that would make the locket spring open. Still, I knew a picture rested inside. Painted on a paper so old that it curled at the edges was a little girl with bouncy curls and sea-blue eyes.

A rush of air splashed my face, my gasp echoed in the distance. Then it started. Like colorful projections against a black screen, my visions flashed in and out of focus. Shady as a déjà vu, or the vivid recollection of a dream, I saw a woman in a coral colored dress holding a little girl who had perfect blonde ringlets falling to her shoulders. A shadow passed over the glowing sun. It shivered into focus, and I saw a man with auburn eyes lean down to kiss the woman's cheek.

The scene evaporated.

In that first moment I am always lost. Alone and trapped in the darkness. I took a deep breath and listened to it break, then the screaming started. In front of me a pentagram with a candle burning at each of its points spun like a ferris wheel. A gunshot cracked the silence, and another harrowing scream followed. The man came back into focus, but his demeanor had changed. The eyes—unblinking and whitewashed—bulged like his face, both swollen and bloated in death. In tufts of evaporating steam the image dissolved, and I saw a fresh grave. The woman knelt beside it, her dress now raven black. In one hand she held a bundle of flowers, and in the other, the small, pudgy hand of her daughter. The child reached out and placed a rose on the grave.

I dropped the locket and opened my eyes. The look I saw on Larry's face was one I had seen many times. A look of equal parts hope and dread. I always wanted to tell them that they did not need to dread. I loved them…so I kept the horror to myself.

"It belonged to your great grandmother. Or great, great? I can't say for sure. I saw the pentagram," I said that last part for myself. If it involved Bellingham or Fairhaven, the pentagram always appeared. "The miniature inside is your grandmother, right? It feels at least a hundred years old. She was a beautiful little girl."

"Yes, she was," Larry whispered, stunned but pleased. "I won't ask you how you know about the picture inside. Thank you Cara, you're an angel."

I tucked my hair behind my ears and averted my eyes. Their thanks always brought out my shy side. "I did nothing Larry."

"You did, and a kind soul you are. I don't know much, but…" he paused and scratched at his chin. "I know that everything costs something. I'm thanking you for the price you pay." He shoved the locket back into his pocket. "I'll hang onto it for now."

"You should. It was special."

"Like you," said Larry. I smiled and continued blushing a rather hot shade. "A treasure," he continued. "Yep, some folks may say different, to the rest of us, that is what you Wynter women are—treasures. Can't remember a time when people didn't go on up to that big manor house of yours for one thing or another. They didn't always leave smiling, but you can just bet their problems were solved. Yep. You could be damn sure of that." He took a bottle of whiskey from the rack on the wall behind him and poured me two fingers. "Where's Lily?"

"Home," I said, and my voice sounded sad. *In the library or up in the attic buried under a pile of books, trying and failing to figure out what is wrong with me.* The thought added to my misery. I took a sip of the Whiskey.

"How long have you been able to do that?" asked Larry after a moment of silence. "Touch things I mean and know what they're about?"

"I don't know," I said, suddenly finding a tiny divot in the bar interesting. "Always, I guess. When I was little, it was off and on, it got stronger after Hanna disappeared. Lily says I have super powers, but Lily is a warrior for the bright side."

"She's right. It's a gift and you'll do real good with it one day. Hell, you have already! Without you my niece would be dead. It's a blessing."

"It's a curse," I shrugged. "Sometimes the good is worth it," I admitted.

Larry smiled, his cheeks flushed the color of his beard. "You're so much like your aunt Hanna, same wild flames for hair, and eyes so green they look like jewels. She didn't want her gift either, hard to see those terrible things and not be able to do a thing to change it. She would come in here, back in the day, a little thing, just like you. Would sit on that same stool you're sitting on now with her dark thoughts, chugging her—"

"Cheap Vodka," I finished, and we both laughed.

"Damn!" he said. "But she could clear a room back then! Not a body in town wasn't afraid of all that red and black hair, the way it seemed to move around her on its own—and those eyes! Enough to knock a man clear off his feet. She was really something. Pretty as a picture."

"A scary picture," I said. Hanna was the last person I wanted in my head. She was a giant abandoner, and some things are better left in the past.

"Scary to some, an angel to others," said Larry. "I know she ain't dead," he continued. "No sir, not her, a woman like that don't die. Not in these parts anyway." He dropped his voice to a whisper. "It's the earth up here. It keeps em' alive. That big manor you call home, it keeps them alive too." He gave me a wink. "Yep, treasures, all of you. I'm gonna go make my rounds, I'll come check on you in a spell."

Larry left me to my solitude. I picked up my glass and sighed. Golden liquid swished from side to side and I stared into its depths. *Hanna,* my mind said. I remembered everything like it happened yesterday…

It had been a dark night, the ominous kind that could not be shaken from Wynter Manor no matter how many lights we flicked on. Lily had fallen asleep in the library clutching a book. I sat on the front porch, watching the seething dance of rain clouds over Fairhaven. Hanna walked down the porch steps, settled her dress and sat beside me.

I remember her clothes in vivid detail. Knee-length, red rubber boots, and a long empire-waist coat that hung from her small shoulders like a cape. She smelled the same as always, lilacs and rain. The wind lashed her wild hair about her face, and the aqua in her eyes flashed when she told me in a quiet voice that she was going for a walk.

I had not thought it strange. She always walked in the forest when it was storming. I never imagined that my childish, dismissive goodbye would be my last.

She leaned down and kissed the space above my forehead. Her fingers chilled the air like icicles. "Don't wait up, Cara. I'll be back when you need me." I remember the red rubber boots, and the way the wet stones in our driveway crunched under her feet as she left. She never walked through our door again. The cops combed the forests for days and found no trace of her. Lily and I had not imagined they would. Popular consensus was that she drowned in the Puget Sound—they even put it in the paper that way: *"Drowned in the Sound."*

The next morning I had a seizure and spent a week in the hospital. 'Nervous breakdown', the psychiatrist called it. I did not leave the manor for a month. Better to hide in the comforting darkness of my bedroom, than face the unending torment of the outside world.

Aunt Jane—our second aunt, twice removed—convinced Lily I could not keep skipping school. She is an older woman with silvery white hair, a sharp disposition, and an eternal supply of potion bottles hanging around her belted waist. It was not in me to disobey her, so I made myself adhere to the mandatory attendance and learned to avoid people. I would slink from class to class, arriving first so I could find a corner to hold my head in my hands, zone out to the best of my ability, and pretend I was dead. My condition worsened until any physical contact became impossible for me. In the beginning it was just a sense, when I hit my teens, I only needed to close my eyes and touch a thing to know where it had been, and to whom it belonged. The pain had been surprising, the visions even worse.

I went to take another sip of whiskey. Realizing my glass was empty, I set it down and folded my hands in my lap.

Lily is the only person I have touched in the last ten years. Her touch does not give me pain, quite the opposite, she is my ballast against the storm. Her explanation for my strange flaws is that we are descendants of great witches. This, however, is her explanation for everything. Our ancestry is her obsession, and she often tells me I should be proud to be the heiress of such powerful genes.

I want to be proud, but all I have to do is remember those red, rubber boots disappearing into the dark folds of a Washington storm, and I am never sure if I should be proud or scared out of my mind. Sometimes, in my quiet moments, it crosses my mind—the witch thing—as it is pretty much the only logical explanation for the literal ghosts in my closet. When we were children Hanna would tell us we had magic eyes. Eyes which could see the shadow creatures who only breathed at night. This sounded mysterious and exciting to Lily. I would always hide under my covers on the full moon when the wind would howl at the windows like an invisible intruder, and my dead aunts would wake up. Singing as they ran down the long oak hall to the kitchen, laughing and talking until the sun came up, then they would fade back into silent shadows…watching…waiting—for what, I can not say. Lily thought it was cool. To me, their cold hands and opaque eyes inspired only terror.

So did the unusual books previously cluttering our house, covered in strange markings and filled with stories that could not possibly be true.

On my seventeenth birthday I stuffed all those books into four iron trunks, sitting in the attic, empty for years. I combed my home for items normal people would not find in theirs. The result: two black garbage bags stuffed to the brim with what Hanna used to call 'wicca shit'.

Feeling the whole time like I was performing a type of cleansing ceremony, I dragged it all up to our attic, chucked it in the idle trunks, and locked the door on my way out. I did it because I wanted a life. I wanted a normal easy existence void of ghosts and their stories. For a while the house was still. There was no more screaming laughter in the moonlight, or creepy encounters with the dead. Yet, occasionally when my side of the world sleeps, and the haunting sounds of night drench the air—I feel them. I have begun to think it is the house that calls to them. It was not all bad, of course. There were beautiful things in my life, like the taste of Fairhaven air before the sun has touched morning, the wonderful sound of Lily laughing, or getting chills from a good Stephen King. Recently, though, the beauty of those things has begun to fade, recently there has only been the dreams.

■   ■   ■

A man sat down on the bar stool beside me, his youth clear in the smattering of pimples on his forehead, patchy beard and long, lanky arms. *Like a perfect scarecrow.* My mind whispered. I smiled. He saw the smile and mistook it. "Whatcha drinkin'?"

"Whisky," I said, trying to sound kind—desperate to be left alone.

"Can I get'cha another?"

This time my smile was for him. "I'm alright for now, I have an in with the owner."

"My name's Jake Summerton," he said, and held out his hand. A network of scars criss crossed his knuckles and dirt, oil or a mix of both, blackened the short nails. I waved.

"Cara Wynter," I said.

He dropped his hand and rocked back on his heels. "So Cara. About that drink?" The persistence in his voice made my stomach tighten. "I'm alright." My phone rang. Lily's face flashed on the screen. During my audible sigh of relief, I sent up a silent prayer of thanks. "I'm sorry, need to take this," I said.

My gloved hand reached for my purse beneath the bar, I stood up, turning my back to him. He caught my bare, right hand. His naked fingers closed hard around my own. "Hey, don't be like—"

I screamed. Pain, vivid and piercing, sliced through me. My left hand thrashed out, knocking my glass off the bar. It fell slow as a feather and time stood still around me. My second scream washed over the sharp sound of my shattering glass. He moved his fingers up my arm, and I fought for consciousness.

"You can't! Let…let go…" The voice—my voice—came out weak, a pitiful parody. I lived in a single moment of pure pain, like a thousand red-hot daggers stung my bleeding eye sockets, and peeled flesh from my bones.

"What the—?" Larry and Brett, the bouncer, arrived seconds before I crashed to my knees. The man let go of my arm and threw up his dirty hands in a sign of surrender.

"What? Man, I didn't do nothin'. That girl's a freak!" he said.

"Get out!" said Brett. I did not understand the boy's garbled response, I was too busy gulping for air.

"Cara? You good?" Larry stood over me, the scar-like furrow in his brow running up and over his balding head.

I did something with my chin that passed as a nod. Remnants of the boy's fingerprints lingered like a brand on my arm, leaving pins and needles running rampant over my skin. "I'm…it's…it's okay, I'm alright." I could tell Larry wanted to reach down and help me to my feet, instead he held back, shifting his weight from side to side and wringing his hands. Brett did the same.

"Thank you guys," I said, still stumbling over each word. "I'm alright now. A bad shock, that's all. I'm fine."

An errant gust of wind from the cracked window above the bar sent a shiver through me. I stood up and remembered my phone still clutched in a white-knuckled grip. Lily's pretty face filled the screen. It was time to leave. So much for getting wasted. All I could do was hope the events of this night would leave me too exhausted to dream. I slung my purse over my shoulder and put my glove back on, then I reached for my wallet, took out a ten and placed it on the bar. "Thanks for the drink Larry," I said. "Say hi to Alice for me, and Jerry, he started middle school right?"

"Uh huh, straight-A student, the missus is so proud. Also," Larry took the ten off the bar and handed it back. "You helped me and I bought you a drink to say thanks, simple as that."

"I would accept it if I had helped."

"If I say you did, you did."

I put the ten back on the bar and blew him a kiss. "Goodnight Larry." He caught the kiss mid-air and slapped it on his check. I turned and walked away. A picture by the door caught my attention, a Polaroid of Lily and I titled 'Good ol' Days'. Larry had nailed our fake IDs right under our photo. To the left, he garnished the wall with a red smiley face. I took a step closer and ran my fingers over the crooked red smile. I hardly recognized the Cara staring back at me from that frozen image. Beneath the heavy eyeliner and overly thick mascara was a wide eyed innocence I lost when the dreams began.

Head down, I opened the door. In the back of my mind I heard a little girl crying. I ignored her, took a deep breath, and stepped into the rain. While my feet took me to my car, I whispered the little phrase repeating in my mind for these past twelve days.

"Last night I dreamed of pain. Now, I dread the peace of sleep, for fear the dream remains."

CHAPTER 2

DON'T WORRY MY DEAR…IT WILL BE JUST FINE

I lay my head on his chest. Our bodies entwined on a golden altar. His warm breaths ruffle the damp curls on my forehead. I kiss the hollow space beneath his jaw and hear him whisper my name. In the distance, far beyond the borders of my golden room, an owl hoots in time with a wolf who lets out a jagged howl. The howl sends a shiver down my spine. In an instant the numbing chill of terror threatens to overpower my desperation. I have to hold him. I have to touch him one last time before I die.

    I run my hands down his naked chest, his skin is like fire under my palm. I look up and see the cowled faces, dark soulless eyes and cracked lips that chant out my death. Their hands grab my bare limbs and pull me away from him. The fiery pulse slashing across my wrists turns to ice, I bleed pure fear. A fist strikes my face. I spit blood, rough hands tilt my head, I taste the poison.

    He is moving, coming for me, he will save me. Save me. The poison they force down my throat makes me want to sleep. I wonder how I can even want such a thing when I am already dreaming.

    He is running to me, I see him, and it makes the fear worse. He is beautiful, muscle bound and sculpted like a god. I am dying, but it is not quick enough to suit the goddess. In a swirl of blue mists she materializes in front of me. I scream. Sharp pain lances through my chest. In shock I look down to the source of agony. Droplets of blood hang from a strange bone dagger sticking out of my heart.

    He reaches me with that impossible speed found only in dreams. I hold my arms out to him. My blood pools under me in a spherical pattern, spreading around my head like a grisly halo.

He takes me in his arms, and I all I can think about is him.

"Stay with me," he whispers.

Pain, anger and the burning ache of death assault me. I feel it all inside. Outside I am numb and lifeless. For a moment his strong hands cup my face, only the earth and sky remain. A moment is all I have.

I scream out his name as I die.

I woke up with a start, my scream still echoing in the room. I experienced a moment of weightlessness before I crashed onto the floor. Breath shot from my lungs, and the side of my head *cracked* against the sloped leg of my nightstand.

I lay dazed in the moment it took my mind to retreat from the horror and pain. I heard his voice in the ringing of my ears, and a fissure of agony opened somewhere deep in my heart. Pulling myself upright, I blinked the sleepy fog from my eyes. I touched the spot above my right eye, my fingers came away hot and sticky, my red blood gleamed a sickly black in the moonlight.

Lily burst through the door. "Cara!?"

"Here," I whispered. Lily knelt beside me, a purple candle in her hand. She breathed on the wick, and a little flame flickered to life. Lily sighed and set the candelabra on my vanity, then leaned in and touched my forehead. I winced.

"Don't move darling. It's quite terrible this time. I'll get the kit." Lily rushed out of the room taking all the light. I crawled in bed, trying to choke back a sob, it escaped in a whimper. I raised my down comforter to my chin and snuggled into its fluff. Every night I died, every night I woke up screaming and bleeding. It was too much!

Lily floated into the room a moment later, set the candle back down, and began the work of bandaging my forehead. I lay still, battling tears. To have the horror of the dreams was bad, making Lily experience it with me—so much worse.

"This is the thirteenth night," said Lily despondently. "Same dream?"

"Kind of… not really… elements of it are the same, I suppose." I hissed at the sting of peroxide then let out my breath in a huff, the sting faded away. "I'll be fine, though. It was just a dream."

"That's what we say, isn't it?" sighed Lily. "When we're right at the end of our mental endurance, that's the time we say how fine everything is. But it's not fine. It's getting worse." Lily searched my face. "Your screams are getting louder. You're sleeping less too."

"It's not the best," I said. I did not want to tell her it grew more vivid every night. I did not want her to know each time the knife fell I took so much longer to die.

Lily smiled and kissed my forehead. "Sorry, Cara."

"I'm sorry! I hate putting you through this."

"None of this is your fault. None. There may be blame to throw, but I am sure it isn't yours. There, all done." Lily closed the first aid kit and slid it under my bed. "I'll leave this here, hope for the best and prepare for—well you know."

The luminous dial on my clock read 4:20. One more hour until sunrise, I did not expect to sleep through it.

Lily saw my crestfallen expression. Her hand stroked my hair. "Cara? Want me to stay?"

"You don't have to. Go to bed Lily, you must be so tired."

"Not really," she yawned, "I know I don't have to, I want to. I hate leaving you like this." I scooted over and made room for her to climb in bed beside me. It would have happened either way. She curled up and wrapped her arm around my shoulders. The pieces of my drifting soul came back to earth. We lay like that for an hour, neither of us speaking or moving. I clung to her presence like a drowning soul to a life raft. Without her, I feared I would lose my mind. I feared I would *want* to.

Still, relief washed over me when the first rays of sunlight filtered through the window and danced over my skin. Lily shifted to look down at me. "You going to be okay?"

"I—I don't know, I'm freaked that I'm going crazy. People say mother was insane. What if I'm like her, what if it runs in our blood?"

"Look at me, Cara. Focus on my voice. I didn't really listen to you before, after tonight…" Lily gave a long, tired sigh. "I know these dreams are scary. Once, I had one about a walking tree trying to kill me… I would run and run, but its legs were so long…"

"Yeah, that's the thing about trees," I said. "Most known for their long legs and speed."

Lily giggled. "Okay, not quite the same. What I am trying to say is you're *not* losing it. Or rather, I will not let you lose it. I can find answers. We're growing up, perhaps our powers are doing the same."

I took one of her slender hands folded in her lap. The sleeve of her nightgown poured over our linked fingers, under the hazy morning light the red silk rippled like blood. I looked away and searched her face, there was no comfort in that beautiful visage, she looked exhausted and afraid. "Oh, Lily, I want so badly for you to be happy."

"I will be, soon. First, I have to fix these dreams."

"Why Lily? This drama isn't on you."

"It's on me, because it is you and me, Cara. According to the town's stories, Hanna and mother didn't much care for each other. They had no one to lean on. No one to care for. I have you. I will not lose you, Cara. I will do whatever it takes to solve these dreams. If I can't? Well, what is the point of living this life, in this place?" Lily gestured to my opulent bedroom; the vaulted ceiling covered in a mural centuries old, the paintings on the walls, featuring women performing random magical acts. A haunting one of a woman burning at the stake hung above my ornate headboard. It always creeped me out. However, it held that exact spot for over two hundred years, and I was not about to be the one who moved it. I always thought the clear, beautiful smile of the woman in the painting taunted the little people in the crowd starting up at her, their painted faces rapt as they waited for the witch to die.

"You have magic," said Lily. She picked up the candle and blew on the flame. It died. She breathed on the wick and brought it back to life. "So do I. That little girl, Larry's niece…Cindy. The one you found in the woods, she would have died without you. I remember the look on your face when we found her. I remember what you said."

"Painful, but worth it," I supplied.

Lily nodded. "Magic is difficult, otherwise it would not be magic."

I threw my arms around Lily and rested my cheek on her shoulder. The flames in the 18th century painting seeped out of the frame and licked across my ribboned wallpaper. I ignored them. "What would I do without you?" I asked her, meaning it with my whole heart. Lily returned my hug. I gasped when her emotions rushed into me; her determination, her resolve, her passion. She was so strong, so complex. It was like this even when we were young, it would only take one touch from her to calm me.

"I'll go make coffee," I said.

Lily stretched her arms above her head and yawned. "Kay. Use cinnamon, it's a stress reducer."

"Ah yes," I said. "Cinnamon will fix everything." I opened my closet, retrieved a pair of jeans and a black T-shirt which proclaimed in bold writing that I 'couldn't adult today'. I pulled my wild hair into a top knot and started for the kitchen.

■   ■   ■

Lily was right as usual. Somewhere between a banana muffin and cinnamon-spiced coffee, a little of the night's horror faded. Lily took my coffee mug, she set it down on the sink, giving me one of her looks. "You know, Cara, this cut is the worst. We should get it stitched. It might leave a scar."

I smiled at her and shrugged. "I never scar. One of the many wonderful things about being me."

Lily laughed, and some of the tired left her eyes. They were the prettiest eyes, only right now dark shadows framed them—courtesy of my dreams. A wash of guilt rushed over me, I turned away so she would not see it. I did not want to force her to tell me again how 'okay' it was for me to ruin her life.

Wetting the edge of a paper towel, Lily blotted my forehead. I took her busy hand and held it. "Don't stress, love," I said.

Lily uttered a dramatic sigh and handed me back my coffee. "Fine. What are your plans for today? Stay home maybe? Sleep? Oh wait, don't you have Mr. Clarkson this afternoon? You told me your class is reviewing Homer's Iliad, that should make you all kinds of happy."

She was right. I loved the literature courses I took at the University of Washington. College differed from highschool and for that I was grateful. In college, everyone was so lost in their own world that they stayed out of mine. On a normal day, I would run around, desperately trying to brush my hair while thinking about what to wear, or I would take a long nap before class. Just the thought of that made me shudder.

I shook my head. No way, no sleep. If it were up to me, I would never sleep again. "Yes, it does make me happy, I refuse to let this dream nonsense ruin my day. I have a paper due, and I promised aunt Jane I would bring her that old Ming vase in the library. I told her the other day it was authentic."

"Is it?"

"I'm pretty sure yes."

"I see," said Lily, a twinkle lighting her eyes. "And it occurred to her that it would look incredible on her mantlepiece, even prettier in her bank account?" Her smile was sardonic.

"Something like that, yes. Fine with me. That thing has seen more blood and battle than the Holy Grail. I'll be glad when it's gone. You don't mind do you?"

"No!" Lily gave a fake shudder. "It's creepy."

I dropped my empty coffee mug in the kitchen sink and headed to the door. When my hand reached for the knob, the bell rang. I jumped back, startled. Lily laughed, then stopped herself.

"Sorry. It's not funny." She tried to school her expression into a stern one, it was too no avail, her lips trembled.

"You liked that? Wait and see what shadows make me do," I said, and her giggles kicked in again. I had a silly smile plastered to my face when I opened the door. A cop cruiser idled in our driveway, I waved to its owner, detective Gary Saint, a volatile jock who grew up down the street. Apart from Lily, Gary Saint was the only other soul in the world I called *friend*.

"Hey Gar, I like the beard," I told him, because I did.

"Hey Cara, Marsha does too," he said, scrubbing at his chin.

"She is a woman of sense. I would listen to every word she says."

"Well I married her, so I suppose I swore to do just that. Oh, good morning Lily."

Lily stepped in front of me. "A fine morning to you too detective," said Lily in a sunny fashion. Her cream dress swished around her slender ankles as she walked outside and leaned toward him. I stepped back to let her kiss his cheek for the both of us. "What are you doing in Fairhaven?" asked Lily. Golden curls whipped around her face, and Gary looked lost for words. "Marsha told us you were working a case in Blaine."

"I am. Man!" Scratching at his chin again, Gary gave us both a look. "You girls may like it, but it's uncomfortable as hell." Gary shifted the bulging, canvas bag he held from one hand to another, looking ready to speak, yet, not knowing what to say.

Lily turned to me. "This one's for you. I'll be in the library if I'm needed." She waved goodbye to us both, fluttering off like a butterfly wearing wings of fuchsia and gold. Gary stood on the second tier of the stairs leading to the marbled pink archway framing our front door. Wind tousled his hair giving him an uncharacteristically rumpled look; from the deep creases lining his pants and button down blue shirt, I suspected he had slept in his clothes. I took a step onto the dias and closed the door behind me. "What's up Gar?"

"It's a case," said Gary. He towered over me, even though I held the higher ground. He stepped toward me, I stepped back, my reaction unconscious as it was automatic. Gary, as always pretended not to notice. "So sorry to just bust in on you," he said. "I tried to call."

I patted the front pocket of my leather jacket and did a brief survey of my purse. "Sorry. I must have left my phone in the room."

"Never mind now," he said. A ragged haze tugged at his strong features, a pinched exhaustion born of sleepless nights—I knew it well, I wore it myself. "Someone murdered a young girl last night in Blaine. Rose Miller, she was thirteen. It seems the potential killer may have connections to Fairhaven. I brought over a few of the victim's things, and I hoped you could—do your thing?"

"My thing?" I repeated.

Gary gave me a tired smile. "Don't hate, I haven't known what to call it since high school."

Gary set the duffle on the ground and rifled through it. After a moment, he produced a ziplock bag holding a clutter of pink, glittering items. I took the bag and knelt down. "I'll try," I said. "To do my thing, that is. It doesn't always work, though." That was a lie. It always worked. Most of the time it was easier to tell them I had seen nothing. I touched the dead girl's things, carefully setting them in front of me, one by one. A pretty pink hairbrush, the handle wrapped by a sparkling ribbon. A necklace dangling a butterfly pendant, and a diamond Disney pin featuring Cinderella at her first ball. Apparently, before this miniature froze her in time, 'make it pink' was the last spell cast. I took off my right glove and lifted the brush, blackness seeped into my vision. I let my eyelids fall closed. The light show began.

"She knows the killer," I whispered. "They had strawberry milkshakes and a good laugh…talked about a play she loves—Snow White, I think. He kissed her under a street lamp, she's smiling, the light falling on her face is golden." I set the hairbrush down, my movements automatic and stiff, I was a sleepwalker lost in a dream. My shifting fingers touched the small butterfly pendant. A spray of blood marred the delicate wings. The images came again. What I saw made my own nightmares seem tiny and far away. "He stabbed her twice in the throat then stroked her hair and told her he loved her while she died." I let go of the necklace and opened my eyes. The world swirled into focus, I swayed with it.

Gary reached for me like he could not help it. An instant before he made contact, he snatched back his hand. "Sorry Cara," his voice was rough and he cleared his throat. "It kills me to watch you do this."

"It's okay," I whispered. "I *can* do it, so I have to. Your killer has brown hair and dark eyes, he's about your height, thinner though—almost youthful. He has a tattoo of a lizard on his neck. His clothes smelled like blood even before he killed her."

"So a butcher, or a doctor?" asked Gary. I did not hear a shred of mockery or doubt in his voice, and I loved him for it. I touched the Cinderella pin, it felt wrong to me even before I understood why. "This isn't hers," I said. "The girl who owns it isn't dead yet. She will be—soon, dead because he loves her. He loves them all."

I opened my eyes again. Now Gary looked befuddled. "Cara, we found that pinned to the collar of our victim's coat."

"Then he pinned it on after he killed her. It belongs to another little girl, the same age as the one who died. Maybe he's telling you who he plans to kill next." A sudden wash of sickness made me drop the pin. "This guy is a psycho, Gar. He's taunting you, telling you he's better at the game." I shuddered. "It's definitely a game to him."

"Lucky I have my own secret weapon," said Gary. He wanted to reach out and take my hand—badly. I could feel the fiery crescents his nails left in his palms as he clenched his fists in restraint.

"That Cinderella pin belongs to a girl named Lorna Parker," I said. "She lives in Edgemoore."

"On Briar road," Gary finished. "She went missing last night. Cara, how can you know all that?"

I shrugged. "You remember that awful black and white slide projector Mr. Fuller insisted on using in every class?"

"I'm told I slept through the worst of it," said Gary.

I smiled at him remembering his daytime snoring. "Well, it's like that, only the colors are bright—otherworldly." I cast my eyes to the ground, tucking my hair nervously behind my ear. It was hard to speak this candidly to anyone except Lily. The fear of being mocked for what I could not control ever loomed above me in the form of invisible, angry clouds. "I sound crazy don't I?"

"Not crazy." he said. "Just amazing. How do you know her name?"

"I heard her mother calling it."

"You can hear during this…slideshow?"

"Sometimes." *Always,* my mind corrected. I stood up and put my glove back on. "Your killer, he might live in the woods, I saw Cedar lake and the evening outline of Mount Baker. Sorry Gar it's not much to go on—"

"It's everything, Cara. Thank you. I mean it."

"Anytime, you know I'm here, it gives me a purpose, a reason to put up with all the rest of this." I motioned to the marble pillars and reclining verandas of Wynter Manor. "Go get the bad guys, you always do. Can I hold onto that Cinderella pin for today?"

"Of course." Gary handed it to me. "I'll be back for it."

"Okay," I said. Gary made to leave, then stopped. He turned back and looked into my eyes. "Cara," he whispered. "About Marsha…"

I put up my hand to stop his words. "She is perfect for you Gar, I'm so happy for you both." I meant it and tried to let him see the truth in my eyes. He did, and a smile broke through his pained expression. "She really is, isn't she?"

"Yes," I avowed. "Perfect." I watched him walk away like I had done a thousand times. In second grade he fascinated me, in junior year I fantasized my crush would last forever, and in that last year of school I understood the truth. There was no future for two lovers who could not touch.

I took a deep inhale, not caring that it burned my raw throat. The fresh air soothed my battered face. I climbed into my car and started the engine. I drove for a while, time and trees flashing past me. I thought about the knife going into the little girl's neck. My heart ached for her, for her family. Then, I thought of my dream and of the painful reality of the blade, I remembered what it felt like to die. A confusing torrent of emotions burned in my chest; pity for the dead child and who she might have become, hope that the owner of the Cinderella pin still lived, and fear that she would die screaming—that we both would. Another image filled my mind. Him, leaning over me, a look in his eyes that spoke of an emotion deeper than love, his beautiful voice twisted by agony, begging me to stay, pleading for me to fight the cold finality of death. For Lily, the answers were out there, hiding somewhere between the stars. I could not agree. Night was falling, with it, came only darkness.

CHAPTER 3

IN THE WEEDS

The drive from Fairhaven to Seattle took over an hour. I used the time wisely by singing Taylor's *Cruel Summer* in time with the radio, loud as my lungs would allow. I was on my way to see our aunt, I needed all the good vibes I could get. Aunt Jane moved out of Wynter Manor when we turned eighteen, telling us she missed the city, that life in Fairhaven would age her prematurely. Lily and I had voiced a few protests, however, we were glad to have the house to ourselves. I had never formed the bond with aunt Jane that I hoped would be a product of our being forced to live under the same roof—even if that roof covered almost thirteen thousand square feet—most likely due to watching her kill a baby lamb in our backyard when I was eight years old. For a lifelong vegetarian, it was traumatic. I cried for two days, and in my dreams that baby lamb cried with me.

Raindrops splashed my windshield, and through them the bruised clouds looked bejeweled. Behind their dark cloaks the sun seemed drenched and swollen, it crouched against the horizon like a lonely, injured thing. I sang each word of the next song, refusing to let my mind wander—*dark thoughts bring dark events*—it was Hanna's line—I am pretty sure it's true.

I turned onto Blake Avenue where aunt Jane's house sits on the street corner like a gothic masterpiece. Only the tips of her castle were visible behind an iron fence draped in green ivy. Twined through the ivy were the last of the autumn leaves still painted scarlet and gold. Two stone pillars framed the double gates, naked vines wrapped through the bars and only bloomed black roses. I got out of my car and walked to the gate. To access the doorbell, I had to lift a thick web of ivy away from the center of the first pillar, I struggled, then shrieked when a black thorn pierced my forefinger. I snatched my hand back and saw the thorn had cut straight through the leather of my glove. I felt a hot bubble of blood expand under the material. The job of holding back the ivy and locating the intercom—and its tiny button for the doorbell—took two hands and my full concentration. When I finally found the button and pressed it the sound that ensued was terrible. Like all the doorbells in the world had come together to die, and this doorbell's music was permanent record of that event.

"Yes? Who is it? What do you want?"

"It's me Aunty, Cara, I brought you that vase you wanted and some apple pie."

"Is it from *Culinary Confections*?"

"Yes ma'am', I stopped in on my way over. Ms. Sherry wishes you a lovely day."

"I am sure she does nothing of the kind, sweet of you to lie though…" The intercom crackled. "Come in dear you're getting soaked." Another piercing crackle, followed by a prolonged buzzing. The echo of the doorbell death cry. I picked up the cardboard box which I had fetched from my trunk, it held the old vase, the apple pie, and the little Cinderella pin I took from detective Gary. Stepping carefully, I weaved my way through the garden. I tried not to knock over a cauldron, trample on a fresh bundle of sage or— saints forbid— step on one of the many red X's littering the ground. The click and release of a latch made me look up in time to see the kitchen window fly open. My aunt's silvery head popped out. A pair of wire-rimmed glasses hung onto the tip of her nose. Leaves and a mess of thin black vines tumbled down from her wild topknot. Her weathered lips were pink and glossed to perfection. "Don't step on the garden gnomes. I put X's where they like to play."

"Yes Aunty, I remember," I said.

"Fine. Put the box down on the porch and come in for tea."

Aunt Jane met me at the front door, kissing the air on either side of my face as was our custom. "Great ghosts child! What terrible dreams you've been having. No! Don't picture them, I don't want to see any of that. Now come inside, you're soaked."

"The rain agrees with me Aunty. How are you?"

"Oh well, I'm too ornery to be anything but good," she said primly. Turning in a flourish of vines and leaves, she led me down the hall, her footsteps soundless. Reaching the kitchen, aunt Jane paused like she meant to change course, then thought better of it and went inside. I followed her, ducking under a low-hanging batch of herbs, only to have another smack me in the face. I pushed it away, coughing, and batting the hair and leaves from my eyes before looking around. Hints of fresh chamomile fused by sage and honeysuckle filled the space. All manner of witchery lay strewn over the counters and tabletops. Three cauldrons bubbled on the stove, each of them belching out fragrant clouds of colorful steam. Mice squeaked in their wooden cages, and homemade candles poured their scented wax over the rushes and vines that crisscrossed the floor.

"Yes, yes I can see you like what I've done with the place," my aunt said, moving to retrieve a tea service balanced precariously between a jar of dried witch hazel, and another stuffed to the brim by what I could only assume—was a couple dozen gooey eyeballs. "Ugh, Aunty, is all of this really necessary?"

Aunt Jane ignored me and used her elbow to knock a basket off the table, it did a flip in the air and two wooden dolls, a spool of yarn, and a knife fell out. She placed the tea-set in the spot she had made. It was a delicate, porcelain confection, its lid, and spout covered in a smattering of little blue forget-me-nots. More flowers wrapped the ornate cup handles and danced around their rims.

"Move those books to the floor, Cara. Take that chair by the door. It's impossible for me to think, when you're looming over me."

"I am five foot five, Aunty, I don't think I can *loom*," I said, but did as she asked. Aunt Jane put a steaming cup of tea in my hand.

"Thank you," I said, taking a sip. Warmth ran down my throat, it seeped into my chest, and felt wonderful— doing much to dispel some of the ever present Washington chill.

"Drink more!" aunt Jane commanded. "After, you can tell me about your dreams, and describe who's coming for you."

"No one is coming for me, Aunty, it's just a few nightmares. They'll pass."

"Cara!" Her blue eyes sparked flame. "You are a Wynter, it is never just a dream." She used a manicured nail to flick her glasses back to the bridge of her nose. Her lips drew together until each one of her wrinkles stood out in harsh relief. "Someone is coming for you. They leave shadows in your aura."

I set the saucer on my lap, the base of the cup clattered against it. Lowering my eyes, I used the handle to spin the cup in circles. "Thank you Aunty," I said. "That is both terrifying and depressing, so I won't think about it at the moment." I said that last part for her, and myself. "Right now I need your help. In the box by the door is a Cinderella brooch. I need you to put a protection spell on the little girl it belongs to." I was not always sure aunt Jane's hocus pocus worked, I did not however, want that little girl to die. My talents were seeing, not saving, I figured anything was better than nothing. "It's to help Gary."

The namedrop was to sway her. It worked. Her old eyes lit up and she leaned forward resting her creaking elbows on her wobbling knees. "How is he? He is such a sweet boy, pure good all the way to his toes." She swatted away a stray vine that broke free of her hairdo to tickle her cheek. "Fine consider it done. I won't do something for nothing though, I am not you, I don't just give magic away."

I rolled my eyes. "I don't give magic away, whether I even have any is still up for extensive debate, and it's not for nothing," I argued. "I try to help people in the only way I can, besides…I get something back."

"Pah, smiles and thanks, I never!"

"What? I love it. It's like a virtual hug. Name your price," I said smiling. I knew she would name nothing too crazy, despite her bark *and* bite, she was an old sweetheart.

"I want you to read your tea leaves for me. That is my price."

"Ummm… I don't know how to do that."

"Look into your tea cup, and clear your mind," commanded aunt Jane. I obeyed trying to prepare myself for her theatrics. I dropped my eyes and stared down at the golden liquid littered in white, floating petals. I watched it swish from side to side, a low buzzing welling in my ears. The saucer quivered in my lap shaking the delicate cup, as it shook, it elongated becoming a misshapen oval, or a gaping mouth from a horror film. The liquid in the mouth splashed, a golden wave reflecting a glowing pair of red eyes. It felt like I sat in a dazzling spotlight, gazed into the soul of a monster and felt it gaze right back. Green flames now edged the mouth of the cup, it turned skeletal, opened wider and screamed.

Next thing I knew I was on my feet, the tea cup lying in shambles around my boots. Stumbling back a few steps I reached out to the wall for support. I felt my mind kick into overdrive, trying to make sense of what it had seen. *Not real.* I told myself, then I whispered out loud. "Not real."

"Easy, Cara," aunt Jane's soft voice said. I could feel that she wanted to reach out and touch me. "Every witch can do it," she soothed. "It's so easy that little girls playing around at tea sometimes pull it off. I didn't mean to scare you, I only wanted to understand your dreams."

"What was that?" I gasped, shaking my head, trying to clear it. "What did I see?"

"In the tea leaves we view our unchangeable fates."

I realized I was panting. I put my hand to my heart. "I see," I said finally, sitting back down. "I don't believe in that kind of fate. I think we always have a choice, an ability to change our destiny."

Aunt Jane's old eyes crinkled at the corners and she shook her head. "You are too young to make such statements," she avowed. "Your fate will come for you, whether or not you prepare for it. Believe in yourself Cara. I have always said you are so much more than you think you are."

I could hear her trying to console me, it was clear my reaction had upset her. It was not what I wanted, yet I could not believe that creature—her glowing eyes reflecting off that deadly knife—was my destiny. The room started to close in on me, snatching my breath, I had to escape. I grabbed my purse, babbled some lame excuse, ran through the garden and out the gates like the house was ablaze.

I drove aimlessly, no destination in mind. The roads were slippery, the wind morose. The sun stayed behind its misty cloak of clouds, leaving the day windblown and dark. After an hour of driving nowhere in particular, I saw the tip of the space needle hovering just above the clouds, and I knew where my mind was taking me.

Large raindrops bounced off the sleek surface of the car as it roared into third. I made a sharp left onto Broadway, then waited for the light to turn green. Gorgeous architecture decorated the walking streets on either side of me. I could see the tips of the colorful street market tents poking up against the bruised sky, the smell of the salty bay and fresh fish was heavy in the air. Lovers linking hands strolled past busy coffee houses, ignoring the pockets of homeless, stepping around their bursting shopping carts and dirty plastic bags.

A particularly filthy man stood a few feet shy of the crosswalk, locked in a screaming match with the air. One hand industriously picked his nose, the other brandished a filthy stick like a sword. He screamed an obscene word at an ambling couple who promptly jumped out of his way. My eyes found his, and the yelling cut off abruptly. His bloodshot gaze locked to mine. He took a step toward me. Skin dripped from his jaw, his eyeballs popped free of their sockets, and one just hung there, swinging against his cheek from gooey red threads while the other rolled down his chest. I heard a wet splat as it hit the pavement. A sickly green liquid oozed from his empty black eye sockets liberally mingling in the blood pumping from his gaping jaw. Hand waving, the grungy stick morphed into a sword. He hurled it at me. The sword arced through the air, picking up speed, it flew directly toward my face.

I screamed, slammed my foot on the gas pedal and gripped the wheel to keep my hands from shaking off. My car skidded through the intersection, my tires squealing shouts of warning. I half-expected to hear the *thud* of my bumper striking the monster, but none came. My pounding heart was audible.

I glanced in the rearview mirror.

The street was empty.

"Oh, what the hell?" I moaned. I risked another wary glance over my shoulder. The rag man had disappeared. I slammed my hand on the steering wheel. That irrational action sent jolts of pain up my tired arm. The city flashed past me in a blur. I felt like I was breaking…shattering into a million pieces….

CHAPTER 4

FIRST TOUCH OF DARKNESS

The ride to the top of the Space Needle took forever, I held my breath the entire time counting to one hundred—eight times. Sighs were audible as the elevator finally pinged and the doors slid open, I hung back for just a moment before following the crowd onto the observation deck. No matter how often I came here, the view took my breath away. Loving the Space Needle—all the tourists and their guides—was not very native of me, but I did. On all sides the world stretched out like a patchwork quilt of color and light. Snow-capped mountains edged the foggy earth covered by teeming black lakes, and countless pines.

I found a quiet corner free of camera flashes and chattering people. I zipped up my jacket, hunkered down, and allowed myself to simply exist. For the longest time I drifted, safe in my nothing box. A polite cough snapped me back to reality. Blinking against the setting sun, I looked up.

An attendant's wrinkled face stared down at me. "Miss?"

"Yes," I squeaked. My hand flew to my throat, I cleared it and tried for a normal voice. "Sorry. Yes?"

"Everything all right?"

I nodded. "Needed some peace, I think."

"No problem at all, miss, we all have those days." He shoved his hands into the pockets of his grey uniform pants and studied the view. "It is lovely up here. Best place in the city, I say," he turned back to me. "Just thought you should know the observation deck closes in fifteen minutes."

I looked around, surprised. A couple leaned against the wall to the right of me, and they cast long shadows against the ground, shadows that wavered in the fading light—besides them, and the polite bearer of bad news—I was alone. "Yes. Sure. I'll be down in a few. Thank you." I tried to smile and my hand hit the air in a pathetic impression of a farewell wave. He hesitated, staring at me for a second longer than politeness required, a question in his eyes. He took in my tear-stained face and offered me his own sad smile. "I'll expect you, then?"

I nodded assent and he waved goodbye. I did not have another pleasantry in me.

Twilight now lay over the city like a velvet blanket. I had zoned out longer than intended. Thunder rumbled somewhere in the distance, followed by a bright flash of light that threw electricity across the sky. Another growl boomed just over the horizon, and this time the flashing light imprinted on my eyes. I stood up and ambled toward the rail. A high pitched buzzing rang in my ears, my movements felt graceful and not exactly my own. My body knew where I was, but my mind was pulling me down a dark tunnel, the tunnel took me back to another time. A long time ago. A time when I stood in this exact spot, beside Hanna staring up at the angry sky, full of swollen black and purple clouds racing, and spinning over our heads.

Hanna had spent the day—Lily and my thirteenth birthday—exploring the city. We shopped, browsed through the market stalls, visited old libraries, then finished with a lobster dinner and a trip to the top of the Space Needle. Yet all happy memories of the day faded beneath the force of the tempest. Tendrils of lighting had sliced across the sky that night. Swollen rain drops splashed against my merlot silk dress and shiny mary-janes.

I had looked up at Hanna and thought her the most beautiful thing alive, a pale face that seemed forever young, lit green eyes flashing more brilliant than the storm. She turned her palms to catch the droplets falling from the sky, raindrops broke against her flawless skin. Water ran down her face, mingling in tears. Those tears surprised me, because I have no memory of Hanna crying before, or after that time.

"What's wrong, Hanna?" I had asked. "Why do you look so sad?"

"I'm sad because I'm sorry, Cara. I am so very sorry because I…I love you. I never counted on that." Her words filled me with a confusion and awe. They always had.

"I am sorry," Hanna said again. "Because strange things are coming for you and there is nothing I can do to change them. I'm sorry because I am powerless to give you any more help than I already have, and I am sorry because I must leave you." She leaned down and held her hands beside my face, not touching me. Never touching me. When her attention focused on me it seemed the storm calmed.

I saw two dry, amber leaves tangled in her dark red hair. A streak of mud ran across her white cheek, but otherwise she looked like a queen in her high-necked black dress and puffy pink pearls. Her lilac perfume — drenched the air.

"You're leaving us?" I reached for a leaf, it was crunchy and broke apart in my hands. "When? Why?"

"Soon."

"Why are you telling me?" Anger bubbled in my voice. "Why don't you just leave in the middle of the night like mother, now I will dread every day because it might be the day you abandon us as well."

"You will not dread the days Cara, not because of this reason anyway. You won't even remember this conversation tomorrow, you will only remember the storm. And, I leave because I must," she said. "I need you to be strong."

"I am not strong, just scared," I said. "I don't think I'll ever be strong."

"You are, Cara. Much stronger than me, you have such a power in you. Don't lose yourself, okay? Your soul is so special." Hanna shook her long, wet curls.

"I will try very hard not to," I said, and tasted tears on my lips.

Hanna smiled, flashing a sharp row of white teeth. "Good girl." She turned to go inside, back to the fat buttered lobster and Lily. I remember the moment she left, the storm hushed.

I opened my eyes. *"Hanna,"* my mind called. It sounded like a prayer. *"Hanna, where are you?"* The wind brought the rumble of thunder and the chill of the evening breeze. *Strange things,* Hanna had told me, now they whispered in the wind. Dark thoughts slithered into my mind beckoning me forward. In my ears the ringing continued to increase. I peered over the edge and looked into… nothing. The open landscape faded to an endless void of nothing, the nothing called me. I could not fight the call. It was so strong, like it tugged on a cord in my soul. More importantly, I did not want to fight it. My hands gripped the rail. It felt like I stood outside myself, a silent spectator who watched a poor girl climbing to her death. I saw myself swing my right leg over the guardrail, then the left. The buzzing was everywhere, it vibrated the ground, rippling the air beneath me. Down in the folds of the swirling nothingness where the city had once been—I heard voices. They whispered my name.

NO! my mind hollered. *NO! fight it!*

I did not want to. It would be so easy to jump, to end all the crazy. Just fall into the blessed darkness, no neon lights, or images I did not want to see, no ghosts calling my name, just darkness. I wondered if I would be as much of a misfit in the next life as I was in this one. The thought made me laugh. A bolt of lightning split the sky and my body swayed. A scream—mine, I realized—competed with the violent thunder. I did not understand my scream. There was no fear in the trance, only the need to jump. To fall. To sleep, perchance to dream—for in that sleep of death what dreams may come? Dreams. They did not need to come for me. I barely survived in the eye of their storm.

No! The voice in my mind tried to regain control. *Cara! Open your eyes! Wake up!*

"No!" Another voice—this one real and strong—sounded behind me. "Wait!"

An arm linked around my waist and for a second my own arms windmilled like I intended to take flight. A hand gripped my right shoulder, dragged me off the ledge and set me on the ground. Reeling and beyond dazed I shook my head to clear the fog. I could still feel the call, and slowly—like it crawled backwards through a malfunctioning time machine—my mind receded from the twilight zone. It felt kinda like waking up from a faint. I lifted my body, resting my weight on my elbows and looked up. A man, dark hair hanging in his eyes crouched over me. He exuded an aura of power and there was something noble in his stance, as if he stood sentinel.

"Are you alright?" he said. His voice rumbled over my skin like waves of electricity, enthralling me. He smelled like the storm, leather, and something undefinable, dark and sensual. I felt my mouth go dry and I swallowed nothing. "Y...Y-Yes, I'm fine," my voice sounded strangled and weak; like it came from very far away, maybe still trapped somewhere in my endless tunnel.

"Sorry I startled you. I called out a few times," he said. I heard fear in his words and imagined I could also hear his beating heart.

"It looked like you were trying to jump." A new voice—purring, silky and feline, sounded behind me. I swung my head. The light streaming from the twin glass doors back-lit the woman, shining on a silver blonde cap of hair, curling around her ears. Her lashes were long and black, thick gloss painted her lips a bright ruby color that matched her six-inch heels.

"No," I said, and looked down, flushing, of course. "I mean I wasn't trying to. I think I was literally day dreaming. Thank you, I'm fine now." There was that one word fast becoming a main character in my vocabulary. *Fine.* I thought how strange it was that a single word could tell such a lie.

The pretty girl *hummed* at me and flicked the nail of her forefinger against her thumb as if an unwanted piece of dust had the unfortunate audacity to land on her. "No harm done, you were never in any real danger we saw you walking toward the rail."

"At least one of us did," I mumbled. She heard me and laughed. Then she gave my prone form a once over like she was inspecting something she intended to buy or, throw in the nearest dumpster. I wondered what she saw. I knew my hair had fallen from it's knot and I wanted to push it back into place, maybe pinch my cheeks. Instead, I did nothing. Just sat there and looked at them.

"Regardless, that was scary as hell," she said.

I closed my eyes. "It really was. Thank you for saving me." I turned back to the man, he had moved away and was now sitting on his haunches regarding me. The fluorescent lights ignited the amber in his eyes. He stood and brushed his hands over a pair of dark jeans. "Can my sister and I escort you somewhere? Your car maybe?"

I tried to stand—a clumsy effort, what with my knocking knees and spinning head. After two embarrassing tries, I gave up and stayed on my knees, wishing the floor would just open and swallow me. "No. Thank you. I'll go back down now. I've stayed up here too long. It was so… I just got—lost." I bit my lip to stop babbling. My blush got hotter. I made myself meet his eyes. I searched his strong features and knew they would forever leave an imprint in my mind. There was a memory in the sound of his voice and I felt the tunnel again, swirling, a kaleidoscope of encroaching colors, pulling me back to the dream.

"Suit yourself," the pretty girl said. She set her purse on the ground and rifled through it. "You want an advil or something? You look like you could use one."

"Yes. Thank you. My head might have a knife in it." In the corner of my vision I saw the man squeezed his eyes closed, something ticked in the curve of his jaw.

"I'm sure I have some," she mumbled and continued the search. Finally, her bangled hand broke free holding its prize. I took the pill, giving her a grateful smile. She returned the bottle to her purse before attacking the scattered shrapnel, courtesy of the purse explosion.

I shivered and realized I was soaking from the waist down. "Oh," I gasped, twisting so I faced the man. "We landed in a puddle."

"Not surprising," he said. His face was rigid. "This State is full of them."

I burst out laughing, he smiled slightly, but I still saw fear in his eyes. Water continued to seep through my jeans, I jumped to my feet and immediately regretted it. The world swayed, fuzzy black spots cluttered my vision and the urge to throw up what remained of my breakfast made me grind my back teeth. I swallowed stomach acid and rain. He took my arm to steady me. I registered his touch the same instant I braced for the pain. It never came. I looked up. His face was inches from mine.

"How are you? Make no sudden movements," he commanded. "You're in shock."

"Am I?" I whispered, too spellbound to move. His hand grazed my forehead, checking my temperature like it was nothing. A thing only Lily had ever done.

"Your skin is chilled. You sure we can't take you somewhere?"

If I said no, I would have to step out of the circle of his arms, so I said nothing. An icy wind struck us. He took a step closer until there was nothing but a wisp of air between our bodies. Raindrops spilled around us in concentric patterns and the heat of him radiated waves of warmth through me. I do not know how long we stood there with time frozen like a broken clock. Eventually, the pretty girl cleared her throat and we both jumped. I took a step back, my nervous movements clumsy. His hands fell away from me, for a split second we were in my tunnel together and his reluctance to leave me felt powerful as my need to run back in his arms. *What the hell is wrong with me now?* I brushed my hands over my jeans, realizing my brief sojourn in the puddle had soaked my gloves. I took them off and stuffed them in my purse. About three feet of empty space stood between us now, he hesitated for a moment, before closing the distance. He took my hand, his fingers linked through mine. If I had not been in shock before, I certainly was now. "Be careful," I thought I heard him say.

They left and took the remaining warmth. I let out a huge breath and gasped it back in. "What the crap was that?" I whispered. Uneven breaths doing battle in my lungs, I took a step toward the door, my foot struck something and I looked down. A paperback, dog-eared and bent by age, lay beside my foot next to a cherry lipstick. Not thinking I bent down and picked it up it, barehanded. Before I could stand the world blackened, and the puddle was once again my home. I saw a palace and pillars of blushed marble. A sun setting against sands so white they glowed. I saw the broad back of a man holding a golden sword, crimson blood clung to the gleaming blade. In the distance I heard the screams and raucous cries of thousands.

"Wait!" I unzipped my purse and put the book inside, when I let it go, reality returned. "Wait!" I got up and stumbled through the glass doors, then ran to the elevator. Nothing greeted me but the whirr of its dissension. I was alone.

I rode the next elevator, putting on my gloves and taking the book out of my purse. Gilded, stylized letters scrolled across the top, proclaimed the title: Blood and Shadows. A heroine sporting crimson hair clung to a half-naked, god-like man. His hair was a mess of long, dark locks, beneath the wayward curls smoldered a set of amber eyes. I held the book against my chest, not caring about the mud splatter it left on my jacket. It mattered not to me that touching it had nearly knocked me senseless—I loved it anyway. The first book I finished cover to cover was a period piece set in the early 1500s. Unattainable, desperate passion between a princess of Normandy and a Saxon knight. They loved, they hated, and they touched all the time. I read them for the touching. I could live vicariously through the beautiful women of days past. Those women always shared a commonality. Touch brought pleasure not pain.

I stepped outside and pressed the book tighter to my chest, trying to shelter the pages from the fresh falling rain. If I ever saw that pretty girl again, I would give the book back. Until then, I would read every word and most likely love them all. I forgot the trance and my desperate need to jump, forgot my aunt's predictions of fate, my pain, and my dreams. There was nothing in the world like a new book. I ran back to my car. For once I could not wait to get home.

■   ■   ■

I pulled into the driveway in time to see Lily fling open the door. Her hair glowed a soft gold touched by the light of the foyer. I got out of my car and grabbed my purse; taking a moment to pick up Blood and Shadows and tuck it under my sweater, wanting to protect it from the elements. I smelled cream-and-tomato risotto and my stomach hollered. I breathed, took in a full gulp of air and felt my chest expand. No pain. I exhaled. I could not say it aloud, I would not jinx it, but something nameless floating in air made this night feel somehow different from the last thirteen.

Lily swung the door wider and pulled me into a warm hug. "It's so late. You smell like the storm." She drew back regarding me from quizzical eyes.

"Were you up on the Space Needle again?" She did not let me answer. "You know, for someone who doesn't like crowds…" She let the sentence hang.

"It's different up there. So many people it makes me feel alone."

Lily shrugged. "Yeah, I kinda get that. Come, love, I made…"

"Risotto," I finished. "I can smell it. I am starving to death!"

She giggled her signature sound. "Always. How was class?"

I sighed. "Didn't go. I went over to see aunt J, she made me read tea leaves and scared the life out of me."

"You poor thing! Why would you even agree to do something like that? It's unlike you."

"I didn't exactly agree."

"Ah," Lily shook her head. "That woman needs to get out more."

"You should see her kitchen, it's ten times worse than the last time we were there."

We sat down at the old rose wood dining table—three centuries old if I could believe Hanna's tales—cuddled together at the end of the giant thing, and like always, we inhaled Lily's masterpiece.

"I totally saw that book you took from the car, BTW," said Lily, chewing behind her hand. "Who is it this time? Cowboy? Pirate?" She popped a piece of cheese in her mouth and spoke over it. "A debonair Duke?'

"I don't know. Tonight I will enter a world of dashing passion and fall into wild, dark dreams."

"Not too dark," said Lily. I looked at her and smiled. I refused to jinx it.

We went through a whole bottle of chardonnay. Talked about everything and nothing. Eventually the topic rushed to the Space Needle and I tried not to tell her, I honestly did.

"You what?! Well what the…wha…" Lily spluttered into silence.

"That's how I felt. I don't even remember what happened. Safe to say I'll steer clear of heights for a while."

"And so…? You were standing there and blacked out? Then what? Just tried to jump?"

"It's like I am in a dream, but a waking dream where I know what is happening, except my body belongs to someone else. Everything in that space is so far out of my control. I was thinking about Hanna. I had this memory of her, something from a long time ago, I forgot all about it, I think she wanted me to forget. The memory came and then, I don't know, I don't black out, at least not really. I just kinda go far away. I'm there, but like a vapor, a shadow—I know it sounds…"

"Don't say strange! We are placing a ban on that word in this house. Strange is for normal. No one I know has *ever* accused us of being such a terrible thing." She smiled. "So you were standing there, and that guy just came and grabbed you? Are you alright?"

I paused unable to even believe my own words. "There was no pain." I shrugged and threw up my hands. "Maybe I was just so out of it, I didn't feel it. I felt calm. His touch—gods, Lily, it was soothing, and warm… sexy." I stopped talking. Blood rushed into my cheeks.

"Sexy?" repeated Lily looking straight into my eyes, her own widening in disbelief.

"Yes, sexy." I said, when her incredulous look continued. "What? I can think a guy is sexy."

Lily tossed her head. "True, anything's possible."

She put her hand on mine. Her hesitation obvious, I grabbed her fingers and just squeezed. "What the hell, Lily? He touched me. A man touched me and I didn't scream, pass out, or die."

"What do you think it means?" asked Lily. "Do you think the dreams healed you? Like a rite of passage or something?"

"Passage to what?" I answered.

Lily had no reply and it seemed to put an end to the conversation. She kissed me goodnight and went upstairs to her room in the south wing. She slept in Hanna's old room. It was by far the most lavish room in the manor. Lily offered it to me first, but I could not. Besides, it felt right for her to be in that room, she *was* at least a minute older. I put my Victoria's Secret jumper on and burrowed into my freezing bed. I kicked my legs around until the sheets lost their coating of frost, shivered, and sighed. The rainy breeze set my curtains swishing, and the moonlight played tricks on my eyes. Through my window, I glimpsed two stars outshining the others in the night sky. They glowed an odd amber light that made me think of his eyes.

My fingertips caressed the cover of the novel. "He touched me," I told the ebony haired beauty on the front. "He touched me." I lay my palm flat against the book—ready for it this time—closed my eyes and let the darkness take me. Colors instantly splashed across my vision. I saw a boy, his feet buried in sand. He drew his head back, eyes alert, his stance guarded. He held a sword made of light and swung it, a harsh battle cry escaped his lips. In most instances, I was outside my visions, like a shadow meant only to observe. This time was different. The same warm sand covered my own feet. I stood at the gates of a temple, eyes fixed on an owl circling the sky. Ocean wind played in my hair, a white dress fringed in delicate lace blew through my legs. I heard a song in the air and realized I knew the words. "Take me to the place that be," I whispered. "Far across the golden sea. From the gates of Tartarus take us away. To live, to die again. In the mists of that fated day." Still wrapped in the colors of my vision, I opened the book and started to read.

ANCIENT CHAPTER I

BLOOD AND SHADOWS — SPARTA, 1204, BCE

"It is dark in this room where I sit, quill and parchment under my hands and an ache in my heart. I can hear water dripping down walls that were golden such a short time ago, now nothing more than molten ash. Draken is silent…I think he sleeps, if such a thing is possible for us now. I can't be sure…I fear waking him. He is cradling his dead love in his arms and I am alone.

I have written nothing before, but I will attempt it now and hope it survives the passage of time. It is that, or run mad in this desolate place. Perhaps if I write down my story, it may help to clarify details which blur before my eyes…either that, or it, too, will drive me mad. It seems sanity will slip from my grasp either way.

I could keep my story, I suppose, keep it in the silence of this grave where it belongs, but if I did that, it would be soon be forgotten. Everyone is dead. Only two other eyewitnesses besides me remain alive, and I doubt they will ever again speak of the events of this day. No.

This is my story and I will tell it. Then, maybe I will die… if I can. What does it matter now? He is gone. Locked in a dimension out of my reach—locked together with her. I see a strange sort of justice in that.

So here is my story.

If you are looking for beauty, this tale will never do. It is not a beautiful story.

It is a story of a world that existed long ago, in a time before time. It begins many eons before man had ever tasted breath. In a world where the

Titans roared across the seven seas and earth was nothing more than a gaping void of fire and wind. It was a time of power and chaos. The ruling gods tore apart the heavens in their battle for the Olympian throne, and the earth itself teetered on the brink of extinction.

Then came Zeus, lightning in his eyes and the strength of the ages in his hands. Using the help of his brothers, he broke the Titans' hold, overthrew their father, and claimed the throne. After which, they drew lots and divided up the ruling world and all of its magic. Poseidon went to the seas, and Hades to his underworld.

For a space in time, Zeus' choices seemed sound, and in the beginning of this age, there was beauty and life. Man was grateful for the gift of a soul, and there was peace. It was only after the much abused Pandora scattered the contents of her box at Zeus' feet—evil and death went out into the world. Then, men fought to take what was not theirs. For centuries their battles tore the earth as they poured the blood of their children into the sands. Long years, they slashed at each other, and the ruling gods reveled in the gore. So came the age of men, the age of legends. So began the golden age of the gods.

I know that no matter whose hands this falls into, or in what time they live, they will have heard the stories that shaped my time: stories of Hercules and his awesome strength, or of Helen and her kingdom-felling beauty. Or even of Achilles, his battle with the great Hector and their fall together into the world of the dead. Stories of valor and strength and of man's triumph even in death.

What if, however, there was a story where nobody was the victor? Who has the heart to write it down?

They are the ones that remain only as memories swept under the tide of time where they become the untold legends—the darker tales where man bled and suffered under the whims of the gods. Maybe it is better that way, for who wants to hear a story where there is no glory—only pain and agony in a dark, breaking world that had left hope in Pandora's box?

I do not wish to be buried alongside the unknown dead. I am Princess Androsia, daughter of a goddess, prize, and pride of the Spartan dynasty. I refuse to be included in the masses of the forgotten. For I was beautiful and worshiped…I was divine…I will not be forgotten."

SPARTA, MARCH 1ST, 1202, BCE

Twenty years after the fall of Troy

"You ready to suffer, prince of Sparta?" Malkalimos's call carried a clear taunt. "Or perhaps you've changed your mind?"

Draken squared his shoulders. They always taunted him, *god-blood* they whispered. It was a game to beat him. He would never let them. He felt fear like any other creature. The only difference between him and them was he had vowed they would never see it.

"Only four Igori?" Draken asked. Proud he kept the tremor out of his voice. "What? The rest bow out?"

Malkalimos frowned. The expression pulled the deep scar above his lip into a snarl. Malkalimos stood as the right hand of the king and captain of the Igori—the most elite warriors in all of Greece. He had the barreled chest of a bear and the face of a minotaur. Draken could not remember a day in his life in which that scowl did not play a prominent role.

"These four will have you eating sand before Apollo shifts in the sky," said Malkalimos. His voice boomed off the hot bricks of the stands lining the training grounds. Draken looked up to judge the time. The sun was at half mast, nearly dead center in the sea of pale blue. It beat down on his bronze skin, pulling droplets from it. He passed his right hand over his brow to wipe them away, his left fingers—slick and sweaty—tightened around the hilt of his sword.

"We waste valuable light exchanging this riveting banter," Draken said. "I came for a fight."

Movement at his left shifted the sands. To the right, a long shadow edged his view. He closed his eyes and listened. A light breeze, like a sigh in the air, brushed his face. Two men at his back. One more, the shadow coming at him from the right. So be it.

The first warrior, Phelios—a huge brute, shoulders sloping, and legs like tree trunks—rushed him, crying fiercely. The sword the beast held was short and wicked sharp. Draken crouched and lifted his shield from the sand. The Spartan roared and lunged, his sword bearing down like a berserker's mace toward Draken's head.

Instead of dodging the bashing strike, Draken braced himself and leaned into it. Seconds before the cold steel connected with flesh, he drove his shield into the man's extended gut. The Igori's swing went wide and he stumbled. His feet shuffled for a wild moment, then he lost the battle and crashed down on his backside. A volcano of dry sand burst up and swirled around the fallen Igori.

Draken gained his feet before the sand settled. Another. Behind him. He spun left. Cold steel rang against his own. Draken growled and put real strength behind his next swing. Again, the blades met in the air. His opponent nearly went to his knees. The man, however—dark and wiry— was quick as a panther. He bent at the waist, dodging Draken's next cutting blow. To the left more sand shifted. Uneven footsteps and ragged breathing came from his right.

Adrenaline surged in Draken's veins. Another lunged at him. Agathon. A seasoned warrior and a friend. The world froze and, for a space in time, he could see each movement seconds before it happened. Like he was a creature standing just outside time. In a fascinating daze, Draken ducked under a decapitating strike, his movements fluid, almost slow. Each action calculated and controlled. Draken raised his sword arm to meet the next swing. He braced his legs and cut upward. The blades clashed again. This time, the Igori's sword went flying. The next warrior charged, the first struggled to regain his feet. A new blade arced towards his legs. Draken brought his sword down and turned the low thrust aside, then slammed his shield into the chest of his attacker. The hit lifted the man off his feet and sent him flying. Enveloped in a dense cloud of sand, the warrior crashed to the earth and did not move.

One down. Draken told himself.

The enraged face of the first Spartan obstructed his view. A hard fist came at him from the right. Draken saw it. It struck his jaw anyway, the middle knuckle catching him at the base of his lip. The hit snapped his head back, but he did not falter in his stance. He flicked out his tongue and tasted blood. In the sky, he heard an eagle scream. He lifted his shield, and the muscles in his right shoulder clenched as his forearm absorbed the next blow. Then they were on him. Streamers of hot sparks flew off the razor edges of the kissing steel. His mind was in control now. His body only followed.

Defend. His right arm hoisted his shield.

Attack. His left raised the sword and cut the air.

The sun moved in the sky.

Draken pivoted on his right heel and threw himself in a forward roll. He felt the air shift and the Igori's sword passed harmlessly over his naked back. Then, he stood fluidly, returning to his guard stance. The remaining three circled.

"Today is the day, prince," was Agathon's friendly taunt. Draken saw the determination in his friend's eyes. He could feel each beat of his own heart pulsing in his palms. The scene whirled around him, the world still in its strange, frozen state. Each frame of movement existing in its own space and time. The eagle screamed again. A keening cry followed by an endless echo.

Draken slapped the flat of his sword against the plain, wooden face of his shield. "Come at me then!" he roared.

They rushed, running feet kicking up great clouds of sand into the still air. To his left, the dark warrior took the first swing. Draken feinted right—causing the Spartan to pivot and lose his stride, then slammed his left elbow into the man's ribs and heard the breath shriek as it left his lungs. Draken left no time for the Igori to recover, instead he vaulted into the air. When the jump reached its full height, he twisted his body to the left and brought the flat of his shield crashing down into the base of the man's skull. The Igori went limp and fell to his knees. His body slid to the ground.

Draken hurled his shield at Agathon. The metal rim caught the man square in the chest. Agathon's body spun under the momentum of the shield, and gasping for air, a hand pressed to his bruised lungs, he fell. Draken turned to his final opponent. Phelios's sandaled feet shuffled his big body from side to side, then he let out a strained battle cry, showing Draken a disturbing number of absent teeth. Draken braced his frame and watched in genuine interest as the man's movements played out in slow motion. Phelios flexed his beefy arm and stabbed at Draken's midsection intending to run him through, Draken twisted his body to the side. The thrust cut nothing but air. Phelios threw finesse to the wind and ran at him. Draken studied the warrior's enraged expression and felt nothing but real boredom. He did not bother to move out of the way of the haphazard attack, he went down on one knee, lifted his shield so it covered him from head to elbow, and let Phelios run into it. Draken legs trembled under the impact but he ignored them. Using the solid placement of the shield, he lifted Phelios off the ground and stood up. Phelios hung there, face down, arms flailing and feet aiming useless kicks at Draken's chest.

Last one, he thought, and brought his arm around. Controlling the force, he threw the Spartan to the ground. The resounding thud rippled the sands.

Draken stood. Waited. Let the world return to normal, living momentarily in the strange silence that always followed a battle. Applause broke out across the training yard, startling him. Draken turned and bowed to the crowd of colorful figures seated in the stands.

King Menelaus stood and smacked his meaty palms together. "Well done, my boy. Well done. It's as if I stand on the beaches of Troy and watch Achilles cut through the hordes."

"Hardly a horde," Draken called out. Walking to Agathon, he held out his hand and helped the man to his feet. "It was a good fight," Draken said.

Agathon spat out a mouthful of sand. "You didn't even break a sweat."

Draken slung his arm around his friends shoulder and smiled. "A little one," he said.

"Don't listen to your father," Helen of Troy sang out. "You are altogether far more handsome than Achilles. Magnificent, Draken."

Draken crossed his sword arm over his chest, bowing to his parents in the ancient way. "Thank you, Father." He bowed again, this time dropping his eyes to the sands. "Mother."

A beautiful girl ran onto the sands, her dress white and wild flowers twisted through her silver hair. Sunlight turned her skin to pure cream and a soft mist of honeysuckle perfume clung to the surrounding air.

"Androsia!" called Helen. "Come back here!"

Androsia ignored her mother and ran into her brother's outstretched arms. "Draken! That was so incredible!"

Draken smiled at his sister and tousled the curls tumbling over her arched brows. "Do you really think so, Androsia?"

"Yes!" said Androsia, head bobbing, and eyes sparkling. "I loved the way you threw him at the end." A stream of giggles poured from her cherub lips. "And that sound it made when his body hit the ground. *Kerthud!*" She mimicked the Igori's fall, flinging her arms out behind her while making her body go limp. "*Thud, thud!*"

Draken tugged on a curl looping over her ear. "Well, I'm glad someone liked it." He raised a dark brow, looking at Malkalimos, who came to a lumbering halt in front of them. "I think winning was not enough—it looks like I am about to receive a scolding," Draken proclaimed.

Malkalimos rolled his eyes. "Would you scold the sun for shining too bright? Or the wind for its violence?"

"I do not even understand what that means," said Androsia, her pretty face twisted in confusion.

"The words were not meant for you, princess," replied Malkalimos.

"Well, then," she sighed in mock sorrow. "They were truly useless words, for I fear they also soared over my brother's ringing head."

Malkalimos nodded, a grave expression tugging at his scar. "I fear you are right, my lady."

"They speak of me as if I were not here," Draken said to no one in particular. When silence greeted his outburst, he turned and shaded his eyes against the sun, exhaustion tugging at his muscles.

A team of Pegasi broke through a line of sparse clouds and galloped across the sky. Massive black wings cut the air, and jets of fire billowed from their nostrils leaving a path of silver smoke trailing behind them.

"Androsia, we have company," Draken said.

Androsia followed the line of his gaze and sighed wistfully. "Pity. Mother was in such a flowery mood. Bring on the storm," she said.

Draken lifted his hand and waved at Ares. The god of war landed his team of beasts and jumped down to the sands. "I hear the din of a young Spartan prince playing at being a warlord," called Ares. He reached them in two strides and bowed low to Androsia. "Princess, you grow more beautiful than all the stars."

"And you, sir, grow ever more proficient in your flattery."

Ares clapped his right hand to his heart. "I am wounded. Deeply."

Draken snorted. "Doubtful."

Ares tossed his shoulder-length black hair, a good deal of it waved around his face, making his sharp silver eyes even more brilliant. He stood just below six feet tall; had wide shoulders, a barrel chest and a strutting posture, which added to his height. He wore no armor and the gilded face of his mirrored shield reflected the sun, making silver rainbows in the sand. The sword in his hand curved in a wicked edge, it gleamed in the muted light. He pointed the razor tip at Draken. "You know it is not wise to challenge a god," rumbled Ares.

"Young princes are never wise," Draken returned. He tried to pull his face into a matching scowl, but a smile broke the mask. "Damn, but it's good to see you."

Ares burst out laughing, he threw his arms around Draken, giving him a bone-crushing hug. "You might not want to say that too loud." Ares used the point of his chin to gesture toward the queen. "Your mother looks to have swallowed a lemon. Her expression is terrifying."

"Oh, yes," whispered Androsia. "She saves that face for you."

"I never will understand why that particular queen hates me. Did I not give her my allegiance in the end?"

Androsia sighed. "It's not just you. She hates your entire family with a strong equality. The exception, of course, is Aphrodite—who she loves to distraction—the only reason she tolerates you, I think. She says you ruined her life."

"I?" Ares put his hand on his heart and threw Androsia a look of pure hurt. "I did nothing to that woman, except bleed for her and, of course, nearly lose my own life in defense of her. Spartan queen turned Trojan princess, now Spartan queen again. For the life of me, I cannot keep track of her thrones."

Draken glanced at his mother. Queen Helen was exquisite in her gown of blue silk. An emerald chain around her neck made her eyes shine like the sun-soaked ocean.

Androsia pulled in a long, broken breath. "It appears she is leaving. Good day to you both, I must attend her."

"Take care of her, Androsia," Draken whispered.

"Yes," she returned from over her shoulder. "I always do."

Draken closed his eyes to block out what he did not know how to change, then he turned and slung his arm around Ares's shoulder, throwing off his pensive mood. "What brings you to Sparta? I thought you were in Tartarus with Hermes?"

"I grew bored of his games. Besides, fighting alongside the dead is tiresome and pointless. There are other things in this life that call to man and god alike."

Draken followed Ares's gaze toward the shores of Aphrodite's temple settled atop the white rocks like a radiant crown. Seashells and mother-of-pearl lined the base of the rocks, it wove up the high stairwells and pillared terraces. Curtains of pale, aquamarine silk flew from open windows flapping flirtatiously in the cool breeze. From this distance, the temple resembled a pale blue-green bird hovering on the rocky lip of the brilliant cliffs. Roses and wild lilies ran rampant up the pink-veined marble walls, and white doves sang as they wove through the thorny vines.

Draken elbowed Ares in the ribs. "How furious do you think she'll be?"

Ares shrugged. "No more than usual. Aphrodite is the goddess of love in *all* its forms. Every flame casts a shadow. Desire possesses the fascinating ability to morph into jealous rage in mere seconds. In the essence of herself, Aphrodite is dangerous as she is beautiful. And yet...."

"Yet, she is yours," Draken finished.

Ares looked at him, a somber tic in his jaw. "It appears so, yes. I returned not only for her. You mean to compete in my games?"

Draken squared his shoulders. "I do."

"May all the gods—aside from my noble self of course—smile on you." Ares stepped back and faced him off.

"They have already done so," Draken avowed. "I have yet to fall."

"You are young. Your time will come."

"I only await its pleasure," Draken taunted.

"Has it come to this?" asked Ares in mock animosity. "Do we finally meet on the sands?"

"Yes!" Draken said. "The only thing I've wanted since the first second I held a sword."

Ares reached out his hand and they clasped arms like brothers. They stood in charged silence, the shining face of Apollo sealing the bond between them. Ares inclined his head to the diamond-encrusted surface of Aphrodite's shrine. "First, I have to survive what promises to be an interesting reunion."

"Will you attend the feast tomorrow night? We hold a banquet in your honor. A celebration for the god of war. More wine and food than even you could want."

"Miss my own feast? Never once in these last thousand years. I will see you, cousin," said Ares, and ambled back to his chariot. Taking hold of his team's golden reins, Ares turned to give Draken a formal bow, topped by a jaunty twist. He clicked the reins. Braying and tossing their glorious manes, the fire-breathing Pegasi vaulted into the sky.

Draken felt his shoulders sag as the previous exhaustion returned in force. The training and worry over his mother had sapped his energy. Stowing his gear on the rack, he strode through the golden halls of the palace corridors leading to his room. The servants had yet to light evening braziers and soft afternoon light tumbled through the arched windows.

A familiar voice rang out behind him. The passage hollowed-out the sound. "Does the young warlord seek to avoid his lesson as he does the enemy blade?"

Draken groaned and turned to face the man hobbling toward him.

Leandros arched a wispy white eyebrow. "What have I always told you?"

Draken grunted. "You tell me many things, old man."

Leandros held his brow suspended until Draken re-buckled the sandals he had undone. "A warrior's greatest weapon is not his arm or his sword…."

"—but his mind." Draken finished.

Leandros waggled a slim, gnarled finger at him. "You cannot outsmart an enemy unless you are smarter."

"The gods bow to your wit," Draken said, falling in step behind his ancient tutor.

Leandros carried on in his dry tone as if Draken had not spoken. "If my platitudes bore you so, you may simply attend me and observe."

A crisp chill bordered the edges of the wind, warning the approach of a cold night. Despite his ancient legs, Draken thought Leandros kept a punishing pace.

"You are young, Draken," said Leandros, his scowl bolstered the crow's feet stamped with papery finality at the corners of his eyes. "You want to be a god, but yours is a dangerous path."

The gold pillars framing the Spartan tribute to Apollo threw their shadows on the ground. Leandros creaked in every joint as he bowed to the massive statue and pressed his lips against the feet sandaled in bronze. Draken inclined his head at Apollo, keeping the scowl off his face for the benefit of Leandros alone. The tutor shot him a look for his lack of reverence, but held his tongue.

"In our lesson today," said Leandros, pulling himself up to full height. "I intended to cover the Phoenicians and their economic and political contributions to the modern Spartan life."

Draken mimicked a long, drawn-out snore. "I know about the Phoenicians and their questionable contributions. I also know you have repeated these things to me for years. Is there nothing more? Perhaps I am young, but I believe I am too old for this drudgery."

Leandros cleared his throat and sent a gob of spittle arcing out over the sand in a wavering stream. "Not yet. Be careful, Draken, that your thirst for battle does not cause you to drown. See here."

Leandros drew his attention to a mural, roughly painted and weathered by sea air and age. The image splashed across the wall on the right side of the staircase leading to the altar of Apollo, standing proudly in the center of the temple dais. Deep carvings and lines of sweet beet juice laid in place by thick, uneven strokes told a story he knew well. Perseus, son of Zeus, champion of the gods. The mural narrated a few of his heroics.

In the center of the piece, three men crouched inside a marble whirlpool encased in ice and fire. Perseus stood among them, arrayed in peasant's armor, yet the artifacts he held transformed him into a god. On his head sat Hades's Helm of Darkness and strapped to his right arm was Athena's shield. In his right hand, he carried a sickle of fused adamantine, a harpe, which Gaia had made to protect herself from her husband Uranus so many years ago. In his left hand, Perseus held the severed head of the poor priestess Medusa. The girl who had traded love for death. The snakes still writhed, the eyes in Medusa's tormented face bulged white and sightless from their sockets.

Leandros cleared his throat again. "You seek glory?"

Draken knelt down and ran his fingers over the rough, gold paint outlining the harpe. "No," he breathed giving the mural the obeisance he denied Apollo. "I have no place, Leandros." A darkness echoed in his voice. "I will reach my eighteenth year in only a few days. I have traveled the world, seen the kingdoms of Greece, Thessalia, Ithaca and Thebes. Not two years ago, I fought the barbarians in our borderlands, I pushed the Thracians back, and I watched many men die. I have received tutelage from Odysseus and," he inclined his head toward his tutor, "the great Leandros. I am strong. Too strong. There are rumors of my birth and I hear many say I am not the true heir of Sparta." Draken flicked a heavy stone, it skipped across the sand. "I don't belong here," he continued, squinting to meet the old man's eyes. "I don't know if belong anywhere."

Leandros motioned to the mural, using the broken nail of his forefinger as a pointer. "Perseus won his right to belong. He was born beneath a dark curse which tarnished his name. Many of the legends are. You feel you have lived, yet you are very young, Draken—a thing the youth hate to hear, I know. Listen to an old man, huh? It can take many years to find your place in this world."

"I am a soldier, a prince, a bastard—I have no place. On the battlegrounds I long for home, yet each time I return, I feel farther away," Draken said. "Mother no longer looks at me the same, she sees the outsider in me. It has eclipsed image of her son."

Leandros twitched his lips into a smile. "Women are tempestuous, boy. A lesson not learned in the classroom."

Draken stood and stretched his arms up above his head. The events of the day had depressed him. He needed a bath, some good music, and a large drink. "I must go Leandros. I fight Ares in the games tomorrow."

"I see." Leandros gave him a wary look. "You think battling the god of war will help you find your place?"

Draken smiled, imagining Ares's blood on the edge of his sword—anticipation was a battle cry throbbing in his gut. "No, but it will not hurt."

ANCIENT CHAPTER II

THE ISLE OF APHRODITE – MARCH 2ND, 1202, BCE

Fires crackling in marble braziers bathed the rose-gold walls of Aphrodite's temple in soft ocher light. Sage and cherry root incense burned beneath brass bowls where lilies swam in pools of rosewater, releasing sweet perfume that drenched the air.

Two girls lay next to each other in the only beds they had ever known. Eleven other girls slept in the room, Alora, and Arias hardly noticed. When they were together, it was just them in the world anyway. Arias reached across the little isle of space between their two beds. Alora took her hand.

"What are you thinking?" Arias asked, her whisper soft and well practiced.

Alora sighed. "Same thing I always think of before I sleep. Tonight is worse, though."

"Because of your birthday," Arias said. It was not a question.

"Yes. Just a few more hours now. I don't think I will sleep at all." Alora sat up, perched at the head of her bed, and wrapped her arms around her knees. "For so long now, I have held onto this strange hope that they would take us together. I've prayed every day for it, begged Aphrodite not to let us go alone," said Alora, and smiled a weak, sad smile. "I told her Hades and his dog scared you."

"The god of death is frightening enough, why does he have to have a three-headed monster dog?"

"Maybe none of the single-headed ones wanted to live with him," Alora said.

Arias laughed, but it died. "I don't want to exist without you, Alora."

"It's just the most horrible thought. Maybe they won't take me right away. Perhaps the goddess will have mercy… give us a few more days? We can hope?"

"Hope," Arias repeated. It was a strange word that had very little meaning to her. She was not born to hope.

Alora fluffed her pillow and lay back down, then let out a sound that was a mix between laugh and groan. "They say it will be beautiful."

Arias snorted. "They say a lot of things."

Neither of them spoke for a long time. When Arias finally felt her eyes close, and her body tumble into sleep she heard Alora whisper her name.

"Arias?"

"Yes?"

"I love you."

"Love you too."

They did not speak again, but they did not sleep—just held hands and waited out the remaining hours till dawn.

■   ■   ■

Thirteen girls in white robes knelt in a circle around the ivory altar. Thirteen beautiful voices raised in haunting, harmonic sound filled the hall.

"Take us to the place that be
Far across the golden sea.
From the gates of Tartarus take us away
To live, to die again
In the mists of that fated day."

Arias bowed to Migora. "Lord high priest," she said, rising to her feet. The priest inclined his bald head in her direction. Arias again knelt and reached her hand into the basket of white roses that rested at his feet. She picked her rose, no hint of thorn or a single bruise should mar the pearly white petals. It must be perfect, like her goddess.

"Take us to the place that be," the girls behind her sang. "Far across the golden sea."

Arias knelt and set the rose at the base of Aphrodite's ivory altar. After a moment of reflection she stood and lifted the knife resting on the altar's face. Mother-of-pearl coated the surface of the blade and a golden serpent—staring out of ruby eyes—coiled around the hilt. Arias lifted her gaze to the beautiful face of her goddess. She placed the tip of the blade against her heart. It sliced through the thin fibers of her white gown and drew a single drop of blood from her porcelain skin.

"Blessed Aphrodite, hear my prayer. My soul and spirit belong to you. I am your oracle, in life and death." Arias kissed the blade and returned it to the altar. She returned to stand beside Alora in the circle and took up the song. One by one, her sisters stood and mimicked her actions.

"Blessed Aphrodite," Arias chanted. "Hear my prayer…" The words spilled from her mouth as they had for everyday of her life that she could remember.

After the last girl finished the homage to Aphrodite, the high priest raised his hands. The chanting fell silent.

"Today one of you is chosen." His words were like the crack of a whip laid across her back, Arias felt chills break out down her spine. Her empty stomach plummeted to her feet as her eyes flew to Alora.

"At nightfall," continued Migora. "The chosen oracle will attend her *Herati* to prepare for the *Aphrodisia.* When her skin is bathed in milk, hair, and body perfumed, she will travel to the Pandemos and give herself in sacrifice to Enisis."

Arias sucked a breath into her lungs and held it there.

"Alora, of Thrace, the *Aphrodisia* choses you. Praise Aphrodite." The white-robed priests lining the wall echoed the cry.

Arias watched Alora's eyes fall closed and thought she might be sick, right there all over the golden floor.

■ ■ ■

Arias found Alora sitting on her bed hands folded in her lap. She faced the window and her expression looked serene. Arias knelt down beside her friend and rested her head against Alora's knees. A breeze wafted from the garden, carrying the perfume of gardenias, crocuses and lilies.

"Do you remember a time when we used to dream about the honor of being sacrificed?" asked Alora.

"Yes, age destroys all fantasies," Arias said.

"I feel we must believe it is beautiful, otherwise the fear of it all will be too much."

"Oh, it's just not fair! If they will kill us, why not at least let us die together?"

"We were not born for fair," said Alora. "We were born to honor Aphrodite, to submit to her spell and whatever man she choses. We were born to die on her altar." Alora shook her head as if she tried to shake the sad thoughts out of it. "I know it is a great honor and a noble death, but I am still so afraid. Long as I can remember, no one besides you has ever touched me. Now I must take off my clothes to let some man touch me anywhere he wants?"

"We will be under a love spell," Arias said, then dropped her voice. "I think you might want him to."

"Enough to die for it?" asked Alora. Arias had no answer. "What if it isn't enough?" sniffed Alora. "I'm afraid and I'm ashamed."

"Oh please, you have nothing to be ashamed of," Arias said. "I think we're all a little afraid. I can't even fathom what it would be like to love a man. I've never even seen a proper one. I don't believe the priests count."

"Do you ever think of life before all this?" Arias asked, when the silence got too heavy.

"No. The temple is the only home I remember. Do you?"

Arias shrugged. "I don't know. Some nights, when I can't sleep, I see the face of a woman. She has soft ebony hair and sapphire eyes. I think it might be my mother. Every time I dream of her I wake in tears. She is probably dead now." Arias shrugged. "I don't know. At least we're dying for a cause."

"Yes," said Alora. "At least there is that. Aphrodite promises to take us from Hades and bring us to the shores of the sparkling mist. Our beauty will not fade, we will live forever."

Arias had heard it before. Migora had explained that her mortal body was a cocoon, and death would free her to be a gorgeous butterfly. Her body, however would be dead—burnt down to nothing but ashes—so how would she be beautiful?

"I am going to miss you so terribly," Arias said. "You were the sister I got to choose. I am grateful for you if nothing else."

Alora moved away from Arias and reached under the bed. After a moment she brought out a velvet bag. Alora loosed the beaded drawstring, reached in and took out a little knife.

"We can be sisters for real." Alora pressed the knife against her palm. "Blood sisters."

"Yes," Arias said. "Blood sisters, in this life and in all our lives."

Alora sliced the knife over the soft surface of her palm, the blood flowed and made a little pool. Arias took the blade cutting herself in the same spot. She dropped the knife and they clasped hands.

"Sisters," they said. "In this life and in all our lives."

They stayed that way, fingers linked and heads resting on each other's shoulders. Soft voices whispering their spell, they waited. Waited until it was time, and the priests came to take Alora away.

ANCIENT CHAPTER III

Draken stood at the entrance to his ancestral family home and searched Hades constellation in the blackness. Dark clouds obscured the sky, which rumbled and belched midnight vapors. An eerie muttering touched the warm breeze that blew through fire-lit halls of the Mycenaean Palace. The soft glow of the torches did little to dispel the hanging shadows; dark mists weaved through the golden arches, whitewashed walls, and marble terraces, muting the rich velvets and lavish decor. Draken turned toward his father's chamber. The sound of his footsteps on the marble floors seemed hushed.

Light shone in the king's antechamber. Draken bowed as he entered. "Father."

"My son." The king's stony face held no expression. "You fought bravely today," he said. "I hope you fare as well in Ares's tournament."

Draken bowed again. "Thank you, Father."

King Menelaus waved to a nearby chair. "Sit, drink, then tell me your purpose. I'm sure you've better things to do than visit an old man."

A flaxen-haired girl stood by the door, a jug of wine and goblet in hand. Menelaus absently snapped his fingers, and she walked toward them. The white cloth draping her slender frame made her skin glow almond in the firelight. She filled the goblet and leaned down to place it in front of Draken.

"Thank you," Draken said. He smiled at her, she flushed, and her eyes fell to study the ground. He turned back to his father. "I've learned this particular *old man* serves the best wine in Sparta."

Menelaus chuckled. "Helen gave you her wit. At least that's something."

Draken lifted his wine. "She gave me a shouting the other day, is what she gave me."

The king nodded, his old eyes wrinkled, twinkling from his smile. "If nothing else, the queen excels at that." Silence held the room in its grasp for a time while Draken studied the man he called father.

"Tomorrow the games begin," Draken said. "In thirteen days when a majority of this insanity has concluded, I will have my ceremony." He sighed deeply; dragging his hands through his hair, dark curls burst between his fingers. "I do not know what I will do with my years, or where the gods will take me, but I have to know." He set down his glass of wine, then stood up and paced the room, stirring the darkness. "I've heard the stories, of course, that I am the son of a god. Poseidon, Hades, Apollo, I have heard them all. According to the Mycenaeans, I have many fathers."

The King pursed his lips. "Yes, stories abound in Sparta like flies on waste. Only few know the true story of how you came to me. Perhaps it is time you are one of them. There have not been many good things in my life. Raising you has always brought me pride."

Draken halted, then looked up at his father, eyes locking on the old face. The king seemed lost in the memories that danced in the room's layered shadows. Battles and blood. Screaming, tortured souls. "In the years after Troy, the world for Helen and I, was one of only darkness and pain."

"Why did you take me?" Draken asked.

"I didn't," said Menelaus. "You were a gift I could not refuse."

"What do you mean? Who gave me to you? Was it Hades? Is he my father? My coloring... I favor Hades."

Menelaus rumbled out another sigh and motioned for more wine. "I went to the Fates, one night almost eighteen years ago. I remember the moon, pulsing silver light, high above my head. Waves crashed into the rocks at the base of Themis. It sounded to me like the rocks were screaming. I wanted to scream with them. I didn't, instead I climbed those black rocks one painstaking step at a time."

"My nightmares taunted me on the long climb, even the wind mocked me. 'Ruler of the world, it whispered to me in its cold, old voice. Ruler of the fatherless. The desolate. The dead'."

Menelaus scrubbed the silver stubble smattered between the scars on his jaw. Pain replaced the faraway look in his eyes. Draken walked back over to his father and sat down, wine forgotten.

"I ignored the brutal pain of the rocky shards as they cut into the flesh of my palms, sank their razor tips into the bones of my knees. It meant nothing to me. I would have done that and more to speak to the Moirae—those ancient, rotten corpses. Crusted crones who hold the fates of the world in their scaly, blistered hands. It had been a few years since the Trojans fell to Odysseus's wit. We dove out of the belly of that monster horse and put an end to that proud city. I went home to months of madness haunted by screams, and violent dreams. Death everywhere I looked. My brother and I had been the monsters. He was dead. I was cursed." Menelaus closed his eyes, flexing his weathered hands. "Nothing rent my soul like Helen. The girl lay in my arms for months weeping for a dead boy. A silly prince."

"She truly loved him then?" Draken asked.

"Aphrodite, Athena and Hera thought it best to destroy a nation over a beauty contest. The judgment of Paris," scoffed Menelaus over more wine. "Helen's heart was the prize. She loved Paris because she was under the spell of a goddess and could not do otherwise. I watched her die a thousand deaths over him. What could I do? I had nothing to give her. On the sands of Troy, I traded my honor for vengeance."

"You fought for your wife," Draken interrupted. "There is nothing more honorable."

"For all the good it did me. I won the battle, claimed the bride, but I had no woman in the night. Only horror. Listening to her scream out her dead lover's name; I prayed for death, but couldn't bring myself to do it. Without a king, what would become of the world my brother and I destroyed? It didn't matter. For years I fancied myself in love with her spellbinding beauty. I couldn't listen to her heartbreaking screams any longer. The Fates would give me some form of answer, or they would cut my thread. I didn't care."

"I reached the first peak and a scream shattered the night. A thick cloud of noxious steam billowed from their mountain top. I climbed and imagined them crouched around their azure flames, that old eyeball bouncing between them, while they cackled and cut the threads of life."

"The night was deep by the time I reached their cave. I remember their choked voices. They crawled on the wind and sent shivers of ice slivering down my sweat-soaked back. 'We hear your approach oh King of the fallen. We have what you seek'."

"Dread froze my muscles. The gods themselves feared the prophecies of the Fates. Even Zeus must bow a knee to their power. I thought they would kill rather than speak to me, a mortal man. The moon's light does not touch that craven place. Darkness hung so thick, I imagined myself thrust back in the belly of that wooden horse, trying not to inhale the smell of fear and feces, while the very men we meant to kill wheeled us through the Trojan gates. I remembered the haunting screams of women and children torn apart by bloody soldiers who had abstained too long."

"You cannot regret the sins of war," Draken said. "You have taught me that since I was a child. What is done on the battlefield is with purpose and honor."

"Yes, that is the dream, is it not? The thing we teach our children." Menelaus clutched the bridge of his nose between thumb and forefinger. "There was no honor on the Trojan sands. It was a massacre of violent proportions. Agamemnon was enraged, his starving men even more so. We behaved like animals. I felt like each disgusting act lay bare before them, black smudges on my soul. I stumbled over more rocks and wheezed like the old man I am now. I called them. The silence that greeted me terrified me more than the screams."

"I stepped into the cave, the reek reminiscent of a field three days after battle, where the guts of fallen men rot in the sun, and the excrement of death lies baked and crusted against the blood-soaked ground. Fire burned in my nostrils. I remember I opened my mouth to call out to the Fates again, but my words died as a heinous, ear-shattering sound screeched out around me, echoing though I stood under an open sky."

"Out of the folds of the inky night came the Fates, the wriggling eye flying before them like a talisman of power. It shone in the murky black. The figures stepped into the meager slice of light that seemed to emanate from nowhere and everywhere. Long streams of flesh dripped off their black, rotting bones. Empty eye sockets gaped like wounds in the center of their vulturine faces. Beneath long, pike-like noses, their lips split apart like ruptured boils.

"I recoiled in horror. Disgust. My stomach lurched. The foremost fate moved, her curling yellow toenails scraping against the glass rocks. The sound of it echoed like their laughter bouncing off the empty air. A hand oozing pus thrust the writhing eye beneath my nose. The stench made bile rise in my throat."

"'Ask your question, King of kings,' they chorused, laughter bubbling from bloody lips. 'We know why you are here, and we know how you will *dieeeee*.' I swear to all the gods the very air around me reeked of unending misery, eternal suffering and death. As if the ground itself shouted: 'Abandon all hope ye who enter here'. My words, when I finally could form them were honest at least. Death holds no fear for me, I told them. I wonder why I am yet alive."

"'You are not alive!' squealed the first fate. 'You are living a cursed half-life, you and your golden deadly queen...'"

"Another pressed her hand to my cheek and caressed my stubble, leaving a trail of slime. 'We have something for you,' she told me. Worms crawled in the center of her empty eye-socket, chewing at the loose pieces of dangling flesh."

"'Payment!' screamed the third. 'What do you offer us in payment?'" Menelaus shook his head and rubbed the heel of his hands to his eyes. "The Fates circled me, sack gowns rustling, crumbling bones creaking."

"From the folds of my thick cloak, I drew out the fist-sized ruby that had graced the pinnacle of King Priam's crown. The Fates screamed in glee. 'Trojan jewels! We have not yet received Trojan jewels. Priam did not favor us.'"

"'Ancient whore!' the first cawed. 'No one truly favors us. So we destroyed the mighty Priam. Ah, how we destroyed him!' The three swirled in a circle around me, lifting the hems of their robes to reveal a great deal more of their decaying flesh than I ever wished to see."

"They raised their hands high and shouted to the moon. 'Severed his spine...cut his string...we should have taken his thing...Ha! Severed his spine...cut his string...we should have taken his thing...his thing. Ya hee hee...taken his thing...'"

"I roared at them, told them to look at me, see past the shadows in my soul to the man I was. I wanted to run. Fear and anger held me fast." Menelaus coughed, his brow remained furrowed when the fit was over. He took a sip of wine. Then another.

"They mocked me," he said, sounding disgusted by the remembered events. "'How he commands us,' they cackled, 'our innards are all aflutter.' I thought of telling them, their innards were spilling through the holes in their robes, but held my tongue. The bloody eye careened wildly as the old witches bathed it in their steamy, putrid breath. The endless spinning drew my own eyes, numbed my mind with its hypnotic gaze. The Fates spoke, their words ran around me. Touched my skin. Crawled along the back of my neck."

"'In twenty-three years, when Pluto and Mars align, a man will come bearing the steel of death—a mortal man and a child of the gods. He will change destiny, his fate will alter the structure of this world.'"

"I yelled, told them I had not even asked my question. 'Horse's *ass*!' One hollered. 'Why would you ask what we already know? Stupid human king. You want to know what will happen if you take your own life, coward that you are.'"

"'Yes, coward king, we will tell you, then. If you die, this child too will die. If he dies, the gods will destroy humanity!'

'Not a bad idea,' yelped the first. 'Kill the child, we should. Kill the child,' moaned the third. 'Yes.' The three said together. 'Kill it, kill it, kill it. Kill the demi-god!'"

"What child? I shouted. The very essence of the place tugged at the last remaining threads of my sanity. Their long, cracked fingers pressed a squirming bundle into my arms. 'Athena gives you this child,' they told me, 'in revenge against Ares for what he did to her on the sands of Troy. You are to take him and raise him as your son. If you do not, the goddess swears she will have your life, as she should have ten years ago. Or, you could simply kill the child. We don't care either way. Better for us if he dies. Better, much better. Kill the child,' she screamed, 'take his thing!'"

"Now, mind this my son, I had not gone there for a child. However, when I moved to cast you back into their arms, the tattered edges of the filthy cloth fell away." Menelaus leaned back in his chair, templing his fingers over his chest. Deep lines cut grooves in his old face, the sunken eyes tired and sad. "You stared up at me innocent of it all. Large, golden eyes searching mine. Then you yawned and gave a half smile. I felt a thing I thought long dead. I didn't want to let you go. Who is this boy? I asked them. I brushed the hair off your face, you cooed, blowing little bubbles, and popping them between your baby teeth. They told me you were Draken, son of Hades, son of Cronus, son of Gaia."

"To my shame, I recoiled. Born of a dark union? I asked. He is evil? Whispered laughter followed my words. 'Who is to say what is evil? Not you, great miserable King—killer of children, defiler of women.' They mocked me again, laughing and spewing insults, staring at me from their crawling wounds. 'Evil?' they hissed. 'No, not evil. Cursed, perhaps. He will follow in his father's footsteps, he will rule the dead. Any more we can not say, raise him, love him, kill him—we do not care. Just take him away. Far, far away. He infects us. We are…afraid.'"

"I backed away, holding you close. The first fate held up a rancid finger. 'A word of warning, human king: if ever harm should come to the one he loves, there will not only be bloodshed in the realm of men. King of the undead, king of the forgotten. He will be the death of you, too. If you kill this child now, you will live to see many long years. Allow him to live, and in twenty years you will die.'"

"I took my cloak and wrapped you against my chest, then began my descent. I didn't know why or what possessed me, yet I was certain you must live. The depressive cloud of the fates grew thinner, I picked up my speed, desperate to be free of their stench and appalling predictions."

Menelaus looked at Draken, meeting his eyes perhaps for the first time. "They cursed me, in my last moments on that mountain. A strange curse. I do not understand its meaning. I will, however, never forget it. 'Allow harm to come to the one he loves,' they told me, 'and the contents of Pandora's box will seem kind compared to the horror he will bring.'"

Draken sat back, his jaw slack, his eyes burning. "W-What does that mean?"

Menelaus sank further into his chair and finished his wine in a single gulp. "Who can know the mind of the Fates? Not even Zeus. When you grow old, you learn to leave deep mysteries alone."

"Even if it means I cause your death?"

"I expected to die that night. Instead, I got a son. An heir, a thing Helen would never give me. If it means one day I must die, so be it. It is a small price to pay for the sanity you have brought me. You made Helen smile. The night I brought you home, my Helen looked a heartbeat from death. Beautiful as ever. Hair spread about her like a blanket of silver moonlight, her soft white limbs resting against lush Byzantium silk. She smelled like jasmine and amber musk. She wanted nothing to do with me. For two years, since the day I carried her onto my ship and took her from Troy, she had not spoken a single word to me. When she looked on you for the first time, however, that light returned. She laughed again, the sound of her singing often rang through the halls. Helen, Queen of Sparta—my true love," Menalaus gave a rueful smile. "My eternal bane."

"So Helen is not even my mother?" The thought churned in his gut. "Does she know?"

"That you are the son of Hades?" Menelaus nodded. "One look at you, anyone would know the truth. The rumors are foolishness, petty stories to entertain children."

"Did you tell her of the curse? Of your death?"

"No," sighed Menelaus, his voice a whisper in the darkness. "No, I did not. Your mother is the daughter of Zeus. Her immortal beauty will never fade. Once I am gone, she will be free to begin her life again. Knowledge of my impending doom would only bring her pleasure. I know I deserve much, but I could not stand to see the light such a knowledge would bring to her eyes."

Draken stood up, staggering only slightly put his hand on his father's slumped shoulder. "Son of Hades or not, you will always be my father. Tomorrow I fight to honor you in the games."

"Then, for both our sakes, son, I pray you are victorious."

ANCIENT CHAPTER IV

THE ISLE OF APHRODITE, MARCH 3RD

Sunlight sparkled off marble, filling the staircase with dancing motes of light. The orchids and water lilies breathed heavy perfume into the air. The piercing song of the blue jay echoed around her, but Arias noticed none of the beauty as she climbed the stairs to Aphrodite's chambers. It felt like every pore in her body wept. She missed Alora, with an ache that grew inside her like a disease. Knowing she would never see her smile again, never fall asleep, the last whispered giggle still lingering on her lips, just—never.

    At this moment, Alora would be in the final stages of preparation, her Aphrodisia would begin when the sun fell. Arias knew she should be happy for her friend, and perhaps the happiness was there somewhere, just deeply buried under the knifing pain ripping through her heart. They would celebrate tonight. Alora, however, would not be there to share it, because the celebration would be for Alora, and Alora would be dead.

    Careful of her deeply kohl-lined eyes, Arias tried to wipe away the smudges of exhaustion beneath, and pinch some semblance of color back into her cheeks. Her sleep had been terrible.

    All night, her mind had strayed to the world outside the temple. What was it like? A day in the life of someone not already slated for death? All day, her eyes roamed over the city of Sparta, its gold, and marble frame coiled around the base of Taygetus like jewels in a crown. The tips of the diamond towers caught the sunlight, a row of prismatic rainbows filled the sky.

Arias had not voiced her concerns to Migora or the other priests. It was pointless. They would give her the same answer: destiny, a gift, not a curse. Aphrodite would know the answers. Arias had to speak to her. The goddess of love and beauty—*her* goddess—would mend the fraying edges of her faith. One look in her eyes would make it right.

In the past, she and Alora visited the opulent golden chambers to party, drink honeyed wine, and hear stories of worlds long dead. Those visits had been full of laughter and games. That was all gone, Alora's absence hung like a pall in the perfumed air.

The climb to Aphrodite's tower stole Arias's breath and turned her legs to water, but she persisted. After what seemed an eternity, she reached the golden door that lead to the antechamber. A gift from Aphrodite's husband, Hephaestus—her wedding gift, so the legends told. Carvings of nymphs adorned the surface, dancing among images depicting the four seasons and Uranus, Aphrodite's father, rising from the shattered face of an abalone shell.

Arias touched the twinkling waves brushing along the base of the shell, ran her fingers over the tiny diamonds buried in the golden ripples. It was a beautiful creation. She sighed. Alora had loved the Seasons. Arias lifted her fist to knock on the door, then froze, hand poised in the air like a frightened cobra chickening out of its strike. She could not do it! What could she say? *I don't want to die? Give me back my friend?* Most likely the goddess would simply think she had gone mad and burn her to purge the body of its insanity. Arias dropped her hand and in a flurry of white silk, turned and ran back the way she had come. She cut a sharp left down a slightly unfamiliar corridor—voices sounded in the distance. Gulping her next breath she pressed her body against the wall. The voices increased in volume. Her cheeks bulged as she fought to hold in that breath. They were getting closer.

Oh, what does it matter? Arias thought in pure frustration. *What am I afraid of? What is the very worst they could do to me?* Her hands folded over her stomach and she let out the breath in a low whistle. Wicker soles squealed against the tiles. The voices halted. Arias stepped out from the shadows.

"Arias!" screamed Migora, his tone high pitched and feminine. A hand flew to his chest. "Goddess, child! You gave me a fright! What are you doing on this side of the temple?"

Arias shook her head and tried to giggle, it was a forced noise, and she feared she may have snorted. "Nothing at all, lord high priest. I simply wished to speak to the goddess, then reconsidered." On an afterthought she said. "I did not wish to disturb her with my mundane ramblings."

"'Tis good of you, child. It is always Aphrodite's wish to be spared the monotony of others."

Arias inclined her head and kept silent.

Migora reached into the front seam of his robes and extracted two glimmering white scrolls. "Today however, it seems the stars themselves whisper in your ears."

Arias could see a small jewel hanging from an engraved rope strung around the middle of the larger scroll. "The stars, my lord?" Arias asked, still staring at the pretty jewel.

"Hum, yes. It appears I have a message for you."

"For..for...for me, my lord?" Arias stuttered. A first time for everything, she supposed.

"There were many levels on which I too felt confusion, yet it's written in the goddess hand, my orders were clear. Take it, the other is for your sisters. You will gather them in the garden and read it aloud." Migora's words trailed off. He held the scrolls out to her. Arias took them slowly. The parchment was cool under her fingers, soft as feather down.

The priest, loitering behind Migora like a misshapen shadow, took a step forward and cleared his throat. "Yes," said Migora, seeming to agree with the phlegm-filled cough. "On your way, child."

Arias stumbled back a few steps before dropping into a clumsy bow. "Yes, my lord."

"Today, child," said Migora over an exhausted sigh. "Today."

Arias turned and fled.

She ran, no thought in her mind. No direction. She felt so lost.

Lost. Arias looked around in confusion. She was lost. She had left behind the white marble halls reserved for the Leisha long ago. Now, she strode through tunnels of crimson stone. Droplets of water leaked from the close, rocky ceiling, and small rivers ran down the walls. The flickering light of torches failed to drive back the damp chill that permeated the corridors. She made to turn back, only to find herself uncertain which way she had come.

Arias rubbed her hands over her upper arms. It did nothing. Chills raced up and down her skin. The circles she spun in only further twisted the jumble in her mind and did not magically point out the right direction—it seemed the only thing they aided was nausea. Her hand went up to cover her mouth and she stopped spinning. A gust of wind sent an eerie howl pouring through the tunnels. She shuddered again.

In desperation, Arias turned and ran from the sound. She made a sharp left, then another. With every step the howl grew louder. It was not the wind that howled, there was no wind down in this endless room of pure night. Arias stopped running and doubled over, trying to catch her breath in wheezing gulps that watered her eyes.

Someone screamed. A scream like she had never heard before. Then a voice, a tearful pleading voice, getting louder and louder. Arias knew the voice, all her soul she wished she did not, but wishes were for fairies and nymphs; she was neither, therefore had none. It was Alora.

Gone was the cheerfulness, the bright notes of sound Arias knew so well. Fear echoed in Alora's voice. Fear and mind-numbing panic.

Arias needed to get away. Far away from that voice as she could. But it was Alora, and all she could do was move closer to the terrible sounds. Alora's tortured voice let loose another scream. Shattered words laced this one like bitter almond.

"I don't want to die! Please! Please, you can't do this!"

"Silence, child!" A male voice screeched out. "You will bring the wrath of Aphrodite upon us all!"

Arias rounded the corner in time to see Alora receive a punishing blow to the face. The crunching sound of fist striking flesh made her want to wretch.

Six priests in ceremonial black cowls wrestled with a bloody, writhing Alora. The girl seemed to have lost her mind. Violent spasms shook Alora's body, and her voice broke over ragged screams.

Arias froze, terror stricken, the scrolls forgotten in her shaking hands. Before her eyes Alora morphed into a rabid beast, kicking, and biting like a wild animal. Clumps of her dark hair clung to a long, bloody gash on the side of her painted face. Hands twisted into claws, she dug her nails into the fleshy face of the priest who had struck her.

Arias screamed, rushed forward, and threw herself over Alora's body.

"Arias?" asked Alora. She looked crazed, shots of blood speared her eyes, a trickle of it ran down her chin.

"Yes, it's me. It will be fine. Look at me, Alora."

"I don't want to die," bawled Alora, renewing her struggles. "Please take me out of here."

A priest grabbed Arias's arm and hauled her off her friend.

"NO, PLEASE!" Arias screamed. "Please don't hurt her!"

"Silence, girl!" The black-robed priest bellowed. He dealt her a firm backhand and Arias's body crumpled. Pain exploded in her cheek. Arias battled for consciousness, she shook her head trying to clear her dusky vision. The priest who hit her took Alora's arm and twisted it up behind her back.

"This is your duty!" The priest hissed in Alora's ear, and Arias could see streaks of sweat running down his cheek.

"Please," entreated Alora, fresh tears running down her face. "I want to live." Her wide, frightened eyes reflected the twisted face of her murderer.

Arias wrapped her arms across her stomach—a place where maggots writhed and acid sloshed from side to side—wracking her cloudy brain. A drink, there should be a drink. Diluted adder venom. Why was Alora not drugged? The priests always droned on about how the drink dulled the pain and erased the fear. All the songs promised feelings of ultimate beauty. Beauty was nonexistent in this horrible place, not one thread in the dying struggles of her friend.

Alora went limp and sobbed. "Please let me stay in the temple. I want to live. Please don't kill me."

One priest dug his hand deep in Alora's black hair, he tilted her face so a second priest could use his grimy fingers to pry her mouth open, and pour a stream of venom down her throat.

Alora gave one final scream before her tense limbs relaxed and fell to her sides. Her head rolled back and her eyes glazed over. The priests released Alora's battered body, it crumpled to the cold stone floor. A seizure ravaged her limbs and her head twisted so it looked like her neck had broken. Like a retreating nightmare, Alora's fear and terror faded, replaced by a serene, stupefied calm—the promised courtesy of the venom. Arias watched Alora's mouth twist into a placid smile, a horrific contrast to her bloody face and broken lips.

"What are you doing here?!"

Arias screamed and looked up to see an evil raven, black robes hanging over its gaunt frame—a parody of broken wings—she screamed until she realized it was a priest who towered over her, poisonous fury raging in his eyes.

"I—I..." Arias stuttered.

"I asked you a question, *girl!*" shouted the priest.

A wail burst from her throat. "Migora—a message, Aphrodite." Sobs shook her shoulders. Her mind felt like it lay shattered in pieces at her feet. Her soul? *That* was forever charred. "I got lost."

"Easy," anger faded from the priest's voice. "This is no place for you, child. Let me take you back to where you belong."

Arias followed the priest through the endless maze of dark corridors. Her every step was an uneven disaster and she tried to press her hands over her lips, hush her sobs, but they bubbled through her fingers and splashed her buffed nails. Arias hardly noticed when they emerged into the perfume-soaked gardens. Leisha ate, played, and read. They laughed and sang with the birds. Arias felt like they had all gone insane. The priest's instructions to sit floated through her mind and she obeyed, falling to her knees.

Nyla, a pretty girl, wearing ribbons twined through gold braids, knelt down in front of Arias. White and yellow daisies tied off the ends of the braids. Nyla pressed a cup of hot wine against the back of her hands. Arias smelled cinnamon and the musky tang of cloves.

Others clustered around, hurling questions at her. Questions that were just empty sounds in the wind. Her mind stayed locked in the room of perpetual nightmare. The images of Alora; her terrible smile, milky white eyes, blood-stained broken mouth—were there, lurking behind her closed eyes. Gone. The girl she knew—gone. Aquamarine jewels sparkling against a crisp white shore. That is what Alora's soul had been to her. A jewel of unearthly beauty. Gone.

Arias felt the scrolls tumble from her cold hands, she gathered them back into her lap, her fingers wooden and clumsy.

"Where did you get those?" asked Kayla. Arias looked up. Lovely blue eyes stared down into hers.

"What happened? You look so strange. You have dirt on your cheek, did you know that?"

"Kayla!" giggled Nivia. "If she knew that it probably wouldn't be there."

"Did you fall?" asked a soft voice from over her shoulder. Arias could not put a face to the gentle whisper. It was no matter. Night had fallen. The ocean long ago swallowed the crimson sun. Braziers scattered through the gardens held pillars of ocher flames and fireflies danced in the twilight. Arias twisted her fingers around the bejeweled little rope wrapping the scroll, then tugged on it. It fell off easily and the smooth cylinder of paper expanded in her hand. Like a captive in a dream, she unrolled the scroll. Golden writing glittered. Little letters swimming in and out of focus.

Gasping giggles, sighs and squeals disturbed the path of the dancing fireflies.

"Oh, Arias!" gushed Kayla. "The goddess asks you to attend her in the stands during tomorrow's games."

"Such an honor." A voice to her left.

"No surprise—you've always been her favorite," said Nivia, taking the parchment from Arias's unsteady grasp. "She wants you to actually stand beside her," Nivia continued. Then she leaned in close until Arias could see the specks of glitter clinging to the tips of her lashes. "We all die," whispered Nivia. "Don't cry over Alora. Don't cry."

It was a command she could not obey. More tears fell, dropping on her knees, seeping into the soft silk of her white dress. Her life had been a dream, reality was coming for her. Arias looked up at the open face of the pearly, haunted moon and wondered for the first time in her life if maybe, just maybe, she did not want to die.

CHAPTER 5

FAIRHAVEN, WASHINGTON, NOVEMBER 9TH, 2019

I blinked and the dreams faded. Sunlight poured into the dark corners of my room—no thrumming rain, only a flock of yellowthroats harmonizing. No screaming. No bleeding. No dying. The death I dreamed last night was not my own. I smiled, burrowing deeper into my cozy duvet.

"Ouch!" My nose smacked something rough. I felt around for it. My hands touched the beautiful book. Sighing, I hugged it to my chest and closed my eyes. When my lashes fell against my cheeks, I saw his face.

"*The Aphrodisia*," I whispered. The word tasted strange in my mouth. At least I did not taste blood. I laughed, kissed the book, and vaulted out of bed. I put on a silky white shirt, a pair of blue jeans, then fluffed my hair. I even added lipstick and mascara. Sunlight hit the mirror making rainbows sparkle in the glass.

Today would be a pretty day.

I put the book under my pillow, straightening the tattered pages almost absently.

I left my room and started down the hall, my footsteps echoed softly. From the gilded frames of their portraits hanging on the walls, my aunts looked down on me. A group of stern women if there ever was one. Once, in my childhood I made myself walk down the hall and look directly into each of their eyes. I never did it again. I found no laughter in that crowd of old eyes. Only eerie power and distant pain. I picked up my pace, rows of chills trickling down my spine.

Lily stood in front of the coffeemaker, the silk of her pink robe matched the flush in her cheeks. She saw me and her eyes widened so big that her lashes brushed her brows. "You look like happiness," she said.

"You look like, Grace Kelly," I returned.

She beamed and poured me a cup of coffee.

I inhaled deeply. Pain free. "Oh, Lily, I feel so much better today! I actually slept last night."

"No dreams?"

"A few. I didn't mind them though. Someone else's drama."

"You fell asleep reading that book, didn't you?"

"Course I did."

"Well, it's wonderful that you're feeling better! Does that mean you'll go to class today?"

I nodded. "I will. I slept. I have a good handle on my crazy today. Today will be a beautiful day."

■   ■   ■

It was a terrible day.

My sense of euphoria died a slow, two-hour death on the freeway. I had a devil of a time finding parking due to my tardiness. On my walk from the courtyard to the English Lit room, I realized I was wrong: one good night's sleep did not wash away two weeks of hell. I got bumped twice on my way to class, then cornered in the hallway by two sweet girls raising awareness for something I barely heard. They were both incredibly passionate about the topic, the barrage of jumbled emotions made my head spin, and a strange splatter of black and white spots glowed behind my closed eyes. By the time I sat down in class I had a nasty migraine. I wiped my sweaty palms on my jeans, then opened my ancient copy of the *Iliad* to book one.

In my opinion, the best opening scene in literature, when Achilles, loses his love, Briseis, to King Agamemnon. *'Fate stands now upon the razor's edge.'* I lifted my gloved hand, it seemed the pages flipped on their own accord. This time, it was Helen's voice that came up at me from the italic ink. *'There was a world…or was it all a dream?'* I always wondered what she had meant by this? Did the dream become a nightmare, the nightmare a reality? Is that what was happening to me?

I ran my fingers atop the typed words, shaking my hair over my face, praying for invisibility. Professor Clarkson called on me twice. Answering his questions was hardly the end of the world. It was easy; I had nearly every word of the subject committed to memory.

The end sucked, the part when he took my hand and asked me where I had been? Why was I skipping classes? Did I think I could complete the week's assignment? His concern rocked me back on my heels, but his misery over his divorce, and his fear for his little girls—obliterated me. He felt their pain, his family's pain, and his own. I felt all the pain so strongly it forced me to close my eyes to keep them from rolling. Agony radiated up my arm, sent sickening shock waves to my brain. I mumbled something, and he let me go. I have no memory of the walk to my car. I remember nothing of the drive back to Fairhaven. My brain's autopilot took me to Larry's.

Lily would want me to drive straight back to the manor, yet, I just could not bring myself to turn the wheel in that direction. She would see my eyes, the fearful black splotches under them, and she would know. Today had started so well; I left her happy, if I went home I would take the smile out of her eyes, a thing I could just as easily do tomorrow. I parked my car and cut the engine. It purred into silence. Twilight brought more rain. I watched the droplets bounce like little disintegrating crowns on my windshield. I wanted to go back home and read *Blood and Shadows*. I wanted to go deeper into the tangled lives of Draken and Arias…the demi-god and the Leisha. I got out of the car and clicked the beeper. The security lights flashed blood and gold.

"*Cara.*"

I spun around, my eyes scanning the edges of the dense forest.

"Who's there?" I took a few steps toward the forest. "I said, who's there?" Rain whispered through the pine leaves, clashing against the sounds of laughter emanating from Larry's bar.

"*Cara.*"

"I heard that!" My broken whisper made me jump. "Well, it's true!" Nothing came back at me from the darkness. Just the haunting tone of silence, and the rich scent of lilacs. I shook my head, gave the forest one last, forlorn look, and walked to the bar. *Freaking lilacs!*

Inside Larry's, a good chunk of my fear slipped away. Brett offered me a polite, "good evening" and pulled out the bar stool for me to sit.

"Larry here?" I asked.

"Around. Still having storm trouble."

"Sorry. I'll have a house merlot," I told him.

"Alrighty, I'll see what we got." Brett squatted down before a cabinet holding an assortment of wines. He coughed and his pants slipped a little too low. I politely looked away.

Larry chose that moment to appear. "Hey, Brett, I'll pour fer her." He smiled at me. "Bad day?"

"Truly, made even worse because it started out so good."

"Well, a good start is always important even if it ends badly. Heard you were helping Detective Saint on that Lorna Parker case." Larry shrugged his big shoulder before I could say anything. "Word travels fast in a small town. It's awful good of you Cara." He poured me a glass of wine and cleared his throat violently enough to make a few droplets of wine splatter the table. Something hissed under the bar, followed by a low crackle, the old register sparked. Larry rolled his eyes. "It's been crazy here today. Phones going wild, lights flickering, bulbs exploding."

"Yep," I agreed over a dry sip. "That kinda day."

"Be right back." Larry put the uncorked bottle by my glass. "Help yourself."

I did. The faded bulb overhead pulsed, emitting a low, steady hum. I watched the little filament dance until a bright yellow flash ended its life, and the bar fell further into shadow—so did my mind.

The light in the room turns golden, and I am on the altar again. I do not yet jerk my arms. I know golden cuffs hold them locked above my head. I also know that soon those cuffs will cut gouges in my wrist. I tell myself not to struggle. Men in black robes howl at the invisible moon. I recognize the chant for what it is. They sing and their blackened lips pull back, showing me yellowed teeth scaling rotting gums.

"'A breath of life from the mouth of death,' they say, and a distant part of me understands. The stench of rot burns my eyes and throat. The chanting stops and I look for the shadow of the blade. I tell myself to be still, but I fight until the golden cuffs are slick with my blood. My screams echo around the room, taunting me. Death is coming. I can taste the metallic tang of fear on my tongue.

Suddenly, she is in front of me, her beauty a thing beyond reality. All of her is gold, save the lush red lips and violet, flashing eyes.

Her singsong voice rises in her final chant.

"Asha avda, meshia envier
Karat me mortando,
Tresea dianda miyha Leisha encada."

The girl in my mind whispers, "thirteen days." I hear her, but do not understand.

The blade falls. It cuts through my skin. I hear my ribs crack a second before it pierces my heart.

I scream his name.

He is beside me. "Don't leave me," he whispers, and buries his dark head against my bleeding chest. "I need you. Please don't leave me."

My punctured heart heaves and I cough, my blood sprays his cheek. I try to scream his name as I die.

"*No!*" I shouted. My voice sounded distant. Powerless. Quick as they appeared, the golden altar and deadly knife faded back into the shadows. Dozens of eyes from around the bar stared at me. My wineglass lay in shattered fragments on the sawdust-covered floor.

"Cara?" Larry bustled toward me. "What happened? Did someone—?"

I shook my head and held my hand out in front of me, warding off his approaching comfort. His voice faded to a faint buzz. The eye patterns were back, neon flashes fogging my vision. It was so vivid. I had to look back at the broken bulb just to make sure the goddess had disappeared. The name! Why could I not remember the name I screamed before I died?

Throwing a bill on the counter, I rushed from the bar into the pouring rain.

My steps slurred like my thoughts as the world fell on its side, whirling and twisting about me. The bad wine clawed at my throat, trying to rush out. I screamed in frustration. My thumb hit the clicker a few times, my beamer yelped at me from somewhere, and for a second the sky flickered crimson and gold. *Blood and gold.* I kept walking.

"Where the hell did I park?" my voice made me jump again. This time my scream was more of a miserable groan. I shivered and wrapped my arms around myself. Freezing rain soaked the silk of my white peasant blouse and plastered it to my chest. I hit my clicker again, and the beep came back at me from every corner of my world. The slouch heels of my beater boots dug into the soil. A sharp branch struck my cheek and a pinecone crushed under my foot.

"Great!" I was in the forest now. I had walked too far. I turned around and looked for signs of Larry's neon lights, sought any hint of their reflection in the sky. Nothing. Only the wet wind running down my cheeks, pine, and the smell of lilacs.

Lilacs…

I took two steps backward, my hands flew out, groping for something invisible. "Hanna?" I covered my mouth when the word slipped free. In childhood I would call her name at night; when I woke screaming from a horrible dream, a random ghost sighting, or drowning in the sorrow of missing my mom, her soothing presence had always comforted me. I stopped calling for her a long time ago. On the day she left us. Now, her scent was so strong, overpowering. I could not help myself.

"Hanna?"

I ran back and forth, sniffing the air like a wild animal. "Hanna! Hanna! Hanna!" The sweet perfume of lilac oil saturated the air, thick, musky, and so haunting.

"Cara."

I did not ask who was there. I did not need to. I had recognized Hanna's voice the first time. In the twilight zone, anything could happen, and I was in that world now, the place where reality and fantasy merged. It was her. Here. Hanna. I was sure.

I opened my eyes and searched the forest. Heart pounding, I delved into every shadow. I did not expect to find her, but the scared little girl hiding inside me, hoped.

"Please! Where are you?!" I shouted.

"Cara."

The wind threw back my name in response. Chills ran riot over my skin. A fearful part of me realized I had no idea where my car was, and that I was standing in the middle of a pitch-black forest behind a dodgy bar, a place little girls like me leave in body bags.

A howl loud enough to rival the storm echoed behind me. I backed up, ready to turn and run, but my heel caught the base of a root, and I stumbled hard. Sharp pain cut into my knee when it twisted and I lost my battle with gravity. Arms windmilling, I shrieked and landed hard on my back. I lay in a daze, the dark canopy of forest swirling over my head. The rain was really coming down, it soaked me to the bone in moments, I was so furious, I could not decide whether to scream or cry.

Groaning, I tried to get up. The ground shifted in the same instant I did. Like a wave, it rolled me forward, knocking me to my knees once more. When I tried to stand, it happened again. The strength of the next ripple made mockery of the first. I screamed as the earth itself hurled me through the air. My body slammed into the ground, my head struck a rock, and a pained cry escaped me. I lifted my hand to the back of my scalp. It came away wet, blood shining a sickly black against my trembling fingers.

I had only a split second to wonder at the absurdity of it all, before another violent wave sent me crashing into the base of a solid pine. My head struck wood, and stars danced in my vision. I spider-crawled my way backward until the bark of the pine dug in my hips. Wet dirt flew everywhere, and twigs groaned when they snapped. The muddy ground splashed up in stringy droplets that formed more broken crowns.

Wiping dirt out of my eye one-handed, I clung to a wet, hanging pine branch with the other.

Anger morphed to horror, rooting me in place. Lighting split the shattered black clouds, then reality faded and was no more. The earth beneath me quaked and rolled like a drunken wave. Jagged cracks broke out beneath the moss covered puddles, shooting off in wild furrows that raised the wet dirt. Then, like pus from a wound, a dozen skinless creatures oozed out of the broken ground. Wet, empty eye sockets hovering above bloody grins appeared first. I could see chunks of rotten tissue and sinew dripping from dirty, ivory bones, flapping in the night wind like old flags wrecked by age and ready to burn. Frozen in pure shock I watched the creatures climb to their feet. I gasped in silence, I may have prayed. Disjointed limbs clacking, the living corpses shuffled toward me.

I screamed, a terrible scream that scratched my throat, then another, and another.

Run! the girl inside my mind cried. I agreed.

Pine needles stabbed into my hand, I heaved my body up and a surge of adrenaline drove back the pain. The dead drew within a few feet of me, giving me a clear view of the wet flesh swinging from their rotting bones. The smell of decay enveloped me. I gagged, screamed, then gagged some more. A hand shot up from the ground and clamped down on my thigh. I screamed like I would never stop.

I fought with all my strength, kicking my legs frantically, the bony fingers continued to dig deeper. Panic ate through my stomach as the skeleton's index finger ripped my jeans. My skin tore under the pressure of the blackened nail as the grip became so tight I wondered if it would snap bone.

Run! my mind shrieked at me.

"Oh, screw you!" I said, feeling helpless. "I would if I could!" I gripped the hand and fought to pry the fingers apart, gobs of dripping flesh slid against my slick gloves, confounding my efforts.

"Awe, CRAP! This is disgusting!" I moaned. "This has to be a dream! Just a dream! It's not true." My voice grew hoarse. "I am *not* being attacked by zombies! *Not real!*"

Low and dirty like something out of a Hitchcock film, the dead groans wove a mesh of terror around me. I froze. The grip on my thigh slackened, the dead stopped in their tracks. Leaves and mud clung to their skinless faces and the old blood on them looked inky in the storm light. Green goo gushed from the empty sockets of their eyes and dripped down their mutilated cheeks.

The grip on my thigh tightened again. I howled in pure, undiluted rage. "Get off me. Get *off*!" suddenly, it obeyed. The fingers loosened their hold, the hand retreated into the ground. I gained my feet with all the grace of a severed marionette and bolted.

"Cara, Cara, Cara!" Behind me, the dead screamed my name, a sound far more terrible than the eerie shrieking of the wind. More terrible than anything I had ever heard. I did not look back to see if they were chasing me. I lowered my chin and ran for my life.

The flashing yellow of Larry's sign painted the distant rain, spilling sunny colors over the stormy sky. I was so close. A stunning wash of relief left me dizzy, for a split second I lost my focus. My toe hooked another root and I went down. My forehead smashed into a rock, my eyes rolled back into my head, and a high ringing resounded in my ears. I tried to focus my eyes under the onslaught of blinding rain. I coughed out a sob and felt my bottom lip split. Hot, sticky blood trickled down my chin.

I rolled onto my back. A shadow loomed over me, large and misshapen, amber eyes gleaming in the darkness. Amber? The shadow reached for me. I meant to scream, but it stayed lodged in my raw throat.

"Shhh," the shadow breathed. Fingertips brushed my cheek. I waited for the pain. Waited for the scream that would not come. In the beginning, the rough fingers of the stranger brought a soothing chill, a numbing of the throb in my mouth and head, then… something else. Little winged creatures of pure fire danced over my skin. Shadows distorted and the bringer of the fire faded into them. The world went black.

CHAPTER 6

BLOODY IS BREATHTAKING.

Hundreds of tiny explosions went off in my head at once. I jolted upright, only to crash back down to…my soft pillows?

I lay on my bed, in my room, I was sure. And, surprise, surprise, I was alive. The pounding in my head made my legs mutiny. I moaned and slid down my duvet to collapse on my knees. I did not fight the fall; this seemed to be the new way I got out of bed now. At least I had not reopened the gash on my head. That was a plus. I lifted my hand, my fingers encountered a new strip of gauze framing a band-aid above my left brow. Lily?

Holy Hell! My head throbbed. My knee was stiff. It felt uncomfortably large, and tiny stinging cuts crisscrossed the backs of my hands. I gripped the edges of my vanity and hauled myself into a half-kneel, favoring my uninjured leg. The mirror showed me its secrets and I groaned again—my face looked horrible. The gauze bandage above my left eye was a lot larger than I first suspected, and two more cuts not deep enough to warrant a band-aid slashed across my cheekbone. A purple bulge stood in place of my bottom lip, and there was a deep gash on the right side of my chin that looked like it could use a stitch. Bloodshot streaks marred the white of my eyes, standing in contrast to the grey shadows beneath them. I sighed and touched my bottom lip. There was no fixing this. I did not even bother using mascara. I just brushed my hair while I searched the floor for my slippers.

How did I get home? Did Lily drive to Larry's to find me?

Memories of the forest played behind my lids every time I blinked. Hideous skeletal faces and broken bones morphing into clinging hands. I tried to put away the images of them bursting from the earth, intending to think only positive thoughts, but the golden woman's horrible chant was on repeat in my head. I had no idea what the words meant, yet I knew if I was to say them out loud my pronunciation of the dead language would be perfect.

On the topic of spells, I knew more than most, and it sure sounded like she had cursed me—right before she stabbed her knife into my heart. I put my hand to my chest, trying to rub away the invisible ache. I finally found my furry slippers and stood up. Pulling on my soft, rosy bathrobe—a thing that has graced my wardrobe since the ninth grade—I left my room, and limped down the hall toward the west wing of the manor.

Sizzling smells of hot olive oil, garlic, and crisping chives made my stomach roar, driving me onward. I ignored the judgmental portraits of my aunts and limped down the hall. Before I stepped into the kitchen, I heard a deep male voice twining alongside Lily's delicate laughter. I made a quick stop, my knee twitched and squeaked out a cringy, grinding sound. I gasped, grabbing the wall for support. Pain gnawed at my nerves.

Unimportant, I had no time for it. I leaned in as far as dignity would allow and tried to distinguish word from sound while a whirlwind of questions spun in my mind. *A guy spent the night?* That was strange, Lily never brought guys here. 'This is a woman's place,' she would say. 'It always has been. I know you don't believe in all this, but we should not allow just *any man* to walk through that door'.

Recovering what poise I had, I ran my hands through my hair and stepped into the kitchen. The male intruder was leaning against our kitchen sink, eating one of Lily's omelets, a dish I consider among the most delicious in the known world. A heavenly scent drifted up from the coffee Lily poured into his cup.

The man was tall, four or five inches above six feet, wearing dark fitted jeans and a tight black T-shirt that emphasized the broadness of his shoulders. A giant silver watch sat on his right wrist, and an intricate-looking group of tattooed symbols traced their way up the underside of his arm. His black hair ended in a natural curl that softened the hard cut of his jaw and firm lips. From my vantage point, I could not see his eyes.

Sunlight trickled through the dining room from the wide French windows leading to our front courtyard. I squinted against the brightness of the kitchen. Self-consciously, I ran my hand through the long, tangled strands of my hair again trying to twist it into order.

Lily paused mid-laugh and looked up at me through a wide fan of sooty lashes. For a terrible second, she and the stranger were creatures of a pure, incandescent light, and I felt like a wraith crawling out of a cave of death.

"Good morning, love, I'm so glad to see you up and walking around," said Lily sweetly. "Coffee?"

"Dear gods, yes!" My voice was scratchy, maybe from lack of use, or maybe from all the screaming—I assumed it was the latter. I limped to the nearest bar stool, pressed up against the marble island in the center of the kitchen, and sat down. I buried my head in my hands while Lily poured me a steaming cup of coffee. She took the seat beside me, nudging a plate against my elbow. "I made you breakfast."

"Thank you. It looks so good. I'm starving!" I took a bite, scalding my tongue.

"Careful! You'll burn…"

"Worth it," I said, gulping down another bite.

Lily smiled. "Fun night?" she whispered.

"Hilarious. I need painkillers."

"Want to tell me what happened?"

"I just went to Larry's, I meant to come home at a decent hour."

"But…?" Lily prompted.

"But, I had another dream, or a vision, or something," I whispered. "How *did* I get home?"

Lily threw her thumb in the stranger's direction. "Meet your knight in shining armor, my lady." She gave me a silly bow as if she had done the rescuing.

I rolled my eyes at her, took a deep breath for my nerves and swiveled around in my seat. I needed to see his face. For no logical reason, I felt compelled. Our eyes locked, and my breath came out in a whoosh. *Him.* I stared transfixed as a bell rang in my mind. *Him, him, him.* His irises were a deep ebony shot with pure amber, the dramatic tilt of his eyes set off by dark slashing brows. It was him. My dark stranger. My rescuer from the tower.

"Drake," he said, his voice almost excessively deep. "It's nice to meet you, Cara. Again." He held out his hand.

I looked down at the large, tanned hand. The moment lengthened. In my head, the bell rang louder and the silence went on, so many seconds too long. I wanted to take the hand hanging in the space between us—so strong, not a single tremble touching the firm lines—to see if it would be the same as the last two times. That beautiful chill. Those fire butterflies.

Instead, I gripped my coffee cup like it would shatter if I relaxed even a fraction.

"It's nice to meet you too," I smiled, hoping it would suffice. "Again."

With a smooth movement, he put his hand in the front pocket of his jeans, and returned to leaning against the sink.

My stomach made a loud, rumbling noise, and heat flared in my cheeks. *This is the worst! Just the worst.*

Lily pushed a cinnamon roll beside my cup of coffee. The sugary smell set my stomach churning. I moved it away, grimacing I turned my attention back to the omelet.

"Drake had to do some detective work to get you here," said Lily.

I saw Drake's shrug out of the corner of my eye.

"Not really," said Drake. "I checked you for ID, to no avail. The bar's upstanding citizens were less than helpful, they all just kept saying: 'That old manor on the hill'. I'm not from around here," he was smiling now, "and, from what I can see, Washington state has more than a few hills." The smile touched his eyes. He was beautiful. "A gentleman by the name of Larry, wanted to take you home. I was quite insistent that it be me. I needed to be sure you were alright. You look much better this morning, Cara." His words sounded loud in my head. The longer I looked at him, the more I felt the cluttered pieces of my world falling away until only he existed.

"Thank you," I said, exasperated with myself, and life at large. I took another bite of omelet and barely tasted Lily's glorious creation.

Drake pushed off from the sink and stepped in my direction. "If you don't mind me asking," his voice was cautious, "what happened? You were lying *on* the road. I almost hit you."

My cheeks burned and I studied the black depths of my coffee. "I don't know, really. I parked on the street, went in for a few drinks, and when I left I couldn't find my car. I must have walked too far, because I ended up somewhere in that black forest, crazy lost. Got spooked and ran—I guess." I shifted in my seat, and the movement sent spikes shooting through my knee. I winced but did not take my eyes off the man in front of me. "I fell. I remember falling." I touched the bandage on my head. "I hit my head," I winced. "Hard."

"I wasn't sure if you were alive when I found you. You were so still." He said that last part more to himself, and I felt something from him, an ache, the same ache I felt when I lost something precious and knew I would never see it again.

"I was pretty surprised myself, this morning," I breathed.

Lily came and sat beside me. She moved the cinnamon roll and gave me a hot scone instead. I picked at it halfheartedly. Drake walked over to the percolating pot to refill his coffee mug.

"Are you all right, hon?" asked Lily, whispering too low for Drake to hear.

"Yes, it's nothing," I muttered. "I just drank too much." That was a lie, but I did not want to talk about the rest of it right now for fear Drake would overhear me. The sheer awfulness of my second impression was more than enough at present; seeing the first had not been great either. There was no need for my gruesome visions to add to the crazy.

"I was waiting up for you in the library. I must have fallen asleep. It was two in the morning when Drake showed up, carrying you all passed out and bloody. I, of course, thought he was a murderer. I asked him to give you to me and leave immediately. Life, it appeared, prepared Drake for the "murder" assumption, he held you in front of himself like a white flag." Lily took a breath. "Gave me his card before he left just in case I needed anything." I could see Lily trying to keep herself from giggling. Drake had walked back over to us, steaming coffee in his hand. Lily knew he was listening and raised her voice a little for his benefit. "With all that's been going on, I thought we might need a murderer in our lives, so I called and invited him for breakfast."

Drake knocked back the rest of his coffee, saluting Lily with the empty cup. "On that happy note I will take my leave. Lily, that was the best omelet I've ever had, I thank you. I won't impose any longer."

"It's no imposition," I blurted. "And, true about the omelet."

Drake smiled at me. There was that pull again, right below my heart, stopping my words, stifling my air.

Lily lightly touched his hand. "Let's all have dinner sometime. Cara and I really only have each other, so I am rather in your debt."

I wanted to take his hand as she had, and thank him for what he had done for me, like any normal person would—I hated that I could not. That little *glitch* about myself had not bothered me for years, today it made feel cheated.

I looked up to find him watching me. "Yes, let's have dinner," I heard myself say, then, "thanks, for being my knight in shining armor."

"You're welcome, Cara."

Wearing her kindest smile, Lily let go of his hand. Drake walked to the front door, his steps echoed in the empty hall. I watched him put on a pair of black boots and jacket—a matte black, fur-lined coat. It had a flat biker collar and a raised silver buckle. An intricate phoenix—wings spread in flight—emblazoned the back. The hard style of the stitched leather suited him to perfection. "I'll take you up on that dinner," he told us. "It's been a long time since I had a home-cooked meal."

"Well, you're in luck," said Lily. "I'm an *amazing* cook."

He winked at her. "I can't wait."

"See you later, Drake," Lily threw him a dainty wave.

His dark gaze lingered on me for a long second before he turned and closed the wide oak doors behind him.

The moment he left Lily turned on me, her eyes wide as saucers. "*Oh my goddess*!" she mouthed. "How beautiful is that man?! I mean…?"

I dropped my head back into my hands and groaned at the horrid humiliation of it all.

"Cara, the way he carried you in here! He was *so* worried about you. I thought he would have a fit. He held your hand for like an hour after we put you to bed. Touching you like it was nothing."

"I thought you said he left."

"I white lied, obviously! I didn't actually say he left right away," argued Lily. "Just that he gave me his card when he did. It was crazy. He paced around like a caged tiger the whole time. And the way he looked at you…" She fanned herself. "Just thinking about it makes me hot!"

"Who is he?" My voice cracked over the last word. The scratch in my throat was turning into an acute ache—definitely from all the screaming.

Lily got up to pour herself some more coffee, then came back to me. She gave me a strict look. "I don't really know. He's foreign, I think—you can't always hear it, when he's upset he has a slight accent. His father owns some banks here or something like that. Or he does? I'm not sure. It was really late and I was worried. You looked like death, white as a ghost, all covered in sticks, leaves, and mud. Blood all over the freaking place! My heart nearly seizured when I answered the door and saw you lying unconscious in his arms. His overall gorgeousness disarmed me, of course. His voice, and that mouth!" She faced the white-framed window over the sink, her eyes drifting toward the headstones of the Wynter graveyard—Wynter haunt as Hanna called it—just slightly visible through the swaying trees.

"Why did he say, *again*?" asked Lily. "Nice to meet you, again."

"He's the guy I told you about, from the space needle. I thought I recognized him last night. I wasn't sure. He reminds me of my dream man…so I thought, well I assumed, I was just falling headlong into another nightmare, or something. Who freaking knows, anymore?" My head went back in my hands.

"No. Way." said Lily, spacing out her words, very little surprise in her voice. "So *that's* why you weren't twitching in your comatose state. I thought maybe you were healing. But, it's not all touch, then. Just his?" She tapped her chin. "Such a coincidence."

I knew where she was going with this. "No, Lily."

"Yes!" She grabbed my hand. "We know for a fact there's no such thing as coincidence."

"We do not know it as fact," I argued. "One must have collected data to form a fact. We have nothing but the word of a bunch of old crazy women."

"Whatever, all crazy means is special, and Hanna made us promise we would never say that word."

"Crazy?" I asked, confused.

"No coincidence. So," Lily continued in a voice that told me she would ignore whatever I said on the topic, "if there is *no* such thing… then it is fate."

Lily held up her hand to stop my next words. It was unnecessary. I had none. "Fate wants you to have him," she said and gasped. "Oh! It's so romantic."

"Have him? Honestly, Lily, romantic? *Nothing* about this has been romantic. And, no, to answer your other question before you went off on a tangent."

"A *looove* tangent," said Lily, dragging out the word.

I smiled at her and she squeezed my hand. "It's not all touch. Mr. Clarkson took my hand and nearly knocked me out yesterday, I was even wearing my gloves. Drake…" my voice cracked on his name. I coughed, wincing. "It's different with him. I feel him—though not in the same way I feel others—the pain should be there," I shrugged. "It just isn't. There is heat in his touch just like anyone else's, only it doesn't burn, it's just so…" I broke off, unsure how to explain what it felt like to have his hands on me.

"Hummm, so," Lily lifted her right hand and held up her pointer finger. "You meet twice in two days." Another finger went up. "We are quite a distance from the Space Needle," Lily raised a third finger. "And there are no coincidences." She dropped her hand. "Conclusion? He is here for you. I wonder if he knows?"

"You could've asked him last night."

"It slipped my mind—you being unconscious and all. Besides, I didn't figure it out until just now, I was missing the space needle info. Also, I didn't ask him many questions. I thought I should take you to the hospital… I know how much you hate hospitals, and I didn't want you to wake up in one. Nothing seemed too serious, so we just talked about you. Anyway, we can thank all our stars he was there. I mean, otherwise this is just getting scary. Hanna used to tell us werewolves lived in that forest. What the hell happened, Cara? Were you just wandering around and…?"

A sad wave of my hand cut her off. "I don't know what to tell you, Lily. It's all going to sound so crazy. I got lost, and then…I know it sounds stupid, but I could swear I heard Hanna calling my name."

"Seriously?" Lily rolled her eyes." Obviously, seriously. You wouldn't say crap like this for fun."

"I heard her like five times. It's why I walked into the stupid forest in the first place." I rested my head on Lily's shoulder and told it all to her, even the dripping flesh and green gooey eyes.

When my torrent of words finally stopped, Lily sighed and stroked my hair. "Enough. Let's go for a walk. Forget class today. Mr. Clarkson will just have to understand."

That surprised me.

Lily saw it in my eyes. "What? You matter more than some silly class."

"What did you tell him about me?" I asked self-consciously.

"Who? Mr. Clarkson?"

"No, Lily, Drake."

Lily giggled. "I know. Just simple things. I told him about the literature course you're taking, and we talked about the books you like. He asked strange things, like your favorite color and our best birthday memory. He seemed sad when I told him about Mother leaving us when we were babies." She got up again and put her cup in the sink. I stood, ignoring my knee and helped gather the rest of the dishes.

"I'm glad you invited him to dinner, Lily." I said, almost under my breath. "Thank you."

"I know," said Lily again, and I heard the smile lingering in her voice. "You're welcome. I'm going to brush my teeth. Meet me on the deck in five?"

"Sure," I said, and she kissed my cheek.

"Don't let your brain talk you out of all that truth I just laid on you."

I burst out laughing. It made everything hurt and that made me laugh harder. It felt a little hysterical; it also felt good. Lily left and I stared out the window, finishing the last few sips of my coffee. I did not believe he was here for me. I had not, however, believed in zombies or undead monsters either. Or did I? Maybe somewhere deep down I believed in everything around me. Somewhere in my soul I knew there was more to this world than meets the eye. Maybe I knew that spells could alter time, that women could survive flames and drowning. That some carried strange powers, even the ability to negotiate with death. Right now I did not care about immortality, power, or dark magics, I did not even want to know if he was here for me. I wanted to know why his touch, of all the people on earth, brought me pleasure instead of pain.

CHAPTER 7

IF THERE IS NO TIME…WE ARE ALL IMMORTALS?

The November rain had finally let up, and small slivers of sunlight bravely fought their way through the swollen grey clouds dominating the sky. We were not sure if we would need them, but we shrugged into our raincoats and grabbed umbrellas for good measure. One could never predict the mood of the Washington skies.

    We walked in silence up the cobbled driveway, and I clung to Lily's arm, trying not to slip on the slick stones. Having another knee go out was not something I could afford, I was already limping like a peg-legged pirate. We stood together at the top of our long driveway, enjoying every moment of the weak morning light.

    "This place is such a picture in the sunshine," said Lily.

    It was. Four red wooden towers—each facing the four corners of the wind—speared up into the sky. Fragile golden frames laced the four tower windows, and the hand-blown glass panes painted rainbows on the front lawn. From our high vantage point, the four attaching wings looked like thatched dollhouses. On the high roofs, the red tiles were missing in places, leaving little gaping holes. The holes were about the only thing left that showcased the true age of Wynter Manor. Built in 1853 as a haven for the abused Oregon witches, Hanna had often boasted that Wynter Manor was standing before Washington became an official American state.

    The manor still sparkled beneath violet-threaded vines wrapping their way through the balconies and wide French windows. After Hanna left however, it seemed the manor had lost much of its glow. The quilted ivy that crept up the high oak beams and stone walls had turned dark, spreading sinister fingers into every crevice.

We walked, nowhere in particular, just strolling, our hands interlocked and the rare sun warming the eternal chill that hung over the Wynter grounds. Images from the previous night dancing through my mind, my thoughts returned repeatedly to Drake. When I closed my eyes, I could feel the way his skin burned against mine leaving a trail of fire winged butterflies.

Lily filled her lungs and let out a slow exhale that ended in a groan. "Ahh! It feels good to be outside. I can't believe it actually stopped raining. Come on!" Her smile made her face shine.

We crested the hill east of the Wynter property and began our descent. The Wynter towers—each facing their own element, wind, earth, fire, and water—faded in the distance.

"Did you know that, *that*," Lily pointed. "Is my favorite place on the Wynter lands?"

I followed her finger to the base of the hill where Wynter haunt—our family's graveyard—crouched in its own shadows.

"Oh, Lily, you're too blonde to have a graveyard be your favorite place! You're supposed to like clubs and fancy house parties."

"I like those things, and I don't like all graveyards, just *this* one."

"It's not a graveyard, really," I said, suddenly exasperated. "It's more like a remembrance yard. All the women aren't really there. You know all those caskets are empty, right? If there even are caskets at all. And, according to Hanna, that 'graveyard' is older than the manor. If that's true, that's like…" I threw up my hands as I tried to calculate. "I don't know, like three hundred years! A lot of time for a lot of women to die. This place is terrifying. It's not even a place!" I growled. "It's just a numinous space on earth, a structural break in time where the laws that apply perfectly well to everything in the real world, just up and stop applying in there." I pointed my finger at the offending spot. "Maybe it would be better if there *were* women in those graves. I think our aunts lefts those headstones in there just so they could have something to come back and haunt. Maybe if their bodies were there, they would have somewhere to sleep and be at peace…stop wandering around in the middle of the night." I ended my tirade in a giant gulp of air.

"Maybe," said Lily lightly, and skipped away.

Two gargoyles sat atop twined metal pillars, guarding the entrance to Wynter haunt. Behind them, an iron arch curled through a mesh of low-hanging tree branches. The trees on these grounds were void of leaves. Just empty branches reaching up into a sky that shed darkness where no darkness should be. The graveyard did not begin here, but its shadow did. Any grass that dared to grow died soon as it tasted air, falling prey to the vaporous swirls of mist creeping across the ground.

Only the roses remained in constant bloom. Velvet petals boasting the enchanting color of bloody snow, and inky night. I knew the black roses blooming along the headstones looked violet in the moonlight.

Lily ran ahead of me and I stopped to stand under the twisted metal arch. Electricity thrummed in my blood when I was near this place, yet I was unsure when the fascination had morphed into fear. The wind blew colder here and the mists devoured what little light trickled through the clouds.

I ran my hands over the statue standing guard before the arch. It was the figure of a woman, done in green marble, ruby-flecked hair twined through the crown of living roses on her head. She knelt atop a fountain of gold, wrapped in yards of brittle vine. The stone plaque in her hands read, *Wynter women at rest.* I always found it ironic; they never rested.

I sighed, a little forlorn. The histories of the Wynter women were tales of pure tragedy—stories full of death, burnt bodies and drowning mothers. Then, of those same women walking again. Coming back from the mists, bringing more magic with them. Also, bringing evil. The stories say they brought lots of that back. They were not always sisters, yet Wynter women shared a commonality: the ability to control an element, bend it to their will. It bonded them enabling survival through the centuries.

"Cara, you coming?" called Lily.

"I really don't want to," I said, trying for some defiance in my tone. I failed. "I will."

"Cara, nothing will hurt us in there. What if," she said, adding a spooky tremor to her voice, "we are the last of our bloodline. If we die, so does the line of the fabled Salem witch."

"Lily, if that's true, I will cry!"

"Why? You don't enjoy being a witch anyway."

"I don't enjoy being the last of *anything*." I shuddered and zipped up my jacket. "It sounds like a death sentence."

Lily walked back to me and took my hand. Her other hand stifled her bubbling giggles. "You big baby," she said. "We haven't been here in ages." Hands linked, we stood under the arch, I felt the mists reach up and wrap long, diaphanous fingers around our ankles.

Lily looked down at her toes, invisible through the white froth. "How old were you when this placed stopped giving you the creeps?"

"Stopped?" I snorted. "I am still terrified."

"You are not," she laughed. "You know you love it here. Don't you remember when we were little and used to come here all the time?"

I shook my head. "No," I said. I remembered, but I did not want to tell her.

Lily continued on undaunted. "Yes, come on," she cajoled. "You do. We would steal Hanna's oils." She mimicked our stealthy childhood moves. "We'd get all that sage and rosemary and those salt crystals."

I gave her my best confused stare and remained mute.

"Oh, you are totally messing with me!" Lily nudged my waist. "I would always pretend to command the sad flame of our little makeshift fire. You tried to control the winds and my mind, what was up with that? I think it actually worked one time. Don't you remember?"

I remembered. Pure magic flowed in the air back then; back when there had been no pain, no dreams and no soul-rending fear, but as they say, that was then and this is now. Now it was just haunting trepidation and an overwhelming darkness touching everything. "Yes, I remember," I said, smiling at her. "Some of my best memories, you know that Lily."

Lily gave me a triumphant smile. "It's one reason I love this place."

Together, we stepped under the arch and the churning mists closed in behind us.

At the entrance to the cemetery the rows of headstones sectioned off into four groups of eight. Two groups lay on either side of a pathway, once fresh marble tiles, now nothing more than jumbles of broken shards jutting from the torn earth. In here, the wrought iron fences poking up from the ground and brittle, forlorn vines wrapping the headstones—some cracked and crumbling—all, gave the impression of extreme age. Most of the headstones and crypts beyond, remained standing, though covered in rambling vines threaded through blankets of moss and ivy.

Lily rested her hand on a particularly well-kept headstone. The inscription read: *Agatha Duvon Wynter, born 1563.* Like all the others, the stone bore no date of death.

Lily saw the path of my eyes and bent down to read the inscription. "Wouldn't it be amazing if all the women who had their headstones here *were* actually still alive?"

"No. It would be freaky," I countered. "Though Larry said something strange to me the other night. He told me it's the ground up here that keeps us Wynter women alive."

"Maybe," said Lily thoughtfully. "I think they just put stones here to remember all the women in our family who have passed through the manor. Now they've moved on, perhaps to the Wynter grounds they are dead."

"Sounds mean."

"Well, Mother has a grave here, but I'm sure she's not gone, like *dead* gone. I still see her in my dreams, and I read somewhere that it's very un-wicca-like to dream of the dead."

"What about Hanna?" First time I ever thought of this. "Have we ever bothered to look for her grave?"

"I don't think it's here. Maybe that just means she plans to come back to us someday."

I looked away from Lily's saucer eyes. "She'd be ashamed at how crazy I've gone in her absence."

Lily scowled. "You're not crazy, Cara. It's not insanity. It's power. Gods, the vibrations here!" she said. Arms raised above her head, her slim body arching with her stretch. Her eyelids fell closed. "Don't you feel it?" she whispered.

I did. Overhead a bird screamed and I started. I gripped Lily's hand tighter and she squeezed back. We turned in stilted silence and continued walking down the broken path, deeper into the haunt

We walked to the largest crypt on this side of the haunt and sat down on stairs so weathered and forgotten they looked ready to disintegrate into dust. Lily wrapped the ends of her long coat around her legs and huddled in its downy folds, then she fluffed her hair and rearranged her coat. Unsatisfied, she stood up and dusted a few vines off the stairs. When she finally settled, she reached into her pocket and pulled out a piece of paper that smelled like an old gym sock. The mists grew deeper, the long swirls thickening in the changing light.

"I found this in the Book of Shadows?" said Lily, and her voice sounded apologetic when she continued. "I know you wanted all this stuff up in the attic, Cara, but we *are* witches whether or not you like it, and every good witch—even if she doesn't know how to use it—should always have her coven's Book of Shadows nearby." She sighed. "Look at the paper. See this? The text is Slavic, maybe Romanian—it's hard to tell with those Eastern European languages." She shook it out before holding it up to the light.

"Careful, Lily. It looks ready to fall apart." I glanced around at the spooky, overgrown grounds. "Matches this place."

"I know, right?" Lily turned it in her hands.

I took off my right glove and touched the tip of my finger to the edge of the page. My world did that darkening at the edges thing—momentarily spinning my dizzy head. I snatched my hand back and returned it to its safe zone inside the glove. "It's so old," I said, hearing a quake in my voice. "There should be wear and tear in more places."

"See down here?" Lily pointed to a tiny nick at the base of the page. "I tried to rip a little piece off yesterday. I couldn't—not didn't—*couldn't*. The paper wouldn't tear. Look at these symbols running along the border. Aren't they beautiful?"

"Yes," I said. "They really are. Do they mean something to us?"

"Well, I was reading and—oh!" A harsh wind rushed past us ripping the parchment out of her hand. It hovered in the air for a weird moment, fluttering back and forth as if it had a little pair of invisible wings. I reached out to snag it and encountered a big handful of empty air right where it should have been.

"What the heck?!" gasped Lily. "It just jumped out of my hand!"

Lily bolted. She chased it off the path and into the jumble of fragmented vines where the ground became impacted, slippery from days of wet and cold. Her hair streamed out, violet ribbons cast by the dimming light threaded through it. Lily dodged a broken headstone lying prone in her path, then cut sharply to the right, and vanished behind a rusted iron arch.

I imagined I heard the tattered headstones howl. The chilling sound rose the hairs on the back of my neck. Though I dared not turn around, I felt a presence behind me. The shiver that ghosted over me was so violent my teeth clacked.

Don't turn around, the voice in my head shrieked. I ignored it and looked behind me. My eyes found only empty shadows and dimming light. Nothing moved, not even a breeze. In the darkening sky overhead, the angry bird screamed again—this particular sound made me break out in a run. I dashed after Lily. My toes skidded when I reached the wrecked arch. My body came to a flailing halt. We never strayed into the north of the haunt. This, where my feet stood, was the oldest spot on the Wynter lands, so old in fact, that crypts here had no dates at all. They sheltered the names of women who, if actually still living, would be within their right to lay claim to the title of goddess.

I closed my eyes like a child, took a deep breath, then darted under the arch.

One eye still squeezed shut, I rounded another group of dilapidated headstones—replete with upside-down crosses wrapped by interlocking rings—and stopped before the largest mausoleum in the graveyard. Tales of Grandmother Rosen's crypt filled many of my bedtime stories. I had seen it in pictures, but never stood at the base of these crumbling Roman pillars. Shorter than I imagined, stout and covered in deeply carved parallel lines, the pillars framed a set of massive double doors. More of the same carvings ran onto the ground and down a set of steps leading to a wild group of sapphire roses.

Lily stood under a separate arch soaked in intricate vines. Black roses in full bloom climbed up the vines, they framed a solitary gargoyle dominating the pinnacle of the arch, watching our drama through impassive eyes.

The parchment circled Lily's head once, twice, on the third time she swiped at the air—cussing beneath her breath— her fingers finally closed on the flapping thing.

"I can't believe you chased that over here," I panted. "You are breaking all Hanna's rules. You know she said never to come back here."

"Well…Hanna said a lot of things." Lily's breaths came in gasps. "She isn't here to stop me, is she?" Lily sat down on the crypt's crumbling stairs, her eyes never straying from her captured prize. She unfolded the paper and pressed it down onto her drawn-up knees.

"Look here, see all the markings?" Lily employed the same tones she used in a chemistry final. Studious, low. "If you stare for long enough, you can see them fading in and out, like the paper is breathing." She tilted it. "This circle in the center, this line tracing down the left side of the page, and these two small lines running parallel across it. I think they make a symbol." She scrunched her nose. "I'm missing something."

My blank look was sincere. "I'm missing everything." A crash sounded behind me. "Lily!" I jumped. "Did you hear?"

"We know spirits haunt this place. What are you freaking out about?"

"I'm not freaking out, yet. It's just…" Thin streamers of white smoke seeped out from under the intricate metal base of Grandmother Rosen's crypt. "They are *definitely* waking up."

"I hear them," said Lily.

"I want to get out of here. I haven't seen a single ghost for over a year. Please don't let me break that incredible record today."

"Just a moment longer… right here!" Lily pointed to a brownish, yellow divot in the center of the parchment, the whole thing, however, was so littered by signs of age I could barely distinguish one mark from the rest. Besides, my focus lay elsewhere. Ribbons of mist now oozed from beneath the heavy doors.

"Blood will give life," something moaned.

"Lily, did you hear?"

"I heard it!" Lily sprang up off the ground. "*Upside down!*" she shouted. "I've been looking at this thing upside down." The moment she flipped it, a bubble of dark ink spread from the center. "The lines, Cara! Do you see the lines?"

It was impossible not to. They spread out in every direction until the thing resembled what I think a map of New York's metro system might look like. Behind her head, a smoky silhouette rambled over the interlocked arch, threading itself through the rose vines. It stopped under the gargoyle, who glared at it with unmoving eyes. I dragged at her arm. "Lily, we're out of time!"

"It's a map!" Lily fell to her knees and spread it out in front of her. "A map. I can see it now. These lines…"

I hunkered back down beside her. I could not help it. The lines on the map moved independently of each other, drifting strangely across the page, propelled by some supernatural locomotion.

Lily's breathing was erratic, and she had picked up a dirt smear across her cheek. Half her hair had come free of its braid. She shoved the locks from her face. Limbs shaking worse than my own, she crawled over and held the map against the etched symbol on the crypt door.

"The symbols are the same," I stated. Not feeling, I thought, the appropriate amount of shock. "There, in the center of the paper."

Still more tufts of mist gusted from beneath the doors, accompanied by soft screams, and the scratching of fingernails against iron.

"I think whatever is behind these doors wants out, Lily."

Lily waved her hand. "Oh, ignore it! You need the blood of a Wynter woman to open these doors. Besides, they're solid steel."

"Iron, I think."

"Whatever. Nothing is coming through. I don't feel like giving up any blood to release the howler. I…" Lily's words dried out on her tongue. "Oh! Blood," she breathed. Excitement thrummed in her eyes, I could feel it heating her veins. "Blood will give life—it wants blood!"

Lily began frantically combing the ground. "Are you going to cut yourself?" I asked, appalled.

"If I can find something sharp enough," she shot back. Map clutched to her heart, she rushed to the edge of the crypt, shoulders jerking, her breaths shrill and irregular. Reinforced by a possessed insanity, she rifled through loose cobblestones to find a chiseled edge.

"Lily, please, let's be civilized about this!"

Long trails of grey moisture bubbled down the steps, pooling around Lily's knees. Like ghostly hands, the mists twined themselves around her jeans and she stopped moving. Hand hovering over a sharp rock, Lily stared at the semi-transparent, and nebulously luminous shadow lurking beneath the watchful gargoyle. She gasped in a shuddering breath. The shadow moved toward her.

The cringey sound of nails scraping on iron morphed into long, pronounced screeches. The leafless trees cast shifting shadows on the mist soaked earth, the balmy air clung to my skin, I felt a drop of sweat trickle down the back of my neck. In the circle of churning mists, Lily knelt.

More shadows crept out of the stillness—ragged figures that slid over the crumbling gravestones and bramble-strewn pathways. My heart thudded faster in my chest. I closed my eyes. *Not going to stop them from appearing,* my inner voice said. A spooky cry rent the air, and my eyes flew open.

Lily sat motionless, her head slumped back—braid now gone—her golden hair poured against the ground. Tendrils of mist crept into her eyes, hiding the brilliant blue beneath an opaque surface. "Blood," her voice echoed like the dead.

I fell down into the warm mists and touched her shoulder. "Lily?" I shook her, then again. "Lily?"

Her head spun, she cocked it to the side with a quick bird-like movement, then looked right past me. Long milky trails ran down her cheeks and into her open mouth.

I screamed. *"LILY!"*

CHAPTER 8

BLOOD WILL GIVE LIFE.

Lily picked up a jagged piece of marble. In stupefied horror I watched her slice it down her palm. A little crimson pool formed in the hollow of her hand. She showed no sign of pain—no expression at all. Lily turned to look at me, a dazed confusion in her unblinking eyes. Opaque liquid trickled down her cheeks in long, milky streams.

Blood dripped from her palm and onto the map discarded at our knees. Like the first melancholy strains of a symphony, the aunts took shape in the mists. Their apparitions formed from the feet. Clothed in styles of dress that spanned the ages; Grecian togas, garlands, and wreaths threaded through pale curls, Victorian gowns flaring at the waist, then dropping into deep décolletages, and frothy silk skirts. Their pale skin dripping jewels and diamonds, shimmering with a soul's inner light.

A plump bubble of blood dripped from Lily's wound to splash against the map's open face. It hissed audibly, as the old, yellow paper rippled. The markings of age faded, and a velvety mauve light issued from the black lines writing across the page.

Dazed, Lily placed her bleeding palm against the map.

Our world exploded in a cacophony of dizzying lights. Throbbing symbols flowed off the paper and soaked into the cobblestones. A globe of light formed around us, bathing us in the lustrous blaze of a thousand stars.

Lily stared, transfixed. The wind seemed to blow the fog from her eyes and the blue shone through. "I knew it!" she breathed. "Oh, I love magic!"

Our family crest of interlocking links spun above our heads, and in the middle junction of the three revolving rings, our family's flower glowed like a white-hot flame.

"It's a lilac," Lily breathed. "Hanna's pendant."

"Her perfume," I whispered, and heard the pure awe echoing in my voice.

Small pearlescent links ran off in all directions from the center and banked against the sphere's border, which appeared to hold more symbols than a Book of Shadows. The whole contraption moved when another gush of blood pumped from Lily's hand. The border rotated clockwise, independent of its counterpart, and the lilac floating in the middle of it all pulsed.

Lambent light and the throbbing mists played upon the apparitions of my aunts, lending them a greater secrecy, an aura of veiled mystery. I rested my head on Lily's shoulder. "Sometimes," I whispered. "Rarely…I love magic too."

"Look, Cara." Lily patted my head. I made a sound of denial and burrowed further into her shoulder. "Get up," she persisted. "See this." I lifted my head. Her eyes were clear; no hint of what she had suffered visible in the cornflower blue.

Lily moved until only her toes rested on the revolving ring. Shadow and light played across her face as her feet followed the sphere. "That one's Polaris. The North Star," she said, pointing into the whirling circle. "These constellations surrounding it—Cepheus, Ursa Minor—this has to be the Northern Hemisphere. This is so strange. Why would there be…?" Her sentence dropped off, she did not speak for a time, just continued to pore over the sparkling lines.

I noticed there was blood soaking the silk of her sleeve—it dripped off the tip of her forefinger, and she had a few big drops on her shoes. "You're bleeding all over yourself, Lily. Can't we just go home now? Neither one of us knows what this means, and I'm sure your hand will still bleed by the time we get back to the house. We can always turn *that* thing back on."

Lily stepped back in the circle of light and bent down to the map. She took the opposing edges and folded them together. The spinning stars retreated. "I found this in the Book of Shadows, stuck to a beautiful old drawing," she said. "I wanted you to see it," she laughed somewhat nervously. "I had no idea it would do all that. I haven't been under a spell that powerful since our eighth birthday."

"Ah, the butterflies," I laughed. "Is that the birthday memory you told Drake?"

"Oh yes, I told a complete stranger that we woke up with colorful wings, when our aunt made us butterflies for a day. Please, that's a second meeting kinda story." Lily linked her arm through mine. "I will never forget being that beautiful for an entire day."

I touched her bleeding hand, I thought she was most likely the prettiest girl in the world. "Oh, Lily," I sighed.

■   ■   ■

Two hours and a pot of coffee later, we lay in the library, buried under a mass of books and family photo albums. Lily gave me the task of translating some Romanian scrawled at the bottom of an ancient photograph, taken using the camera obscura sketch. Two miserable-looking women stood together, hands interlocked, and hard years bracketing the corners of their pretty mouths. Beneath their puritanical bonnets, their hair hung wild and windblown. Due to the scratchy quality of the black-and-white image, the ocean looming behind the women resembled an ominous death trap.

In my best estimation, the text read: *Leaving the black shores of Corvin Castle, 1708. Rosen Duvon and Hanna Wynter."*

"Do you know where Corvin Castle is?"

Lily glanced up from her book. "Yes. I think it's in Transylvania somewhere. Why?"

"This picture of Hanna and her Grandmother was taken there."

Lily busied herself laying out the map, then unwrapped the light layer of gauze from around her hand. I bolted up. "Lily, don't!"

"Why?" asked Lily and pressed her palm to the parchment. The dome of light exploded through the room, brightening every dark corner. She threw me an innocent look. "You said we could start it up back at the house…you know, I think Hanna was born in Romania." She moved under the sphere and held up her hands to what looked like a mass of shattering galaxies.

"Do you think that's where a lot of the Salem witches are from?" I asked her. "From Romania?"

"Possibly," said Lily, gnawing at her lower lip. "But, it wouldn't have been Romania. From about a hundred A.D. until the early two hundreds, most of Romania was part of a Roman province called Dacia."

I tilted my head up to her and tried to see through the light. "Huh? How old would that make Hanna? I mean," I held up the image, "if this *is* her." I studied the grainy picture. It looked like her, only colder and more weathered than I remembered.

Lily gave me a pointed look. *"Too* old. We're talking *hundreds* of years here. Ownership of Romania swapped hands over the centuries. After the Romans, the Bulgarians. Then, the freaking Inquisition. The Inquisition pretty much brought the death of every woman who knew anything about anything." She lifted her hands and played out *"dun-dun-dun"* on an invisible, floating piano, before she continued. "In the 11th century the Hungarian empire absorbed Transylvania. After the Russo-Turkish War of 1820 something, the area went under the control of Russia." She took a deep breath. "I just read most of that today." She preened, sounding incredibly pleased with herself. "Romania, as it's known, only became a kingdom after the Congress of Berlin. The old legends say the landscape changed under various masters. In times of darkness and carnage, when blood ran like rivers through the fields, land folded into itself and died, unable to bear the evil. Even the stars altered their course. Unless I've missed my guess, this isn't just a map of Romania. This is a map of Romania in all its stages of evolution—past, present, maybe even the future."

"I must admit, that's pretty cool."

Lily pointed to the picture in my hand. "Up in the attic are a dozen more pictures just like that one. Tons by that beach, and a bunch more inside this Corvin Castle itself."

"I know. I put them up there," I muttered. If she heard me, she still had nothing to say on the topic. I gazed down at the photograph in my hand. Like everything else in these books, it should have faded to dust a long time ago. Yet it had persevered. Age had not eaten its surface. Even the ears looked unable to properly dog and crumple. A memory frozen in unaltered perfection.

Strange little spell. Strange little time spell, the girl in my mind chanted.

"Maybe this Corvin Castle was their haven before Wynter Manor," I said and thought about how afraid they must have been. So much power, so hard to hide. "I mean, if the Inquisition was already in full murdering swing, they would have needed something, right?"

"I think so, Cara." Lily bent down and folded up the map. The light dissolved, casting the library back in shadow. "Come, I want to show you the page of the book this was in." Lily walked to the cluttered oak table in the center of the room and opened the black-and-velvet Book of Shadows.

"I found this map of light, or whatever it is, right here stuck to this symbol. It's a lilac," she whispered. "I stared at this page all day yesterday."

I peered over her shoulder. Where most of the pages in the book were littered in markings, this page had a simple charcoal sketch of a beautiful castle poised on sharp black cliffs overlooking an endless sea. I ran my fingers down the page. "It's gorgeous."

Lily turned to me. "I want to go here."

My fingers touched the edges of the chalky sea. "Me too. It looks haunting, like a dark fairy tale."

"You know," Lily flipped the page, "there is a spell here about understanding dreams and one for sleepless nights."

"No!" I told her. "No spells. I will deal with my nightmares."

"Just one little spell, Cara. Come on."

I hesitated.

Lily rose on her tiptoes and hopped in place. "Yes, please! Come on, just do one. Hanna always told us we have more power together."

"What about the cost?" I whispered. "What if I don't want to pay whatever price that spell will exact from me? Hanna also said there is always a cost."

"Will it be worse than hitting your head, or waking up screaming the house down?"

"Lily," I tried to reason, "it's been years since we've done anything like that."

"So we'll be a little rusty…"

I threw up my hands. "I don't even know if I have any magic. I don't know how to transfer fear and agony into a superpower."

"Maybe *they* will know how to help us, here." Lily flipped back to the charcoal-smeared page. "At this Corvin Castle." She sighed. "I will go up to the attic and bring down the rest of the stuff you hid up there."

"Lily, don't…I…"

"Cara, I have to figure out if this is where they came from." She stared in my eyes, and I saw her plea for understanding. "Maybe knowing where they came from—Hanna, Mother, Grandmother Rosen and all the other laughing shadows—will help us figure out where they hell they went." Her face was becoming all sharp lines and angles. "We have power from an ancient bloodline. I think it starts here." Lily slammed her fingers on the dusty drawing of the castle drawbridge. "We have money. Besides, it's not just you. I also…" She went silent.

"You also, what?" I demanded.

"Never mind. I just want to know what our powers are. Or if we even have them at all. At this house, there is no one to teach us. Somewhere out there is a network of Wynter women still alive—I *know* there is! I remember the coven meetings late at night, when they would strip and dance under the full moon, I remember all our sisters, ethereal and mortal. Maybe *that's* where we'll find them."

"In Romania?" I said, tasting the foreign name.

For once Lily dropped the veil layered over her eyes. Simmering below her confidence, I saw trepidation and uncertainty. "We can't just stay here knowing nothing. Surrounded by all this information we have no chance of deciphering, no hope of understanding." Lily dropped her voice to a whisper, her fingers caressing the lines of the black ocean. "I think Hanna is here. Don't you want to find her, Cara?"

This *was* her trump card, she knew I did.

"This is our only lead," said Lily, when my silence continued.

How could I argue when she offered exactly what I wanted? Clever, clever Lily.

■   ■   ■

The floorboards outside my bedroom door creaked and I jumped at the shadows. I threw my clothes, still covered in dust and Lily's blood, in my hamper and turned on the shower. I wiped a circle in the fog that ghosted over the mirror. My reflection bled into focus and I winced. The gauze above my eye hung from a dirty piece of tape. It seemed my lip had doubled in size, and the cuts on my cheek looked inflamed. Wincing, I ripped the gauze off and tossed the blood-soaked cotton in the trash. Favoring my good leg, I stepped into the shower. I sighed as the hot spray of water rushed over me, and my thoughts turned to the cold black walls of Corvin Castle.

Hanna, my mind whispered. "Hanna," I said aloud.

If she *was* there...my mind stumbled, unable to finish the sentence. Lily knew it would be easy to convince me. If Hanna was somewhere in that forlorn place, she knew I would walk over broken glass to get there.

I missed Hanna. She could tell me if I had powers like Lily believed, or—I was simply losing my mind. More than the rest, she could tell us why she left two little witches alone in a giant ghost house of puzzles.

Heat flushed my skin when I finally turned off the shower. I snuggled into my pink bathrobe and put on my slippers. I thought about taking a brush to my mane, but opted to tying my hair back instead. The encroaching curls could do their worst. I straightened my boots at the foot of my four-poster bed and picked up a few of the books buried in my scarlet shag rug. I felt the smile go to my eyes when my fingers encountered the ragged cover of *Blood and Shadows*. Not stopping to wonder how my new favorite book jumped from bed to floor, I snagged the tasseled throw blanket from my bed, then ran back to the library. The hall was very dark and my footsteps echoed. I had the horrible sensation of being chased, goosebumps broke out on my skin, and a freezing chill slid down my spine. I came to a skidding halt in front of the huge double doors. The oak beams towered over my head, I thought I saw the little cherubs—burnt into the vaulted moldings—twitch. I closed my eyes and shook my head.

"Oh! There you are!" Lily peered over my shoulder. "What? Are you okay?"

Fire crackled in the hearth, the smell cherry root and sage filled the room. I stepped in and closed the door behind me. "No, not really. With the dead guys chasing me, the traumatizing hand cutting and sobbing apparitions, I seem to spook rather easy."

Lily smiled and kissed my cheek "Bite my head off, then. You smell nice and look incredibly comfy. I made a fire and tea."

"Oh, you are a true angel," I purred, and went to curl up on the chaise lounge closest to the fragrant golden flames. I fluffed the cushions behind my head and snuggled down into my fuzzy throw.

Lily sat beside me and put a steaming cup of chamomile and honey tea in my hands. I took a sip, let the warmth run down into my chest, and drive away some of the graveyard's lingering chill. Her cup clattered as she set it on the red brick framing the hearth, then she lay down beside me. She twined both her hands around my upper arm and pressed her cheek to my shoulder.

"I can't look at another word," Lily yawned, daintily patting her mouth. "Read to me."

"Do you want me to tell you the story so far?"

"No," she yawned again, and her lashes fluttered against her cheeks. "I'll catch up. Just read."

"Okay." I kissed her golden hair. "Love you, Lily."

"Love you, Cara," she whispered, already dreaming.

I opened *Blood and Shadows* to chapter five and read…

ANCIENT CHAPTER V

SPARTA, MARCH 4TH, 1202, BCE

The setting sun brought the evening dew. It wet the faces of red roses trailing through the lush gardens of the Mycenaean palace. Color soaked flowers twisted between the marble pillars, climbed down the spiral stairs, and ran through the fire-lit courtyard. They left their petals scattered over the white marble floors like drops of velvet blood. In the courtyard music flowed freely as the wine. Tonight, the gods would feast alongside the mortals, and tomorrow, take their blood offerings. The games had begun.

Draken leaned against a pillar, twirling a petal between his thumb and forefinger. He felt exhausted, having somewhat surprised himself he made it here at all. Ten more feet and he would be in the center of the madness. He had no will to summon the strength it would take to weave through the opulent daybeds and jeweled dancers. Soon he would be missed, for now however, he could observe the revelry, yet not experience the crush. Bodies everywhere—draped in gems so rare they glowed a living light—sparkling in gold and crimson gowns. The air rang laughter and shouts of encouragement for the two Spartans battling it out in the center of the courtyard. Draken wanted to leave, go to his bed and dream a dreamless sleep. More laughter and hard sounds of fists meeting flesh. He wanted to leave it all.

The clap of leather on the polished floor sounded behind him, he felt a firm hand slap his right shoulder. The hit was hard enough to make a few drops of wine jump from his goblet. Draken watched the escaped drops splash to the ground.

"A warrior who does not watch his back?" said Ares, pure censure in his tone.

"In my own home?" Draken asked, regarding his assailant through wary eyes. Ares wore his hair loose so it fell past his broad shoulders. A thick gold chain crossed his bare chest, from it hung a violet robe, leather braces encased his forearms, and in each hand he held a jug of wine.

"Boy, that is where one must watch it the most."

"You lead a sad life, Ares."

"He says, lurking in the shadows," Ares returned.

Draken looked around the empty garden. "You were what? Stargazing?"

Ares tilted his dark brows at the crowd. "It is a lot of bodies crammed into one attitude."

"They seem to love it," Draken observed.

Ares took a long gulp from the jug in his right hand. "Humans," he said. Draken heard the slight distaste in his friend's voice, he felt some hidden part of himself resent it.

"I looked in on my stallions," said Ares, unaware of Draken's shadowy mood. "All the noise makes Aithon restless—he wonders why he hears screaming and does not taste blood. After calming him I found myself quite lost until I hit the training grounds. Couldn't miss it, that rather appalling rendition of Apollo points the way. The thing is enormous, overbearing really. Near touching the stars."

"It is excessive," Draken said, and cracked a smile. "My uncle Agamemnon had it commissioned before he sailed to Troy. Thought it would please the golden god."

Ares snorted. "Obviously it did not, since Apollo sided with the Trojans."

"Obviously," Draken said.

"Seriously, why are you out here brooding in the dark?" asked Ares.

"This is a well-lit garden, more torches than fireflies," Draken replied.

"Ah! It's fear then," said Ares, nodding. "Thoughts of our fight tomorrow fill you with unreasonable terror."

"Are you taller in your dreams?" Draken asked. "These dreams in which I fear you? Or, are they rather visions riding strapped to the backs of Nightmares? Visions in which I beat you senseless?"

"Are you accusing me of having sense?" retorted Ares.

Draken barked out a shout of laughter, and a real smile lifted the corners of Ares's lips.

In front of them the party roared. The din shook the little cherubs frolicking on the gilded ceilings, while fresh screams bounced off the polished marble floors. The warring Spartans were taking a brief intermission, and each member of the crowd cheered for their chosen competitor. Crystal waterfalls edged the makeshift sparring sphere. Droplets overflowed the tiled basins and ran on the floor. Shaking and battered, the two Spartan champions dragged their bodies across the wet ground, as blood seeped into the water, spreading out like pink dye.

"They look done," Draken observed.

"Unfortunate. It would just be rude if I challenged them now."

"Ares, it would always be rude."

"Funny, though," said Ares.

Draken scowled. "Just another thing for the gods to laugh at in men."

Ares shrugged. "It is not our fault mortals are so entertaining." He gave Draken a wry grin. "Well, not *always* our fault."

Draken nodded. After the story his mother had told him—of how Ares and Athena had used her in their war, and how the Fates had given him to Menelaus as Athena's weapon against Ares—he found himself less than pleased at the gods' meddling.

Draken took a jug of wine from Ares. He brought the cold rim to his lips and drank deeply, then wiped his mouth on the back of his hand. "I think, if you look hard enough you'll find greatness in more places than you expect. Even the most unimportant of mortals may surprise you."

"I am rarely surprised," stated Ares. "And, never by humans."

Draken gave a tight smile. "Never?"

"Never. Well, perhaps once. Prince Paris surprised me. Less by his actions, more due to my own stupidity. I underestimated the power of his love for your mother."

"It is hard not to love her," Draken said. Helen glistened in pearlescent beauty at the King's right side. A crown of sapphires encased her head, adorning her brow in sparkling vines. She smiled at Draken, though the hard edge in her eyes sharpened when her gaze roamed to Ares.

"She whispers in your ear, does she not?" asked Ares, swigging more wine. "Tells you the gods manipulated her? That the love between her and Paris was Aphrodite's doing?"

Draken raised an eyebrow. "Is she wrong?"

Ares smiled. "No. Not in that. Aphrodite likes her little games. I love war and battle. It is our nature, and we cannot act otherwise. Queen Helen, daughter of Zeus, made her own choices despite the will of the gods."

Draken heard the story from his mother many times. He had seen the bitter regret in her eyes as she spoke of the Trojan War, of the thousands of men and heroes fallen in a battle over her love. She tried to forget Paris, had given him and Androsia all her affection, still, she never could erase the suffering caused by her actions and it visibly weighed on her.

"Remember, Draken," said Ares, his expression somber. "There is a darker tale that often lurks behind every story. The truth may differ vastly from legend."

Draken grinned. "I've seen that black chariot of yours, and those four immortal, fire-breathing stallion fiends."

Ares chuckled. "Perhaps one or two of the stories are true." He shook his head. "Yet the tales that I consume the carcasses of the men I kill? Or that I murdered Adonis because of his infatuation for Aphrodite? These are not true. Not entirely. The shadows of time conceal many truths." He raised the jug. "Enough of this maudlin talk. Let us eat, drink and celebrate. Tomorrow my games began, and your first defeat at my hands."

Draken laughed. "Keep drinking, Ares, you will need the spirits to bolster your own, after your crushing defeat tomorrow, on your sands, on your birthday."

"Painful, Draken," said Ares, then; "Ah! Here comes the most dangerous of you all."

Androsia stood at the entrance to the hall, framed by golden pillars and waterfalls. Her ivory gown hung off one white shoulder, pink ribbons, and fuchsia pearls hung from the ruby clasp holding it in place. Mother-of-pearl lined the necklace of flat stones strung around her neck. The sparkling rocks dangled low between her breasts, a matching chain wrapped her waist, stressing the curve of her hips. Steps measured—careful not to collide with a glassy eyed party patron—Androsia moved to the edge of the courtyard and onto the terrace. Her eyes met Draken's and she shrugged her shoulders in an exaggerated sigh, flinging her hand up to her forehead as if she meant to faint.

Draken had noticed a marked change in her these last two years. The child who told him stories of nymphs and ogres, chased him up trees and forced him to collect an endless stream of shells, stood replaced by a young woman who turned the head of every man in Sparta.

"Your sister is ten times more beautiful than her mother," muttered Ares, following the line of Draken's sight. "That—no matter how you view it—is not good for anybody."

Draken nodded. "Do *not* let the queen hear you say that."

"I doubt she could hate me more than she already does. Yet here she sits alive and well after it all, high queen of Sparta. The luscious playground of the immortals, where the great gods all come together in one place to make man free." Ares's laugh was sardonic.

Draken swallowed his arguments—there was no point to them. It only dragged him back to all he did not wish to think on. Hades. The name blazed through his mind. He hefted the wine jug and took another long drink.

An ear-splitting roar from the crowd brought his mind back to the present.

"The fight begins again. Isn't that Phantias?" asked Ares, pointing to the bald man who had just landed a solid kick to his opponent's jaw. "He won the title during last year's games?"

"Yes, The other is Hyrtachus. Young and strong as a bull. He will go far in your arena tomorrow. Providing he makes it out alive tonight. Watch him," Draken said. "He's quick."

Phantias recovered his feet. Stumbling slightly he righted himself. Hyrtachus charged him. Using desperation over skill, Phantias ducked the second blow.

"Here he goes," Draken said. "Quick as lightning." Draken's feet shifted, mimicking the warrior's moves. He stepped forward, bending slightly at the knees. Phantias spun to the right, made a sharp half-circle and landed a hard punch to Hyratachus's gut. Winded, he stumbled. Phantias gave him no chance to recover. He jumped up and bending at the waist, returned the kick. Hyratachus went flying. Blood and spit sprayed from his mouth, splattering the ground in tandem with his body. Phantias dove for him. Hyratachus put his hands up to protect his face, fingers flexed, his expression rapt and fearful. Phantias did not go for the face. He landed two solid blows to Hyratachus's right rib cage. Bone *snapped* on the third. Phantias hollered, and Ares cheered.

Hyratachus curled around his injury, agony twisted his face. He ground his teeth and spat more blood.

"It's over now!" shouted Ares.

The crowd surged and cheered as the huge fighter attacked his fallen opponent. Phantias swung a terrific blow that shattered Hyratachus's jawbone.

Draken reached for Ares and took his arm. "It's done." Draken handed the jug of wine to Ares. "I'll take my leave of you, warlord. I have an errand before the night is out."

"The fight…only a few moments more…"

"I must. Androsia will keep you company until I return. Though I don't understand why you don't go and mingle. It is your party."

Draken scanned the room for his sister and found her hovering at the edge of the crowd—a silent a golden shadow. He motioned for her to join them.

"Good evening, brother. Bloody fight," said Androsia, and went up on her toes to kiss his cheek. "I can hardly watch it, each time a bone breaks, I feel one of mine has also shattered." She laughed, prettily. "Well, perhaps not quite. Though that sound makes me shudder."

"It is a sign of good sport if it makes a princess like yourself shudder," said Ares, giving her a low, courtly bow.

"Because one like myself must grow accustomed to the sights and sounds of the bloody games?" asked Androsia.

"Yes," said Ares. "Such sights should be nothing to one who might someday be queen."

"I shall not be queen for many years yet, so the sight still brings horror."

"Then we shall walk and fetch you some wine." Ares held out his arm to her. "Come, let me ease the pain."

Draken accompanied them through the feasting hall. He had a task to be about, yet hesitated to leave Ares and Androsia alone. Her tinkling laugh unnerved him. He knew well that her infatuation for this god had been a lifelong thing, and Ares revelled in the attention.

"Every eye in the room holds you enviously," Ares told Androsia, head bowed, lips near her ear.

Androsia peered up at him through thick lashes. "They are welcome to be envious. However, I think they direct their looks to you, my lord."

Ares turned to study her. "I think not," he said, gaze fixed on her mouth. "Your eyes glint like the crystal sea at dawn, and in that gown you rival the beauty of any Olympian lady."

Androsia curtsied. "Thank you, my lord."

The next bone crunched louder than the others. Androsias winced, and Ares changed the subject. "Did you ride today, princess?'

"I did, my lord." Androsia took the goblet of wine he offered her and sipped it slowly. She swallowed, making a sound of pleasure. "I saw your horses earlier when I went to saddle my Vessus. Magnificent beasts—you know I love each one of them."

"And they you, darling."

"I think, the soul of a horse holds far greater value than that of a man," said Androsia.

Ares laughed and smacked Draken on the shoulder. "Your sister is right. 'Tis true for many a horse and many a man." He lowered his voice to a conspiratorial tone. "Now it's the half-man, half-horses you must watch out for. The centaurs have all the power."

Androsia's laugh sang out again, more heads turned in their direction. "I would love to meet a centaur," she whispered back.

Ares shivered. "No, you wouldn't. Nasty buggers."

"I've always tried to guess why you named your stallions the way you did," said Androsia. "Aithon is 'red flame' due to the color of his coat, so that one is obvious. Phlogeus is blacker than night, as a child I couldn't fathom why you named him 'flame', until one day I startled him and he nearly set me on fire. Konabos is the smallest, and the wildest—which is why you named him 'tumult'. Phobos, the cobalt one, is the largest. A monster to be sure. They say men die at the mere sight of him. So you call him 'fear' because that is what he inspires." Androsia paused and lifted her brows. "Well? Am I at least close?"

"You are perfect!" Ares avowed. "And, yes, Phlogeus breathes fire when he is in a mood." Ares placed his finger beneath her chin and tilted her face up to his. "Have you studied my beauties, Androsia?"

Androsia moved her head, batting her lashes in playful flirtation. "Perchance," she breathed, leaning close to him as if to whisper a great conspiracy. "I know all the stories… 'And on the shield stood the fleet-footed horses of grim Ares…he was red with blood as if he were slaying living men, and he stood in his chariot. Beside him stood Deimos and Phobos, eager to plunge amidst the fighting men'."

"Draken, your sister thinks to quote Hesiod to me. Little minx. I was there when he inscribed those words." Ares wagged a finger. "Never pay attention to the fantastical writings of a born storyteller."

"I wonder if my Vessus could match Konabos in speed. I hear Konabos in flight is faster than Wind herself. I think Vessus has outrun a cold northerner a time or two."

Ares cupped her chin. This time, she did not move away. "I promise I shall race them." He ran his thumb across her jaw and touched the tip of her nose. "I think I would promise you anything, little princess."

Draken cleared his throat loud enough to draw their attention. He threw a look at Androsia, she shrugged it away. Pink cheeks flushed, and eyes glowing laughter, she stepped closer to Ares.

"Vessus and Pluto—Draken's Pegasus, were gifts from Zeus to my mother," said Androsia. "According to her, the only gift he ever gave her."

"If one of them even came close to beating my Konabos, the pair would have been a gift worthy of a king." Ares's mouth pulled downward, his eyes dropped away from Androsia. "Zeus is too kind to all his bastards," he said absently.

A hint of steel flashed in the cobalt depths of Androsia's eyes. She removed her chin from his hold, this time there was no playfulness in the gesture. "Is that a bad thing? I happen to prefer kindness in a man over violence."

Ares searched her eyes, then reached for her. "You are an impertinent girl." He took her slim white hand and held it between both of his, then leaned in close so his warm breath fell against her cheek. "And, *I* am much more than a man."

"Easy now," Draken said, trying to make his face hold a stern glare. "I'll not be long. I trust you can control yourself until I return?"

Ares did not look at Draken—his eyes remained locked on Androsia's face. "I promise," he said. "Now leave us, we return to the fight. I will tell you who won. Though I think it is obvious Phantias owns the day."

Draken strode away, a smile tugging on his lips. He went through the eastern courtyard that faced the training grounds and led to the temple of Apollo. The night wind poured off the ocean and blew fresh gusts against his face. He breathed in the salty air while the sounds of the party faded away. The look on his sister's face stayed in his mind as he rushed between the stacked *halteres,* and sandbags lying strewn between the training posts.

He reached the front steps of Apollo's whitewashed shrine. The golden figure stood on a diamond pedestal at the head of the stairs, just facing the entrance to the temple. The giant diamond caught the early morning sun. Legends say, the person who knows the code can decipher the truth of time in the patterns cast by the diamond's various cut lines. In his youth, Draken tried master it, a task which proved to be impossible, the instructions of its mathematics were long lost to time.

Draken stepped inside the torch-lit antechamber. The wooden chests and marble desks littering the room were free of dust, the floor freshly scrubbed. Boughs and palm leaves lined the base of the altar which stood tall in the center of the room. Draken picked up a lantern from its hook beside the door and struck the wick aflame. A warm glow spread out around him, casting light on the pieces of parchment, inkwell and feather quills strewn across the ground.

"Leandros?" Draken called out.

"Here, my prince." The response was weak, the voice dry from lack of use. Draken rounded the altar and found Leandros in the furthest corner of the room, nearly obscured by two teetering stacks of mismatched books and dozens of loose manuscripts. His tutor's spidery fingers leafed through an aged book, there was a plate of roast lamb pushed off to the side.

Draken ran his free hand through his hair, then cleared a space to set the lantern.

"Over there on the floor, boy," barked Leandros. "Just not near the…"

"Parchment—I know…this was my classroom for many years. I am well aware paper and flame do not mix to your satisfaction."

Leandros grunted, though he was smiling. "*See* that you remember it." Movements hampered by the halting pace of old age, he closed the manuscript and gave Draken his attention. "It's good to see you boy, Apollo misses his offerings.'

"I am sure he does," Draken said.

"Do not take that tone near me when you refer to the gods, lest they judge this old servant guilty by association."

A pair of footsteps broke the charged silence. Leandros stood, a pained expression darkening his age spots. Draken imagined he could almost hear the old bones creak. It pained him to see the man withering so, Leandros would take a great deal of knowledge to his grave and the world would be lesser for it.

"Leandros."

Draken recognized the voice and stood.

"Walk your mother to the altar, boy," commanded Leandros. "She comes for her evening prayers."

"Strange to find you here, son," whispered Helen. "I thought you would toast Ares till Dawn flew the skies."

Draken leaned down and kissed the top of her silky head. Helen touched his cheek. "It pleases me you have found a friend in this difficult world." She sighed in exhaustion, her light touch brushing a wayward curl behind his ear. "If only it were not him. I would kill that one, rather than shake his bloody hand. Watch out for him. That is all I ask, he breaks promises and kills his friends, Draken." Helen lifted on tiptoes and kissed his cheek.

"I love you, Mother," Draken whispered. "Should I kill him for you? I would if you told me to."

Helen lifted a sculpted brow. "In the arena tomorrow, perchance?" She smiled. "No, I would not raise the conflict even though all of me wishes that god dead. No matter now darling, there is nothing to be done for it tonight. Come walk me to the altar. I am tired, I must offer Apollo my prayers before I sleep."

Helen placed a ruby jar of peach oil, at the base of the altar. Beside it, she put honey cakes and a stoppered jug of pomegranate wine. She went down to her knees, and Draken knelt beside her.

A cherry log popped in the fire releasing a burst of sparking flame. Helen crossed her hands in front of her chest and her bracelets danced down her arms. "Now this is an honorable god. Apollo did not betray his friends. He fought beside Hector. I watched them fight Achilles in rivers of blood." Helen's face pulled into a scowl. "Ares swore to Aphrodite, to Hera, and me he had switched sides, would lend his sword to the Trojans, but in the end he was not there." Helen turned to Draken, staring into his eyes, she placed her hand on his chest. "In those last days only Ares could turn the tide." Helen's eyelids tumbled closed as she relieved it. "That horrible night when the children were dying—our beautiful city in flames—when we needed him the most, he broke his promise and broke the world. By the time we heard his battle cry it was already too late." She opened her eyes and looked directly in his. "We were already dead."

Draken knew Ares had his own side, but his mother was unshakeable in her fury.

"I am sorry, Mother. Sorry for every single thing putting such a sadness in your eyes…Ares, however, is the least of my problems. I spoke to Father."

Helen's closed her eyes again. "So you know."

"I know about Hades. Athena."

"Do not utter her name!" barked Helen. Draken watched her hands ball into fists. "Do not—"

He held up his hand. "I'm sorry, Mother. I only want to say, Father told me everything."

"So he told you about the curse?" she asked. Draken heard a sad resignation in her voice.

"He said you didn't know."

"I know. Your father talks in his sleep. He will never forget that night, it exists forever buried in the darkest places of his mind, only resurfacing in dreams." Helen unclenched her fists, releasing another long, pent-up sigh. She bowed low, pressed her lips once more to the polished feet of Apollo, then stood and settled her silky, violet robes around her. "Leandros," she said. "I will take a glass of wine. Or a stronger drink, if you have it."

"I do, my queen. We have honeyed mead, and blanched melon liqueur. Combine a few drops of poppy oil," Leandros nodded, already agreeing with his next statement. "Either will send you to the vale of dreams."

"That sounds divine," said Helen, and took the seat Draken vacated. Leandros bustled over to one of the smaller chests, took out an earthen jar encased in a piece of stitched hide and poured a cup of a violet liquid for Helen.

"So, what is your plan?" asked Helen, when she had settled. "I know you son. I am sure you have one."

"Can you tell me how to get to my father?"

"I could, yes." Helen accepted the proffered goblet with a nod of thanks and sipped in silence. "As a mortal, once you pass through the Elysian Fields you must die to cross River Styx. For you?" Helen looked at him over the rim of her drink. "You would not have to die to cross the River. You would only have to convince Charon to take you. Charon sleeps on the Riverbanks. Once you have put him and Styx behind you—there is Cerberus."

Helen set aside the drink and took his hands. "Don't go yet, Draken," she said. Tears pooled in her eyes. "Not yet. I can't lose you to that fate, yet. Stay till the priests conclude your ceremony. Aphrodities spell, and Athena's promise will enhance all your abilities. If you leave now, I will worry each second into a year."

"All right, Mother," Draken said.

Helen threw herself into his arms. He held her and stroked her back, pressing another kiss to her brow. "I will stay, I promise."

Thirteen days. Thirteen days until his Aphrodisia was complete. He would find Hades and get his answers. When that day came, all the tears in the world would not change his course.

ANCIENT CHAPTER VI

MARCH 5TH, FIGHT DAY

Apollo shone bright for the day of the games. Sunlight beat down on the bleached tents and thatched roofs of the colorful market stalls. Carriages rumbled over hot cobblestones while drivers tried to navigate skittish teams of horses through the crush of bodies. Jasmine incense from the silk vendors rose in the hot air, mixing in the rich fragrance of tender honeyed mint-roasted pork, and almond pies with cheese filling. Piles of fish flopped in the huge copper buckets which stood in front of a cluster of blue tents, slimy bodies writhing as they slowly died in the baking sun. Coins of gold and silver exchanged dirty hands, and people shouted out bets, intermingling curses and cheers.

Arias walked three paces behind Aphrodite and watched in awe as the crowd parted for her goddess. A pair of pure white doves sat on her shoulders, speaking to each other in soft coos. Aphrodite's gold hair pulled back from her face and twisted into a mound of lustrous curls strung by diamonds and white rubies. Her saffron gown clung to every curve, its hue matching the color of her eyes. On either side of Arias, two high priests clutched the hem of the goddess's gown, struggling to walk and bow, tripping over every step. They coughed dirt, yet could not wipe their white-rimmed lips for fear of allowing the goddess's robes to brush earth. Arias swallowed a giggle at the way the sunlight bounced off their protruding rears.

"Ithacan silk!" a vendor behind them shouted. "Woven by Athena herself."

Arias never imagined so many people existed. In front of her, she could see a line of beautiful women, thick chains encircling their wrists and throats. A man cracked a whip and shouted at them to move. Wiping sweat from his bulbous nose, he turned and called to a group of men. Arias realized they were negotiating a price. A price for the life of a girl. Arias could not help but wonder what *her* price had been. Suddenly, the day was too hot, the jasmine clogging the air too sweet. There was a scuffle and Arias ducked under the flailing hand of the priest about to topple. He crashed against a stone wall behind a small set of steps leading up into a curtained portion of the arena.

"This way, My Lady!" the uninjured priest called out to Aphrodite. "Up these stairs. We can enter through the *maenianum primum* and on to your esteemed seating. We will move quicker, free of this throng."

Aphrodite breathed a vexed sigh. "Come then Arias, think of it like a rite of passage. We must battle through the dirt gods to see the golden ones."

"Yes, my lady," Arias said, keeping her eyes locked to the ground. The snow-white silk of her veil was terribly dusty, and her delicately sandaled feet so caked in grime she feared they would never recover. "Sparta is very…overwhelming," she whispered.

"Isn't it, though?" gushed Aphrodite. "I love it here. Come, the King and Queen await me."

"Yes, my lady."

When they entered the *royal primum*, the pre-game was just reaching its bloody conclusion. Two groups of warriors stood locked in combat. The sun hit the gold and silver of the Spartan armor, pouring light into the sands as slashing swords drew blood. An eagle screamed and whirled through the dust clouds bursting up from the violent battle raging in the center of the arena. Arias tried to catch legible words in the crowd, but curses and praise clashed together, forming a sound similar to the desolate howl of a stalking beast.

The shield wall which the silver Spartans had been fighting to maintain—broke with a grinding crash, the warriors decked in gold rushed forward to defeat their remaining foes.

Even in her wildest dreams, Arias could not have pictured such a spectacle. Men, bronze and beautiful in the sun. Born to sweat, fight and die in honor of the gods. She imagined herself locked to a different fate. Down there, battling in the sands instead of submitting on an altar in a golden temple. Dirt and blood between her naked toes as she stood her ground, prepared to die a different death for the same cause. The image made Arias swallow a smile. She tore her eyes from the sands and drank in every detail of the strange world. A sense of desperation filled her. She had to see it all, something told her she would not have another chance.

Menelaus paced the front of the *primum*. Near him, Helen sat enthroned, her lily-white fingers tapping on the golden arm rest. Seeing Aphrodite's crest riding above the gilded marble stairs which led up the right side of the wreathed podium, she stood and bowed low. Aphrodite inclined her head and held out her hand. Helen took it in both of hers. "My house welcomes you Goddess."

"Thank you, Helen," said Aphrodite, and brushed her fingers across the Queen's crown of threaded white gold. "You are the picture of perfection. As always, you put all other creatures to shame."

Helen smiled and bowed again. Aphrodite seated herself, and Arias took her place standing on the right side of the goddess. Arias dared to glance up through her lashes. Helen was more beautiful than rumored, creamy skin framing eyes brighter than sapphires. Menelaus instantly terrified her, the way he stalked the royal box like a tiger on the prowl.

"Sit down!" commanded Helen. "Stop pacing. You will irreparably fray my nerves."

The king whirled on his queen. "Where *is* he? Even a god should know to not be late to one's own tournament." He thrust a thick finger at the stands. "Zeus knows these brutes are doing little to entertain the crowd."

"I am here," said Aphrodite. "Where he commanded me to be. He will be here. Late enough so all eyes fall on him alone, notice his poise, nobility, and of course his sense of fashion." She threw up her hands and laughed. "We are talking about Ares, yes?"

"You see?" scolded Helen. "Cease your worrying, Menelaus. Sit, drink." She held out a wine goblet. "The sands belong to Draken next. Ares will not miss it for the world."

The last of the silver Spartans held up two fingers in the symbol of surrender. The crowd rumbled half-hearted cheers, while the men in gold gained their feet, staggering painfully. Standing proud, they chanted the ceremonial words and dedicated their victory to their god of war.

"Androsia!" cried Helen, jumping to her feet, she rushed to her daughter. Arias watched Helen take the beautiful girl's hands. "Where have you been?" demanded Helen. "You almost missed your brother's glorious entrance. He would never have forgiven you."

"I know!" wailed Androsia. "Today is just the worst! I could not find the right dress, my chambers are a shambles, and this crowd!" Androsia rolled her eyes and fanned herself. "Insanity!"

A cloud crept over the sun's face, and darkness fell over the stands. Under the reaching shadow, an expectant hush descended on the crowd. A solitary figure strode onto the sands. Small beams of remaining light bathed his naked sword, and the metal flamed where the light touched it. The man turned, bowed to Menelaus and Helen, then shot a wink at Androsia. He struck the broad steel blade to his chest and saluted. Then, raised his arms and let out a long war cry.

The wild beast slumbering in the center of the crowd stirred, then roared.

"*Draken! Draken!*" it chanted. "*Prince of Sparta. Prince. Prince. Draken!*"

Arias shuddered as chills traced her skin.

"Who will fight me?" shouted Draken, brandishing his sword. When no reply came from the crowd, he laughed. "Men of Sparta! Afraid to face me? Let me fight two at once. Or three, or ten. I will fight as many as dare!"

No answer. The beast waited.

Menelaus leaned forward, grunting he tossed a heavy sack into the arena. "For the victor!" he shouted. Gold coins spilled from the bag—a challenge to all.

Draken bared his teeth in a feral smile, then lifted his arms and roared again. The crowd echoed his name. Head held high, he moved to the center of the sands. The heavy silver armor of his rank spilled from shoulder to wrist like dragon scales, and his cloak of Spartan red flowed down his back.

Arias felt like she hovered somewhere just outside her body—pins and needles attacked the soles of her feet, her hands felt clammy, her lips dry. Realizing she held her breath, she exhaled—air dashed from her lungs in a *whoosh* that made her stumble. She closed her eyes, it did not block the sight of him. His naked chest stood branded in light behind her lids.

"Perhaps the men need more incentive," rumbled Menelaus. Lifting his arms, he shouted, "a kiss from my daughter then. A true kiss from the mouth of the fair Androsia, and a place at her side tonight during the royal feast!"

"Father!" Androsia went pale.

"Menelaus!" snapped Helen at the same time.

"Oh, hush woman! No one has ever defeated Draken. You have nothing to fear."

"And, what if he loses?" asked Helen.

King Menelaus shrugged. "Then, Androsia receives an education on the life that awaits her." He turned to the princess. "Your beauty will bring many men to Sparta, my daughter. Know full well that *I* will choose the one you are to marry."

Helen's gaze was cold and anger bracketed the corners of her mouth.

Real fear contorted the perfect lines of Androsia's face. "Please, Father," she whispered.

The king spared her a quick, irritated glance. "One night with the daughter of a demi-goddess," he shouted out again. "A gift for the victor. Who will take up such a challenge?"

Helen's eyes grew wide until they were violet beacons in her face. Arias followed the queen's gaze. A new warrior stepped on the sands dressed like a foot soldier, wearing leather braces instead of silver, and a wide leather pleated skirt that fell to mid-thigh. Golden links fastened a red cloak across his shoulders. Arias knew from the stories that he did not wear the color to honor Sparta—they called the garment 'his bloody shadow'.

Ares, god of war, had come to battle.

The world seemed to fall strangely silent, save for the hollow pounding sound in Arias's ears. The hot fingers of the sun pulled sweat from the pores of her neck; it trickled down her back, sucking the silk of her gown to her skin.

Aphrodite beamed. "Arrogant bastard."

"Great Ares," returned Draken. "This is an unexpected honor. I feared you would hide yourself until I left these sands."

Ares roared with laughter and the crowd screamed.

"I would not miss this for all the world, boy." Ares raised his sword. "Now this prize… a kiss?" He laughed. "From the well-guarded lips of your sister?"

Draken's teeth flashed again. He pounded sword on shield in the steady war beat of the Spartans. "Only if you can defeat me," he said, soft and deadly. "I think it's more likely, Androsia's virtue is safe for another day."

Ares strode to the box where Aphrodite stood, he moved past the goddess and turned his blazing glare on the princess. "Fair Androsia, what say you? A kiss if I win?"

"Yes," Androsia breathed, blushing. "I mean, of course, my lord. *Only*, however, if you can best my brother."

"Best? The question is only how long he will last…" Ares bowed to her. Finally, he faced Aphrodite. A beautiful smile painted the goddess's lips. Arias knew it was false. The hands of her goddess shook, the knuckles white and clenched.

"My lady," said Ares, in a deep tenor that rocked the very dais. Arias did not miss the sardonic twist to his brow. "You honor us by your exquisite presence."

Aphrodite's blinding smile competed with the sun's brilliance. "You are late," she said tartly, pausing for dramatic effect. "The king worried."

Ares cocked a brow. "Did *you*?"

"Certainly not. I know how you love to make an entrance. If this day proves to be yours, I fear there will be no living with you."

Ares laughed, Arias thought it a chilling sound. He moved to take Androsia's hand and turned it over slowly. "Now," he whispered into her palm, "I have *two* reasons to fight." He kissed the spot heated by his breath.

Cheeks flushed, Androsia fell back in her seat, giggling. "We shall see," she told him in a breathy whisper.

"Will you do something Menelaus?" screeched Helen when Ares retreated. "You know how I despise Ares. You cannot give him my daughter!"

Menelaus gripped the bridge of his nose. "I beg you, be silent, Helen. I do not hate this god. I owe him my life. Give me a moment of peace. Besides, I cannot take back the offer."

Helen's beautiful face contorted in a paroxysm of rage. "He is responsible for the death of everything I loved; him and his insatiable thirst for blood. You have promised my daughter to a monster!" she spat. "I was wrong to think you could have changed. You will always be nothing more than the septic spawn of a whore who stole my childhood. Only evil will come of this, mark my words!" On her last word, Helen stormed from the *royal primum*, her gold and indigo robes flying behind her like butterfly wings in the wind

Arias held her hand to her pounding heart. She would never forget a single moment of today, she knew it. If the Fates forced her to walk the mists for all eternity, she would never forget. Never.

On the sand, Draken, and Ares circled each other. The crowd rumbled.

"What say you god of war?" called Draken. "A fight to first blood?"

"To first blood!" Ares confirmed.

Draken charged, his bellowing war cry shook the stands. The ring of shield on shield echoed through the arena as god and demi-god crashed together. The god of war stood firm. Draken rebounded off Ares's shield, staggering from the force of contact. Ares struck out. Draken parried, catching Ares's blow on the flat of his sword.

Draken's expression grew sober. He dropped into a low crouch. Shifting sands shuffled in the wind. Between breaths, Ares struck, fast as a darting cobra. Draken met the attack and countered in a blur of movement, which ended in a lightning slash.

The crowd gasped. Draken had knocked Ares back—a single step.

"Not bad," heaved Ares. "For a boy," he finished, and slammed a sandaled foot into Draken's shield. Draken stumbled back and went to one knee. His raised sword barely turned aside Ares's next strike. Draken gained his feet, retreating under the war god's powerful onslaught. Step by step, he gave ground.

"Come on, Draken! Is that the best you can do?" panted Ares. A drop of sweat rolled in his eyes, he ignored it. Ares spun, his foot caught Draken in the stomach. The force of the kick sent Draken hurtling toward the arena wall. Draken twisted mid-air, brought his shield to guard his chest, then landed—exploding particles of disturbed sand—on one knee.

Ares sped forward to continue his attack. Draken would not yield. He ducked behind his shield and absorbed the punishing blows. Ares raised his sword for another strike. Draken leapt from behind his shield and slashed upward. His sword passed dangerously close to Ares's throat. The blow would have severed any mortal man's head. The god of war jerked aside, head twisting to avoid the strike. Draken's blade cut so close, Arias imagined she could hear it slicing the hairs off the tip of Ares's nose.

"How's that, old man?" huffed Draken.

The song of steel on steel rang out in the auditorium as god and prince dueled across the blood-stained sands. Metal glinted on the ground behind Draken. The spiked tines of a fallen pitchfork protruded from the sands. Arias dug her nails in the soft skin over her heart, swearing she could feel it stop. One more step and Draken's sandaled foot would land directly on top of a wicked-looking spike. Arias flung her hands out in warning and screamed. "Draken, look out!"

The piercing sound caught Draken off guard. His feet stuttered. Ares brought his sword across in a terrible blow that sent Draken stumbling to the right. Away from danger.

Growling, Ares retrieved the fallen pitchfork. Draken's eyes widened at the sight of the weapon.

"I will *not* have our battle spoiled, by something so mundane," said Ares. His muscles bunched as he hurled the trident across the auditorium. The force buried the tines two hand spans into stone.

Draken's eyes rested on Arias. She leaned over the railing, hands thrust out, the echoes of her cry still reverberating through the air. To Arias it seemed the voices of the crowd faded, the dust clouds stilled. Time rushed ahead without her at an incredible speed. The world disappeared and there was only him. Fire burned in his eyes, his lips forming silent words meant for her alone. Words she would have died to hear.

Arias watched the expression on Draken's face change. A hush fell over the arena. Even the noisy vendors ceased screaming out their wares. All eyes remained fixed on the two gods. Arias lost all ability to breathe, and her damp hands grabbed fistfuls of her dress.

Ares launched in a series of swift, deadly strikes, but Draken refused to meet his blade. He twisted aside only to return moments later, slinging powerful slashes of his own. Ares stumbled backward, lost his balance, and fell to one knee.

The crowd gasped. Draken did not give Ares time to recover. He swung, a vicious downward chop which blurred through the air—its speed such, the god of war had no time to block. Ares caught the blow on his silver arm brace and fell in a sideways roll, a move Arias thought—looked more desperate than skillful. Ares jumped to his feet, sword extended. Draken knocked it aside and raised his own, Ares spun out of the blade's deadly path and dove behind Draken's back.

The blurred motion of battle turned to utter stillness. Ares held his blade pressed against Draken's throat. A single drop of blood trickled from the cut.

Silence reigned in the arena.

The whispers started slowly, even before the dust had settled. "First blood," someone chanted.

"First blood," another cried.

"*First blood! First blood!*" The beast moaned.

Menelaus yelled over the din of the crowd. "We have a victor. Ares, god of war!"

"*First blood!*" the beast yowled. *"The god of war has drawn first blood!"*

"Wait!" Draken thundered. He raised his sword high. A visible streak of crimson clung to its razor edge. Draken flicked his wrist. A single drop of blood fell to the sands. The silence of the moment was deafening.

Ares looked in open shock at the droplet, then slowly upwards to a small red knick, maring his upper thigh. A trickle of ran from the wound, the blazing blood a scarlet banner of victory.

The mob went wild. *"Draken! Draken!"* they chanted, throwing flowers, scarves, and other unmentionables.

Ares smiled, stepped back, wiped the blood from his thigh, and sheathed his sword. "You fight like a god, Prince of Sparta."

Draken dropped in a bow. "I've trained under the best, my lord." He winced and touched the cut on his neck. "Not so bad yourself."

"I demand a rematch," said Ares.

"Always," Draken returned. The two men clasped arms, then turned as one to the king.

"Name your winner, Father," said Draken.

Menelaus looked dumbfounded.

Androsia stood and blurted. "May I decide, Father?"

The king's expression changed to surprise, he nodded. "Let the prize declare the victor."

Arias commanded her body to remain still, it disobeyed, moving to Draken like a loadstone. He stood—chest heaving and eyes laughing at Androsia—in front of his father.

"Well, Androsia?" asked Draken, sheathing his sword. "The choice is yours."

"Hmmmm," Androsia hesitated, a painted nail worrying at her lower lip. "'Tis a draw," she declared. "A draw where both walk away victorious. Draken, prince of Sparta, you leave the sands knowing you made a god bleed."

"A feat few men survive!" shouted Ares.

Draken inclined his head. "You are generous, sister."

"And you, Ares, our proud, patron god…walk away with a kiss." Androsia descended to the marble edge of the dais leaning over amidst cheers and shouts, which rose to a soaring crescendo. Ares strode to Androsia, he took her shoulders in his rough hands and crushed his lips to hers. Ares gripped a handful of soft hair and drew her closer. Androsia caught her breath when he broke free. She pressed her fingers to her bruised mouth, smiling. Ares bowed to her, then winked.

Draken laughed. Silver curls blew around Androsia's face, to Arias she looked enchanted. Arias let the scene play out before her, but she had eyes for the prince alone. Sensing her scrutiny, Draken's gaze fell on her. She had no power to look away. She felt her short breaths in each thud of her heart, an impossible organ that seemed to have fallen to the very pit of her stomach.

Ares looped his arm around Draken's shoulder. Together they bowed to Androsia. Draken blew a kiss in her direction before Ares hauled him away. Arias watched them walk until even their shadows disappeared, then closed her eyes.

That could not be the last time she saw that man. The Fates would never be *that* cruel.

ANCIENT CHAPTER VII

TONIGHT, THE HYADES WEPT.

Swollen droplets of rain splashed against the ground and ran in rivulets through the cobblestones. Under the crimson light of the setting sun, the water wove through the stones like a thousand throbbing veins.

More tears ran on the marble floors and into the hot pools of the palace symposium. Foggy steam swirled through the tinkling harps and raucous laughter. A hundred cinnamon and cherry-scented candles surrounded the banquet tables set low to the ground, they dripped wax on the multicolored furs and velvet pillows strung by satin threads. Tiny lights glittered overhead, twinkling in the leafy canopy climbing over the ceiling tiles.

Draken and Ares lounged at the head of the largest table. A hog fresh from the spit lay in front, an apple stuck in its mouth. Androsia sat nestled between them, lounging cross-legged on a mound of velvet pillows. The three had long ago abandoned their goblets and now drank wine straight from the jug.

"You do *not* line your bed with skin," Androsia repeated, her voice only breathless, tumbling giggles. "That would be the most awful thing!"

Ares fluffed a pillow beneath his head and took a deep pull from the jug. "It's incredibly comfortable."

Androsia smacked his bicep, Ares gave a mock flinch. "What?" he said, looking impossibly innocent.

"What?" echoed Androsia. "I know you are only trying to make me blush. Human skin, icky!" She shook imaginary flesh off her hands.

"It is such a pretty blush," said Ares against her cheek.

Androsia's eyes fell closed and the rings on her fingers caught the firelight when she tried to straighten the chain of blue roses draped across her forehead. "You are too close, my lord. I do not recall owing you another kiss."

Draken took Ares by the shoulder and dragged him free of Androsia, chugging wine as Ares fought to retain his seat. "Off her," Draken chuckled.

"Shall I obey your brother, my love?" asked Ares.

"No," said Androsia.

"Great surprise there," Draken said. "She's smitten."

Androsia gasped. "That's not true. I am nothing of the kind, Draken!"

"'Tis the only reason you named him equal victor—my cut landed first."

"That *is* true, my lord. Perhaps you should give me the kiss back," said Androsia, giggling sweetly when Ares buried his face in the slender curve of her neck "Ugh! Draken!" She pushed at Draken's intruding arm. Her shove upset his questionable balance, and he fell laughing into the pillows.

Ares picked up a strawberry and put it to Androsia's lips. She bit down. The sweet fruit burst in her mouth and a droplet of pink juice ran onto her lips. Ares leaned in and kissed it away.

"You shouldn't, my lord!" whispered Androsia against his mouth. "We'll be seen."

"Yes," Draken said, mock fury dripping from his voice. "By me. It will force me to fight for your honor Androsia, and I am far too drunk."

"You will not beat me a second time," said Ares, absently twining Androsia's silky hair between his fingers. "I know all your weaknesses now. One thing is certain. I will never call you *boy* again." Ares raised his jug. "To the most fabulous draw in history!"

"It really will be," said Androsia. "Told and retold so many times. Look, Draken," she continued, "you are already becoming a legend."

Minutes passed and they drank in companionable silence, then Androsia rose to her feet. "If you will excuse me, I will take a moment to freshen up. Ares, you have quite destroyed my hair. Come me with me, Draken. I have no desire to wander this party alone."

Draken stood reluctantly, and together they weaved their way through the wild crowd. Two fire dancers sprayed mouthfuls of flame in the air, Draken saw Helen through the golden glare. He had not laid eyes on her since she left the sands. Anger twisted her features, she looked exhausted and worn. Ignoring him, the queen walked to Androsia, took her arm, and swung her around.

"How could you?" hissed Helen.

"What on Gaia!??" said Androsia.

"How could you bear the kiss of that serpent after the stories I've told you?" said Helen, her voice enraged. If they were alone Draken imagined she would have shouted.

Androsia pulled her arm free of Helen's painful hold. "It was a good fight Mother. You shouldn't have left. Draken won the hearts of the people, so I figured we wouldn't want to offend the god of war. He cut Draken nearly at the same time. It was only fair he receive his prize, besides it wasn't me who offered my mouth."

"You had no right!" cried Helen.

"I had every right. It is *my* mouth, Mother."

A loud, stinging slap rang out. Androsia screamed and Draken felt his jaw drop. Androsia gripped his arm to steady herself as she stared up at Helen in pure shock.

"How dare you?" screamed Helen. The sound faded in the party. Helen held the hand that had struck her daughter at an awkward angle as if it pained her.

"Mother!" Draken found his voice.

"I can't believe you did that!" whispered Androsia.

Helen took a step closer to her shaking daughter. "I told you he was my enemy!'

"He is not *my* enemy!" wailed Androsia. "Show me proof of what he has done. You are the only one who says he caused the fall of Troy. Everyone else tells me it was you. You and your lover!"

Draken stepped between the queen and princess.

Helen looked ready to rip skin from bone. "This is not about your childish lust. You have no idea what is at stake."

"Like you?" Androsia shot back.

"Yes, just like me! I had no idea. I loved Paris with all my heart, but my romance was nothing more than a love spell, a great big, painful lie manipulated from the start by those monsters who call themselves 'the gods'. Aphrodite gave me to Paris before I even knew he existed. We were in love before I ever saw his face."

"Oh, Mother!" groaned Androsia, she touched her hot face. "Oh, Mother, you are hateful! I am not you!"

Helen's hand flew to her mouth to stifled a sob. Androsia whirled away and darted back toward Ares. Draken stood, uncertain which weeping woman to follow. Because he had no idea what to say to Helen, he went back to Ares to find Androsia weeping on the pillows.

"Obtuse!" spat Androsia. "Biased and obtuse."

Ares stroked her silver hair. "Hush, Androsia."

"I can't hush and I certainly can't be seen near you anymore. I fear she might kill me. Take me out of here, Draken. Please! I just want to go to my room."

"Come now, Androsia," said Ares in consolatory tones. "Stay a while longer, and her anger will fade, by Zeus it has to, does it not?"

Androsia whirled on him. "It will never fade! She hates you beyond reason."

"I know," crooned Ares, all laughter gone from his eyes. "I'm sorry, Androsia, I know."

Shaking fingers wiping at her eyes, Androsia sat up, and rounded on Draken. "It will be up to you to fix it when the games are over. She hated the thought of you fighting him too. She didn't even watch it you know."

"Yes, Androsia I'll fix it." Draken pried her hands from her face. "That was quite the slap. Your cheek is swelling."

"Argh! It is the most painful thing I have ever felt in my life. The whole side of my face is on fire. I hope her hand is in agony. She is so cruel! Her stories…!" Androsia threw up her hands. "You would think she was the soul of innocence, when really she should have just stayed with Father instead of running off with that stupid—Draken, you're not even listening to me!'

"I am listening to you, but I know you Androsia, you would fight until death to be free of a man you hate. In that, you are not much different from Mother."

"I am nothing like her," said Androsia.

There was a tussle followed by an angry shout, and a fight erupted in the center of the room. Ares jumped to his feet.

"Are you going to take them all on, oh fearsome warlord?" sniffed Androsia.

Ares picked up his sword. "There are only a dozen. Come, Androsia. Cheer for me, it will take your mind away from this personal tragedy."

Androsia folded her arms. "I will do no such thing. I will not cheer for a dust cloud of flailing limbs. Draken, let's watch the fire dancers in the garden." She gained her feet and tugged her brother's arm. "Come on, Draken. Take me out of here."

The wine spun in his head, lurching in his gut. Draken allowed Androsia to pull him upright.

"Come, Draken!" yelled Ares, already running—fists at the ready—to join the fray.

Androsia continued her relentless tugging on his arm. "Do not go. Take me to the gardens. I just need some air before I sleep."

Draken tossed a rather forlorn look at the group of warriors battling in the hot pool. Ares had two men pinned against the pool's marble stairwell and pummeled them each in turn.

Draken shook his head. "Battle is breath to that god." Throwing a final glance of pity to the fallen warriors, he followed Androsia into the gardens.

Rain fell in light, drizzling waves. Androsia blinked at the sky, and droplets crowned her lashes. Draken led his sister toward the pale blue light reflecting off the courtyard fountain.

Androsia took deep breaths of the night air and closed her eyes on a sorrow filled sigh. "Thank you, Draken. I love the rose gardens after a rain. The droplets make the flowers look bejeweled."

Draken reached for a thorny stem. Plucking it he twirled the rose between thumb and forefinger. "Beautiful," he agreed looking at her. "Beautiful and delicate. You know, Androsia, Ares is not for you. Give him your smiles if you will, if however, you care about your heart at all, don't give him any more than that."

A pout puffing her lower lip, Androsia ripped the rose from his hand. "Beautiful and dangerous." She corrected. "I am stronger than you think, Draken."

"He will hurt you. He will not mean to, yet he will. It is his nature."

"Oh, really?" said Androsia, shooting a sharp look at her brother. "I don't believe that."

Draken tugged on a curl bouncing against her ear. "Why not? Because he dazzles you?"

Androsia sat on the fountain's edge and ran her hands through the glittering water.

"You are a total liar if you deny it," Draken said.

Androsia rolled her eyes, though she did not deny it.

"I don't want to fight, Androsia. I just want you to be careful." Draken tucked the curl behind her ear. "You are one of the few things I care about in his world. Your pain would be my pain."

Androsia's eyes misted as she stretched up to kiss the tip of his nose. "Fine. I will be careful. I don't know what everyone is freaking out about! For Zeus's sake, it was just a kiss."

"I know," Draken winked. "Your first?"

Androsia smacked his chest, scandalized. "Draken! I will tell you no such thing. Why are all the questions directed at me tonight? Who have you been kissing?"

"No one," Draken admitted.

"Fine, I assume there is someone you want," Androsia returned. "Who is she?"

Draken hesitated. "I want no one."

"You're thinking of someone."

"I'm not."

"You are."

"I…" Draken cleared his throat. "The girl standing beside Aphrodite today…?"

Androsia raised an eyebrow. "Who?"

"The stunning dark-haired girl. Dressed all in white, brilliant green eyes."

"Oh, her," Androsia's face scrunched up. "I've never seen her before, but if she stood near Aphrodite, she must be a priestess of some sort, I think. Mind numbingly dull, didn't utter a single word."

"Except to warn me," Draken said.

Androsia shrugged. "True." She gave him a mock stern look. "A priestess, Draken? There are *thousands* of women around Sparta who would suit you better. Like her, for instance."

Draken turned to follow Androsia's finger. "Who?"

"There!" Androsia pointed to the edge of the rose garden. "That woman in a black cloak. Don't you see her? Under the peach trees lining the carriageway. She is quite stealthy. Do you think she is trying to steal into the party?" She crinkled her nose again. "That's rather cheap. So maybe not her, then." She dropped her hands. "Whatever—there are tons of other women."

Draken's eyes finally found the cloaked figure standing in a pile of fallen fruit and scattered wildflowers. Her slim, elfin face obscured by the waterfall of black hair tumbling free of her cowl, running down her past her hips. Each perfect ringlet had a rich crimson sheen in the dim light.

"So tiny," whispered Androsia. "Perhaps she's a sprite."

Draken barely registered Androsia's hand waving before his face, or her singsong voice saying, "Gaia calls for the return of Draken." His breath came fast and he gripped the fountain's edge. The marble—white as his knuckles—groaned and cracked. An owl flew through a coil of smoke whirling up from a dying torch. The bird soared, higher and higher above the girl's head until darkness nearly swallowed it. The owl flew a final time before the girl's face, spread its wings and soared into the night.

"Draken?" Androsia's voice was a distant sound "She's pretty, not *that* pretty. Perchance the hits you took today were worse than we first suspected."

Draken tore his gaze away from the girl and focused on his sister. "I- I'm fine." He forced a smile. "Just lost in a moment, that's all. And, Ares hits like an untried boy—you may tell him I said so." Heaving a tremulous sigh, he pulled her in his arms placing a kiss on the tip of her nose. "Go make peace with Mother, will you?"

Over Androsia's shoulder, he saw the girl move. She took two steps up the ornate staircase leading to the symposium. Golden slippers covered in tiny pearl ribbons flashed out from a slit in her gown. Suddenly, she flinched like a startled deer and retreated down the steps, nearly stumbling in her haste.

"Go. I want to talk to that girl."

Androsia shook her head making ringlets fly about her flushed face like dizzy fairies. "You chase strange shadows in dark gardens…I am berated for a single kiss." She whirled in a flurry of silk, leaving him to his own devices.

Androsia's movements happened at the periphery of Draken's vision. The girl diminishing in shadow filled his world…

ANCIENT CHAPTER VIII

LOVE AT FIRST SIGHT.

Arias wanted to run. She was foolish to sneak away. The temple was safety, a haven of soft music, silks, and gold. Here, warriors fought, and dancers spewed fire on a pack of squealing ladies swaying to the violent drums. Through the torch smoke she could see silhouettes entwined in pleasure, and she realized safety was ignorance. She had seen so little, lived so little in her eighteen years.

Just a glimpse of the prince was all she wanted, yet she dared not enter the party, too many opportunities for touching—she was *Leisha* the right to touch her belonged only to the man who would be her pleasure and her death.

Arias teetered on the tips of her toes, unable to pick him out from the crush of glittering bodies. She sank back down on her heels and a sigh of defeat passed her lips.

And if you find him? her mind queried. *What then?* This was beyond stupid. She turned to run.

"Stop!"

The sharp voice nearly caused Arias to jump free of her skin. Her hood fell back on her shoulders. Arias only heard that voice on one other occasion, but she would have recognized it anywhere. It was him, she knew it.

"Don't go! Please," the prince said. Arias felt him stop a few paces behind her. Warm, ragged breaths brushed the back of her neck, and gooseflesh broke out across her skin.

"Who are you?" asked Draken, his voice was deep and luminous as the firelight kindling the liquid amber in his eyes.

Arias took a frightened step back. "N-No one important. Just…just a girl."

Draken closed the remaining distance between them, crushing fresh peaches and crunchy autumn leaves under his feet. "I remember your face from the stands. You stood in the sanctum beside the goddess. I felt your eyes on me before you called. Your warning changed the fate of that match. I believe I owe you my victory."

Arias tried to keep her voice airy—it came out desperate. "You owe me nothing. You fought like a god. Still…" her eyes dropped to the earth, and she laughed, "I had a strange feeling that if I looked away, you would fall." *That's a foolish thing to say,* her mind told her. She tossed her hand in the air feeling her cheeks warm. "I have little experience of these things, but I believe that fight will grace written works for many years to come. It was extraordinary."

Draken moved closer. "Will you at least tell me your name?"

Arias took a stumbling step back, she held her hand out in front of her. He could come no closer. He was far too handsome when he smiled. One look at his face and Alora would have labeled him a *'heart crusher'*.

"My name is Arias." She looked over his broad shoulders to the throbbing symposium. "It sounds like a wild night." Music filled screams of laughter rose around them, followed by the ring of clashing swords, and the crunch of fists meeting flesh.

"Why are you here? Sneaking through the gardens, I mean?" Draken held out his hand. "Come and join the party."

"I am not sneaking," Arias said, then sighed. "Well, maybe I am. Normally I only walk the temple grounds, tonight I heard the music and all the laughing…I thought if I could just get one look at the beautiful women in their colorful silks and jewels…" She touched her bare curls self-consciously. "I only caught the smallest peek, I think they glow like stars." *And to see you.* Her mind whispered the words she could not say. *To look in your eyes, hear your voice.*

"Temple?" asked Draken, breaking her reverie. "So you are a priestess of Apollo?"

"No." Arias shook her head, setting her curls—violet-threaded by diamond raindrops—blowing across her face. "Aphrodite is my goddess. We are to the west of Apollo's shrine."

"So you came from over the Agora?" His eyes widened. "You walked all this way?"

Arias shrugged. "It's not far, and I love to walk. I stay to the forests and hidden mountain paths. I am rarely seen. Now, I…I have to go." She pulled her cloak tighter around her slender shoulders. "I will be missed and forced to come up with a credible excuse if I am to avoid a scolding."

"Going?" asked Draken, appalled.

"I must. I should not be here with you."

Draken shot her a quizzical smile and reached for her hand.

Arias spun away, crying in alarm. "No! Do not touch me. I am *Leisha*. It is forbidden."

"You are a priestess of the *Aphrodisia?*"

Aris said nothing, she did not believe his choked question required a response.

"How old are you?" asked Draken.

"I am eighteen," Arias told him. "Today is my birthday."

"Then, you are to be sacrificed?" Draken's eyes hardened. "When? To whom?"

The rain had slowed to tiny droplets cluttering the early morning mists. Pale blue light soaking the horizon bled into black shadows turning them grey as shrouds.

Arias shrugged again. "I don't know. No girl knows the exact time," she paused. "Don't look so horrified, Prince, you know it is our duty to respect the old ways. The gods demand it." To Arias, her words sounded hollow and forced, still, she continued. "Death, life, rebirth and death again. This is the circle of the gods."

Draken's voice was low, his eyes searching. "Are you afraid?"

"Sometimes," Arias whispered. "Not when I was young, as a child it was all I wanted. Now?" She shook her head. "It is my destiny. It contents me to know I serve a purpose beyond simply living and dying." Even to herself it sounded like she recited some sad old rhyme. The thought was depressing, and she shook her head to drive it away. The movement only rattled her brain and sparked a slight ache between her eyes. Suddenly, she wanted her bed, her home, the safety of the priests, the marble walls of her gilded cage. This world full of mists, and his golden eyes would only bring her pain, when she returned to her own world—so very void of those things.

"I should really leave now," Arias whispered. "I must be back before Apollo wakes. There are no dark paths left for me to walk when he rises."

"May I see you again?" asked Draken, a hint of desperation in his voice. His hands hovered in the air, so close to her, she could feel their warmth.

"No. It's impossible. We are standing in a moment never meant to occur. If anyone ever discovered me," Arias sighed. "Well, I can't even imagine what would happen. I do not believe there is a precedent set for these things."

"I will see you again," vowed Draken. "Even if I have to sit outside the temple every day."

Arias laughed. "Nonsense. You will do no such thing!"

"I cannot let you walk all the way alone." His hand hovered over her jaw, not quite touching, yet so close she could feel the heat of his palm. "I must see you again."

Arias closed her eyes. "It's impossible."

Arias twisted away again, this time he did not follow her. She drew up her hood and the mists transformed her into a phantom—a fantasy only touched in dreams—and she vanished from sight.

■   ■   ■

Arias walked up the familiar stone stairs carved into the tallest of the Mycenaean cliffs. To her right, the rocks shot into the sky and their tips brushed the puffy clouds. To her left, the city of Sparta slumped at the base of the rocks, still fast asleep. She looked up at the sky, judging it to be about an hour more until her world woke. Despair flooded her. Arias knew she would never make it back in time, yet forced her aching legs to keep climbing.

While Arias walked she tried to think about anything other than him and found it impossible. She felt way worse off now that she knew the sound of his voice, she also knew that for as long as she lived she would never forget those eyes. *I will go back to Aphrodite,* she told herself. *I will beg her. Maybe once it is all over, once I've completed the Aphrodisia and done whatever I am supposed to, completed whatever soul-wrenching act they demand from me, maybe they will let me run into these hills, hide in the rocks like Medusa. Disgraced but alive... maybe."* Her useless thoughts faded to silence. It was a broken dream—she would not see him again, and she *would not* survive the Aphrodisia.

Arias stepped off the path of stairs to the expanse of patchy shrubs and cold sleeping rocks. She walked to the tip of the cliff until she could curl her toes over the edge. Her arms spread wide, the wind caught her cloak and flung it behind her, before slapping her cheeks and tossing her hair around her face. Arias closed her eyes, let the wind play havoc.

"Take us to the place that be…" she chanted softly. "Far across the golden sea. From the gates of Tartarus take us away. To live, to die again. In the mists of that fated day."

The chant made her feel slightly better, helped her remember if her destiny was sacrifice, it was only the end that would hurt. Draken had just been another glowing moment in her perfect life. Now, she could die remembering his face and voice.

Somehow, impossibly that same voice came at her from the dawn. Her name rang sharp and clear. So close. Shocked, Arias whirled and her left foot slipped. Draken's dark face appeared an instant before his arm wrapped around her waist and hauled her into the air. For a moment of unspeakable terror, she hung suspended from his arm, the wind stealing her breath, the earth looming far below.

"Put me down! You can't touch…you can't…"

"I am not touching," said Draken. He lifted her up into his saddle, seating her in front of him.

Arias panicked and grabbed handfuls of black mane. When she had one hand buried in the horse's thick hair and the other slung around the stallion's neck, Draken held his hands out to his sides in a gesture of innocence. "See? Not touching. No skin. Only your cloak."

"What?! Wh…what are you doing?" Arias's voice stumbled out in breathless gulps.

"Saving you," said Draken.

"By nearly killing me?" she cried.

"You were standing at the edge of a cliff," Draken pointed out reasonably. "Not the safest place to—"

"I was saying my prayers!" Arias shouted. The wind ripped away the sound of her words. "The only thing I need saving from is you, and this…" Arias looked down at the creature under her. It was ink black, had an impossible wingspan, and gigantic shod hooves that seemed to be cantering on thin air. "This monster!"

"Pluto is no monster." Draken reached across her and patted the beast's neck. "He is a blue-blooded Pegasus. Isn't that right, Pluto?"

The horse nickered at him, its lips drawing back over a set of teeth that looked like sharpened knives.

"He is terrifying," Arias retorted. Trying to link her arm around Pluto's neck, Arias took a deep breath through her nose. Pluto dipped once, banking hard. Arias screamed again and buried her face into the billowing mane.

"I will not let you fall," said Draken in her hair. "I won't touch you. Just hold on to him and open your eyes."

Arias shook her head and burrowed deeper.

"We are above the clouds, Arias." Draken spoke her name like a prayer. She opened her eyes and turned to look up in his face. Behind him pink and cerulean blues flushed the sky. Fluffy clouds kicked into smoke by Pluto's heels swirled up around them. Between the break in the clouds, she could see pieces of the city flying by, distant specks on the horizon.

"Oh!" Arias gasped, and struggled to sit up, trying to look everywhere at once. "This is…"

Pluto dove and the dewy clouds splashed up in her face, misting her eyes. She screamed again, this time in laughter and delight. Arias spread her arms, the way she had on the cliff. This was magic. Here, there was no death, only breath, life, and flying.

Draken's arms encircled her, careful not to touch he tried to recapture the reins, then he pulled up. Pluto followed his rider's lead, and they soared higher.

Cooing out soft sounds of wonder, Arias threaded her fingers through Pluto's damp mane, and stared in rapt silence for a long time. For a single roaring moment of untainted astonishment, she forgot everything about her life, and all that came with it.

Draken watched her face. She blushed and turned away to study the whitewashed pillars spearing up in the distance. The gold framing the temple courtyard caught the sun, and Arias threw up her arm to shield her eyes. Draken fed slack to the reins. Pluto snorted and began a slow, circling descent.

Arias watched the sun crest the mountains to their east and wash the white shores in effervescent color. In her heart, she knew she would do her duty, fulfill her destiny and honor her goddess— still, in that moment she accepted she would miss this earth and all its beauty. She did not want to walk forever in the land of forgotten phantasms.

Pluto's hooves hit the ground, and he galloped flat out across the open expanse of empty land edging the chiseled face of her temple. Rocks spewed out of their path as Pluto kicked up dust clouds that left a fine brown mist on her cloak.

"Around back," Arias said, her voice hoarse from screaming. Adrenaline ran through her, making her breath come in little pants. "Take me to the south entrance. You can let me off near the hanging gardens. I can reach my rooms easily from there."

Draken reined in. Pluto snorted, nickering at the air as he slowed to a walk.

"I can keep flying, you know," said Draken. "Take you away. Anywhere you want to go."

Arias said nothing as he dismounted and led Pluto in silence through the garden. A statue of Aphrodite stood in the center of a sparkling fountain. The goddess held a vase over her shoulder, pouring water down to the marble basin. Pluto stopped and lapped at the sweet water. His ears fell back in pleasure, his wings folded and brushed against the ground. Arias slid down Pluto's side and stepped on the lip of the fountain.

"You are a good boy," she told him, hands running up and down his slick neck. "Good boy."

Pluto stopped for a second to push his wet nose against hers, then went back to drinking.

Arias teetered on the edge of the fountain, emitting a little scream she jumped down. The fall was further than she expected, her teeth smacked together, clicking audibly.

Draken chuckled. Arias tossed a handful of water at him, hitting him in the face. He laughed out loud.

"Shhhh!" Arias said in a whispered shout. "Someone will hear!" She took another handful of water and splashed it over her heated skin.

A few droplets ran in bracing rivulets down her neck, falling in the hollow between her breasts. Draken's gaze followed the crystal drops.

"Please say you will meet me again," he rasped.

"You know I can't." Sadness soaked her voice. "I will never forget today, though." Arias reached to touch the space over his heart, her hand only a breath from his chest. "Thank you, prince. You gave me a beautiful dream. No matter what happens after today, all I will have to do is close my eyes and remember flying."

Arias left Draken for the second time that day, she wanted him to call out to her, yet prayed he would not. Gardenias brushed the hem of her sleeve as she rounded the garden gates. The moment she passed his line of sight, Arias spun, pressed her body into a fragrant bush and watched him. Draken stood in a ray of sunlight, his face upturned, his eyes following the path of a screaming owl circling the skies. His shoulders sagged and his eyes touched the ground. Arias watched every step Draken took as he led

Pluto out of the garden, mounted up, and kicked in his heels. Shaking his vibrant mane, the Pegasus spread his wings and vaulted into the air.

Arias watched man and beast—both dark as night—vanish into the light. "Goodbye, Draken," she whispered. "My beautiful, impossible fantasy."

CHAPTER 9

FAIRHAVEN, WASHINGTON, NOVEMBER 10TH, 2019

At least once in your life, you will want what you cannot have.

We woke up still curled on the couch, Lily's hand clutching mine. Rain pounded against the windows and we could hear the drops shattering against our oak terrace.

Lily stretched, flexed her toes and yawned hugely. "Ah, a storm. Our world is back to normal." A violent shiver punctuating her words, she got up to stoke the fire. Red coals still simmered at the base of the grate, and the flames started up. Lily glanced at the clock on the mantelpiece and squealed. "It's one in the afternoon! Oh, Cara, we have to cook."

My back arched under the shaking force of my yawn while I tried to rub the sleep out of my watering eyes. "Why? Do you have a hot date?" I said, my voice layers of sleepy sarcasm.

"No. *You* do." Lily slapped my foot.

That got my attention. I sat up. "You invited Drake?"

"Yep, and his sister," said Lily, as always, sounding incredibly pleased with herself. I swung my feet over the edge of the chaise, and something thumped on the ground. I reached down and picked up a book so thick I needed both hands to lift it. I had fallen asleep still wearing my gloves and inside them my palms felt sweaty. "Wow, Lily," I gasped, laying the tome on the throw beside me. "A little light reading?" I tilted the book so I could see the spine. *A History of Rome: The Fall of an Empire.* "Jeez, Lily."

Lily shrugged. "I couldn't sleep in the middle of the night. Not sure what woke me. So I figured I'd read for a few hours. I think I found every book in this house even remotely related to eastern European histories."

"And?" I asked over my second yawn.

"According to this book, Hanna *is* from Dacia. Look!" Lily opened the volume and rifled through the pages. "Where is that photo you found last night?" she asked absently.

"I don't know. Why?"

"Because," Lily stopped flipping suddenly and smacked the page, "here is the same obscura photo, all grainy black, and white lines."

"What the hell?" I yelped. Awake now, I stared at the dark, roiling waves and the somber faces of my relatives looking daggers at me from the pages of a history book. "Read the inscription at the bottom of the photo. It's the same." Wonder drenched my voice. "It's word for word, except…" I sprang to my feet and dashed for the cluttered table and the Book of Shadows. Wax sculptures poured down in suspended motion from two engraved candle holders balancing precariously at the table's edge—the candles burnt down to stubs—Lily had read all night.

My hand passed over the Book of Shadows's mauve velvet casing touching the embroidered lilac preening in the center of our three interlocking rings. A shiver flowed up my arm when my gloved fingers contacted the flower. I moved the book out of the way and found the old photo.

"I was right." I held it up, triumphant. "It dates our photo of Hanna, 1708, and the photo in the book, 1604."

"So the book is a little off," said Lily. "We are talking about a *loooong* time ago."

My shoulders sagged in defeat. She had me. I was totally interested. "Did you go up to the attic last night and take the rest of the stuff down?"

Lily smiled, still engrossed in the page. "Yes. I found a ton more pictures. Look, there is even a family tree here." She opened to another page that held a mass of tiny names and connecting lines, which created a stacked family timeline dating back to A.D. 106. I ran my finger through the sectioned branches.

"Gods, here it is!" It was impossible to keep my voice from shaking as I read aloud. "Lenora Rosen, Princess of *Dacia Traiana* and Rome, A.D. 203 to unknown."

I read forty or so more names I did not recognize. Princesses and kings from Austria, Bavaria, Denmark and Rome. Then, at the bottom of the page, no descendants, she was there: Queen Hananka of Transylvania, A.D. 1222, to unknown."

"Insane, right? Impossible. So classic Hanna!" Lily flipped the pages back to the photo of Hanna and Grandmother Rosen. "There are two dates almost a thousand years apart for the *same* women."

I made a squeaking sound in my throat as Lily read the words again aloud. Maybe just to hear her own voice cement the reality of the impossible.

"Queen Hananka of Transylvania," Lily read, "born A.D. 1222, death unknown."

I pointed to the base of the family tree. "It spells Hanna's name differently here. Maybe it's a coincidence. Maybe this *Hananka* is just a distant relative." I disbelieved the words as they came out of my mouth.

"It's possible," Lily allowed. "We do however, know one thing for sure." Her fingers touched the dark sea in the photo, she smiled at Hanna, then walked over to the ladder resting against the eastside of the library— it stood in the middle of a bookshelf spanning nearly the entire wall, holding rows of books stacked from floor to vaulted ceiling—Lily climbed it, inspecting each row as she passed. Four rungs up she found what she sought, jumped down from her perch, and ran back to sit beside me. She opened the book and scrolled through the index, then turned to a page holding a detailed map of the ancient Roman Empire. Using a pink highlighter, Lily circled from Bucharest to Transylvania. "We know for certain both *Hannas* were born somewhere here, our Hanna certainly stood on the shores of the Black Sea." She made a pink X on the Corvin Cliffs. "Right here. That castle was once her home. Much more, I think, than Wynter Manor ever was."

"Even if that's true, what makes you think Hanna returned to her roots?"

"Well…" Lily sighed. "Even if she didn't, roots are a good place to look."

No arguing that, my inner voice said, and I let it go.

"Did you know Grandmother Rosen was a Roman priestess?" asked Lily. "There are more pictures here, carvings on St Anthony's Cathedral, her name inscribed on a tombstone at the Louvre, these tapestries." She returned to the book holding Hanna's photo and flipped to a page filled with paintings of silken embroideries. "Our family crest, here," she flipped again. "And here, all over items dating back a millennium."

"So what? Are we immortal?" My tone was sarcastic, yet her eyes were serious when they bored into mine.

"What if we are?" asked Lily. "I don't know. One of the plethora of things I want to ask Hanna when I find her." Lily glanced over her shoulder at the massive iron clock hanging on the cherrywood wall. "Crap, we have to cook. We can open another bottle of wine while we work and I can tell you about everything I found. Maybe I can even convince you that an adventure in Eastern Europe is the best idea for us right now. I've always wanted to see Prague."

She did not need to convince me. Though I would not tell her that now, her argument was solid. If this was the first breadcrumb to Hanna, I would follow Lily wherever the trail led—straight to the evil witch who would eat my heart.

Immortality made my mind go to *Blood and Shadows,* to the fate of the priestess Arias. If I were her, I knew I would not have made the same choice. I could see myself wrapping my arms around the handsome prince's waist, begging my dark stranger to run away with me. He would kiss me—untouchable be damned—and together on his winged monster we would make for the sunrise. It would be pure poetry. Not the death that was coming for her. Coming—I suspected—for both of us.

A thousand miles I would run if I had to—to find the love of my life. The beautiful lyrics played in my head. I hummed the tune as we walked.

In the kitchen, Lily went to turn on the lights. I stood alone at the little arched window over the sink and peered through the rain. A vivid blaze of lightning split the sky. The metal arches of Wynter haunt flashed pure white, illuminating the shadows that lived and moved beneath them. Ghostly shadows of my aunts, dark figures in the pale storm light, motionless under horizontal sheets of rain. I stared at them, gripping the edge of the sink until my fingertips throbbed. A dozen eyes stared back at me—in anger at my willingness to leave them—or encouragement, I could not tell.

■   ■   ■

We spent three hours in the kitchen, drinking wine and talking about women that should be dead. The smell of garlic broiling in pesto oil and aerated mozzarella melting through the fresh roma tomatoes engulfed us. Our stomachs rumbling, we waited for the edges of the lasagna noodles to crisp and curl. We sat together at the edge of the kitchen island. The oven's heat fought back the chill of the storm, making everything feel cozy and warm. I sat on the bar stool closest to the stove and swung my foot absently. The wine had done little to help my nerves.

"Calm down, Cara," said Lily, startling me. "You're making *me* jumpy."

"Maybe inviting him over was a bad idea. What if the 'no pain when he touches me' thing was just a fluke? What if I faint or…?"

"Don't say it! You're just putting bad juju into the air. We will have a wonderful dinner and *nothing* will happen. It *is* possible to engage in normal activity in this house!"

"Are you speaking from experience, or is this a legend you read somewhere?"

She ignored me and looked at her watch, then slid off the bar stool, taking the red velvet cushion with her. Lily growled, picked up the cushion. "Every freaking time." Then, "Cara, your shoes! Did you know you have half the forest clogged in your soles?" She put the cushion back on the seat and smacked it for good measure. "We need to change." She lifted her arm and sniffed at the air. "I for one, smell traumatizing. Please don't wear those shoes to dinner. No arguing with your elders!"

I smiled. "You know, you're only like a minute older than me."

"An eternity," said Lily

"Which makes you the boss of me?"

Locks of blonde hair fell in her eyes. She smiled and tucked the curls behind her ears before bending to unlace her boots. "Self-ordained, of course."

"Of course," I said.

"If there is no time," continued Lily, "how long is that minute really? Try *that* mental Rubik's cube out!" Thunder rocked the kitchen. The lasagna in the oven popped and sizzled. Lily kicked off her boots and gave me a knowing look. "Whatever, I know you want to be pretty for him." Standing in fuzzy pink socks, she finished the rest of her chardonnay in a gulp, the gesture somehow made dainty by the mud-soaked boots slung over her shoulder. "There *is* something about him, though. That night he brought you home, he sat beside you for so long. The way he looked at you—well it was downright worshipful." She glanced down at her watch again. "They'll be here soon." Lily left a kiss, and a jaunty wink floating in the air behind her, and sauntered out of the kitchen.

As usual, she was right. I wanted to be pretty for him, gorgeous even. I ran my hands through my ever-tangled hair and touched the cut above my eye. It felt slightly less tender. I walked down the hall to my bedroom, thoughts of a foreign, dark land prominent in my mind.

I kicked off my shoes, and picking up my brush from the vanity, sauntered into the bathroom to attack the ends of my hair one-handed. I used my other hand to splash cool water on my face.

"Immortality," I whispered to my reflection. My voice seemed distant. The women in those books were strangers. If I closed my eyes, however, Hanna's face, her perfume, and that rare beautiful smile were so real. I remembered her like my own reflection. She told me I was the strong one. I did not believe it. Every woman in my family had strange, incredible abilities. It had always been the way—I just could not believe my defect may someday morph into a superpower. I might live in a haunted mansion, but my world was not drawn on the pages of a comic book.

In my room, I slipped into a little black dress. It had flowing sleeves, which belled at the wrists, and an old lace trim at the hem. I had not worn the dress since high school. I spun to face the mirror, hoping for the best. I let my breath out in defeat when I saw my reflection. There was not a whole lot I could do about my cuts and busted mouth. I abandoned the lipstick and focused on my eyes.

The doorbell rang when the mascara wand hovered just a breath from my eyelashes. Lily's footsteps clattered across the wood floors, echoing down the hall.

"No!" I hollered. Standing on my tiptoes and wielding the mascara at top speed, trying not to poke my eye out. "I'll get it! I'll get it!"

I dashed out of my room, pulling on my gloves as I flew down the hall with a strange, running limp that made Lily giggle. I took a bracing breath for my impossible nerves and threw open the door. The pouring rain lifted mist off the ground in steam swirls. I saw him through the haze. Raindrops glittered like diamonds in the thick locks that fell over his forehead and curled around the flat collar of his leather coat.

"It's nice to see you again, Cara," said Drake. His whole face moved when he spoke, eyebrows arching, slanted eyes flashing. "You look beautiful tonight."

A great swarm of winged creatures burst free in my stomach.

"I bring gifts of wine." Drake raised two hefty brown paper bags. "I didn't know what either of you liked, so I chose a selection."

"We accept any form of fermented grapes in this house." I pulled the door open wider. "Come in, please. I'm sorry dinner isn't quite ready yet."

"Don't be," he winked. "I'm in a drinking mood."

"Perfect. That makes two of us. And… I promise to do my best to stay conscious all evening."

My bad joke took some of the animation from his gaze. I felt something from him, finally. A burning sadness that touched my chest. It flickered briefly through the air, guttering out in seconds like a bad bulb. He smiled again and stepped to the right. His sister stood behind him snapping her umbrella closed.

"Hi," she said, her voice slightly irritated at her ongoing struggle with the umbrella. She kicked the little metal spoke fixed to top, spraying raindrops across the foyer. It clicked shut, and she let out a pent-up sigh. "Sorry we're late. It's my fault."

"Oh, no problem, we just finished getting ready. Please come in. You're both already soaked."

She stepped inside beaming at me. "Thank you. I know we met the other day, but the circumstances were…less than perfect."

"They were weird," I said. She laughed.

"A little. It's nice to meet you. I'm Andi."

"Cara," I replied.

Drake stepped inside, set down the bags and took off his coat, careful not to drip on Lily's calico welcome mat. Andi shook the rain out of her hair, the short disheveled cap shone a silvery blonde, and instead of being a complete mess the hairstyle looked like it had taken hours to achieve. I heard Lily's footsteps clipping behind me, Andi's silver gaze trailed over my shoulder to lock on my sister. She smiled, real pleasure filled her eyes. I turned around. Lily had pulled her gold curls into a stylish topknot, and her cherry lip gloss matched her empire waist dress. I sighed at how beautiful she was. Her fashion sense was ethereal.

"Hi," Lily held out her hand to Andi. Her sleeves fell in pinpoints over her knuckles, framing a set of nails polished to a perfect shade of violet.

"I'm Andi." The girl reached past me to take Lily's hand, but she did not shake it, just clasped it between both of hers. Under her long fur coat, her small body sagged in relief. "Oh, if this city has a creature like you," Andi nearly swooned at the thought, "perhaps you will convince me it isn't so dreary. I feel like I may drown at any moment."

Lily let go of Andi's hand and reached out to take her coat. "I wish I could say you are visiting in the rainy months. Welcome to Washington State." Lily hung the faux-fur on the coat rack by the door. "You have such a pretty accent," she said over her shoulder. "Where are you from?"

"Eastern Europe," said Andi.

Lily paused mid-motion, the glittery pelt spilling over her arms. "Oh," she said. I heard the catch in her breath. I could almost feel her excitement thrumming through the floorboards. "Whereabouts?" Her voice was the soul of casual.

"Romania." Andi made the word sound exotic, like the name of an extinct bird, or rare ballad. For a second that seemed to drag on forever, the word hovered in the air.

Lily hung up the coat, then turned. "I have always wanted to visit Transylvania, I dream of Prague fashion."

"Prague is amazing," said Andi. "I know every good store in Mala Strana. This is only my third time in America. New York once, and Cali—I loved Cali! Drake wanted to drive up here. The drive from Huntington Beach really was spellbinding."

The sky spat out another lightning bolt. Thunder rolled over the grounds and a sheet of rain blasted in through the open front door. I walked over and closed it. The latch made a hollow clunk as it fell in place. Drake met my eyes. All the windy, creaking sounds of the old manor seemed to go mute. He hefted the brown bags. "Where do you want these?'

"Uh," I swallowed. "In the kitchen. On the island. Come." I led the way down the hall. Lily and Andi chattered a million miles per hour, flinging their hands around their faces. In the bronze lamplight, they looked like ladies from another time. Their heels clicked in rhythm, their laughter filling the hall. It was nice. I thought this hall could use some laughter.

"Your sister left her book at the Space Needle," I told Drake when the silence between us got too thick. "I forgot to give it back to you…last time you were here." My voice sounded so nervous. I mentally rolled my eyes. "It was just sudden." I stopped and looked at him. "I was so unprepared to see you here in the manor the other morning. I…I just forgot. Also, it's a historical novel, so I was dying to read it." I smiled and did not care that I blushed, I was strangely proud of my romance obsession.

"I didn't know she left anything," said Drake. For the first time, I noticed his accent—just a slight inflection to the words—nothing garish or glaring, only an intelligent diction that gave his speech a lyrical tone. The world got brighter as we rounded the hall into the kitchen. Drake set the bags on the counter.

Lily waved a hand. "There are glasses over by the wet bar, in the corner." She craned her neck to get a better view at the contents of the bags. "Is there a Chardonnay in there?"

"Two or three," he said.

Lily pulled out bottle after bottle, commenting on the year and vintage. Her pretty brow went up at Drake. "What nice choices." She lifted one that had a gold swirl on the label. "I am saving this one for my next skirmish with the Book of Shadows."

"You have a Book?" asked Andi.

Lily threw up her hands, motioning around. "Look at this place. I think a Book of Shadows comes standard with a three-story library, a graveyard and a spook attic."

"Drake," Andi buzzed, blowing him a kiss, "I love this place."

He smiled at her. "I thought you might."

"So…?" Andi's hands made a rotating motion as if she was trying to pull Lily's words from the air. "What's in the attic?"

"Thanks to Cara, all the good stuff." Lily gave me a fake pout and poured me a glass of Chianti.

Andi turned to look at me, a frank expression turning her mouth down at the corners. "Why would you hide all the good stuff?"

"To be normal," I said.

She waved away my words. "Normal is so boring. The most beautiful women in the world have all found themselves offended by the word *normal*. It used to be normal for women to play with wind and fire, bend elements to their will, using nothing more than a breath and a prayer." She rolled her eyes, but smiled at me. "Fuck normal!"

"I think we should bend to the elements," said Lily. "Obey and respect them. I think *then* they lend us power."

Andi shook her head. "That's that theory of Wicca. Modern witchcraft," she huffed.

Lily threw her hands on her hips and off they went into a heated discussion of Wicca versus just plain witch.

Drake busied himself settling the wine in the fridge. The oven beeped, and my mouth watered. I turned to inform Lily the lasagna was ready, and instead I just stopped and watched Andi's hands fly around her exquisite face while she talked. When she reached for her glass, her sleeve brushed the cuff of Lily's dress. The black of Andi's sweater turned to liquid crimson and ran down the back of Lily's hand like thick blood drops. I watched the droplets fall from Lily's fingertips on the floor, splashing up. More morbid, bloody crowns.

Lily turned and met my eyes—hers were gaping black wounds. The bloody holes had charred, smoking edges. Crimson poured from her empty sockets in grisly streams. My hand went to my mouth. Little rivers of blood carved down her face, and streaks of hard ochre light split her skin. Flames exploded over her neck and jaw. Lily burned.

I spun away, gulping back my strangled sound. Head spinning, I reached out for the barstool to steady myself. My hands met empty air and my legs buckled. A knife of agony sawed across my ribs as I crashed into the edge of the marble island. Lily screamed, and the world went a misty grey.

Calm. The girl in my mind cautioned. *Not real,* she whispered. *Just breathe.* Objects bled back into focus. I shook my head, trying to clear my ringing ears.

"Cara, are you alright?" Lily's panicked voice came at me from the end of a long prism colored tunnel. I shook my head and wished for the tunnel to just swallow me. Drag me down the proverbial black hole before I died of embarrassment. I tried to steady myself. The force of Lily's worry staggered me, her fear for my well-being set my stomach churning. I willed my eyes not to tear. It would be the last straw if I cried and passed out in front of a man I had known for less than forty-eight hours.

"Cara, what's wrong?" demanded Lily.

"I'm fine," I said. My shaky, breathless voice did not know the definition of fine. I grabbed onto the stool and tried to pull myself upright, but my arm wobbled, useless. I crashed down again.

I felt Drake's control snap a second before I saw him lunge for me. Andi caught me first. The pain was instant. Blinding. Acid fire raced through my veins. My spine arched and I screamed. Crimson flashes of hot light filled the tunnel. Lily's voice echoed in the pain.

"Andi, no! Don't touch her!"

"For the love of Zeus!" gasped Andi. The pain receded when she let me go. Darkness sucked the colors out of the tunnel and my world.

When I came to, Drake was holding me—No pain.

One big hand gripped my waist, and the other was hot on the back of my neck. His arms cradled me against his chest. Warm air swirled between us, loud with my shredded breathing—No pain.

We stayed that way without speaking. I held a fistful of his shirt and he lifted me off the ground—easily as he had the paper bags—and sat me down on the stool that had defeated me. I could not understand it.

No pain?!

Only a bone-melting heat searing my veins. His touch felt like hot sunlight on my face, or velvet on my naked skin. Drake's fingers brushed the back of my neck when he moved his hands from me. Those fire butterflies ran rampant.

"I'm so sorry," said Andi, softly. Awe echoed in her voice. She studied me like I was a strange creature she had discovered. "Touch causes you pain?"

"Yes, it always has," I said.

"I didn't know," said Drake. His voice was polite, if a little reserved, as if we danced at a masquerade and he wore a mask fashioned just for me.

"It's okay," I whispered.

"All touch?" he asked.

"Yes," I said.

"But, not my touch?"

"Apparently not," I admitted.

"That is very…" The mask slipped a little. "Interesting." *Interesting* did not sound like the word he wanted to use.

"And Lily," I said, and noticed my voice had lost some of its quiver.

"Twins," said Lily lightly. "It's a special bond thing." She came and kissed my cheek. "Sorry, Cara," she whispered, then to the room at large. "The lasagna is ready and it is perfect. Cara made a kale and strawberry salad."

"With goat cheese," I said, in desperation to have something normal to attribute to the room.

"Oh!" Andi clapped. "Goat cheese, a Book of Shadows, *and* lasagna! This place is paradise."

"Andi?" Lily opened the oven and the rich smell unfurled in a cloud of steam. "Could you go to the china cabinet and grab some plates? We can take everything in the dining room, just through there." Lily pointed her nose toward the French windows while she pulled the bubbling tray out of the oven and set it on the stove top with a clang.

"Oh, it looks perfect!" gasped Andi. She reached her finger in the boiling tomato sauce for a taste. It surprised me when Lily did not slap her hand away. Instead, Lily tilted her head to the side, the way she did when she wanted the truth out of someone. Her teeth worried at her lower lip.

"What do you think?" asked Lily, finally.

Andi closed her eyes and mewled in her throat. "Oh, *dios mio!* I am back in Milano. That sauce is divine. You are a true witch!"

Lily tsked. *"Wiccan!"*

I smiled as they launched into a fresh round of hard debating.

I turned my attention back to locating my glass of wine on the now cluttered island. Drake held it out and his eyes met mine over the rim. Storm light moved in the crystal cup.

"Did I hurt you at all?" he asked. "In Seattle, or the other night outside the bar?"

"No, you didn't. I never—"

"Drake, help!" said Lily, a note of genuine distress in her tone.

The rest of my sentence hung in the air, forgotten and unspoken. *For the best,* the girl in my mind chided. *What were you going to tell him? That it felt like a kiss in a dream, like peace and warm sunlight?*

"Maybe," I shot back under my breath.

"Sorry, ladies! No, don't take that," said Drake. Andi tried to reach over his shoulder for another finger of sauce. Drake took Hanna's quilted hot pads out of Lily's hands. "I'll carry the tray."

"Oh, it's okay," said Lily and fanned herself, like a southern belle caught in harsh noonday sunlight. "You're just getting all distracted by Cara, we understand."

"This is the largest tray of lasagna I've ever seen." Drake hefted it. "Are we feeding an army?"

"Yes," said Lily, hands on her hips and a prim tilt to her bare shoulders. "Us. We will eat every bite."

He laughed and shook his head, eyes wide as he stared at the tray. "Impossible."

■   ■   ■

We ate every bite.

The storm had previously released most of its pent-up fury, now it only washed the windows. The droplets splashing on the glass panes added to the comfort of the fire, colorfully dancing in the hearth, pouring light on the red bricks until it seemed the glowing coals had fallen from their grate.

Lily and I cuddled under our fuzzy purple throw, my head rested on her shoulder. In her lap, the Book of Shadows lay open to a *"locating spell."* She ran her nail down the list of ingredients inscribed in thick red ink, which she would need to pull it off, chewing absently on a sweet Hershey's Kiss, while the rest melted between her fingers. I took it from her and popped it in my mouth. The rest of the chocolate lay forgotten in an open box beside Andi, who sat cross-legged on the floor, studying the family tree we discovered earlier today. Drake sat across from us in Hanna's overstuffed leather chair.

After dinner, it was Lily who suggested we sojourn to the library. She tantalized us with talk of stronger liquor, but her destination was the books. The library was freezing when we entered, and Drake immediately set about making a fire. Lily and I smiled at each other while he stripped the bark off the store-bought logs for kindling. He hunched down in front of the logs, his large frame dwarfing our massive hearth. Neither Lily nor I mentioned the little gas lever beside his foot; it was too wonderful to watch him lean close to the tiny flame he made using his engraved Zippo, and fan the fire to roaring life. Now, the four of us sat in companionable silence.

Releasing an exaggerated sigh, Lily placed the book down and went for another Hershey's Kiss. She knelt beside Andi. "You know, Cara and I were thinking of planning a trip to Romania."

I felt like everyone in the room caught their breath, except Lily, who went on undeterred. "Do you know anything about flights? Or maybe you can suggest a good hotel. May I?" Lily held out her hands for the book Andi was reading.

"I haven't seen a timeline like that since I was a child," said Andi.

"Amazing, isn't it?" Lily took the book and flipped. Ignoring the index and ancient maps she scrolled her finger down for something more current.

"Here," she said finally and opened the book to a colorful double-page spread. "I want to stay somewhere around this area. Hunedoara."

"Your pronunciation was perfect," said Andi, no pleasantries in her voice, just a slight hint of awe.

"Thank you," Lily beamed.

"I live right here," said Andi and pointed to a little violet dot on the map. "The university I attend is in Deva."

Lily pulled back and looked at Andi. "Seriously?"

Andi laughed. "Yes, seriously. Drake owns a bank here in Petrosani, but my mother lives in Deva. We have a beautiful home on the southern cliffs of the Transylvanian Alps."

Lily's eyes fell closed. "That's almost exactly where we want to go." She came over and sat down beside me.

"I will make a deal with you." Andi made the word *deal* sound like an exotic, impossible thing to refuse. "You let me stay here for the next few days, instead of that place downtown." She gave Drake a sweet smile. "No offense it is beautiful. But I have no acquaintances here, and it's too rainy to ever go outside. So the hotel feels a little like—" she paused, "can I say 'fancy prison'?"

Lily laughed. So did Drake.

"Yes, you can say fancy prison," he said over a chuckle, then tried to swallow it back. "Sorry, Andi."

"Yes," said Lily. "Oh! Yes that would be so nice. We literally *never* have guests." She jumped back up off the couch, knocking my blanket on the floor. I shivered and reached for it.

Andi laughed. "I haven't offered the deal yet."

"You will extend us the same courtesy if ever we find ourselves in your neck of the woods?"

"We are not quite at the wood's *neck,*" said Andi, confusion painting her pretty face, "but we are very near some beautiful woods that border the base of the Alps."

"You sound like you miss home," I said, wanting to contribute at least six words to the vibrant conversation. I could feel her sadness.

"I really do. America has many distractions, I often find myself quite lonely on our trips here." More sadness. Perhaps deeper than a girl her age should feel.

"Then you're staying," said Lily. "Cara refuses to do spells, I need a second. I'll show you where you can sleep. I'm sure we have everything you need for the night. We can drive into town and get your things in the morning. When do you fly out?"

"Friday," said Andi.

"Cara," Lily sang. "Don't you think a weekend in the Alps would be just the thing?" She let the question hang and I rolled my eyes. She would win in the end. She always did.

The girls flitted off down the hall, abandoning Drake and I to an empty room. The crackling flames enhanced the thick silence. I turned to him. He sat curled in the old couch, the black cotton of his long-sleeved shirt stretched across his shoulders. I thought he looked a little like an idling panther.

"It's possible that Lily's determination may one day conquer the world," I said.

"I'm sure," he replied.

I put a piece of wood on the fire just for something to do with my hands. The fresh log clunked against a crispy one, the latter popped and spat turquoise flame. While I stared into the hypnotic depths of the fire, I felt every step that brought Drake to me. He took my hand and I stopped breathing.

"You have beautiful hands, Cara," he whispered.

I said nothing. We sat frozen in the perfect, peaceful silence. Unable to find any more words, we stared at each other like there was no other place in the room to look. How long we remained like that—a minute or a thousand years—I'll never know. It seemed time spun backwards on itself, then something crashed upstairs. I jumped, startled. My cheeks flushed and I took a nervous step back.

Drake said nothing, only dug his hands into the pockets of his jeans—a trademark move of his, I noted. "If Andi is staying the night, I should get going. I have business early in the morning."

"Okay. Thank you again for what you did for me last night. It's the dreams," I blurted, and once I started, I could not stop. "I don't know what they are—only that they are real! So real! Like memories, or living nightmares. I am always losing, always dying." I clapped my hand over my mouth to stop the flow of words. Gods! I was incoherent and I *was* going to cry in front of him. "Don't worry about it," I said, feeling ridiculous. I tried to wave my shaking hand. "It's just a dream."

Drake took my hand again and closed the space between us. Warmth radiated up my arm. "My people," he said, then corrected himself, "my family has always believed in dreams."

"I don't want to believe in my dreams," I whispered.

"Yes," he said. "I know exactly what you mean. I understand what it is to fear a dream."

CHAPTER 10

WHY DO WE CALL WHAT WE EXPERIENCE IN SLEEP A DREAM…AND THE DREGS OF FOGGY LIFE, REALITY?

I sat for a long time after Drake left, staring at the dying fire. Even after the final coal sputtered its last ocher sparks, I stayed until the cold touch of night removed all remaining warmth from the room, and I shivered under my blanket.

I did not want to sleep. I commanded myself to stay awake. My body rebelled. Sleep came and brought the nightmares. I am Snow White in the forest, only it's the evil queen, not the huntsman who has come for my heart.

For once, I came out of the dream slowly, no falling or screaming. I rolled onto my side and watched the linked pendulum of the grandfather clock over the hearth swing out the hour of four. I sat up slowly, keeping the furry throw wrapped around me, and walked over to the fireplace; it looked dusty and unused in the moonlight, like a relic from a spook house. I turned on the gas and sighed when the flames exploded around the grey coals. I threw another log on. No way could I get back to sleep. One more dream like that and I would be a good candidate for Bedlam.

Deep night enveloped the house in a breath of stillness as it always did. Without conscious thought, I ran my hands over the places where Drake's body had touched mine. These dreams were not normal, they did not fade with time. The more my body shrugged off the fog of sleep, the more vividly I remembered them.

I had to admit it, Lily was right, it would be good to get away for a while. Get away from this house, away from this town, step outside the jumble of my life and view it from a different perspective. I sat down in the chair he had occupied and buried my face in the worn cushion. It was rough against my cheek and smelled of leather and him. I closed my tear-rimmed eyes.

'My pen creates stories of a world that might have been, a world of my imagining.' Bronte's words, written so long ago, came to me, read by that mellow voice I was coming to associate with my subconscious. *'Here is one I am going to tell, but take care not to smile at any part of it…it begins with a stranger.'* All the best stories began with a stranger; a stranger and a dark night, maybe even a dark dream.

I could not hold back the tears any longer. I put my head in the blankets and submitted to them until fuchsia light painted the morning sky.

■   ■   ■

In my years growing up in Washington, I had grown lovingly attached to storms. Now, they were a passionate affair calling to me. I could feel the power in my veins when the thunder clapped. As a little girl, I watched the roiling storm battle in the sky, smiled as the lightning flashed through the black clouds, and giggled at the chills that rushed across my skin. I would play a game in my mind, a game where I was something other than human, an alien creature that fed off storms with the power to right all the wrongs in the world.

"Thirteen days," I whispered. My eyes locking on the misty grounds of Wynter haunt, I searched the dark places between the trees. I put on my boots and walked down the porch steps, following the little stone path that wound through our backyard.

Something cracked and hissed in the sky, but I did not stop until I stood at the tree line. I strained to see forward in the dark mesh of forest, into the shadows, and whatever moved inside. A sense of alertness—not fear, but a wary caution—slowed my steps. Another clap of thunder, and I held still. I glanced over my shoulder toward the house. My heart kicked when I realized all I could see were the trees, and the dancing white shapes made by the swirling rain.

The bushes in front of me rustled. I leapt back. "Who's there?" I hollered over the storm.

A dog howled in response. "This is ridiculous," I hissed. "Obviously shadows are moving. I haven't slept properly in three weeks." I turned and stomped back toward the house. "Everything is just one long hallucination right now."

A giant bolt of lightning split the opaque clouds, and the smoky light on the pathway brightened as if someone had flipped a switch. A flash of gold on the ground caught my eye, then the wind gushed and the raindrops danced away. My eyes watered when a sharp rainbow of color pierced my vision. I leaned down and picked up the source of the glint.

It was a woven gold band and had more than a dozen small yellow diamonds buried in the braid. I had never seen this ring in my life, but my soul recognized it. I took off my right glove and closed my hand around it so hard, the sharp edges of the diamonds cut into my palm.

The green world spun around me. I did not fight the onslaught of visions, even as the dizziness sent me reeling to one knee. Closing my eyes, I let the vision take me.

I stood in a rich forest, the leaves of the trees were deep green, and a beautiful light seeped from their stems like sap. A man took my hand and folded it over his heart. Shadows covered his eyes, but I could see his lips move when he leaned down to whisper in my ear.

"I love you," he told me. "I'll love you till I die, and if that day never comes then I will love you for eternity."

My eyes fell shut. He slid the ring onto my finger and pulled me to him, my heart pounded against his chest and the air crackled from the heat between us.

I woke up gasping. Instead of the stormy darkness and cold, hard earth, I found myself on my favorite couch, back in the library, bundled in my purple blanket. My teeth clinked together from the cold and my eyes burned when I tried to open them.

"Cara?" Lily sat beside me, gripping my hand. Inside her raged such a torrent of anger I felt certain if she let it go it would knock me senseless, again.

"What the hell, Cara?" she whispered, and squeezed my hand even tighter.

"My ring! Where's the ring?"

The hand she held clenched in her lap opened slowly. "This?" Soft gold lamplight splashed against her palm, highlighting the beautiful delicacy of the thing. "*Your* ring?"

"I found it over by the Haunt," I told her defensively.

"Which is where I found you. Passed out and shivering!" Lily looked at me and her scowl crumpled, tears filled her eyes and trickled down her cheeks. "You promised not to walk in the rain anymore!"

"Oh, Lily," I sighed. "I'll never be able to keep that promise. Anyway, catching a cold is really the least of my problems. Passing out in the middle of thunder storm *has* to be a bigger deal."

"You're *joking* about this?" she asked.

I shrugged. "Why not? I don't know what else to do. Maybe I need to see a professional." I sat up slowly, trying to keep every inch of the blanket in contact with my freezing skin. "You know—post-traumatic stress or something."

Lily rolled her brilliant eyes. "I think this might be a *little* more than that." She handed me the ring and I slid it on my finger. It fit like someone sized it just for me. Tears rolled down my own cheeks. I did not wipe them away. "I'm going crazy, Lily," I sobbed.

"No, you're not, Cara! I promise. You just *need* something wild and crazy to take your mind off all of this," her sigh was long and tired. "We both do. Why else do you think I want to go to Romania? I need to get away from here. Get *you* away from here."

"But...." I protested, my words fell away. I could not summon the energy to complete the thought. The thought of leaving Wynter Manor scared me. I had never traveled beyond the borders of Washington State, not outside the pages of a book, at least. If I stayed however, if the dreams kept coming—I conceded. "Fine. I'll go."

Lily's eyes lit up. "What?" She gave me the biggest smile I had seen since I caught her kissing Jake Broody in fourth grade. "You mean it?"

I nodded, trying to wipe my face while she threw her arms around my neck. "Oh thank you, Cara! I am going to go look at flights right now. Maybe we could get on the same plane as them." She jumped up, then threw herself back on the couch and hugged me. I could see moisture glinting in the corners of her eyes.

"You really want to go, huh?" I asked. "You won't change your mind when we get there?"

"Why would I do that? Course I want to go!" Lily lurched to her feet again and paced the library, randomly picking up piles of books from one place and depositing them in another. "Oh, I have to pack. I didn't imagine you'd say yes. I have to pack right now!"

"If we are catching the same plane as them then you have two full days to pack," I told her reasonably.

Lily groaned. "You're right—I will *never* be done in time."

Shaking my head at her I lay back down on the chaise lounge, my head was still shaking when it hit the cushion.

CHAPTER 11

A BEAUTIFUL DREAM

My 'something wild and crazy' came for me after sunset.

I sat at the island in the kitchen tackling my second *Iliad* assignment, reading the sad story of Helen for the thousandth time. I heard Lily and Andi laughing somewhere as they pored over the Book of Shadows. The last time I checked in on them, they sat surrounded by pearl-white candles, piles of herbs, and foul-smelling things in their hands. A thick stem of sage pumped out a curling white stream of noxious smoke I thought smelled a little like sweat.

My eyes fell back to the pages I labored over. *'So long as the gods held themselves aloof from mortal warriors, they were triumphant.'* What I took from that sentence was, so long as the gods butted out, humans stayed alive.

I went to the coffeemaker, tossed out the old grounds, then set about refilling a fresh filter. Rain trickled down the window panes while the coffee boiled. My fingers galloped on the marble countertop when the roar of a motorbike, shattered the stillness cocooning Wynter Manor. Aqua high beams sprayed across the counters and floors of the kitchen. I felt him—in my chest, tingles dancing on my skin—before he hit the paved section of the driveway and killed the throttle.

I walked to the door, grabbed the cold handle, flung it open, and stared transfixed through the rain. Arms crossed and body leaning against the rumbling machine, Drake looked at me and smiled. They were a work of art—the *Corse* sitting proudly on its glossy Pirelli Diablos, and Drake wearing his fitted black coat, wet hair and flashing eyes. "Hey, Cara," he said. I said nothing—only searched around for my breath. He walked to me.

"Andi needed some things." He stopped in front of me, his face just inches from mine. He cleared his throat—I thought it seemed too human a gesture for a creature as spectacular as him—and held out his hand.

This time I took it. Our bare palms touched. "It's nice to see you again," he said.

I squeaked out a reply and fought the urge to throw my arms around him, rest my head on his shoulder and listen to the beats of his heart. Somewhere in my mind lived the impossible notion that I had done it before, countless times.

"Also, I came to ask if you would have dinner with me tonight."

My mind went blank. "I just ate," I said, then mentally kicked myself. *Who cares?? Eat again.*

"I see," he said.

"I'm sorry—I'll eat again." I bit my lip. *Why are you still talking!?*

Drake laughed. A warm sound that gave me more shivers. He let go of my hand and put his own back into the front pocket of his jeans. "We could do something else." I felt his hot breath on my rainwashed cheek. "I could take you for a ride." Drake looked at the bike still idling in the rain, then turned back to me. "You want to?" he asked.

OH MY GODS! HELL YEAH! My mind screamed, so loudly I nearly stumbled. "Sure," I said out loud, trying to sound calm. "I would love to."

Unconcerned by the soaking rain, Drake strolled to the back of the bike and took a pink day bag from the trunk. He stepped under the double door frame and into the foyer, as his arms moved to set Andi's bag on the ground, his eyes went to the ring on my finger and he froze. Rain washed over his cheeks and dripped on his lips. A still moment passed in which I held my breath—he cleared his throat again—it sounded right this time. Human. Almost afraid. A few more seconds ticked by before composure returned, yet he seemed aged somehow.

He held Andi's bag against his chest like a frilly pink shield. The delicate piece of luggage strangely enhanced his masculinity.

"Set it down anywhere," I told him. He did not—instead, he looked at me like I was an alien creature who had just up and sprouted wings.

"May I see it?" he asked, suitcase still clutched to his chest. To say his eyes smoldered would have been a gross understatement and the unbridled heat pouring from them was full of such heartbreaking sorrow, that I felt my own sting. I did not need him to tell me what *'it'* was. I knew he was talking about the ring. I held out my bare hand.

"It's exquisite," said Drake, finally setting down Andi's bag. He said nothing else. I sensed a torrent of words in the air. He touched my fingers and turned my hand slightly to the right. The soft gold band caught the light of the hall lamp, it made the yellow diamonds sparkle like stars.

Heat ran off of Drake and flowed in me. He folded his hand over mine and touched the ring. When he ran his thumb over the winking yellow stones, every part of him went still. "Where did you get it, if you don't mind me asking?"

"I found it," I whispered. "I had a dream about it. In the dream it was mine."

"It looks like it belongs to you," he said.

"Drake! You're here!" Lily's holler made us both jump, and the top of my head bumped the underside of his chin.

I winced. "Sorry." I imagined I felt him drop a light kiss on my hair.

"Andi," called Lily. "Your brother is here." She took my shoulder and spun me around, then pulled me into a fragrant hug. It was an unexpected gesture and my arms hung in the air for a weird moment before I returned the embrace.

"What's up, Lily?" I whispered, giggling.

"You happy?" she asked in my ear.

"Yes. Why are we hugging?"

"Well, I didn't want Drake to hear and I am worried about letting you go."

"You're the one that called him?" I broke free of the hug and gave her an exasperated look. "And how are you worried? We rode our Ducati's all the time in senior year. It will be much better this time—this time I get to sit on the back, my arms wrapped around *that* guy." I turned, wanting to see if Drake heard my gushy words, he had abandoned us to our nonsense, and bent his head down to Andi saying something I did not hear.

"I think I'm happier than you are," said Lily. "Cara," she leaned in to whisper in my ear, "this is your first date."

On a motorbike. Classic. I told the girl in my head to shut right up. I could not believe this was actually happening. I had never seen romantic adventures in my cards—in high school the only thing they had voted me 'most likely' for—was to die a virgin.

"It's not a date, but thank you for doing this for me, Lily. Thank you, thank you!" I pressed a kiss to her cheek and seized my jacket. My own helmet sat beneath the coat rack, its ruby red surface dusty from lack of use. I grabbed it. Drake opened the door for me, and we rushed out into the rain. The bottoms of my jeans got soaked, and I could feel my curls plastering to my face, but I did not care. I could not wait to get on that bike.

Drake arched an eyebrow. "What did Lily say?"

"She will worry every minute until we get home, so best we leave before she changes her mind." He did not move though, only stepped closer to me and slowly zipped my jacket.

He slowly zipped my jacket. "It's a good look on you." He said, then gripped my waist and lifted me onto the soft, raised leather seat. One of his bare hands touched my chin, he tipped my face up to his. "Lily told me your own Ducati is rusting in the garage."

This close to him, words refused to form—I nodded.

"She also said you needed a distraction." Drake's voice changed, became low, almost tender. "Same dreams?"

"No," I said. "They're getting worse."

"Don't sleep tonight, Cara," he whispered.

"I tried that last night," I said.

"Then, I will stay with you and see if we can't find something to do to keep you awake."

His suggestive words made me blush. "I suppose I must thank you a third time for rescuing me."

"You kidding me?" he said. "I stared at IRS forms all day. You, my lady, are rescuing *me*."

I giggled and put on my helmet. "Then *you* are welcome, kind sir." The helmet muffled my voice, but he got the gist and winked. Drake zipped up his own coat, then got on the bike. I wrapped my arms around his iron body, and my hands crushed the leather over his heart. He hit the throttle, the idling creature roared to life.

"My bike is nothing like this," I shouted.

"This is more than just a bike—it's an Italian masterpiece!"

"Oh, right," I muttered, and heard him laughing.

When we reached the top of the hill, Drake brought us to a skidding halt. The treaded tires twisted into the ground and sent gravel flying. I could hear my gasping, uneven breaths, but they were not coming from fear.

He turned back and looked at me. "You ready?"

I nodded.

"Press your body to mine and lean when I lean."

I did what he told me. My helmet rested against the wet leather of his coat as he revved the engine and sped forward. The Corse surged onto the twining road leading down from the manor.

I tried to squint through the rain into the foggy night, but the trees lining the road were nothing more than a black jumble blurring past. We hit the I-5 at ninety miles an hour and still we sped up. Drake rode the Ducati like it was a part of him, taking the curves with controlled precision, laying us down so low my knees hovered mere inches from the ground. I could hear the blood pumping in my ears. *Like flying,* the voice in my mind whispered and for the first time in years, I felt no fear of who I was, no terror at the dreams that refused to leave. Drake as my shield, I felt safe.

■ ■ ■

For the fifth time since we stopped I fought to get my hair in order. Between the rain, wind and helmet, my ridiculous locks refused to cooperate. Some of the clouds had blown away to show the knifing ridges of Mount Baker spearing up in the distance. To many people these dark woods seemed a veritable wilderness, but to me, they were the hills of home, their rugged nature comforted me.

I twisted my hair in a messy braid at my nape, trying to hold my helmet and not slip off the idling bike. I watched Drake through a set of dirty glass sliding doors. Since my decision was to fight the dreams with insomnia—I needed coffee, Drake pulled over at the first convenient store before I had time to ask.

A spasm of vibration shook my leg—startled, I nearly dropped my helmet. Rolling my eyes at my overall jumpiness, I set the helmet on my knees, then reached into my pocket for my buzzing phone. Lily's face flashed on the screen. *Have fun, Cara. Don't think about anything. Happy doing spells with Andi. XOXOXO.*

I started to text her back when the corner of my eye caught the shadow of a man shuffling across the parking lot. His clothes dangled from his back, filth clung to their tattered corners, caking the soles of his bare feet. He stopped under the blue light of a solitary street lamp and lifted his head. Our gazes locked. Black bled into the whites of his eyes like spilt ink. He held out his hand, palm up, and curled his fingers. Flesh dripped from them, soft as melting wax—it gushed down his arm. His mouth fell open, bugs crawled on his tongue and a cringy sound poured out of his throat.

"*Leisha,*" I heard him say. "*Leisha.*"

Behind him, the shadows of others moved, they came at me from all directions. Dozens, smiling odd, dead smiles—devoid of feeling or soul. One of them pointed at me, I stared in mute horror as both his eyeballs popped out and green goo ran down his checks. The reek of decay slammed me full in the face. More filtered out from behind the convenience store, half walking, half dragging their skinless limbs.

There was no time to scream. I put my helmet on and kicked the bike into gear. The engine growled as I gunned it. The Course spun, spraying gravel at the nearest skeleton.

"Drake!" I hollered. Tires squealed as the Coarse shot forward. I twisted the handles, the bike skidded again. More gravel flew. "Drake!"

To my left a creature held out its hand. Tilting his head, he opened his mouth and mewled my name.

"Cara?!" Drake's terrified voice spun me around. The harsh light of the store cast him in silhouette, his black clothes indistinguishable from the night.

"Cara?!" He scanned the parking lot. The coffee he held in each hand, fell forgotten to the ground.

"GET ON!" I screamed.

He was beside me in seconds. I felt his arms wrap around my waist, felt the heat of him against my back. "Drive," he commanded. I did.

I twisted the bike to the right, missing a screaming corpse by a breath. Skeletons and shadows held their hands out to me. The thick padding in my helmet did nothing to drown out their haunting wails.

The highway was empty. I turned onto the road that led to Rainy Pass. I could hardly breathe and my vision wavered. The bike was larger than I was accustomed to, and my shoulders ached from navigating the sharp turns. I drove without sight, drove until the creatures faded to black dots in my rearview.

Will you stop!? my mind yelled. *Just pull over!*

I took a bend in the road too fast and felt the front wheel quiver.

"Careful!" shouted Drake.

It was too late for caution. The next curve ended in a vicious hairpin turn. Jerking the handles, I slammed on the brakes—too hard—the front wheel twisted and I lost control. There was an audible *crunch* of rock as the back wheel spun off the ground. The impact lifted me into the air, I felt Drake's arms wrap around my weightless body. A deafening crash blasted through my ear drums, and we slid into an outcropping of rocks. A bright light flashed in front of my eyes, then…there was darkness.

CHAPTER 12

"Cara?"

Drake's voice filtered through the fog in my brain. I lay cradled in his arms, one of his warm hands cupping the back of my head.

"Cara, are you hurt?"

I struggled to open my eyes. My lashes felt capped by little weights as they fluttered back down to my cheeks. On the second try, I prevailed. Drake's stricken expression swam into focus.

"Don't talk, Cara. Let me see how bad it is." Drake touched my face and shoulders, his gentle hands hot in contrast to the freezing wind.

"Sorry," my voice cracked, and I coughed weakly.

"Don't be." Regret burned in Drake's eyes. He pressed on my ribs. I shivered. "Here? Does this hurt?"

My head shook out a negative. My neck ached a little. Though, not bad as it should. The bike lay ten feet from us, something near the tailpipe was smoking.

"Can you move all your fingers and toes?" asked Drake, I heard him struggling to relax his tone.

"Yes, nothing hurts, really," I whispered.

"I think your helmet absorbed most of the impact before it flew off."

"Your *arms* absorbed the impact," I said, struggling to sit up. "Are *you* all right?"

Drake turned his neck from side to side. "I think so, yeah. It wasn't such a bad fall—I've certainly had worse." He helped me into a sitting position. "You'll have one hell of a headache," he said. "I'm sorry I couldn't save you from that."

I rolled my eyes. "I'm the one who crashed your bike."

Drake chucked me under the chin softly. "It's okay, I have another one. I would rather all the scratches be on it instead of you." He wiped a streak of blood off my knuckles. I could tell he wanted to say something—maybe say a lot—instead he touched my hand. "I think it's best we call an ambulance," he told me.

I suddenly found my voice. "No! No hospitals."

Hospitals were the most emotional place in the world. I have never left one better for the experience. The powerful feelings sheltered in those cold walls devastated me. The fear of impending death, all the sorrow, anger, and heartbreak over lost loved ones, made walking in a hospital feel like stepping in a tornado of serrated knives.

"Please," I whispered. "Don't take me to a hospital. I…I'll be fine." I tried to stand. My head spun and I crumpled back in his arms.

"Okay," he soothed. "Okay, no hospital."

"You saw them right?" I looked up, his face was inches from mine, it was hard to breathe, but I continued talking—I had to know. "I'm afraid to even ask you, I know it sounds so crazy, but… you saw them right?"

A muscle twitched in his jaw, he clenched it and his cheekbones looked like weapons. I thought he would lie to me. I felt him trying to find one, a plausible story for the occupants of the parking lot, then he let a pent-up breath go, and his shoulders sagged. "Yes. I don't know what I saw. But, I saw something."

There was still a lie in his words, it was a small one though, and relief washed over me. "Maybe I'm not crazy, I mean if you saw them they must be real."

"I should take you back home." Drake touched my cheek. "You're still bleeding." He said that last part like it was the greatest offense of all time.

"Not yet," I said. "I'm okay—I want to go to the lake."

"If you're sure," he said. I slung my arms around his neck, and he lifted me.

"Am I heavy?" I asked.

Drake looked down at me and laughed.

I placed my hand on his chest and stared at his lips. I wondered what kissing him would feel like. I had never even thought about kissing a man, not really—with my touch problem—the thought terrified me—it was strange to think about it now, strange and kinda wonderful. I clung to him as he walked to the bike. I did not realize how tall he was until he held me. Bike crashes and corpses lurking—I still felt safe. He lifted the Ducati, then placed me gently on the seat.

I saw—in pure sadness—that the crash had left a dent in the right side of his bike, and peeled away a strip of ruby paint, leaving visible the broken shards of asphalt that clung to the side of its body like barnacles on a ship. "You saved me and I trashed your bike."

Drake shrugged. "It's okay. It will be great to work on. More fun when it's a little beat up."

I glanced at the shattered remains of my helmet—still lying on the side of the road—and shuddered at what could have been. Drake revved the engine. It stuttered once then roared to life. He kicked the bike into motion.

Hair streaked across my cheeks and the dewy night wind played havoc through my curls. I lay my head against his back, my body aching—my soul at peace.

Drake made a sharp right and the foliage lining the trail grew denser. The leafy arms of trees linked above our heads until only hints of night sky showed through the canopy. I felt him shift. He pulled on the brake lever, and we took one more mad turn before we were in open air again. The steep cliffs of Mount Baker swept up in the distance. At their base, Cedar Lake rushed against the chalky rocks and boulders blanketing the bowed shore. Drake brought the Ducati to a halt a few feet shy of the tiny, lapping waves

He lifted me off the bike and walked to the water.

"You can put me down now," I said.

"And why would I want to do that?" Drake smiled down into my eyes. "You could have some kind of internal injury. A broken bone you are unaware of. Human bodies are very fragile and that was quite a crash."

I laughed. "You said it wasn't that bad, and I think I would know if I broke one of my bones."

"I have something that might help the cuts on your hand," he said, finally putting me down. I watched him walk to the bike and take something from the trunk.

"What is it?"

"Maybe nothing." He walked back to me, a small vial in his hand. "It's from a lake near the base of my homeland."

"A magic lake?" I joked.

He was serious. "Many think so. People from all over the world travel there hoping to discover the fountain of youth."

"How long have you had it?" The glass had a pink hue and the movements of the liquid inside the bottle were sluggish—more like oil than water.

"A friend gave it to me many years ago. I've carried it ever since." Drake brushed his fingers over my cheek, then walked to the water's edge. He unstopped the blushed glass vial, then poured it unceremoniously in the lake.

I ran to him. "Why did you do that? I thought you said it was special to you? You just wasted it."

He looked at me. "No, I didn't. I finally found a worthy use."

"If the 'worthy use' is me, that was a fail," I said, inspecting the tiny cuts maring the back of my hands, some were fresh—others, from the last time those creatures attacked me. "This is nothing. I'm constantly getting hurt."

Pink liquid folded in the water making the ripples of froth look like cotton candy. All chill had vanished from the air taking the clouds. The moon was out in force—full, and radiant against the backdrop of night.

"Do you want to swim?" he asked, taking off his coat. It hit the rocks.

"Yes," I said. *Moonlight…water…Drake.* A strange sensation of déjà vu gripped me.

"Have you ever swam here before?"

"Once, with Lily, but it was freezing. Now, we don't dare, not even in summer. It looked nothing like this, though. The moon, all these colors… and you." I kicked a rock lodged beneath my toe. "Sometimes I dream about this place. Maybe that's what is happening right now." I said that last part under my breath and my mind went off. *The other less appealing possibility is that you have lost it, and this is your descent into that part of your mind you only like to visit on special occasions. Our 'happy place', if you will.*

The cool surface of Drake's lips brushed my forehead as if he sensed the argument raging. "No, you're definitely awake," he whispered. His hands went to the emblazoned silver buckle on his pants.

"We can't swim here," I said, removing my shoes.

Drake shrugged. "Tonight seems like a night for magic."

I loved the way he spoke to me—it was so poetic it left me feeling like I was lost in a Jane Austen novel. Drake dropped the vial and it let it shatter. The pieces fell forgotten among the smooth rocks. He tugged my torn leather jacket off my shoulders. I let him. I let him take my sweater, too. Dream and reality were mattering less and less to me. I would run with it.

Wearing little more than a few scraps of silk and moonlight, I stepped into the water. The smooth liquid felt sun warmed. Steam drenched my hair, plastering the silk of my cami to my blushed skin.

"This is incredible," I whispered, looking up at him. Our bodies were only inches apart.

"So gorgeous," he said, his eyes never straying from my face. "Incredible, inevitable."

"Inevitable?" I did not like that word. That's very cryptic," I snapped.

"I know." His smile seemed like a lie. I had never felt him like I did in that moment. His turmoil was acid in my gut. He dropped his eyes to the white stones on the ground and I almost slammed my hands against his bare chest in frustration.

"You know something don't you Drake? Know about my dreams?"

He shook his head. "I only know what you've told me." Now he actually sounded like he was lying.

"I don't believe you!" I nearly shouted. "There is a connection here, something strange and unshakeable. I would be an idiot not to feel it!" My breaths raced as I listened to the sound of the water breaking against our bodies, and my sense of déjà vu intensified. I told myself to live in the moment, yet I knew that tomorrow, reality would resurface and this space in time would fade to fantasy. My blood boiled as an unreasonable surge of anger blasted through me. I was missing something vitally important. I felt like Drake knew what it was, and for some reason chose not to tell me. I wrapped my arms around myself and waded deeper into the water.

Thirteen days, my cruel mind mocked, *all the King's horses and all the King's men couldn't put Cara together again.*

I wanted to see Hanna's beautiful, ageless face, then I wanted to pound on it until she apologized for leaving me in this mess. If she had told me anything, I would not be dying to ask some man I just met if: *hey, perhaps I met you in another life?* Or, did *you know the last thirteen nights, I dream you watch me die? At least I think it's you. Yes, it will be fine. Everything will be just freaking fine!*

Drake moved closer making ripples of water break against my stomach. He closed the distance between us and I felt his bare chest hot against my back.

"Cara," his voice sounded raw—I did not let him finish his thought.

"Why were you there?" I blurted. "The other night behind the bar? Or…or at the Space Needle? Why were you there?" I watched the smile on his lips harden into a firm line. He said nothing. I blushed, but persisted. "Lily says you're here for me, is that true?"

Drake's expression turned agonized and one dark brow arched, when he spoke, his voice was cautious. "What do you think?"

"I don't know! I want to think it *was* a coincidence, and that there *is* such a thing." I lifted my hands to cup my hot cheeks, shaking my head so hair curtained my face. I sounded like a lunatic. "It's just all been so crazy, even you… so crazy. I'm sorry," I said miserably. "I just can't even anymore."

Drake tilted my chin up to his. "Stop saying that. You have nothing to be sorry for, Cara."

My anger flowed away quickly as it had come. "Sorry," I repeated. I looked in his eyes trying to *see* him—it was useless, he was hiding again behind that impenetrable steel wall guarding his heart and mind. "You're infuriating!" I sighed. "Don't think I didn't notice you answering my question with a question." The world went quiet for a few moments, the burning radiance of his eyes holding mine completely captive. I thought he might kiss me, when he did not—my crushing disappointment annoyed me. "Forget about it," I said. "Too many unanswered questions already plague my life, tonight I just want to swim and laugh."

"It is such a beautiful laugh," he said in a low, gravelly voice that gave me chills. He held out his arms and threw an inviting look at the water. "May I?" When I nodded, he leaned in and swooped me up. I giggled and wrapped my arms around his neck.

"So, tell me something about you, something personal. Is there a beautiful woman waiting for you in some Romanian castle?" I meant to sound casual but my stomach flipped, and I failed.

His look made me feel more naked than I was. "No, Cara. No woman. Something personal. Let me see…I love Elvis," he said finally. "The man was a genius."

I burst out laughing. "I said tell me something personal."

"That is. It's a secret I tell few people."

"No, something about what makes you—you know—you."

"That would be a long something."

"Just a little thing," I whispered. "I don't enjoy being at this disadvantage."

His brow went up. "What disadvantage? I know nothing about you either."

I did not completely believe that, but I said, "I know, it's just that…well I am used to knowing things, feeling things, touching people and seeing their memories. With you it feels like I've gone blind."

"Very well," said Drake, and went quiet again.

I poked his chest.

"I like good scotch, and Stephen King," he said dryly.

I smiled up in his eyes. "I like him too, a lot actually."

His hold on me loosened, I slid down his body until his arms were around my waist, my toes dangled a few feet above the shifting sand. He held me like that, our faces inches apart. "And, I love being with you," he breathed.

My mouth went dry as my blood ignited. His somber expression cracked in a wicked smile. "Hold your breath," he whispered. Before I could obey, he put a big hand on the top of my head, and dunked us.

Bubbles rushed up around my face, tickling my cheeks. Giggling, I opened my eyes. I expected it to be dark underwater, instead, everything was brilliantly lit, each plant, and creature strung out across the lake bottom like Christmas lights. Drake was beside me, he reached out and linked his fingers through mine. I kicked my legs, we dove deeper and deeper until the luminescent plant life was almost blinding. I forgot my irrational anger. I was so happy I thought *I* might be glowing. I did not even feel the need to breathe, there was none of that painful expanding in my lungs—I simply had no desire for air at all. You would not need to put me back together down here. In this world, I was light as a feather and ageless as time—too spellbound to be incredulous. Later, much later, when he carried me back to shore, I realized what he had done.

Magic bottle or not, he had given me a beautiful dream.

■ ■ ■

Drake refused to put me down until I was in my nightgown and buried under my duvet. The whole ride home I had slipped in and out of consciousness. Even now, I was unsure if I was awake. He leaned in and tucked a stray curl behind my ear. "When was the last time you slept? Really slept?" he asked, his voice was deep, another layer in my dreams.

"I can't remember," I said, hardly recognizing my own voice.

"You need to sleep."

"No!" I turned my head to the side, breaking free of his touch. "I can't…not again. If I see the woman, her knife…" I shuddered, struggling to hold my eyes open. His body shifted. I grabbed his arm like a lifeline. "No! Not yet. Please don't leave me, stay a little longer. My thoughts go quiet when you're here," I said, too tired to wonder why I always say the silliest things.

"I won't leave until you tell me to," vowed Drake, stretching out on the massive bed beside me. He propped one hand beneath his head so his face leaned over mine. "Tell me something personal, something that makes you, you." He smiled, even in the questionable vision of my exhausted, waterlogged eyes—he was breathtaking.

"If I touch something with my bare hands I have visions, sometimes I see the past, other times the future…besides that, I'm not very interesting," I said. "Well, I wasn't until a few days ago, before the Space Needle, the dark stranger, and the Ducati."

Drake laughed, a deep husky sound that made me blink. I smiled in his eyes and watched the way little flecks of gold moved in the depths of the outer rim. "Nothing much has ever been normal around here," I told him over a yawn. "We're a weird family." His touch was so soothing, it scattered my thoughts. "Mother abandoned us when we were babies, then our aunt left us a few years later. I used to think she was dead. Now," I said, my voice drifting like my mind, "I think she might be immortal." *Seriously, Cara?* my mind asked. *Who says stuff like that?* My next yawn tried to dislocate my jaw, it made a long, tired sound.

"Does immortal mean the same thing to you as it does to me?" he asked and tucked the fluffy duvet under my chin. His hand brushed over my cheek. I think he might have touched my lips, but my exhausted body refused to do anything but crash. Reality became a shifty thing. The moment I closed my eyes, I was already dreaming.

We lay together on the mossy floor of a verdant forest, his naked body and mine entwined, moving in time with the keening wind. He kissed my neck and told me he loved me. The picture changed, and we stared at the stars, watched them shift and shoot through the night, then all at once we were flying among them. A black stallion galloped over the clouds. I reached up and threaded my finger through the shifting vapors.

"Sleep, Cara," I heard Drake whisper against my throat, his voice glancing off the earth and sky. "I'm watching over you. No more dreams. Just sleep."

Before I completely dissolved in the arms of Morpheus, I realized that despite the dreams, these last thirteen days had been the most incredible of my life—by quite a wide margin. Without hesitation my mind folded into silence until there was nothing but the memory of his touch. It was all that filled my dreams…and they were beautiful.

Sometime later that night, or early in the morning, I woke up alone. The ever present pain in my heart was in no way gone—but I felt like something had changed, or brought a strange acceptance that numbed it. I threw off my covers and stood up, giving one long look at the indents his body had left on my chaste bed. *Him. Drake. That name...Drake? Was that it? Was his name the one I scream when I die?* The voice in my mind gave me no answer. I felt her silence was intentional.

My eyes flew open as I came fully awake. "Oh my gods!" I dove for the switch on my lamp. "Oh my gods, Draken? Drake?! I'm such an idiot! Coincidence? Crap! There really is no such thing, is there?!" I flung open my door and dashed to the library. It only took me a few seconds to locate *Blood and Shadows*. I fell to my knees, opened the book and started to read. I was two paragraphs into the next chapter when the visions came for me, I went willingly.

ANCIENT CHAPTER IX

BLOOD AND SHADOWS, MARCH 6TH
IT WAS ONLY AN APPLE—
IT HAD NO PART IN THE CHAOS IT CAUSED.

Kyros crashed to the ground, sword, and shield flying from his stunned grip. Draken snarled and leapt atop the fallen Igori, fists lashing out. Kyros lifted his arm, taking the impact on his brace. The thick iron band groaned and dented. Draken lunged again, knocking the warrior's arm from his face like it belonged to a child. Teeth bared, Draken pressed his sword to Kyros's throat.

"Yield," Draken growled.

Kyros spat a mouthful of dry sand, then tapped two fingers on the ground. "I yield," he rasped.

Draken stood and held out his arm. Kyros took it, Draken pulled the Spartan to his feet.

Kyros rubbed his jaw, using thumb and forefinger to shift it from side to side—testing its placement. "You're in a vicious mood today," said Kyros, working at his jaw, groaning when something clicked into place.

Draken tossed his sword on the ground. He felt equal parts enraged and sluggish, as if unable to wake from a dream featuring only one image. One face.

"Draken!" Malkalimos's voice cracked like a whip. "Your rage decreases the number of your father's guard. That's the fourth man to fall to your fists today. What ails you?"

Draken shook his head to clear her from his mind. He peeled off his bracers and unstrapped the leather belt from around his arm. His shield fell against the sand.

"No lectures today, Malkalimos. Practice is over. I am for the baths." His tone brooked no argument, not even from the captain of the guard. The man may have mentored him since boyhood, but he was still the Prince of Sparta—if one more man challenged him, Draken feared he might kill him…like they meant to kill her. That beautiful girl, her scent like roses and sunlight. He remembered her soft sighs tumbling from her cherry lips, saw her delicate fingers threaded through Pluto's mane, the wonder in her eyes when the stallion hurtled through the air.

He wanted to see her again. No, he *needed* to see her again. To gaze down at her elfin features, see the sparkle in her eyes and the mixture of mischief, intelligence and sadness in her smile. To feel the warmth of her body on his, let the barest wisps of her gauzy robes brush over his fingers.

A swollen orange sun hung low on the horizon; already a half-moon appeared beside it in the sky. The distorted shadows looked disorientated in the netted light of the silver moon and setting sun. Draken descended the steps to the baths. Hot steam washed over his face as he unclasped the emblazoned silver buckles holding his chlamys anchored across his shoulders, the cloak fell to the ground, and steam curled the edges of the woven crimson cloth. He stripped off his sweat-soaked tunic and dropped it beside the cloak. Water seeped in the wet cloth the second it touched the hot tiles. Aching in every muscle, Draken climbed down the marble steps to the largest of his three bathing pools. Filling his cupped hands with scalding water, he splashed it on his face and strode to stand under the waterfall. The crystal water fell from golden jars, hoisted on the shoulders of two nymphs, their marble arms interlocked, and the golden leaves in their hair tumbling to the base of the sculpture. Steam poured from the jars surrounding the nymphs in snowy auras. Under the spray of the fall, Draken closed his eyes and let the water wash the sand and sweat from his skin. He wished the water would wash away the horror and disgust he felt at the thoughts bombarding him—that beatific, cherub mouth hanging slack, skin gone grey and cold—it was absurd and horrifying.

Men in the training barracks often spoke of their ritual, stories whispered at night, told by warriors who had experienced their own Aphrodisia. Killed their own innocent priestess. They spoke of dark golden rooms, altars lit by firelight, and power found in the pinnacle of pleasure.

To hear them tell it, the girls were nothing more than beautiful objects to be used and disposed of.

Drake waded through the fountain, water parted for him like a shattering glass veil. He let his legs relax their kicking, and hot water closed over his head. That soft, fragile woman—barely more than a child—taking part such a thing made his heart clench and brought a dark thought. Who would die for *his* pleasure and power?

He had her in his arms, astride Pluto, where he could take her away from the fate that awaited her. He could have soared across the Aegean Sea to the ruined shores of Troy, or the hidden islands of Crete. Never return to her temple. Never deliver her to die. It was the look of steel in her eyes which had stopped him.

"You gave me a beautiful dream, no matter what happens after today, all I will have to do is close my eyes and remember flying."

A beautiful dream, nothing more. She was Leisha, sanctified since birth. She would face her destiny with unflinching courage whether or not she wished to do so. A range of emotions had blazed across her innocent features: fear, elation, and resolve. She would give herself to the Aphrodisia, die for a man she did not know. It was her fate and she would accept it.

"Arggg!" Draken kicked his legs and broke the surface, slapping the water. This angered the ripples and they shot hot droplets in his face. What he had once viewed as a divine ritual was now a thing so horrible he could not bear to think about it.

Draken stepped out of the pool, he ran his hands through his hair, and lifting his cloak from the ground, slung it around his hips. This was madness! He was prince of Sparta. He would *not* let her die.

■ ■ ■

Pluto galloped hard, hooves kicking up mud and shells. Foam bubbles marking the high tide line popped against the moonlit sand. Draken glanced at the darkness stretched across the horizon and tried to mark the time of night.

A snow white owl shot across his field of view. His vision blurred, darkening at the edges. He shook his head to clear the fog and brought his body low against Pluto's straining back. Together, rider and beast moved in silence, a black blur over the bleached sands. In the cloudless sky, the owl kept pace.

When Pluto's pounding hooves ate another five miles, Draken took the lead. He could see the edge of Aphrodite's isles, and her Temple sitting in the cradle of whitewashed cliffs spearing the sky. Artemis shot her bow into the night, the fiery tips of her arrows spewing stars that caterwauled through the darkness. Draken reined Pluto in, the black beast snorted, snapping at the cold air.

"Easy, boy," Draken said, patting Pluto's sweating neck. "Easy now, boy."

Pluto calmed, nickering at the air.

"We will fly to her," Draken said. *Leisha. Untouched.* His mind whispered the words at him like they were filthy things. "We will take her away."

The owl hooted overhead. Pluto shied away from the sound, braying out a screaming challenge to the bird, before rearing up, his hooves slashing at the air. Draken stared at the owl. It folded its wings and landed at the stallion's feet. Feathers floated down from the wings; when they hit the sand, they dissipated into soft golden mists.

Out of the mists, Draken watched Pallas Athena form before his eyes, from her slender ankles to the jewel-studded golden aegis encircling her brow. Bedecked in full armor of starlight and gold, she was smaller than the picture his mind had painted of her. Chestnut locks shot with shining rubies tumbled from beneath the aegis and ran down her back. The soft curls flew out behind her, ghosting over the wind like a cape of pure silk.

"Draken," said Athena. Her words floated on the restless waves, echoing against the constellations and vanishing into the darkness—it seemed the very universe called his name.

Draken dismounted and dropped the reins against Pluto's side. Pluto lowered his massive head to the goddess, his knees slightly buckled. Eyes studying the ground, Pluto ambled over to the playful waves and lipped at the effervescent froth.

Draken dropped to one knee. "Athena."

"Get up, nephew," Athena's voice rode on the variegated trail of shooting stars. "It does the son of Hades no good to kneel. Also, on your knees like that, you are the same height as me, a fact that makes me feel distressingly small."

Draken stood, warily, "How can I be of service, goddess?"

"It is, of course, how I can serve you," said Athena. Waves rushed into the shore, as if eager to be closer to the lilting sound of her voice. "You go to your priestess tonight, and I will not forestall your devotion. I, so deprived of love, can easily spot it in others."

"I fear for her," Draken said. "The Aphrodisia—"

"It is her destiny. "

Draken raised an eyebrow.

Athena's face grew thoughtful. "You know now that it was I who brought you to the Morai?" She faced him and the flash and crackle of her emerald eyes hinted at a violent storm rolling in their depths. "Do not hate me more than you must, you have a powerful destiny, Draken, if you *choose* it. Leave Arias to her fate, and the wheel of time spins on. Follow that woman, and she will be your salvation and your doom. I am not old, Draken, but my years have been long."

Athena stepped close to him and reached out her gloved hand to touch his face. The gold of her fingers felt cool against his jaw. The waves abandoned their charted course, content to run around the feet of the goddess they adored. "If you live, I may die," said Athena. "Yet, I will never have the chance to love, or be loved like you." Her hand shifted away from his face, falling to his chest. "You are from an old, strong bloodline. If any god can succeed, it is you. And, you are a god, Draken. Remember that. Just because I gave you to be raised by a human king, you must *not* forget your blood. It pumps here." She pressed hard against his heart. "Listen to it."

Athena's hands fell away from him. "I have warned you, Draken. Aphrodite will not release her treasure without a fight. Make your choice cautiously." Athena stepped back and spread her arms. Snowy wings broke free from the creamy skin of her back. Her neck twisted as her head spun full circle. When her face snapped back in his direction, her eyes were black and huge. Feathers sprouted from her hair and skin, tips of the effulgent quills burrowed in her pores. Athena's eyes drew close together, and wings snapping to their full length, she launched her slender body into the sky, leaving a trail of golden feathers in her evaporating light.

Draken remained unmoving long after Athena flew away, her warning echoed in his mind. Pluto came at his call. Draken mounted and Pluto soared into the air, climbing until they strode the night skies.

The temple of Aphrodite unfurled below them. The night chill washed across his face, wisps of dewy cloud clung to his cloak. Pluto dropped his nose and plummeted, honing in on one of the smaller towers facing the north of Poseidon's waters. Draken let Pluto take the lead—the horse's guess was as good as his.

Pluto's hooves were silent as they landed on the sands bordering the eastern shore. The horse did not seem to notice anything particularly sinister lurking in the shadows cast by the moonlit cliffs, or the drawn-out howls coming from the depths of the warm waves breaking against the sharp rocks. Firelight played on the curled edges of the waves, and Draken smelled sage and spruce wood smoke. A chant rose from the stillness and lingered in the air.

Draken retreated into the shadows until the sharp corners of the rocks stabbed in his back. Feeling like a strange version of sea crab, he crawled along the rocks, arms behind his back and fingers splayed against the cliff face. Wet sand clustered under his nails and a drop of hot sweat dripped from his brow. He blinked it away. Controlling his breathing, he moved—silent as any nocturnal creature that scaled these cliff walls. Draken rounded the base of a rock and dropped to his knees. Before him, a small alcove glowed under the slice of moon. A fire roared and flickering pieces of burning ash rode the dancing tips of the flames. A cluster of cloaked figures flanked the gyrating fire. The night was full of hideous yells and howling chants.

Close to the flames, so close Draken was sure she felt their heat, Arias knelt, a dozen white roses folded in her hands. Night sounds muted, the crashing waves hushed, there was only the vision of her. Moonlight buried in her auburn hair twinkled as it escaped its binding to pool like liquid silk against the ground. Arias's eyes searched the stars, her porcelain skin absorbing the moonlight. Draken crushed the rocks under his palm. Sand poured from his fist and fell into his sandals.

The fire showed him the priest's faces, the fleshy, flushed cheeks of men severed from their manhood at an early age. Then, the shifting flames changed them to human beasts with sagging cheeks, and flesh gnawed by time until only gaping holes remained. Green puss seeped from the hollowed out eyes, reminding Draken of dancing, venomous cobras. He pulled a silver knife from his belt and crept forward. Arias's tinkling laughter rang out like a crystal bell. Her white gown flowed around her as she stood. Music resonated in her laughter, she lifted her arms—full of white roses—and tossed them at the sky. When she moved the soft gown outlined her slender frame. She turned toward a priest who made a motion over her head, blessing her. Another brought her a goblet to drink from. At the edge of the cove, more girls filtered from the base of the cliffs. They ran to Arias, gowns flowing behind them, pearlescent petals streaming from the flower wreaths in their unbound hair.

A fat priest—gold lines edging his black robes—threw back his cowl. The moon bounced off his bald head, it filtered into his popping eyeballs so they looked like two puddles of milk. He lifted a jug from the sands, the girls laughed, the varying tones lyrically interlaced. The priest raised the jug above his head, the girls lifted bare white arms to their goddess and danced to the rhythm of the colliding surf.

All Draken saw was *her* face.

Draken sheathed his knife and sat down in the cool sand. He watched Arias drink the wine. A drop trickled down her lip and fell against her chin. A girl who had purple flowers threaded through golden hair came and kissed her cheek. Arias caught the droplet of wine on the tip of her finger and put it back in her mouth. Another girl kissed her lips, taking the droplet.

Arias laughed. Her expression bore no anxiety or worry, only peace. She knew her place in this world, more than that—accepted it. Duty above desire, the way of warriors, kings and priestesses alike.

Draken watched the moon fall into the water until time lost meaning to him. Arias sat at the fringes of a dying fire, surrounded by a dozen dancing girls. Clay jugs now lay discarded in the sand, empty of their intoxicating liquid. Arias took another sip from her goblet, she had not yet refilled it. The moon fell lower, its light trickling down onto the laughing girls. One by one they slept until only Arias remained. Legs crossed beneath her, hands folded around the stem of her cup, she regarded the moon through wistful eyes. The few priests who had remained to guard the Leisha, snored. Wine stained their fleshy lips purple, and the pallid light morphed them to hulking corpses.

Draken stepped from the protective shade of the cliffs. His feet followed his heart's verdict; they took him to her.

Arias stirred, torn from her reverie. Her head flicked in his direction, sending her dusky hair cascading over her shoulder. Emerald eyes flew wide when she saw him, her mouth opened for a scream. None came.

"What are you doing here?" she finally hissed.

Draken took a step closer to her. "I needed to see you." His voice changed; something acidic infiltrated his tone. "See if you were still alive."

"You can't be here!" moaned Arias.

"Hush." Draken put his finger to his lips, making her roll her pretty eyes. He dropped his hand from his mouth and held it out to her. "Come and ride with me."

A war raged in Arias's eyes: desire, hesitation, and something deeper fought for dominance. "I can not," she whispered. Her tense hands made fists at her side, and she held her body poised, as if she wanted to scream or run but dared not.

"Come with me," Draken said again. It seemed her taut body yearned to move toward him while simultaneously trying to pull away. His hand hung in the air between them. Arias stared at it, desperation in her eyes.

"I'll have you back before you're missed. I swear it."

Something broke in her gaze. "If I am caught," said Arias, "I'll hurl you from Pluto's back myself."

"You have my word, Arias," Draken breathed.

She rose to her knees and created spheres in the sand when she twisted to face him. Her perfect face showed the depths of her emotions. Pale moonlight glancing off her hand, Arias reached for him. She drew in her breath, a sharp gasp that slashed like a scream through the night. The edges of her fingertips ghosted against his, and Draken heard himself whisper her name, then their fingers curled around each other, he pulled her to her feet and into his arms.

ANCIENT CHAPTER X

MARCH 7TH

FOR HIS LIFE, SHE GAVE HER SOUL;
THERE IS NO LOVE WITHOUT SACRIFICE.

Arias felt her whole body sigh. She rested her flaming cheek against Draken's shoulder and looked at the ocean. In those depths dwelt Poseidon, god of all waters, and Cronus, lord of rocks and mountains. Down there in those black waves, where the earth flipped and the shores of Tartarus began, Arias wondered if they watched her. If they watched her, it was to see lovers embrace against the breaking dawn.

"Come fly with me," he had said, and when she took his hand it was beyond anything. Now, Warm fingers brushed her jaw, then passed just a breath from her lips. His heat poured into her. If she was fated for a horrible death, at least her first touch had been like that. She thought about what the rest would be like with this man, and something inside her melted. The sliver of silver moon had sunk now into the depths of Oceanus. Dawn blazed over the shore.

"Yes," Arias told him. Draken bent his head to her. Arias felt her legs stretch of their own volition, lifting her toward him until she held her weight balanced on the tips of her toes. He was her center of gravity. The solid thing in her spinning world.

Arias had expected a strange form of torture to befall her during her first touch—this yearning to press her lips against his *was* torture in its own way. She wanted to give herself to him here, on these sands, in front of her sleeping sisters and the priests who would kill her.

"Come," said Draken. "Pluto is beyond these cliffs, near the largest of those caves." He pointed to a dark grouping of rocks.

Arias spotted Pluto. The horse's ebony feathers stood in sharp contrast against the pale sand. Draken reached for the reins but the stallion moved away, chomping at the air, then wrapped his soggy lips around Arias's outstretched hand.

"Traitor," Draken told the beast.

Pluto nickered and nuzzled at her soft skin, unconcerned.

Draken locked his fingers in Pluto's mane and hoisted himself onto the Pegasus's glossy bare back. He held out his hand to her. Arias reached for it and clasped his forearm between both her hands. Draken lifted her into his arms.

"That way," whispered Arias, pointing west. "The fires from the *Herati* should be extinguished by now. We have less than an hour."

Arias felt more than saw Draken arch his brow. "*Hetairai?*" he said, badly mispronouncing the word.

"Today I became one of the blessed *Herati*—soon I go to my Aphrodisia."

Draken said nothing, but Arias felt his arm turn to a steel band locking her to him. He made a clicking noise and dug his heels into the horse's side. Tossing his head, Pluto set off at a trot, then galloped forward to the cresting day, wings beating out a hard rhythm that carried them into the dawn.

Taking a handful of Pluto's mane, Arias urged the stallion to dive toward a strip of sand along the rocky coast. Laughing, she guided the horse to land on an outcropping of boulders clawing their way out of the ocean.

Draken leapt down from Pluto's back and helped her to dismount. He set her on her toes and his hands lingered against the soft silk flowing over her waist.

"I can't go far. It's already morning," Arias sighed, a sound full of pleasure and longing. "I won't miss the sunrise, though," she threw up her hands and laughed. "Oh what does it even matter? So what if they miss me at devotions? I mean, how much trouble can I really get into? What are they going to do—kill me?"

Draken's body stiffened. "That's not at all funny Arias."

The sun washed over his bronze skin, turning it a radiant gold. Their fingers touched once more, and he stroked the fine lines on the back of her hand. "Has any man ever touched you, Arias?"

Arias shook herself and took back possession of her hand. "No. Never." The places he touched tingled, she rubbed at them absently. "We take care of ourselves in the order." She flipped her hair over her shoulder and twisted it into a braid. "Perhaps, never is wrong, if it happened I don't remember."

Conscious of his hand dangerously close to hers, Arias moved away from him. "You should not be doing it now, it seems I am lost in the romance of sunrise."

"Why, Arias?" asked Draken.

Arias shaded her face against the sun and met his eyes. "Why what?"

"Why would you allow yourself to be…sacrificed?"

"Do you know the story of Enisis, Draken?"

Draken arched a brow but shook his head.

Arias gave him a beatific smile. "They raised me on her legend. Enisis was a young peasant girl—said to be exquisite as the moon. She was madly in love with King Actheron, an obsession nurtured since childhood. King Actheron was ruler of all the Aegean." Arias flung her hands out to encompass the ocean stretching before them. "The legends say the king had a terrible lust for power. Some say that he guzzled wine and women faster than a—"

"Arias," Draken cut in, "I know who King Actheron was."

Arias shrugged. "Well, anyway, in Enisis's seventeenth year, Actheron insulted his brother, Atheon, who was High King of Sparta. A terrible fight ensued between them. Their battle raged for three days, they fought without food, drink, or rest. At the end of the three days, the gods came and told the brothers to sleep, because they were losing their enjoyment in the now sloppy battle. Enisis was waiting on Athena when she overheard the goddess saying Actheron would certainly fall. So that night, when the moon was full and the sky at its blackest, Enisis went to Actheron and gave him her body." Arias looked up at Draken. "I'm not sure why she did it. I like to think it was because she just wanted one memory with the man she loved. Their time together is said to be one of the most passionate in history—when Enisis was blinded by pleasure—she offered her life to the gods in exchange for her lovers invincibility. Athena gave Actheron strength, and he overcame his brother. Enisis died in his arms."

Draken's face took on a sickly cast. "That...that's revolting!" He passed his hands roughly through hair. "It's the worst story I've ever heard. Actheron was no man if he could live with himself after trading the life of the woman he loved to ensure preservation of his own."

"Actheron didn't love her," Arias threw her hands in the air. "He didn't even know her. That is why her sacrifice was so blessed. She did what she did, expecting nothing in return..." Arias broke off. "And, it is not revolting, it's beautiful!" Anger edged her words. "My sisters, and I are under Aphroditie's spell, it is said, the priestesses of the Aphrodisia feel real love for their intended partner. It is from that love, the power of the Aphrodisia is born."

Disgust still showed on Draken's face. "You are telling me they raised you knowing you will be raped, then murdered—and they have you saying it's *beautiful*?" His fists clenched and unclenched.

Arias found his anger surprising and confusing. "It is beautiful!" The words sounded hollow. "You are a Spartan, you knew about this ritual your whole life. You knew the girl beneath you would die. Why all the rage now?"

"I knew, I just didn't—"

"Didn't think about it?" Arias interrupted. "Didn't think about us as real women with a beating heart and a perishable soul?"

"Ye Gods!" roared Draken, yanking at his hair until it looked like he might tear it from the roots. "Aphrodite condones this?" He shook his head, "That vain creature! What is her vile part?"

"How can you speak about the gods like that?" Arias was all but sputtering now. "Stories of your extensive learning were apparently greatly exaggerated! The old writings say, Aphrodite saw a pure love in Enisis's sacrifice, she took Enisis from Hades and sent her to live in the mists of the in between so she could watch over Actheron all his life. Enisis, grateful to Aphrodite for rescuing her from death devoted the rest of her immortal life to the goddess. It is said her fervent prayers increased the goddess's power. Now, Aphrodite chooses women from across the world to be guardians and give her worship." Arias stared back at the sky, sighing—her longing audible in the breathy sound. "The whole thing has always seemed rather romantic to me."

"*Romantic*?" snarled Draken. "It's the most demented thing I've ever heard! If ever I am king, such ceremonies would never take place—the gods may rage as they will."

Arias reached out, grabbed a handful of his cloak, and pulled him down to sit beside her. "You," she touched his chest, "would probably feel different, if the lives of your people depended on it. No man would willingly bring down the anger of the gods on himself and those he rules. In the choice between war and peace with the gods, what significance is there in the lives of a few insignificant girls?" She smiled. "Nothing. It is not even worth a second thought. We are but shadows…"

"You are not a shadow." The last vestiges of Draken's control disintegrated and he took her in his arms. "I can touch you." He buried his face in her neck. "You are very real to me, Arias."

"I dreamt of you the other day," Arias whispered, leaning back to trace the sharp lines of his face. "I dreamed it was you who took me on the altar," she gave a little shudder. "Sometimes, I dream things before they happen…"

Draken's hands on her skin were hot. He lifted her face up to his, looking deep in her eyes, a mad light in his own. "I would not, Arias. I would not take you before all those men, then leave you to die. Look in my eyes, little one. Do you think I have that in me?"

Arias looked at him deeply. "My goddess drugs you, you will not have a choice. It's not only Aphrodite, Athena, even your father has a part in it. Hades houses us, until the goddess arrives to spirit us away to her immortal shores."

Draken studied her. "Few people know my true origins," he said finally.

Arias gave him a demeaning look. "Your origins are the most gossiped-about topic in the world! Besides, even if they were not, I've read our histories. How does it feel to have the god of death for a father?"

Draken thought about that for a time. "I suppose if Hades was not my father," he said finally, "I would not have the strength I do, it might have made my childhood less bloody—or not. It appears horror is a part of life in our world." He let her go, stood up and walked over to stare into the vibrating folds of water. "It means nothing to me—there have been many divine bastards. I want to meet my father, that is all I know. I have so many questions, Helen wishes me to hold my travels until after my Aphrodisia," he turned to give her a hard look. "Now, I do not believe I will take part at all. I am a god. It is a ritual for men." His words carried the weight of an unaccepted reality. "I don't know. I haven't decided what to feel yet."

Arias came to stand beside him, giving his shoulder a little nudge with her fist. "I'll say hi to him for you, if you like…your father I mean—I should see him any day now."

Draken threw Arias a murderous glare, the light in her eyes faded. "You don't understand, Draken," she whispered. "Everybody dies." She looked at his face and pressed her finger against her chest as if she could touch her soul. "I was born to die and *there* is the difference. I will fulfill my duty as a priestess, and a guardian of whatever man takes me."

Draken was past feeling fury at this woman—it was not helping anything. In retrospect, his best results had never come about by yelling at a woman. Silky hair whipping around her face, eyes wide and trusting, locked on him, she seemed lost and forlorn in a world that wished her only pain. "If I swore to take you away from all of this, would you come with me, Arias?"

Arias did not look at him. "No."

"Why?" Draken shot back.

"Because, prince, I will die anyway. Aphrodite will find a way to take me." Arias met his eyes for the barest of seconds before she turned away from him, her arm trailed out behind, her hand still resting against his chest. "I have already told you, I don't want the hope you are offering me. I don't even want to think about it. I am irrevocably bound by my own honor to keep my destiny. See to your own, prince. It doesn't include me."

ANCIENT CHAPTER XI

MARCH 9TH

Two days since they galloped over the clouds. Two torturous nights since he questioned her destiny and she informed him of his lesser role in it. Many women had flitted through Draken's life. They had always been there when he needed them—a convenience for a prince. He had never known what it was to *want* one. To have their face fill every corner of your mind, feel their absence like a wound in the gut.

Two days ago, he had taken her back to the cold cliff walls of her home and begged her to meet him again. Arias had offered her customary response, cautioning him to the impossibility of it all. He had told her he would wait.

So he did. Waited until the waxing moon held a prominent spot in the star-drenched sky. The waves crashed and the sand shifted over his feet, burying him to the ankles. His desperation stretched through each passing hour. "She will come," he told the restless sea, the taunting corners of his mind did not believe it.

The stars wheeled overhead. Still, Draken waited alone.

"Draken?" The wind brought her quiet voice to him. He whirled in time to see a white figure break from the shadowed cove. His body sagged in relief—she would give him one more sunrise.

Arias said nothing as he lifted her atop Pluto and climbed up behind her. She curled in his lap, and they drifted without a sense of time, past the sprawling beaches that ran alongside the towering city, and the sun bleached road banking the Olympian shores. When they landed, Draken dismounted, and lifted her from Pluto's back.

"Where are we?" asked Arias.

"Welcome to Condora," Draken said, setting her down, he held her until she found her footing, then stepped back and slapped Pluto on the rump, the Stallion went off to find grazing.

"These caves lead to the underworld," said Arias, she turned a sad smile on him. "Don't you think I will find my way there soon enough on my own?"

Draken ran his hands through his hair. "I didn't even consider that. I've never brought anyone here. I wanted to take you to a place that meant something to me."

Arias's perfect nose wrinkled. "Enchanting," she said, mildly sarcastic. "It smells quite awful."

Draken smiled at her. "The air is worse inside," he took her hand. "Still, this place is sacred to me. I practically lived in these rocky caves, as a boy." He squinted into the sun to meet her eyes. "I would come here whenever I needed to get away from the tongue lashings from my tutors, Igori fists, or my mother's tirades at my father. Now, it seems obvious why I favored these caves. I guess, in my soul, I always knew Hades was my father."

"You *must* have known. I knew the moment I saw you. You have your father's legendary coloring."

"You mean my skin is dark and sinful," Draken said in a bitter voice.

Arias laughed at his discomfort. "Dark and beautiful," she breathed.

They found a low rock, smoothed over by time and tides. Draken sat, he felt homeless, without hearth or anchor. A bastard god—not quite human, not yet an Olympian. "Tell me what else you know of me?" Draken asked. "Helen and Menelaus have never been overly forthcoming."

"I know what anyone knows." Arias laughed, and he thought it a ravishing sound. "The real question is, how can *you* not know?"

"The queen and king kept me in the dark on many matters, though I suspected the truth when I fought my first battle. I was nothing like the other men. I always believed, always hoped, I truly was a son of the gods. Ares has called me cousin since our first encounter."

"Well, that's the beauty of a legend. No one truly knows the full tale," Arias shrugged. "I only know the gossips. There is no mention of your mother. It's possible that you were conceived before Hades kidnapped Persephone and compelled her to live in the underworld. Meaning your mother is a mystery, which of course only adds to the fascination. He tricked her, your father did. Tricked Persephone to be his queen. I hear he is quite the trickster."

"I am a fighter," Draken replied. "I have no trickery in my soul. And I would not kidnap my queen. I believe it would stunt the romance."

Arias waved away his remarks. "Athena stole you from Hades—though how she accomplished that feat is beyond me," she shivered. "Goddess of wisdom or not, she frightens me most of all. Athena gave you to the Fates and you ended up the prince of Sparta. Some say Menelaus meant to kill himself the night they gave you to him. A handful of tales say that Zeus is your father. There is very little talk of you in connection with Poseidon. I think a jealous dryad once accused you of belonging to him. Jealous dryads, however, accuse Poseidon of many things, so not much was made of it. I knew though…" she said. "When you stepped out on the sands, I knew which legends were true. I have always felt close to Hades. He is a player in my fate as well." Arias stood up brushing her hands down her silk skirts. She glanced over her shoulder at the yawning cave mouth, breathing shadows and mists. "How far have you traveled into Condora?"

"Never far," Draken admitted in a low voice. "Dark things in those depths frighten even me. I think I've always felt the curse that chases me, the dark bane attached to my name."

Arias took his hand and hauled him to his feet. "Don't we all? Take me into the caves," she commanded, her voice quiet but firm. "I don't have many days left to explore this world."

Draken bowed. "As you will, my lady," he motioned to her dark destination. "Lead the way."

Arias laughed, now it was desperately unhappy sound. "Many fear facing the shades rumored to lurk behind those rocks, yet, standing here, holding your hand—the great heir to the throne of Tartarus—I believe I am perfectly safe."

"I am heir to the throne of Sparta. I do not know yet if I want any part of my father."

"That is for you to say," Arias told him softly. "I believe you will know what to do when the time is right. When you have a reason, perhaps? When it matters."

"I have a reason. I will ask him why he let Athena take me, why the curse? Why the dark fate?"

"I see." Arias stopped and took his hand. He brought her fingers to his lips; they were cold from the wind. "You're not sure if you wish to know the answers to those questions?"

"Yes," Draken said, feeling lost in her eyes. He saw aged wisdom in their innocent, emerald depths.

"Time changes everything for us all, Draken."

Silence walked with them, Pluto followed behind, shying away when they reached the entrance to the pitchy cave. In the darkness, the rocks at the entrance looked like dragon teeth ravaging the fleshy body of some alien creature. Sable light drenched the mouth of the cave so that it seemed violet blood dripped from the rocky maw. Silhouettes writhed between the jagged rocks that made up the old cave walls. Together, he and Arias stepped under the shade of the yawning, bloody teeth.

A transitory dizziness, a kind of cavernous sensation that made the dark passage a portal he could see into—struck Draken. The cave walls glistened. The darkness of before now seemed a strange facade when all around them throbbed a thick green light permeating the air with a metallic taste—one Draken instantly identified with blood.

"There are words," said Arias, and she pressed her bare fingers against a wet rock. *"Why do we loathe Hades more than any god, if not because he is so adamantine and unyielding?"* She smiled. "This writing is recent."

Draken moved to stand at her back. She was so small the top of her silky head brushed his chin. "How do you know?"

"Because, your adopted uncle, King Agamemnon wrote and signed it. He died a horrible, bloody death nearly twenty years ago. Clytemnestra, killed him; she stuck a knife in his throat while he tried to rape her—" Arias spat on the ground and made a cleansing motion over her head. "He deserved his violent fate. A monster if there ever was one. Any man who would kill his own daughter to take a city that didn't belong to him, destroy one of the greatest civilizations of our modern world! Well," she huffed, "he earns nothing but my pure loathing." Arias twirled in Draken's arms and looked up, "Are you adamantine and unyielding?"

Draken grunted, then admitted, "It would not be an unfair description."

Arias smiled and bit her bottom lip. Draken kissed her chilled brow. "Should we go further, you're not afraid?"

She thought on his words for a moment, running hands along the bumpy rock, stopping to mull over the deep carvings and jagged lines of words and pictures inscribed—at time's beginning—into these crumbling walls.

"I should be," Arias said. "Alas, I'm a strange mortal, one trained to crave death." Draken watched her eyelashes flutter down, coming to rest on her cheeks. "I think perhaps if one does not fear death—for that one— death holds no fear. It seems redundant, yet makes perfect sense. In a way this cave is death, or an entrance to its shores. There is no point fearing the origin of the thing I cannot avoid. Death is just the next step of a soul's journey. Before I met you, taking that journey was the only thing I wanted."

"And now?" Draken asked deeply.

Arias did not answer, instead, she turned and went back to study the drawings. Her fingers came away coated in slime, as if she had stroked the trail of a snail.

Draken looked out of the cave's mouth. The sun seemed to have slid down a dark tunnel and come to rest in some distant corner of the sky. He saw the ocean and the glistening rocks bordering it as if through a waterfall. Perhaps these caves, too, were unanchored like him. Lost and outside time. He turned back to Arias. She touched a jagged section of rock depicting images of little people with smiles that pulled back over their pale jawbones and empty, blackened eyes. Bony hands clutched thin spears and short spartan blades. The earth beneath their feet burned in aqua flames. They formed a semicircle in the fire and grabbed the arms of a woman painted to look like a ghost: her arms ended in wisps of smoke, her open mouth uttering its final scream. The haunting image sent a shudder of horror through Draken.

"These are the Nori," Arias told him. "I suppose one might call them priests of Hades, though they serve Aphrodite. Legend says they carry weapons but are not warriors. They can take a soul from earth to the Under Realm. *'One soul in the winter',*" she quoted, *"'owhne soul in the rain. One soul held to his bargain, one soul to die in pain'.*"

Arias's hand fell away. "They are dark, filthy creatures," she wiped her hands on her dress. "I will not touch them or call upon their name," she said, and made more warding gestures over her hair and face. "I would not have villains like that chasing me. It's dark in here," she said absently. "Your heritage is sad."

Draken raised a sardonic brow. "Mine is?"

Arias waved this away. "Mine is not all sad. When I am dead, and the celebration's flowers have wilted, I will go to the mists and watch over the man I love for all eternity."

"The man you *love?*" Draken tried to keep the sneer out of his voice. "The man responsible for your rape and murder, you mean."

"You make it sound so horrifying, Draken," cried Arias. She shook off his touch and rushed free of the cave's cloying shadows. He followed close on her heels. Draken realized he had been correct in his assumption. Time had scrambled on without them. The hot orange sun had sunk into the horizon, spilling bloody light over the rocky swells.

"Oh!" gasped Arias. "It's almost evening. I have lost an entire day!" She rounded on him, unleashing the flames in her eyes. "You swore."

Draken caught her flailing hand and steadied her. "I could take you away from this, little one. Just say you will come with me, we will never set eyes on these lands again." Draken heard the open pleading in his voice, he hardly cared.

A gust of howling wind rolled off the rocks. Arias shivered and buried her face against his chest, he heard her soft whisper. "Do not say such things, my prince. It has been a dark day. I should not have left."

"I want to save you, Arias," he breathed.

Arias jerked and shoved out of his arms. "I do not require saving!" she shouted. "Do not think to save me. Do not think to hope for me. I am already lost." The last statement made the heat rush from her cheeks, sorrow softened her voice. "Take me home, Draken."

Draken took her back in his arms and pressed his lips to her forehead, her cheeks and the very corner of her mouth. "We are so different, you and I. I trust in myself. I believe in nothing. But you, you believe in what you do, don't you, Arias?"

"I did," she whispered. "I do. I love Enisis and I love my goddess. I am not a slave. I chose this."

"Liar," Draken breathed, and watched her teeth sink into the flushed cushion of her lower lip. "Fine," Draken sighed. "Tell me something you love. No more death today."

Arias looked up and smiled at him through a veil of tears. Draken felt the chambers of his heart ignite. "I love music and the wind swirling through the waves," she whispered. Absently brushing the dust from the hem of her gown, trying to shake it from her dainty sandals. "I play the harp, a little, and I adore poetry more than anything."

"I love poetry," Draken admitted. "My teacher Leandros forced me to recite the classics until I rhymed common words. It gained me endless ribbing in the barracks."

Arias laughed, a teary sound. "I still do that—all the time, it seems my soul just wants to rhyme." They looked at each other through the whirling dust and the approaching shades of twilight. Her laugh faded as the moment took on a sad overtone of finality.

"I don't like many things, to be honest, not because I'm picky, I just don't know them," said Arias. She stroked Pluto's warm nose as he lipped at her hair. "I had a friend, Alora. I have no real memory of my mother and father. Alora was the only thing I ever truly loved. She was nothing like me, never thought of any destiny but the one the fates had given her. She wanted to die. In the beginning at least," her voice dropped and she stumbled over her next words. "I saw them beat her, she fought back, it made me think of things which have no business crossing my mind. Things like freedom, choice, and love. Being born with no choice is simpler. A life without choice is a life without fear of consequence. Alora was innocent, she chose life and now she is dead, I will join her soon. Aphrodite tells us we will see each other again in the mists."

"I am sorry," Draken told her, meaning it in his bones.

Arias gulped in a deep, bracing breath. "I have lost many sisters. I will have many friends waiting for me on the other side."

Draken held her face cupped between his palms. His whole soul wished he possessed some way to comfort her and wondered, for perhaps the thousandth time, what she would do if he simply picked her up and carried her away. He ached to kiss her perfect lips, but if he did, if he let go, let his hands and mouth do what they wanted, then he knew he would never stop. Never.

■　　■　　■

They had left the caves far behind, below them spread the shaggy inland plains bordering the coast. Dotting the road was an occasional mansion, outlining pillars turned to shadow, or a shepherd's hut identified by the glow of fires casting gentle light in the dark sky. Sparta was beautiful. *His* land. Not by birth, merely a byproduct of a goddess's vengeance. A chill wind whipped through the frigid air, and Arias shivered in his arms. He tightened his hold, wrapping his cloak around her.

All too soon, Pluto brought them down to the edge of the rose garden framing the temple. Torches flickered beneath the multi colored bushes, making it seem as if they landed in a nest of fireflies.

Draken dismounted and helped Arias to her feet. She could hear laughter and the music of harps pouring over the garden wall. "My sisters!" Arias folded her body in the leafy locks of a weeping willow. "We can't be seen together," she whispered in a threadbare shout. "Leave!"

"I will not leave," Draken retorted. "Promise to meet me again or I will shout until they come running, harps and all."

"You would not dare," said Arias, taking the swishing branches and drawing them across her slender frame like a forest shield. Draken hauled back his broad shoulders, thrust out his chest, and drew up his head for a roar that would wake the rocks.

"Goddess!" Arias ran to him and laid her hand over his lips. "Quiet!" she hissed.

Draken stared at her beautiful face, through the barrier of her palm, he drew in even more air. A stormy rumble started in his chest.

"You will not shout," commanded Arias.

"On the contrary," Draken returned, a smile creasing the corners of his eyes. "Say you will meet me, or I will raise a din to summon the gods."

"Fine!" she hissed. "I will meet you. Will you be silent?"

Draken winked and kissed her palm. She snatched her hand back, smiling at him. Arias retreated again into the folds of the willow until only her emerald eyes glinted from the swaths of green. Between them hung a dancing curtain of leaves whispering to the night wind. A chunk of mossy dirt flew toward him, splattering his chest. He heard the tinkling bell of her laughter and two more chunks of mud hurled in his direction. Draken stepped back, dashing his body left to evade the earthen missiles. He watched the willow branches flicking the air like tiny switches, her pale fingers threaded through the leaves. "Meet me here in two days," her cherry lips mouthed him a kiss. "I know a place." She disappeared and only her voice drifted to him from beyond the leafy veil. "Goodbye, Prince."

"Priestess," he whispered. Only silence replied and the night winds carried his voice away. "Come, Pluto." The stallion brayed at the air and pointed his glossy nose toward the willow branches, still holding traces of her perfume. "No, boy. The girl is like smoke." Draken scratched the bridge of the wet nose thumping his shoulder. "If only she would vanish from my thoughts. It's possible she will drive me mad."

"Tis the way of women," a deep voice rumbled out from the darkness.

Draken knew its owner. The earth seemed to shudder under the weight of the tenor. Ares could not disguise that proud stride no matter what clothing he wore—now it was a plain brown toga that might have draped a palace servant. Ares made the simple cloth look like a robe of state. Androsia clung to him. Her eyes dripped honey on her god while her fingers twined through loose threads on his toga.

"Draken?" Androsia called out, abandoning her perch on Ares's arm. Her plum gown of Egyptian silk caught the first light of the rising moon.

She flipped her hair off her pale shoulder and skipped over to kiss his cheek.

"What are you doing here?" Draken barked.

Androsia ignored her brother's mood and beamed up at him. "Ares promised to take me on a walk through the prettiest rose gardens in Sparta. We flew here on Vessus. It was marvelous," she chattered. "We wondered where you were. You have been sneaking off of late." She tapped a painted nail against her lip. "Have you a lover, Draken?"

Draken saw Ares look past his line of sight to the temple that housed and caged Arias's precious soul. When Ares's eyes returned to Draken, their roiling depths held a knowing look. "They are untouched for a reason, Draken."

"The reason is barbaric," Draken spat. Pluto shied from his master's anger and kicked his hoofs in the air. Androsia screamed and threw up her arms to shield her perfect face.

"Calm!" Draken commanded, and Pluto fell still.

"What is barbaric?" asked Androsia, voice gone breathless from her fright. "What are you talking about?"

"Nothing to concern your lovely head," retorted Ares.

Androsia pouted. "Don't patronize me. I know where we are and to whom this temple belongs. The girls here are *Leisha,* right? Untouched."

Both men gave her an astounded look.

"Don't look at me like that!" Androsia tossed her hair. "I know everything that happens in Sparta."

Ares barked out an unexpected peal of laughter. "Zeus! I hope not."

"You don't look yourself at all, Draken. In fact, you look rather terrible," said Androsia.

He felt their eyes on the back of his neck while he watched the place he had last seen Arias. The space around the willow tree wavered as if touched by noonday heat.

"I do not feel myself," Draken admitted.

Ares placed a hand on his shoulder. "They all die, Draken. Aphrodite is the most jealous goddess I know—and that is no small statement, considering all my sisters and aunts in the equation. She will not let a single one leave her service or her arms. They are hers, from birth through death."

Draken almost hit him. He thought about it. What it would feel like to smash his fist into Ares's jaw, the satisfying crunch as flesh met bone. Yet, Ares only spoke the truth.

"Come back," said Androsia, a nervous tone in her voice, as if she sensed the disquiet in the air. "This is dark talk. Let us away to the games, where we will see some blood and take our minds off whatever is occurring here." She glanced at the cold temple walls, reflecting a pale hue under the risen moon. Her hands came up to rub her arms as if chilled by her own thoughts. "This place makes my skin crawl."

"Come," said Ares. "To my games, then!" He gripped Draken's shoulder. "We shall see what blood they offer to the god of war, and son of death."

"Ahem!" Androsia cleared her throat prettily, a dainty hand across her mouth.

"Ah," Ares stepped close to her and bowed low, his dark curls brushing the silk stretched across her breast. "And, of course, the most beautiful princess in all the lands."

Androsia let him take her hand and draw her to him. Draken watched them amble away. They expected him to join, he resisted, the shadows alive in the night mocked him. Dark thoughts, dark dreams and a dark destiny. Draken threw himself on Pluto's back and let the icy night air chill his rage.

ANCIENT CHAPTER XII

MARCH 10TH

Arias shut her eyes and tried not to tremble. She bowed low. A priest poured freezing water over her head. The others clapped their hands.

"*Born to purity,*" they chanted, their wheezing voices muffled by dark cowls. "*Born to die as a goddess, born to honor the gods.*"

More freezing water cascaded down her hair.

An old priest—leaking eyes framed by a set of wrinkles Arias thought resembled craters—motioned for her to rise. Arias obeyed and kept her gaze trained on the ground, studying the weave of her golden sandals peeking from beneath the train of her white gown.

"You are clean," they told her. Their old, croaking voices made her feel she would never be clean again. White roses lay in the puddle of cleansing water gathered around her feet. The innocence of the rose only heightened the macabre scene. Today, this ritual proclaimed her coming death. They cleansed her to die and she was afraid.

They left her alone to pray. Arias knelt in the water, reached out her hands to the stone feet of Aphrodite's statue, and looked up at the carved face of the goddess. The statue looked back at her through impassive eyes.

"Aphrodite, I don't know if you can hear me," Arias whispered, as her tears splashed on the feet of the goddess. "I will die for you, but whatever man you give me, I know I cannot love him. There is another I dream about," she wiped the tears from her cheeks. More tumbled on her bottom lip and she caught them between her teeth.

Her mind shouted questions at her, refusing to be silent. *"Will the mists even take me if I do not love the man I watch over? Will I even want to die for him?"*

"I am not Enisis," she sobbed. "It is not my Actheron I will die for."

Only silence came from the statue. Bowing lower, Arias pressed her forehead to the marble base, not caring that the water soaked the front of her gown. Her curls fell in her eyes and stuck to the moisture drying in streaks across her face.

Arias lay like that until the sun fell below the cove and the night braziers were lit. Torchlight poured through her tower window, and she realized her once sodden dress was dry. Exhausted joints screamed when she stood and black spots clouded her vision, but she bent and picked up a rose. A sharp thorn stabbed into her thumb. She watched a blood drop form—the little pain solidified her reality, the color of her blood was quite beautiful really, and she liked that. Memories of beauty were all the good that would follow her into the house of death.

Arias pushed the doors wide, and began the tedious climb down the narrow stairwell leading back to the main hall. Torchlight fell in velvety sheets against the uneven stairs, shifting around the black spots still fogging her vision. A ravenous thing growling in her stomach told her she might need food and perhaps sleep, but what did those things matter now? She was already a walking corpse, a girl devoid of choice, nothing more than a fading shade. Each boundary her mind crossed stripped away another illusion, and she feared death would be her last.

Sorrow singed a hot path down her throat, her eyes remained dry. There was nothing left to cry. Behind the torches, tiny windows flaunted the forbidden outside world. Moonlight stroked the cold marble frame of the small outlook. Evening had fallen. Draken would be waiting for her.

"I will not go," Arias told the little fires spinning in their iron braziers. "It will kill me to leave him this time. I will beg him to take me away, then I will be like Medusa, the fool who dared to love a god, forever cursed, forsaken, and alone."

Arias repeated all the reasons she would not go to him, while she rushed to her chambers to bathe her face and change her rumpled dress. The grass was wet beneath her toes when she pulled the pearl hood down over her forehead, obscuring her features. She wore a simple shift and a silk cloak. Bare feet kicking up chunks of wet earth, Arias ran through the garden and the night mists parted in her wake.

In her mind she imagined she ran for freedom, far away from the walls that meant death. Arias reached the willow and rushed through the branches to the old, moss-covered trunk. She braced her hand against the uneven bark and tried to catch her breath.

"Oh, this is madness!" Arias cried. Night air carried her voice and sent back her name in response. She did not need to turn around, she knew who called her. Wind caught the edges of the leaves and pushed them aside. Draken stood shadowed by a backdrop of silver moonlight. He was looking at her, from the slouch in his shoulders and the lazy cross in his arms, it seemed he had been for some time now.

Arias held out her hand and shook her head. "Stay back," she said. "I have not decided yet whether or not to go with you,."

Draken's shoulders straightened and he locked his hands behind his back. "I will not move until you give the command."

Arias rolled her eyes. "Well, we can't just stand here where anyone could happen by! Come!" Turning on the spot, she fled back the way she had come—through a thick growth of low-hanging, thorny junipers that made her feel dwarfed. Draken followed, though with considerable less ease. Arias giggled when she heard a branch whip flesh, followed by a hissed curse.

Arias broke through the trees into a small clearing. A courtyard of cobblestones flared out around a pool of water licking at its white stone border. She sat down against a sun-washed stone shelf at the pool's base and looked past the midnight water.

"Will you run if I come closer, Arias?" asked Draken.

"N...no," Arias said, but she shied away when he knelt down beside her. His eyes held her face. She reached out a finger and wiped a smear of blood from his cheek.

"The branch cut you. I'm so sorry. I shouldn't have run like that." Her voice fell away and she touched another drop of blood. Together, they watched the droplet roll down her finger.

"The blood is nothing. I would give you my last drop," vowed Draken.

"You don't know me enough to say a thing like that," Arias said, but her voice held no heat.

Draken laughed, though there was little humor in the sound. His gaze said he had always seen her, always known her. "I am prince. I believe I can say whatever I like."

Arias turned up her nose at him. "Not to me you can't."

Draken made a muffled noise and she slapped his chest.

"Now you're laughing at me?" Arias challenged.

"Never," he blurted, wiping the smile off his face. "I would never laugh at you, little one. Before you showed up just now, I feared I would never laugh again. I thought you might change your mind and refuse to meet me."

"I thought so too."

"Why didn't you?"

"I don't know. Curiosity, I suppose." Arias rested her chin against her knees and looked to the sky. "Life and its intricacies are a mystery to me. I wonder sometimes if I know anything at all. My beliefs, my prayers have always been the substance defining me, yet, I felt something break inside when I saw Alora die and now..." she shook her head. "I will not go into all that sadness again. Besides, I'm babbling—I'm not trying to feel these things, they do nothing except cause me pain. The fear of death strengthens my mortality, and I am striving for the divine." Arias reached up and brushed a wandering curl off his face. "I blame the majority of my upheaval on you, you know. This is nice, though…being near someone, speaking my thoughts out loud."

Draken took her hands and tightened his grip when she gave a weak show of resistance. "Nice is not the word I would use for this, Arias. I could take you away—"

"Don't say it!" Arias wrenched her hands free of his. "Don't even think it. Speaking to you is the worst cruelty of all. You would try to force hope on me when I have no desire for it?"

Draken leaned over her, she fell back against her elbows. "I'm not forcing. I simply don't want to lose you." His voice softened. "You are too perfect to be part of so dark a ritual. No man should ever have the right to destroy such beauty."

Arias placed her hand like a peace offering against his chest. "You are a prince," she responded. "The Aphrodisia is your birthright. What of the woman *you* rape and kill?" Arias clapped her hand over her mouth, unable to believe those awful words had escaped it.

"You are right, Arias. I did not think of the woman who would die for me. No one will die for me now," vowed Draken.

"You can not say such things, you do not know. You did not think of the woman, because you are not meant to, a spell—like that one cast by Aphrodite—can not be explained, only experienced. Whoever it is I am sure she will be glad it is you she is dying for."

Draken closed his arms around her and lifted his hands to thread them through her hair. "Curse the gods. I will *not* lose you."

Arias let the insult slide in the rush of his touch, the fire of his hands on her neck and face dissolved her resistance. He pressed his lips against her temple then trailed them to the corner of her lips. Arias felt something wild fly apart inside her, she looped her arm around his neck and tilted her head back to look at his face. "Sometimes," Arias whispered, "when the night is dark, I swim here. I even saw a nymph once. She told me there is pure magic in this water. It can heal anything, even change the sky and stars." Arias stood on shaky feet, she reached into the side pocket of her gown and removed a small vial of perfume, unstoppered the bottle and poured the contents on the ground. The heavy scent of roses wafted up around them.

Draken raised his brow in question, shyness heated her cheeks. "What? I want you to have some of the water, carry it always. I believe it will protect you when I am gone." Draken said nothing so, Arias walked to the edge of the pool and filled the little bottle with the clear, shimmering liquid. Could it honestly protect him? If such a thing was even remotely possible, then Arias wanted to dunk his whole body in it. She walked back to him and held out the vial. "Take it," she said.

He did. Arias watched his large hand close over the glass. "Thank you. I will carry it, always." He placed it in the pocket of his tunic, then reached for her. Arias felt herself flow into his arms. Behind them the water lapped against the shore, making its own music—she wanted to dance in it.

"Do you want to swim with me, Draken?" Arias asked softly.

"Yes," said Draken instantly. "I want to swim with you. I want to do anything with you."

Silence enveloped them. In a trance, she watched him reach for the golden clasp at her neck. She heard a small click and her cape floated to the ground. She stood like a statue, watched him kick off his sandals. His hands brushed over her neck and the untouched skin on her shoulders. Arias shivered.

"Cold?" Draken's voice, thick and rough—slid like silk against her raw nerves.

"No, I feel quite warm," Arias sighed. "I'm lying. I am constantly amazed each time you touch me that my skin doesn't simply burst into visible flames."

Draken laughed, then his eyes fell to the golden clasp beneath her breasts. The laugh knotted in his throat when she reached for it. The click of its release was a thunderclap in the silence. The silk dress slid down her shoulders. She felt every inch of cloth glide over her hips, closed her eyes when it came to rest in a pool around her feet.

Draken pulled his tunic over his head, and the low-hanging moon sculpted him in ivory light. Standing there under the giant silver orb, he was a god of gold, each line of his body a testament to his divinity. Arias knew she did not know much about life and love, but she had to acknowledge—had they been in the chamber of Ensis, she would have willingly lived in each moment, and passionately died in his arms. Arias did not know this man, this beautiful warrior who stood on the precipice of mortal and god. If, however, by the purest of magic, she was his priestess—Arias knew she would need no love spell, and at least that part of the legend would be true.

Draken held out his hand. Arias took it and they stepped into the water. In the indigo sky an ocher star shot through a thick patch of its sisters. Arias wished on it, she wished for him. For a time neither of them spoke. Arias thought she felt his inner struggle and wondered if he held back the words that would beg her to run away with him. It was hard to ignore the wild thing in her wanting so badly to say yes. It was quite the worst thing ever Arias realized, if it was her destiny to feel love at first sight—it had happened, only with the wrong man.

"You are so beautiful, Arias," breathed Draken. "You confound fantasy." His mouth hovered over hers. "I cannot let you go to another man. I will not live if they kill you."

"You must," Arias whispered. "If I run away with you, I will be another story like poor Medusa, the girl who betrayed a goddess because she loved a god." Arias kissed his cheek and watched his eyes fall closed. "Don't give it a second thought, in the grand scheme of time, I am already dead."

"The gods have cursed us both. Please, Arias, come with me," his eyes and voice begged her. "We will go where they can't find us."

It was impossible, and illogical, a dream holding a host of a danger she did not understand. Never. She could not.

"Yes," Arias breathed.

"What?" Draken's head snapped up, his light grip on her arms became a vise.

"Yes, I will go with you," Arias said. "It is stupid and I fear I will regret it forever, but, I will go with you."

Draken pressed his mouth against her forehead breathing her name.

Arias reached for his face, brushing her fingers across his perfect lips. "I am lying, again. I would never regret a single second."

Draken lifted her hand and kissed her fingers. "You won't change your mind?"

"I believe I will change it many times," Arias said. "My heart will not change once."

"It will be easy to get what we need and slip away during the insanity of these games. I will meet you here in two days." His hands fell to her waist and flexed against her hips. "Promise you will be here," commanded Draken.

"I promise I will be here. If not, then the Aphrodisia has taken me and it is the will of the gods."

Draken pulled her against his chest, pressed hot lips to the shell of her ear. Arias looked at the stars shooting through the ebony night. Terrible, frightening, and oh, so wonderful—she felt herself dare to dream of life.

ANCIENT CHAPTER XIII

MARCH 13TH

It was the day that signaled the end of Ares's tournament and Draken was blind drunk.

Arias had not returned for three days, all the while he held a morbid sort of vigil, staring at the spot where she had sworn to meet him, drinking jug after jug of wine. On the third day of his watch a young girl who slightly resembled Arias came to him, a white slip of paper in her hands.

"It is from her," the girl whispered. Draken tore the small wax seal apart. The words Arias wrote in beautiful curling script reached down his throat and broke his heart.

They have taken me for preparation. I mean to do my duty. Please don't try to find me...yours truly in life, Arias.

Draken crumpled the note in his hands. It was done. There was nothing left for him to wait for. She was gone.

Now he lay across his bed, staring at the interlocking murals on the ceiling. The wine's effects had washed away his anger until only a hollow sadness remained, a miserable tearing at his gut, sapping the strength from his limbs. He had fallen for her the first moment he laid eyes on her. Poets often spoke of love at first sight, but Draken knew it was more than that. This went beyond simple infatuation or even love—more like recognition at first sight. He had glimpsed her soul in her eyes and recognized a piece of his own.

The heat in the room grew unbearable. Sweat tickled the hairs at the back of his neck, Draken slapped the itch away, walked to his windows and flung them wide.

They opened to an unobstructed view of the south side of Sparta. Lights flared to life around the city. Fresh swirls of dust, upset by the iron-shod hooves of horses and sloppy mules, lifted through the traces of sun filtering down from punctures in the clouds. He moved from the window, stripped off his robes and let the air wash over his skin. It soothed nothing. So, he prowled the room like a wild animal. He filled a cup from a glass pitcher of wine and drained it in a single gulp—immediately wishing for more.

"Gods!" Draken groaned. "This is insanity!" He hurled the pitcher into the wall. The sound of shattering glass brought a sense of angry satisfaction, so he pitched the table as well. The cherrywood split and the joints groaned. Rage settled like a smothering blanket atop him. The chairs went next over his head, followed by his bed, chests of drawers, and everything he could grasp. His breath burned in his lungs as all objects in the room took on a harsh red haze. He destroyed whatever he could find, tearing tapestries off the walls and hurling priceless objects out the open windows.

He would *not* let her die. He was a demi-god. It had to be a simple thing to break into the temple and take her. If she still lived, that was. A lone chair stood the sole survivor of his rage. He grasped the splintered leg and lobbed it into the wall.

Draken stalked through the rubble of his bed, snatched up his robe and pulled it over his shoulders. A sharp pain stabbed in his gut, bending down to strap on his sandals—he tried to ignore it, but his legs turned to water, and he crashed to his knees. The pain in his side amplified as a tremor gripped his limbs. Salty sweat ran like icicles down his spine. His eyes went to the bloody splatter of wine on the wall.

The wine, he realized. *Poison*. It seemed impossible, yet, the proof was vivid in his cramping limbs, in the red haze billowing through his vision, obscuring everything.

Brutally aware of his surroundings Draken could hear every sound in the room, hear the wild rush of the sea and howling wind funneling through the desert sands. He fell on his back, arms wrapped around his stomach. His chamber door opened. Draken registered the individual breaths of the intruders, the shift of glass fragments, the creaking of the floorboards. They moved closer, knelt at his side, and leaned across his chest.

"Prince of Sparta."

Draken recognized Aphrodite's voice. He tried to snarl at her, but his mouth hung slack. She splayed her hands across his chest, leaning close she breathed against the shell of his ear. Draken wanted to throw her off of him, his fingers lay uselessly immobile at his sides.

A sharp fingernail trailed him from neck to navel. "Do you want what's coming, son of Hades?" asked Aphrodite. "In the shrouds of night, have thoughts of defiling your virgin kept you warm? Do you see her writhing on that altar, waiting in fearful anticipation for you to take her?"

Draken had not heard a word past virgin. Everything became clear: the Aphrodisia. Horror seeped into his soul.

"I have someone special for you, Draken." Aphrodite's voice sounded like a moan in the wind. "Beautiful and devoted to me. She will give me many years of faithful worship in the mists. She will be the star in my silent sky of power. It feels like I have waited centuries for her to die."

Draken tried again to lift his arms and experienced the same numbing resistance. Fear tightened his spine and brought acid surging in his throat. His sword hung beside the door, propped up on the wine-smeared wall, gleaming at him in the fading light, acknowledging his uselessness—taunting him.

Aphrodite ran her long fingers through his hair, Draken cringed at the scrape of her nails against his scalp.

"You are strong," cooed Aphrodite. "The powerful spartan who outsmarted the god of war." She let out a high-pitched, humorless laugh. "Wasn't that a sight?" Aphrodite stood. "Prepare his body, the priests are here now."

Draken felt her move away from him. A whisper of steam hissed through the air, signaling the goddess's departure.

Draken heard the clatter of glass jars, and the pop of bottles being uncorked. He heard three women whispering in soft tones, then hands rubbed oil on his skin, and brushed his hair.

Draken had never prayed for strength, not once, he had always taken it for granted. Now, he saw Arias's tear-streaked face in his mind, and silently cried out to Athena for help. Using every ounce of concentration, he willed his hand into a fist. Struggling against the paralysis for what felt like an eternity, a muscle in his finger finally clenched. A tide of relief surged so forcefully through him, he thought he might vomit.

More pottery and shattered glass shifted against the floorboards as a new volley of footsteps pounded in the room. Hands slid beneath his back, the world spun when they flipped him in the air. The sound of his face hitting the floor was a loud thudding in his ears. Six heartbeats echoed in the room, beside his own. Two sets of footfalls moved with lightweight grace, the rest lumbered like monsters. The *Litter* they set on the ground was used for carrying the royal dead. It took a monumental effort, but Draken clenched his fists again. *"Not dead yet,"* he thought. *Not yet.*

Grunting and panting, the priests hoisted the poles of his conveyance on their shoulders, then carried him from his room, through the sleep-darkened Palace, and out in the falling night.

Dewy air hit him in the face, his eyelids snapped back, he ached to rub his watering eyes, yet dared not move. Let them think he was dead to reality—his moment would come. A white moon rose in the sky, he stared at it, seeing her face. Thirteen days elapsed since he first laid eyes on Arias. Thirteen torturous nights since her emerald gaze had imprinted on his soul.

"Is it settled?" the wheezy question came from his right.

"It seems so," a shrill voice answered. "There are suspicions she did not drink the venom, still, the girl is calm, I chained her to the altar myself—as a precaution, of course. It is easier if they drink it before, some choose not to. It doesn't matter much. The result is the same."

The first man chuckled, an old, wet sound. "The prince won't care either way. The men rarely notice."

"Do you think they will give us this one before she dies?" This came from the front of the line.

"Who knows?" the first said. "That is for Aphrodite to decide. I, however, think not. This one is special to her."

Fresh rage surged through Draken's veins at the thought of Arias handled by these beasts. He imagined himself hacking the man's head from his shoulders and feeling the warm spray of his foul blood.

"Nothing can go wrong in this ceremony," another replied. "The last was a disaster. That idiot girl nearly killed herself before the boy finished, she was properly drugged—I poured it down her throat myself."

Garbled slurps of agreement echoed all around. Draken felt the blood leaving his clenched fists, felt his short nails cut crescents into his palms. He would wait to see where they were taking him, let his body regain its strength. When the time came, he would tear out the rotten insides of the panting band of murderers. The priests fell silent again. Draken could feel them pivoting, heard them wheeze and pant when the ground dropped into a steep decline.

When they reached another plateau, the priests picked up their pace. Draken watched the stars come out, concentrating on anything except his throbbing limbs. Less than a minute later, the sky vanished behind a high growth of tree. The dark green mass thickened before they descended a flight of stairs carved deep in the rocky ground. Soft blue light leaked from a small doorway, illuminating his surroundings. They were in a tunnel, a vapid hole chiseled through the rock. One priest snorted and spat a long stream of yellow, it splattered against the wall. "Perhaps we can have her while she is dying," he said, coughing and spitting again. "They are so out of their mind by that time anyway, I doubt the little girl will even rem—"

Draken's fist ended the priest's ill-advised sentence. It smashed through the man's fat lips, knocking out his front teeth. Draken sat up, blinding rage the only thing in his world. He snapped the silken bands around his limbs and lashed out with his right hand. His next blow split the priest's bald skull, and it cracked like an old egg. In the same instant, he drove his foot forward. A sharp sound of snapping bone and the neck he targeted broke—the whole contraption he rode on pitched toward the wall. Draken dove down the stairs and rolled to his feet. His legs rocked like he stood at the helm of a ship trapped in a storm, his muscles trembled and the walls spun. He reached out in the way of the Igori, his mind contacting the pulse in each of his limbs until he could feel the tingling tips of his hands and feet. The tremors faded and died. Draken stood strong.

His eyes fell on the four remaining priests, who lay tangled in a heap of limbs and cowls. One priest gave a long ugly, moan. A snarl built behind Draken's clenched teeth. The priest in front of him had cheeks that hung like great distended cysts, and beady, piggish eyes set too close together. Across his bald head, concave liver spots stretched everywhere like bloody bruises.

"Get out or die," Draken spat. Advancing—teeth barred and eyes flashing.

"You are a madman!" one whispered. He looked at his dead companions, then back up at Draken. Sweat dripped down his face and he wrung his fat hands. "You cannot do this!" he lamented in a squealing imitation of a man's voice. "We are high priests of Aphrodite, and her blessed father Zeus. Surely the great god will strike you dead where you stand. We must carry you into the ceremony; your virgin awaits." Fear and confusion mixed in the priest's expression. "Please, your highness! We must complete the ritual and honor the gods, perhaps the preparation angered you?"

"Perhaps," Draken sneered.

"But my lord," the priest squeaked. "It is part of the ritual. Aphrodite honors you with a priceless opiate of the gods. The effects are stunning at first, but as your mind grows accustomed, it will give you an increase in stamina and pleasure."

Draken leaned in so close to the man that he could feel the heat of his rotting breath against his face. A muscle spasmed in his jaw. He snarled each word. "Get. Out. Now. Or die."

"But my lord— "

Draken let out an ear-splitting roar that shook the walls. The priests made a sprightly decision in favor of self-preservation. They smashed and pushed their giant globs of flesh against each other until they looked like a bowl of thick pudding trying to shove itself through a tiny hole.

Draken forgot their existence the minute they cleared the narrow entrance. He pressed his body close to the wet stone wall and ran down the tight corridor in the only direction available. His pulse hammered in his brain. His limbs felt as if they belonged to another body, like if he let his control slip for just one moment, his arms, and legs would go flailing off without him.

The deeper he went in the damp cave, the more the temperature plummeted until freezing wind buffeted him from all sides. It felt as if he stood in the center of a blizzard. Powerful shivers seized his naked body. He looked down at himself for the first time. Two strips of silk hung from his waist. They had smeared gold paint across his body in weird circular patterns so his hands and feet had a metallic sheen. Draken felt like a prize bull dressed up for the kill. How he had ever imagined he could go through something like this? *Arias! Gods Arias. Dead, dying. Did she call for him? Wish for him?* If he lived in his last moments, he knew he would wish for her.

He climbed a set of stairs, at the dais they plunged to the right. Suddenly, the soggy enclosure opened into a bright rectangular room. Three burning torches hung on each wall, a yellow glow flooded the space. It felt blinding after the murky darkness of the cave. Draken flung up his hand to shield his stinging eyes. A door stood at the far side of the room. He seized a torch and continued running. Paintings of cherubs decorated the sides of the tunnel, fat with flushed cheeks, they frolicked in a cloudy sky. Images too happy for this place.

The tunnel ended in another sharp curve, around which stood a wide doorway. Long, guttural yelps of breath drifted from the chamber beyond, echoing discordant moans. One more turn, one more doorway, and Draken realized he had finally reached his destination.

The room he now stood in appeared like a giant bubble of gold; even the floor seemed to arch into itself. Torches hung from every wall, and wide grates on the ground spilled out hot flames that surged up in the room. The fire made no smoke, just sparkled green and purple light.

Draken took a silent step forward. He had no plan, right now he did not need one. Every person in the room had their backs to him. He counted thirty black cowls, and another for the goddess. Aphrodite stood barefoot atop a pedestal on the south side of the room. She swayed side to side, her eyes closed and lips slightly parted, keeping rhythm to the music of the howling priests. Her robes rode out behind her, and the glow emanating from her long, golden skeins of hair blanketed the spherical room.

Draken wanted to kill them all.

The priests knelt around their goddess. Chanting the prayer of the Leisha, they gyrated against the ground, arms stretched out in supplication and faces raised to the arched dome of the ceiling. They cried out as if they waited for death. In the center of the room, flaring out like a jagged cut jewel, stood a glowing altar.

A sick sense of fatality curled in the pit of Draken's stomach.

On the altar lay the prize, silent and still. His prize. It was her. Of course it was her. Draken whispered the one word branded on his heart.

"Arias."

CHAPTER 13

FAIRHAVEN, WASHINGTON, NOVEMBER 11TH, 2019

The glass of water idling in my hand soaked the tips of my fingers in perspiration. I took a long gulp and looked down at the pair of plane tickets on the counter. Lily booked us for a 10:45 departure Friday morning, less than twenty-four hours away.

I walked to the sink and refilled my glass. Through the kitchen window I could see the late evening mists hanging against the ground; deep black and foreboding, not even the barest hint of grey to mellow their ominous faces. The entire world was one great misty swirl. Sprays of rain blew through the heavy air and clung to the grass while drenching the trees and sloping pavements.

It was dead quiet in my mind. In the North wing I could hear Lily's buzzing excitement. I believe in *her* mind she has already traveled to Corvin Castle a thousand times, explored the old world of Romania, ghosted through the ancient ruins and mountain caves. The thought of actually doing all that—while delving into the Wynter histories, and chasing her halogen map—the freaking Book of Shadows in tow, of course—must be driving her crazy. Andi's presence charged the enthusiasm crackling in the air. Across the manor they twittered like the blue jays that tap incessantly on the windows in the springtime.

I definitely felt the electric charges rippling off the walls, still, I had not packed a thing, trepidation shimmered beneath my excitement. It was Drake. He had changed everything. I wanted to be with him. Feel his hands on me while I listened to his soothing voice. Last night—that strange, impossible night, the heated lake and all that luxurious swimming—he showed me there was something better than the known. The unknown held magic and dangerous thrills, previously found only within the pages of my books.

Drake had left during the night, even though I was pretty sure I had not told him to do so. I had a hazy, bewitching memory of his hand holding mine. Not in the dream—here in the house. In my bed. No one besides Lily had ever done that. Not even Hanna.

Absent his touch, I felt a strange sense of belonging to the man who had stepped out of my dreams. Last night I saw Drake trying, but he could not fully hide it. He felt it too, this strange cord connecting us. I was sure he did.

In my mind I heard Mr. Rochester's words to Jane Eyre as he held her hands in that wind-washed field. His gruff voice, impassioned; telling her that: 'were she to leave him, that binding cord connecting them would snap and he would bleed inwardly'. Two weeks ago, those were just beautiful words. More fool me—now I felt the cord and I feared it would pull me wherever Drake went.

A shiver traced my spine and I belted my robe, my nightgown twirled around my slippered feet. I had finally taken a brush to my hair and it flowed down my back like an auburn cape, lying still for once. I rubbed my bare hands over my shoulders—my gloves sat on the counter beside the tickets, I ignored them and moved closer to the window studying my reflection. I exhaled, the bruises and cuts on my face were almost magically gone. I feared my midnight swim and dark stranger had much to do with their absence. My next exhale fogged up the chilly glass. I lifted my finger and wrote his name in the condensation.

Drake.

I wiped it away and breathed again, this time I wrote:

Draken. Then beside it I put *Goddess*.

No, that was wrong. My hand flashed out and cleared the foggy glass. I put my mouth right up to it and breathed out all the air in my lungs until the glass had a thick film. I wrote again.

Draken

Aphrodite

Arias

The names from the characters of *Blood and Shadows* stood out in the haze of the mist-spattered window. Tiny droplets—crafted by the condensation—edged the base of my finger paintings, then poured down the glass. The light of the kitchen made them look like little golden pearls.

Beside me my phone rang, I picked it up, answering on the second ring. "Hey Gar, how goes the case?"

"Nothing solid yet," said Gary, skipping the pleasantries. "Your aunt came down to the station today and returned the pin."

"She must have kissed your cheeks a hundred times."

"She did."

"I will never know what you did to make that woman love you so."

"I exude natural charm," joked Gary, there was, however, no humor in his tone. "That tattoo you talked about, the one you said might be on the killer's neck?"

"Yes?"

"It's a gang symbol. They call themselves the Fairhaven Warlocks—if you can imagine. You were right about Lorna. We found her last night. It was a total fluke, there was an electrical fire in the warehouse where they were holding her. James and Ryan were on call and went to put it out. They found her in a crate, her head shaved, almost unrecognizable from a beating, but it was Lorna Parker."

My eyes closed in silent thanks. I would bring aunt Jane an apple pie every day for the rest of her life if she wanted.

"There was a guy with her, we caught him trying to escape the flames. Idiot jumped from the second story and twisted his leg. We have him in custody now, he has that tattoo you mentioned, though he is not the killer. A new recruit from the looks of him, a bad guy for sure—not a murder."

"How can I help?" I asked.

I heard him hesitate. "Could you touch him for me, Cara? I would never ask but…" his voice turned sour. "I think they're sacrificing these girls, I have to stop them."

"Yes." I said. "We do. It's hard for me to go to the station…"

"I know. Me and two of the guys will bring him over to your place in a little bit, is that okay?"

"Yes that's fine." I pushed away the fear, there was no time for it now.

"It's pretty wonderful," said Gary.

"What is?"

"Having our very own superhero."

My cheeks went up in flame and a wash of shyness made me laugh. "Whatever," I said. "I am not super, just strange."

"Super," repeated Gary, and then, "you sure, Cara?"

I assured him I was as I listened to the double set of footsteps running down the hall. We said our goodbyes and I hung up the phone. "Lily?" I called out.

"Yes love," she sang back. "Come and have a coffee. Oh! You're already in here. Gah! I can never tell where voices come from in this house." Lily kissed my cheek. "Have you eaten?"

"No." I gave her an accusatory glance. "Have you?"

"No," stated Lily. "Way too excited to eat. I can't stop smiling, my checks are actually cramping." She looked at my forlorn face. "Aren't you even a little happy about this trip?"

I gave her the only smile I could find, and it felt forced. "No, I am. It just feels so—" I broke off. A chill washed in from the little window facing Wynter haunt. My hands came up and tried to rub the chicken skin off my upper arms. "It just feels rushed Lily, I'm afraid. It's a whole new place, an entirely different set of emotions it will force me to acclimate to. You know how terrible I am at that."

"Posh! Terrible isn't a word I would apply to you, and it's not rushed."

"No, not for you, you've been wanting to do this forever." My sigh slumped my shoulders. "I would love to see Europe, and I want to be with you. I want you to be happy, Lily. I want you to find what you're looking for."

"I have! Well, part of it anyway." Lily reached for the book on the bar stool. It teetered on the edge of the red pillow, she snagged the binding before it toppled. "Whatever!" she said, annoyed at the pillow. "I really should just get rid of them and let practicality win out over my decor obsession." She slapped the Book of Shadows down on the bar, it flipped it open on its own.

"A spell?" I queried.

"A spell," confirmed Lily. "Not just any spell though, It's a good one, says it will bring on an instant, dreamless sleep. Which I thought was rather funny—a person just passing right out every time they take a sip—but it doesn't work like that. Andi told me her mother used it on her and Drake when they were kids. The potion calls for chamomile and rooibos root, which are the normal ingredients of sleepy-time tea. How bad could it be?"

"Well, now you just jinxed us. You put a question like that out to the universe and it dares her to respond. Please don't put a spell on me Lily."

"What if I drink it first?"

"No, Lily."

Lily regarded me through thick, sooty lashes. "Yes, why not? It's pretty much just a tea that you drink right before bed. Something you could get over the counter."

"Except it isn't from over the counter. It's from that awful book."

"Nonsense. There's nothing awful here." Under her fingers a page growled and hissed. "Well maybe one or two things," she admitted. "But not this. I will make it, you will drink it and love it, you'll see. It will be like your great brussel sprout conversion in '08."

I giggled at her, it died in my throat when Andi walked into the kitchen. She had a bundle of sage in one hand, and Hanna's teapot in the other. "Hey, Cara."

"Hi." I said. "I see you're also taking part in this witchery." I tried to make the latter word sound evil, but it came off dusky and enchanting.

"I am," said Andi. "This is a simple thing to do. You know, it was not considered a spell or even wicca a couple thousand years ago. It was simply alchemy, medicine and science. In those times there were far more female doctors than male."

I stretched my arms above my head and spoke through my yawn. "I know. I know. That was a long time ago."

Andi smiled at me, something old, and I thought rather sad flashed in her eyes. It danced away and she set to work filling the kettle and firing up the stove. Lily turned another page in the Book of Shadows, a tuft of dust billowed and something mewled.

"Just be careful, Lily. I don't want one of those monster drawings in there to come alive and slither out." I walked over to refill my glass from the kitchen sink. "Still raining," I told no one in particular.

"In my country," said Andi, her accent thickening. "We believe there is magic in the rain. If that's true, Washington must be the most magical land on earth."

I heard Lily's sigh. "That's a gorgeous way to look at it."

On the stove the kettle whined. The rain moved in layers over the swishing grass, while shapes writhed under the persistent beat of water.

You always see ghosts in the shadows, the girl in my mind said reasonably.

The kettle screamed as thunder shook the floorboards. I turned to face the girls. Lily was up on her knees, dangling precariously on the edge of the barstool. A collection of herbs lay scattered around a cast-iron pot. The pot was one of those that hung over the fire in the old days, where the steam from the boiling water would warm the room, while providing endless lakes of tea. Now, it teemed rosemary, sage, sprigs of fresh lavender, and a bundle of chamomile flowers, white-tipped petals catching the storm light. They smiled up at me, dying in calm repose.

"Careful," said Andi. She set the whistling kettle on the bar and climbed up beside it, ignoring the stool. She covered her bare hand with the fur-rimmed sleeve of her aqua sweater and lifted the lid off the kettle.

"And then I put my fate in your hands," I said again, to the room at large.

"Ah the melodrama," returned Lily.

Andi poured a long stream of water in the pot. The kettle wheezed, then belched out cloudy white vapors, I watched the tiny flowers wilt under the smoldering heat.

Lily read out further directions while Andi used a chopstick to stir the cauldron. I turned back to stare out the window. About six years ago Hanna had told me off for not trying harder to fit in at school. I yelled at her and told her I wanted to be normal. Wanted a white picket fence. The next day, right at the edge of the terrace, stuck in a small outcropping of lawn; stood three prongs of an ebony picket fence, she had hastily painted white. Lily and I left the strange piece of décor where Hanna put it because it made us both laugh. I looked at it now. Through the rumbling thunder I heard the forlorn hoot of an owl. I squinted my eyes, trying to peer through the weaving rain. The singsong squall came again, and a snow white owl landed on the picket fence, its sharp claws digging in the uneven paint.

"Look, guys, this owl is amazing," I said, and barely spared a glance over my shoulder. Patterns of rain fell in waves around the bird, not a drop touched the brilliant feathers. Belting out another lingering hoot, she extended her wings, I saw highlights in the feathers painted in mother-of-pearl. Lily came to stand beside me, holding a steaming cup that smelled like sleep and soothing dreams.

"I know. She really is spellbinding, isn't she?" asked Lily, sniffing her brew.

"You've seen her before?" I replied.

"A couple times over the years. At first I thought she was a figment of my imagination, then I remembered I don't really have one. Now I leave food for her right over there, at the edge of the gardenias." Her fingernail clicked against the window. "She mostly stays in the sky."

I followed her finger to the velvet purple flowers growing against the lip of the stone path leading to the dark tree line. A lone figure stood on the path. Lily's gaze must have followed mine, because I heard her gasp. Ten feet in front of us a large cobblestone rattled. The figure moved closer.

The monsters are coming, Cara. The girl in my mind sang in haunting tones. *Run now, princess, run fast and far—the monsters are here.* A violet flash of lightning cracked in the sky. It showed my mind what we already knew. The rock rattled again, a disjointed hand broke free of the cobblestone path.

Lily screamed. The cup she held, fell from her hands and shattered against the sink. Shriveled herbs, and a little bundle of wilted flowers circled the drain. I swallowed a gulp of air and it stuck like a knife in my throat.

Even here on these hallowed grounds, the dead had come for me.

CHAPTER 14

MIRROR, MIRROR ON THE WALL—
WHO IS THE MOST IMMORTAL OF THEM ALL?

Watch out for the huntsman, my mind's voice trilled. *Run away, he comes for your heart.*

My fingers gripped the edge of the sink until the tips ached. "Not real," I said and squeezed my eyes shut. I pinched my own thigh and gasped.

"Open your eyes, Cara!" demanded Lily, the sharp edges of her voice stitched by threads of pure fear. "We're all freaking awake."

Lightening cracked again, while a second hand burst up from the ground. The figure on the path moved toward us dragging each step; he craned his head to the right, his eyes searching the distant horizon, while the exposed bone of his index his finger pointed at me.

"Cara?" Lily's voice quaked.

"They're here for me," I whispered. My own fear made rage bubble in my gut. I lashed out and flung the little window open. Rain laced in flying pine needles slapped us in the face.

"WHAT DO YOU WANT?" I hollered at the limping monster. "GO AWAY!"

The creature dropped his hand, his head rotated in my direction. His hollowed-out stare locked to mine, then he cracked open his skinless jaw, and roared.

Lily lurched past me, shoved the window closed, and latched it. "We need to get out of here." Her lips had a strange blue undertone, and they trembled.

Andi's reasonable voice came from behind us, her tone impossibly calm. "Are there any weapons in his house?"

"Yes. Two swords, a dagger and a forty-five in the library," said Lily. "Yes, the library." She ran back to the counter and grabbed the Book of Shadows. "We can hide in the library. I think…"

The little kitchen window, shattered, cutting her off. A rock—covered in mud and shards of glass—clunked against the floor, lazily it rolled to our feet.

They're coming to take you? You know that, Cara—you know that, right? my mind asked me. "Yes, I know," I told her. The second I heard the words out loud, I understood how true they were. They were here to take my heart. *Suck it up, Snow White, your story is already written—it dooms you to die.*

Seconds ticked by, the three of us stood like statues in a museum, watching the tableau unfold in front of us, as more skinless bodies clawed their way free of the wet earth. The dead guy who roared at me now stood less than ten feet from the window. Skin clung to the bones of his ribcage, rough red tendons threaded the neck, pulsing like a severed artery. Hanging from a chain stringing his neck was a circular pendant. The rim of the pendant had chunks of black showing through the gold, the ornament swung against the creature's gaping stomach cavity, reminding me of the pendulum on an old grandfather clock, punctually chiming the midnight hour. I looked into a long tunnel of nothing funneling back in his cavernous skull. He opened his mouth and reached for me.

"Come," I heard him say. "A gift of life from the mouth of death."

I would be a liar if I said I was not terrified, but—it also fascinated me. I wanted to run, cover my face, and cry until I woke up or it all went away. I also wanted to go to them. Lily's fingers locked over my wrist, she tugged me back.

"Did that thing just speak?!" Hysteria laced her words.

"Yes," I whispered.

"Do you understand it?" squeaked Lily.

"Yes, did you not?" I whispered.

"No."

"They want me to go with them," I said. It was as if I stood outside myself again, a forlorn, severed vision. I could see the little strands of hair at my nape, see the gooseflesh breaking out all over my skin. I reached out my hand. I had no control. I needed to be with them. I wanted…

"Not bloody likely," said Lily, she jerked my outstretched arm. Hard. Hard enough to snap me back. Through the shattered window the wind howled. Drops of burning sweat splashed against my lashes. I wiped them away.

Lily screamed.

It was a traumatizing sound, and her second scream hit the air before the echo of the first had died. A single skinless hand gripped the French pane, the window frame creaked loudly. Long shards of glass pierced through the fingers and the palm of the hand. More glass tinkled in the sink as another hand came into view. It locked itself beside its partner, and inch by inch, the creature pulled himself up. His decomposing tongue hung from a lipless mouth forming one world only. He held out his hand, its center still pierced by a wide slice of glass. "*Come.*"

"NO!" shouted Lily. She grabbed the cauldron from the bar and tossed the contents in the creature's face. Steam hissing against his ruined lips, the skeletal mouth opened wider to let loose another ear-splitting yell. Chamomile infused sage stuck to the bones, dripped down the old rotting teeth.

Lily grabbed the kettle by the arched handle—yelling as I have never heard her yell before—she swung it at the creature's head. It connected with a metallic clang. The impact jarred her—she stumbled back as the kettle fell from her numb fingers. "Screw this," she said. "I'm getting my keys! Meet me in the garage." There was a hollow crash as the creature pulled himself in the sink, the swaying pendant clunked against the marble. Somewhere in the house another window shattered. A series of booms sounded at the front door, like a hundred fists struck it at once. My hand clutched my chest, the erratic beating of my heart snatched my breath.

"I think we're trapped," cried Lily. In front of me, the skeleton thing swiped. His hand clawed the air dangerously near my face. This time it was Andi who came at him, swinging a cast iron pan. She hit his arm, the blow whacked it clean off the creaking body. The arm clattered against the hardwood floor. Howling, the creature turned to Andi, rage further twisting its face.

"Stay away, vile thing!" hollered Andi, she drew back her arms, teetering slightly from the weight of the pan, then slammed it against his skull and the creature went to his knees. More bodies poured through the window, pressing and slithering against each other, all fighting to be the first through the small space. Holding Lily's hand, I backed into the entrance hall. Andi brandished the pan in front of her like a fiery sword.

"*Stai in spate!*" shouted Andi. The foreign words melodic despite her tone.

Footsteps shuffled in the hall. Shadows moved in the small shafts of flickering lamplight. The thud of feet got closer. The sweet smell of rotting flesh filled my mouth, the taste lingered, slid down my tongue to burn the back of my throat.

The front door blasted open. Creatures—soaked in mud, twigs and torn, dead leaves—poured through the entrance.

"LILY! RUN!" I screamed. Already in mid-motion, no one needed to tell her twice. We locked hands and dashed for the library. I heard Andi bat something out of her way, the sound of dry, crunching bone resonated off the walls. Lily shoved the library door open. The fire had long died and its absence soaked the room in grey shadows. Lily's hand felt up the wall for a second while she searched for the light switch. Andi flew inside, slamming the door behind her.

"Does this thing have a bolt?" Andi's voice shook a little now.

"Down there on the floor," I told her. "One of those old foot-latch things."

"Well, that won't help," said Andi, then she leaned down and twisted the rusted lever in place anyway. Lily ran around the room grabbing books. She tucked a few under her arms, while others she pitched across the room like they had angered her. All the while, skeletal hands pressed and pounded against the west windows.

"We could try to make a break for it, the keys to your beamer are over by the front door," said Lily.

"So are the freaking monsters," I rejoined. I reached for a few books on the verge of falling out of her arms.

"So grab a weapon," said Lily reasonably, sighing she dropped the books at my feet. "In the dresser by the window over there, in the bottom right-hand shelf is Hanna's old revolver, if memory serves, it's loaded."

Lily turned away from me, and gave the stack of books on the ground a forlorn glare. "We have to take those, all of them. Andi, will you grab a few?" She picked up a couple and then set them back on the ground. "Where is that sword? That ninja-looking thing Hanna used to swing around all the time when she thought no one was looking."

"I know what you're talking about," I told her. "I don't know where it is—oh wait, check over there under the cushions."

"Why would it be…?" Lily tossed my purple throw on the floor, the chaise pillows followed. "It's here." She tugged it free, deftly pulling the sword out of its curved sheath. The blade was gunmetal grey and looked wicked sharp.

I walked over and knelt in front of the dresser, then hooked the lace edge of my sleeve over my thumb and forefinger, then used that portion of my hand to open the drawer. In the dull light of the library the Smith and Wesson's shiny body glimmered like a snake. I picked it up, the uncovered part of my hand contacted the barrel, the buzzing in my ears started up and the edges my vision darkened. "No!" The clear part of my mind pushed back at the darkness—a thing I had never done in the past— it vaporized almost instantly, the ringing in my ears stopped. I was conscious mostly of surprise. There was no time to think about what I had just done, I lifted the gun and spun the chamber of the .45 my motions clunky, and unpracticed. Hanna made me shoot this piece a few times before she left. Said 'every pretty girl should know how to fire off a decent shot'.

The pounding increased, the voices beyond howling in unison. Then, our beautiful French windows, which have stood strong for over two hundred years against the forces of Washington State nature, gave way to the persistent pressure of a hundred pounding hands—and shattered.

The dead came pouring through.

Branches and slivers of glass rushed in the room on the tail of a wind carrying a host of keening, vile moans.

Andi threw open the library door, nearly dislodging the stack of books balancing in her arms. A chorus of screams echoed in the hall, a bony hand locked in Andi's silver hair. She yelped in more rage than fear, twisted sharply, and used a large tome to brain the nearest monster. The hand fell from her hair, she threw her body against the door, slamming it closed, it smacked back against her head and Andi's eyes rolled.

"Vile creatures!" she spat. "Either give that thing over, Cara, or shoot."

I lifted the gun, my shaking hands, strangely steady. I did not need to aim. A cluster of skinless bodies writhed in front of me, bones wrapped in shreds of glass-studded flesh. I looked a slimy monster directly in its hollowed out, goo-rimmed eyes and squeezed the trigger. The shot rang against my eardrums, much louder than expected, the recoil was incredible. It flung my arms up, bringing the body of the gun dangerously close to my face. My nostrils filled my mouth with the taste of metal and singed hair. My heart racing I leveled the gun, again. A body lay on the ground. My bullet had blown a fist-sized hole in its stomach. The prone body slowed the approaching creatures as they tripped and stumbled over his splayed limbs. I pulled the trigger again. This time, I braced my legs and took the impact in my core. My bullet hit a head. It exploded. Green goo splattered the west wall, and the decapitated sack of bones crumpled to the floor. I felt my lips kick up at the corners.

I squeezed again. Another head popped like I had pressed a hot needle against an over-inflated balloon. Something which sounded suspiciously like a giggle tumbled out of my mouth. Behind me, viscous fists pounded on the library door, somewhere to the right of me, I heard Andi shout out a curse I did not understand. My fingers caressed the dull surface of the trigger for a second before I pulled it again. This time my bullet found a heart and threw the monster back through the gaping hole in the wall. The dead body fell to the terrace, the heart twitching inside the splintered chest cavity. From it, black blood shot in stuttering spurts, spraying the deck and a small cluster of potted plants.

"Andi, forget the door," screamed Lily. A swish and a thud punctuated her voice, followed by the sound of a limb rolling on the ground.

"I can't!" Andi cried back. "If I let it go… I can't. They're too many. We'll never get out of here."

It was silent for a second before I heard Lily draw a deep breath. "Let them come, then."

"I don't have a weapon," said Andi. "I can't keep throwing books at them."

In front of me, a monster screamed. His mouth opened to show me a few broken teeth hanging onto rotting gums like unwanted assailants. I saw clear to the back of his throat and aimed for it. The discharge of the fifth bullet cracked in the air, his neck exploded. I saw the shards of skin and bone fly out around his floating skull in slow motion.

Humpty Dumpty sat on a wall. The girl in my mind sang in a voice louder than the bullets, every note of the song intensified the ringing in my ears. *Humpty Dumpty had a great fall.* The headless limbs hit the floor. Enraged, the remaining creatures roared, pushing each other to get at me. I aimed into the center of the pack. My shot broke a cluster of them apart, wounding not killing.

"Crap!" I howled.

"There's a box of bullets in that same drawer," said Lily. The door banged on its hinges, again smacking in Andi's head—her stream of foreign curses flowed.

"I can't get back to that drawer," I told her, looking at the spot I had stood only moments ago. Two creatures huddled a few feet from the brassy chest, hands still held out to me in what I could only assume was some sort of entreaty.

"I really think they want me to go with them," I said, to no one in particular. "Where do you think they want to take me?"

Lily growled, slashing her sword through the air. An arm hit the ground. She swung again and lopped off a head. A broken body collapsed at our feet. "Look at these disgusting things!" she wheezed on every intake of breath. "They don't want to take you anywhere good."

"I am going for those bullets," I said.

Lily did not argue, turning to face me she hoisted her sword a little higher. Still absent their eternal tremor, my hand grasped the top of the gun. I lifted it over my head, prepared to use it as a club. A shadow rushed past my vision, I flinched away a second too late. Two hands reached around my throat from behind. In the first second all I registered was the warm, slimy touch—like I was in the clutches of a giant leech—then, the hands squeezed. My mouth opened, gasping. Black and red spots burst in front of my eyes and I felt them bulge. Through the strangling haze, I saw Lily's face, her beauty nearly obscured in a twisted mask of rage. She drew back her arm and thrust her sword inches above my head. There was a rending scream as the death grip on my neck dropped away.

I coughed, stumbled, and fell into her arms. Each breath cut at my battered throat. "Okay, maybe I was wrong about the not hurting thing."

"You're right," said Andi, looking at me, something dark and indefinable in her eyes. "They don't want to hurt you. They're calling to you."

"We have to get through the room and out that window," gasped Lily. "It's our only chance."

"I am letting go of this door now," said Andi. "The second I do that we need to run." A massive bang punctuated Andi's words and her body shuddered. A creature on my left whimpered. His mouth chewed a word—his lips moved like he tried to spit it out, but the uneven twitching of his shredded tongue refused to let him.

"Leisha," the voice finally groaned. Then it lunged, two hands racing at me like costume claws in a funhouse. I drew back my arm and threw my fist in the monsters face. Hot skin smooshed under my clenched fingers as my knuckles hit brittle bone. His head snapped back. I hit him again. Still near me, Lily stuck her sword through the broken rib cage of another. Andi was beside us. Her fist lashed out, and she kicked the monster nearest her

in the gut. It stumbled back. Andi spun her body in a full three-sixty and kicked another in the face.

"NOW!" yelled Andi. "RUN!"

We dashed to the window. A hand reached for me, I hit it away with the butt of the revolver. Cold air washed over my face. In front of us the glass curtains flapped in the wind, mimicking the ghoulish shrouds of dead brides.

"Leisha." Voices came to me from the wind; from the droplets of rain from the house, from the ground itself—they touched the core of my soul. In the distance the dark tree line shimmered, blurring in and out of focus. I stepped over the raised lip of the shattered window frame. Glass jutting out of the white boards stabbed upward—deadly, storm-lit blades. Then, we were outside standing in the rain. More creatures crowded the driveway and shoved their dripping bones against the front door.

Something struck me hard on my cheekbone and I saw stars. I felt the skin there split and hot blood spill. I had a terrible vision of landing on the glass, imagining how it would feel as it cut through tendon to slice my spine.

All the king's horses, my mind whispered. *And all the king's men, couldn't put Cara back together again.* A hand reached out and threaded long bony fingers through my hair. This time my scream was giant and full of fearful rage. More of a growl, really. Lily spun and caught my flailing hand.

For a strange second I teetered between Lily's death grip and the hand clawing at the roots of my hair. Then, the monster's fingers splayed, cold fingertips pressed to my skull. The pain was instant, far worse than any human touch. I bit down on my injured lip and tasted blood.

The dead surrounded Lily. She swung her sword at them. With most of her strength focused on holding me, her movements were lopsided and clumsily. Creatures slithered over the wet deck. One reached out and grabbed Lily's ankle. Lily tried to step on her attacker's head while Andi kicked him in the spine.

Clawed fingers dug in my skull. The pain inside my brain was alive. Attacking me. Lily roared and tugged on my hand. I saw the veins in her neck bulge as she gritted her teeth. Suddenly, the hand in my hair let go. The momentum of the release sent us sprawling forward. We hit the deck in a flurry of muddy leaves, glass, and flailing limbs. I blinked and rolled onto my back; an aura of skeletal faces looked down on me, a dozen feet painted in bloody mud closed an invisible circle on the ground. As one, the monsters reached for us.

"No!" said Lily. A hand hurtled at her face, she caught its attached arm mid-air. "No, you will not touch her!" It was like her final word ignited the air. Scorching crimson flames edged in brilliant violet shot from her hands and coursed up the offending arm. The monster turned sightless eyes to the flames and wailed in fear.

Wearing twin expressions of stupefied shock, Lily and I watched her hot flames eat at the screaming creature's loose flesh, gobbling up the old bones. In seconds a small pile of blackened ashes fluttered to the dirty deck at our feet.

I swung to face my sister. "Did you...?" There was no way to finish my own sentence.

Lily gave me a look, one that confirmed the impossibility of it all, then reached for the next monster. Another rush of flames, so beautifully deadly, poured from her hands. Despite the water soaking the ground, the tongues of fire spread, licking over the deck, lighting up the creatures like bushels of dry wheat. Behind us, somewhere in the depths of the gripping darkness, more things moaned and wailed—around us everything burned.

Lily locked her hands on another creature. It tried to shake her, but her flames were too quick. He was ashes before his scream touched the air. She reached for another. "Run, Cara! Get out of here. NOW!"

Lily's eyes rolled back in her head until only the whites remained. Milky liquid rushed down her cheeks and more flames pumped from her splayed hands.

"You will not. You will not take Cara from me." Lily's head fell forward, her golden hair tumbled over her face, spilling across the deck. Through her veil of hair she looked at me out of a pupilless glare. "Run, Cara. RUN!" The flames in her hands died and she pitched forward.

I caught her head before it hit the deck.

"Cara," said Lily one final time, choking on her broken whisper, "Cara. Run." Her slender body went limp and she fainted, open eyes staring sightless at the angry, flashing sky.

I caught her head before it hit the deck, and held her in my arms, engulfed by smoky rings of her dying wildfire watching the last of those who had dared to follow us onto the deck, turn to piles of disintegrating ash. Embers danced around my head like crimson fireflies, or little drops of glowing blood, and I realized our future is not composed of a single thread. Rather, a tapestry of shifting threads, they wove around me, carrying faded memories and broken visions. In that moment, kneeling on bloody knees, a thought came to me. The same one I always have in the dreams; the mantra which refuses to leave me. I did not appreciate the thought, it made me feel weak and so incredibly powerless. Yet, kneeling in this pile of ashes and bones, surrounded by burning cinders, ridding the edges of leaping flames—the desperate thought persisted: Drake will come. Drake will save me.

■ ■ ■

Lily's white sockets stared out to the great nothing, filled to the brim by those milky, swirling mists. A stream of snowy liquid ran from each corner of her eye in thick, gelatinous rivers that cut through the grit coating her cheeks. I pushed a lock of hair off her forehead.

"Lily," I whispered, trying to wipe at the dirt. Under it, her skin was chalk white. "Lily, come back." There was no response. I told myself not to panic, that I had not really expected one.

"Lily. Lily, please wake up!" I shook her and thought about how wrong I had been to let my disbelief and deep denial blind me to what had been right in front of my eyes. *Not real? NOT REAL?* My mind screamed. What an idiot I was. All of this had always been way too real.

"Is she okay?" croaked Andi. I looked up, blinking back my tears. Andi crawled to us on hands and knees, blood pouring from a cut on her cheek. I could see some of her hair stuck in a clump over her right brow, a dark substance clung to it, maybe mud, or blood—perhaps a blend of both.

"Is she breathing? Check her pulse."

"She's breathing," I said. "Her pulse is weak, but I can feel it. She was like this the other day, and she came back." I closed my eyes, tracking each pulse, listening to each ragged little breath. I wondered if Lily knew fire could pour from her hands, and if she had known, how long had she been hiding it from me? The thought hurt, and I felt incredibly selfish. A small pulse of energy flowed from her bloody palm, it was weak and scary.

"Lily." My voice broke over her name. "Lily, come on, please."

"The fire?" asked Andi, and I could not stop hearing that extra note in her voice, that thread I did not understand. "She's done that before?"

"No, not the fire just…just this scary trance." Suddenly, Lily's breath hitched in her chest. I jumped and pressed my ear to her heart, listening to every beat.

"You were brave back there, Cara," said Andi. I could not see her face, but her soft voice sounded surprised that bravery had been one of the flash weapons in my sad arsenal. I did not mind her tone. I surprised myself.

"You know…"Andi cleared her throat. I could feel her struggle so I waited, just looked at her pretty face, and old, sad eyes. There was a hard element to Andi, like if someone wore her down even a little, scary edges would emerge.

"You must feel quite confused," Andi finally said. My sudden laugh was a terrified bark I could not quite keep in.

Andi smiled. "Yes, understatement of the millennium, I know. It's just, I never thought about you as an American girl," she held up her hand, but it was unnecessary. I was not going to say anything. "I mean a girl with her own mind, thoughts and beliefs," she explained. "You know, a strong woman, a self-aware human."

"I am many things, Andi, I don't know if strong makes the list." Then, "when did you think of me at all?"

Andi swayed on her knees, her hand reached for me. I took it. Our fingers touched. Hot pain exploded in my brain and rushed up my arm. I gritted my teeth and ignored it.

"Thank you," said Andi, letting me go. "I'm so dizzy, I almost fainted—" Abruptly, her words snapped off in a squeal, her mouth fell open, she took a breath—a whispered scream. Andi's eyes dropped to her chest, mine followed—I felt them expand in total horror. A jagged blade stabbed out from between her ribs. Time teetered on the tip of that blade. My eyes flew back to Andi's face. Her expression was a strange mixture of rage, pain and shock. Behind her quivering shoulders stood a creature; ominous as a looming tornado, shrouded in a cloak of rain. Dispassionately, the monster withdrew his sword. His head turned and his gutted eyes found my face. Andi crumpled onto the deck and did not move.

Something inside me snapped. I heard a voice screaming her name, over and over. A broken record locked to a single sound. I realized the voice was mine. My hands slipped on the bloody, mud-smeared deck and splinters bored into my palms. I barely felt them. When I got to her body, I pressed my hands against the wound. Shocks of pain attacked my arms, but it was much less than before. Red blood bubbled and pumped up between my fingers, behind me the growls grew louder. Her blood ran over my bare fingers, got lost in the grooves of my skin, my world darkened—I let it. The visions came, and told me who she truly was, I suppose I had already known.

I closed my eyes and saw her standing beside Drake in an elevator I knew well, riding up to save me from throwing myself off the ledge, just a few days ago. "You can't deny me this!" shouted Andi. "She must remember, it is the only way I can have him back. You killed him, you owe me this!"

The visions pulsed and I saw tears in Drake's eyes. "Don't you think I want that more than anything in the world?" he said. "She can't remember, not truly. If Aphrodite wakes, it will all be over. This world is not built to deal with those old gods, it will break. Cara can live without remembering, no one remembers their past lives these days."

Andi shook her head, her eyes flashed silver fire, but her skin was deathly pale. "Arias will be the end of us all," she vowed.

Under my hands, Andi's body shook, I pushed the visions away. "Oh, Andi," I started to sob in pronounced gulps that shook my shoulders. "I am so sorry. This is all my fault." I thought about dashing into the house, finding a phone and calling for help. I thought about screaming for someone. Anyone. Then, I knew not a soul would hear me over the storm, and I would never make it past the monster guarding me, holding the bloody sword. I coughed on the hot sobs in my throat, wracking my brain for a plan. There was nothing, only more bubbling blood, like she was a strange form of spider and I pulled streamers of red silk from her chest.

Andi turned her head to me. Her movements were jerky, and her body shook, making me feel as if I held shock pedals to her chest instead of my hands. A little pool of blood collected at the corner of her mouth and trickled down her chin. I tried to wipe it gently away, but only succeeded in smearing a streak of it down her white neck. "Cara," she coughed, splattering my face with drops blood and saliva.

"No, hush, don't talk right now, you'll be fine." I tried to apply more pressure to the wound to stop the endless flow. It was useless.

"You have too…the book. Blood and Shadows." Andi's voice, small and weak, fell away. The pain from touching her lessened, I imagined I could hear her dying.

"Shhh. Don't talk, it will be alright." *Never.* My mind argued. *It will never be all right again.*

I held one hand tight against the gushing hole in Andi's chest and used the other to unzip my jacket. Moving carefully, I pulled my arm free. I switched hands and repeated the process. One handed I wadded the jacket, then pushed it up against the wound. Blood soaked through the down fibers almost instantly.

I had that dreamy feeling again; the kind where you want to scream but can not, where it is run or die, only your legs are locked by unbreakable, invisible chains. A gentle paralysis shrouded me, it seemed I could do nothing save cry, and watch her die.

The creature took a step toward me. Soul and body numb, my mind came alive.

Run, Cara, run! Don't go to him! Don't let him take us. The girl in my mind cried, I felt her better this time and I wanted to cuss at her. Don't let him take us? Us? It was me he would be taking. My body. My life.

"*Leisha,*" the creature croaked in those broken words I understood, I shuddered at the sound of them. Against my hands Andi's body shook for what I thought might be the last time. The crimson river of silk slowed its flow. The spider was running out of thread. In my head the girl screamed. Painful sounds that dug bloody furrows in my mind. I tried to shut her away. She refused to be silent. I knew any moment I would scream with her.

"*Come, Leisha,*" the creature persisted, holding out his hand to me, all slick and painted in Andi's blood. He stood there, eyeless and dead. It seemed he searched my soul, and I felt he had no right when I could see no evidence of his own. He waited and watched, watched me like an old relic from an abandoned spook house. The lead actor in a ghost story. This however, was no campfire tale. I felt the reality of the moment I was in more vividly than anything I'd ever felt before, the worst of it was, I wanted to go. So did the girl in my mind. A part of me also wanted to I hide my face, crawl over to Lily and bury it in her chest. Listen to her heart beat, count each tiny, halting breath, use my presence to somehow keep her here, next to me. That part was small, the larger part of me knew this had always been coming. Since the beginning it had only been a matter of time. I let go of my blood-soaked jacket and stood up. Even though I tried not to, even though nearly everything in me wanted to run, I filled my lungs full of burnt air, and followed him.

■　■　■

I was a phantom. My feet glided over the grass. I felt that hook attached to my ribs, somewhere an unseen hand held the line and reeled me through the storm like the ghost I was. The ghost of the dead girl who shrouded me. I was the dream. The memory. The specters of my aunts the reality. They stood under the iron arches of our Wynter haunt watching me. When the lightning cracked and spit sparks overhead, the aunts pulsed. They flickered wildly, a white glow that lit the night and illuminated the cobblestones, little flashes that blinked in and out like broken halogen bulbs

Locked inside some dark room in my mind, I was screaming. Every swish of my bare, bleeding feet took me farther from Lily. Lily, who was lying there in the rain alone and hurt. Suddenly, all the little details of her, the ones that made Lily, *Lily* were clear in my mind. I saw soft curlers in her hair, piled up in that way which made her look like a famous actress from a forgotten time. I saw the way she wrinkled her nose as she read, and she way she smiled when she slapped away my '*evil hand*' that always picked at her food. I thought about her crying, laughing and angry, then I thought of never seeing her face again and I did not want to think at all, because there was also Andi dying, the last of the blood slowly draining from the ripped cavity in her chest. I could not even turn my head, look behind me and say goodbye with one last glance. My eyes remained fixed on the creature in front of me, and the globs of skin swaying under loose pieces of wet cloth. The metal arch of Wynter haunt rushed over my head and the plaque by my left hand told me again that they rested.

They are sleeping, my mind whispered. *Resting. You must not remember. We must not wake them. Sleeping.*

If I was not crazy, and I did not think I was—not *that* kind of crazy anyway—then I knew I remembered at least a little. When I spoke my voice had a distant dreamy quality, and it felt right as if one should never use forceful words in a dream. "It's all my mine. Isn't it? It's all ours. The book, the story, Drake, even Andi. Somehow they are all ours. The life of that poor priestess. It's mine. Yours. Ours." In my head I felt the girl give an imperceptible nod, but she said, *it's a fantasy. A story. Nothing more. No reality. No peaceful conclusion. Only death. If you want to live, you must not remember. If you remember, we can only die.*

My eyes searched the darkness of the graveyard. My aunts ghosted along the headstones, their ethereal shadows passing slowly over the graves.

"*Go back,*" they told me. "*Go back.*"

I was angry again—it made no sense. Did they not know there was no going back for me?

Twenty feet from Grandmother Rosen's grave the creature stopped. Time had gouged the cobblestone path in this spot and big chunks of earth framed the thick vines crawling up between old, ruptured stones.

They will take us down...take us so far down! The girl in my mind screamed.

I watched in utter stillness. No running or crying this time. No helpless pleas of denial as the ground once more quaked and roared. I watched it break apart the way it had on that dark night behind Larry's. It curled and rumbled like earth at the base of a rupturing volcano. Tonight, I did not lose my footing because I floated, swayed gently back and forth in the air. I waited, watched, and let it happen. Screaming inside, I waited because it was all I could do.

The ground exploded, attacking itself. A civil war broke out between the dirt, rocks, and flailing roots. The quake hurled a sharp piece of cobblestone at me. I watched it strike my bare forearm, watched the chiseled tip of the rock carve a bloody grove in my skin. A long stream of blood ran down to my wrist, and my right hand twitched wanting to wipe it away, I remained motionless. Only the rise and fall of my chest told me I breathed, informed me I still lived.

The storm light was all but gone now and the colors around me sharpened until I felt like I stared at an over saturated television screen. Green smoke flowed from the deep gouges in the earth, and under my feet I heard the crackle of flames. My mind went to Lily again. I imagined her awake and looking for me. I could almost hear the fear in her voice as she called my name.

There was a popping sound, and a pillar of green flames jetted up from the torn earth. More pillars of the same fire shot up around me in a pentagram formation. I felt my back arch and the jerking movement flung my arms behind me, nearly clapping my hands behind my back. My hair lifted on the wind, I felt the flames run cool fingers through its long strands. It did not burn me.

I hung in a semi backbend, starting at the sky and felt that tug under my ribs, my body moved forward again. Nightgown trailing behind me like a shroud, I drifted toward the center pillar. Even more than the gravestones, the fiery pillars looked at home in Wynter haunt, like they had always been there, unseen behind the veil, the veil that hides all those things we do not want to see, those realities we refuse to believe.

The flames flowed up and down in lava lamp fashion, fat bubbles of oil floating in water. I drifted closer and realized the bubbles were bodies. Hundreds of opaque bodies. They swam in the center of the green flames, clustered and trapped as fish trapped in a tank. Eyes wide and sightless in death, open mouths frozen in their final screams. I did not need to be a mythology major to know what I was looking at. The fabled lake of souls was not water, but fire. Cool green fire and I was swimming in it.

Vines crept up the sides of the aqua pillars connecting them to the quaking stones. It appeared the service of the vines was to feed the fire while simultaneously keeping it stable, grounded to the broken, angry earth that held the portals open. I knew where the portals led. I knew they lead to Cerberus, Hades and the endless lake of souls. All the things Arias feared. I knew these things the same way I knew some part of my soul was unknown to me. I was Cara now, yet some small, hidden part of me was her. It was impossible and insane, but every ounce of my soul told me—once that life and love had been mine.

I continued to drift. Burning air washed over my face as I passed through the pillar of fire to the hollow dark center. I came to a slow stop; my feet hovering over a deep black well of nothing. I was the bulb in the lava lamp. Through the flames I could see the dead army—those who had survived Lily's fire—hobbling to the pillars. As one they gathered their bones and jumped into the flames. The creature who led me here stepped in my pillar. Fire enveloped its limbs before it plummeted to the yawning darkness. I watched its endless fall until the thick blackness finally swallowed the firelight.

"*It is too late,* my mind told me. W*e must fall too. It binds us, we are lost!*

My head snapped back even further, I heard more than felt the breath rush from my lungs. I could see creatures leaping into the flames, watched more flailing limbs disappear into the abyss. I should fall with them. Knew that was the next act. I did not. Slowly, I realized that this unknown thing could call me, even compel me. It could not take me. Not this last final step. Some part of me may belong to a forgotten, dead priestess—the rest of me was Cara Wynter and she had a choice. I knew it and so did the unseen force in the darkness.

"*You're* bound and lost!" I told my mind. "I am not." Through the haze of the green I saw the aunts. Old, young and all ages in-between. They studied me.

"Cara," they said. "Your name is Cara Wynter. Blood of our blood."

"Cara!" called another voice, it was stronger than the rest. This time there was no question in my mind. I do not even know why there had been. It was Hanna. It had always been her.

"*You can not have her!*" shouted Hanna. My wall of fire rippled around me and shot up further into the interlocking trees, beneath me the darkness writhed.

"*She is ancient blood, and she is mine.*" Lightning crackled and the aunts flickered. Hanna's voice trailed on until the wild wind, washed away the sound. "*Cannot have her. Mine. She is mine.*"

In that moment and perhaps for the first time, I saw my life as something precious, a gift given only to me, and I had no intention of losing it. On the heels of that decision I felt the paralysis slowly leave my body, almost as if it had been waiting for me to decide. My body remained suspended, but my limbs were once again my own. I wiped my hands over my face and pushed a skein of hair off my forehead. My skin felt wet and clammy. Suddenly, there was another pull under my ribs, stronger than all the others combined, I battled to resist it.

"No!" I told the darkness. My arms stroked at the air and my legs kicked, as if I were struggling to get my head above water.

I heard no words, no sounds save the crackle from the fiery green lake of bodies, and the surge of the storm. Something stronger, older and more powerful than any of the aunts commanded my descent. Lily's face flashed in my mind. Then, I saw Drake—his eyes burning in the face of every swimming ghost.

"I won't. I won't leave them!" I screamed. The darkness ignored me and I shot downward at an incredible speed. Wind buffeted my face and lifted my hair off my neck. I raised my arms above my head, tried to grab a hold of empty sky, kicking my feet as every ounce of me fought the darkness, fought for my life in a way I had never fought for anything before. The whole episode probably lasted less than ten seconds, but in that space of tick-tocks time was nothing and it felt I battled for an eternity.

A hand shot through my smoky pillar and grabbed my ankle. I shouted out some garbled denial and kicked at it. It was like kicking at a rock. The strength radiating from the grip was unshakeable. I registered the skin under my toes was warm and smooth, not the corroded slime I had been expecting. I stopped struggling and looked down. Through the flames I saw him. The cold wind lashed his hair across his face, but I would have known those amber eyes anywhere.

"Drake."

"Cara! Grab my hand!" I barely heard his voice over the roar of the pillars. He thrust another arm through the fire, I smelled burning hair as his flesh began to ignite.

"No! Let go!" I screamed. "It's hurting you."

Drake ignored my desperate commands for him to save himself. A creature launched from the edges of the shadowed headstones and jumped on Drake's back. Roaring my name he yanked one hand from the fire, reached backward, and took hold of the creature by the neck. I saw his fingers sink in the flesh before he ripped the thing from his back and slung it in my pillar. The burning body shot past me. Then another and another. He fought them one handed, never letting go of me. I pushed at the air. It pulled back. I threw my body toward his hand, gulping convulsively as I felt my fingers lock around his wrist.

"You cannot take her!" Drake yelled at the earth, the flames and the sky. "This is Cara Wynter. She is not yours!" His fingers linked through mine. Tendrils of black smoke shot up from the abyss and wrapped around my ankles like phantom ropes.

"Drake," I said, exhaustion deepening my voice. "I can't fight anymore. It's pulling me down."

"It cannot have you!" he shouted. "Look at me, Cara! Please fight it, little one. Don't let go of me."

I closed my eyes. "Okay. I won't!" I said. I meant it. I kicked with every ounce of fight I had in me. Drake dragged me to the wall of flames. The darkness hauled me back, despair threatened to strangle me.

I opened my eyes. His face was inches from mine. Embers decorated his hair and I could smell more burning skin. "Cara," he pleaded. Then, for a sliver of a moment Cara was gone. The girl in my mind had my eyes and my heart and they remembered him. I knew the curve of his face, the shape of his gorgeous eyes. I knew the sounds he made when he slept. I knew the pain he felt when I died. The same pain that still lived in his eyes. The darkness pulled again. My body revolted. I was no longer in control. It controlled me. The girl in my mind had joined the fray.

Drake yelled my name. It sounded like he called me his love, but the din of the flames and my own heart made it hard to be sure. My arms broke free of the pillar. My left hand grabbed a fistful of his hair. I locked my right arm around his shoulders and dug my fingers into his bicep. A blast of air rocked me. It felt like a giant ghost hand made of fire and smoke slapped me in the back as green flames rushed over my skin, then I was free. The flames and the darkness let me go. Together, Drake and I tumbled down to the freezing earth.

"Cara, Cara," his voice broke over my name. I tried to take a breath, my lungs resisted. I had a thousand things I wanted to say, more questions than I knew how to phrase, I barely whispered his name. He reached out, cupped my cheek. I turned my head and kissed his singed palm. My intent gaze never left his. There was so much in his eyes, so many unsaid words burning there. Instead of terror I felt at home, as if for the first time in my whole life I was finally awake.

Drake made a low sound and took my face in both his hands. My fingers knotted in his hair and I gasped in a screaming breath as his lips touched mine—hesitantly at first, just a breath, a thought—then, we crashed together like colliding galaxies—bright, spellbinding light blinded me. His mouth was scalding hot, his lips firm and wet with rain heated the blood in my veins. His tongue touched mine, I tasted him and I was lost. So lost. His hands sunk into my hair, he deepened the kiss, tilting back my head and drawing me closer. He kissed me for an eternity and when he leaned back to place his lips against my forehead, it was too soon. Our ragged breaths were loud in the echoing graveyard. I touched his cheek, looked into his eyes and I knew I would remember my first kiss until death did me part.

"Drake?" I whispered, too shaken for coherent thought.

Drake made a deep sound in his throat. "I'm sorry. Are you all right?" he asked. His voice muffled by my mouth. His hands did a perfunctory sweep over my shoulders and back, much the same as he had done the night of the bike accident. "I didn't think I would do that," he muttered. I assumed to was referring to the scalding kiss and blushed. "I wanted to," he continued. "Just didn't think I would." He stopped to brush the shell of my ear and run his finger over the curve of my bottom lip. "Do you hurt anywhere? Are you burnt? How bad is the pain?"

"Not bad," I lied. It was not important. His question made me think of Lily's flames, then I only saw Andi. Her eyes wide and bloodshot, a sword thrust through her chest.

"Andi!" I dug my fingers in his back while he rocked me. "Andi. They stabbed her. I tried to stop it, I couldn't. I couldn't even stay, or help her. They took me. Oh, I think that's a lie," my voice shattered. "I...I...w...went with them."

"Hush, Cara, hush. It's all right, she will be just fine. A host of cops already surrounded the manor when I got here."

"Gary, Ryan are they...is everyone...?"

"Everyone is fine," he soothed. "They took Andi to St. Joseph's Medical. Lily's okay too. She's sleeping now."

"Lily," I felt a dizzying flood of relief. "She...she woke up? Her eyes?" Behind his head my hands balled into fists, tugging against the curls that gathered at the base of his neck. "Did you see her eyes? Were they blue?"

Drake smiled and it made his harsh features so beautiful they were alien. "Very," he said. "She wanted to come find you. I convinced her to stay."

"Convinced?" I echoed. "Doubtful."

The sadness in Drake's eyes disappeared, replaced by that brilliant smile of his which lit their corners. "She adamantly refused all my begging and pleading. Fortune alone, made her pass out again when the paramedics got there," he said. "It was a good thing too—she looked ready to crawl through this graveyard on her hands and knees. I had the paramedics check her. Extremely dehydrated, but stable. I have to tell you though—your home is not so stable. It's a battleground."

My hands fell away from him, I sat up, rubbing harshly at my sore eyes. "Yes, I suspect it would be."

"I got there just in time to see you walking away," he said. "I called out to you." I heard censure in his tone. It bothered me.

"I didn't hear you," I said honestly. "I didn't hear much." My voice broke. "Where were you?"

The smile drained away and the snarl returned to twist his lips. "I was trying to negotiate a contract with my father. It's not important now. I failed, at any rate. I have been rejected on many fronts tonight."

The tightness in my throat was nearly unbearable. "You lied to me!" I blurted. "You said you didn't know who I was. I touched Andi's blood, blood doesn't lie. I know who you are." I gulped, hardly able to believe my own next words. "Who your father is."

Drake flinched like I struck him, slowly he closed his eyes. "You remember?" his toneless voice shook, and I heard real horror in the words.

"Remember, no I don't. Not really. But, I was there, so I know. I know you've been lying to me from the beginning. The meeting at the Space needle wasn't chance," I accused.

He reached for me, then stopped himself at the last second. "I never meant to lie, I only wanted to keep you safe."

I gaped at him. "Tell me, when does protection become deception?"

"Cara…I…"

I cut him off. "You know I am going to make you tell me everything," I said, knowing it would not be now, I could not remember a time when I had ever felt more exhausted. I looked at the ground, saw the remnants of fire on the stone. I stared at the fluorescent green goo that now splattered the haunt, and a part of me did not care if he lied, he had saved me, fought for me when I was too tired to battle for myself. "Thank you for coming," I whispered. Taking his hand, I ran my index finger down his scarred palm. "I knew you would."

He chucked me under the chin. "Doesn't seem like you needed me. From the look of your house, you three put up quite a fight."

"Yeah, we did. It was horrible, but kinda awesome at the same time."

Drake said nothing. He turned my hand over and kissed my ring, the ring from the forest that had not yet found its way off my finger. Then, he stood up and lifted me into his arms as if silk and moonlight spun my bones. His lips fell against mine again and I closed my eyes. "Come, Cara," he whispered against my mouth. "I'll take you home."

CHAPTER 15

STRANGE LITTLE TIME SPELL

Giant swirls of steam fogged up the bathroom mirror. I streaked my hand across the glass, then studied my reflection. Just below a new cut on my chin, a band of blue-green bruises decorated my neck like some kind of gruesome choker. I had a vivid, flashing memory of that dead hand squeezing my throat. My every movement was pain filled, each sparking jolt made my nerves jerk and tremble. I took off my thin robe and nightgown—both stiff from mud and Andi's blood—and tossed them in the hamper. I tried to wash the dried blood off my chin. It stung horribly, so I gave up. I let my hands fall to the protruding lip of the sink and dropped my head, exhausted.

My own head fell, the head of my reflection—did not.

The face in the mirror remained upright, staring forward, gaze locked on something in the distance. I stumbled back. My legs hit the edge of the oval tub, my hand clawed at my heart. In the mirror my reflection smiled at me.

I righted myself. My heartbeats bashed against my palm. I squeezed my eyes closed. *Count to ten and breathe. There's nothing there, but the imaginings of your exhausted mind.* I believed *that* even less than I believed everything would be fine. I opened my eyes and turned my head from side to side. My reflection remained still, her vacant gaze fixated on that unseeable thing, a haunting smile flirting along the edges of her lips.

She was me, and she was more. In wonder, I stared at our face, watched as the bruises slowly faded. The cut on my forehead stitched together until there was nothing but a clean strip of skin. Soft red bled into my colorless lips, the green in my eyes lightened until they glowed the aqua of a dawn-touched sea. Golden coins and plump rubies threaded through a strand of pearls, wrapped my forehead like a crown. Around my neck was a slave collar of ivory, and mother-of-pearl. I watched my hair lengthen, darken into a crimson so rich it was nearly black.

"I almost remember you," I told her. "Arias." I felt the truth of the word. "I almost remember."

The image in the mirror shivered like the word *remember* threw a rock in a crystal-clear lake.

In the mirror her lips moved soundlessly, I heard the familiar voice in my mind. *"Must not remember. For us, to remember is to die."*

"Coward," I told her.

"What comes will come, Cara. Over the years I have learned it is the definition of insanity is to fear the inevitable."

"And death is inevitable for us?" I asked.

My reflection shook her beautiful locks, the golden coins clanged together making a sad music. *"Must not remember."*

"Oh?" I said at last, so angry in that moment that I could have happily shattered the mirror with my fist. "Oh, I think we must," I told her. I told myself. "I really think we must." I stepped in the shower and let the hot water spray my face.

■   ■   ■

In my bedroom I put on another nightgown, this one watered black silk, it had sleeves that fell to my fingertips and ribbons on the hem. I pulled it over my head, feeling better when it settled around my shoulders. Over all tonight had not been that bad, a scene from a horror movie to be sure, but pretty alright in the end. I fought monsters—real live zombie things. I battled darkness itself—and I kissed Drake. Thinking about him made that thing clench in my heart again. He had lied to me. Well not lied exactly. Was omitting to mention a truth like mine not the same thing?

I ambled down the hallway I have walked a thousand times, the one that takes me from sleep to food. The lamps on the wall still burned their yellow flames, their halo of light small, all but obscured by the dove-grey morning. Because of the shattered windows throughout the house, I was expecting some whistling wind or pattering rain sounds, the huge manor, however, was dead quiet. The shadows were dim and it took a moment for my eyes to adjust to all the shapes. During the monster fight, something had knocked two rather large paintings off their perch, and shards of crystalline glass littered the floor.

"Sorry, aunt Paula," I said, as I stepped over the first, shattered, face-planted frame. I did not need to see her old, stern eyes, they had watched me my whole life. It was kinda nice to have her starting judgementally at the floor for once.

The doorbell rang and this time I did not jump, scarier things than loud noises existed in my world. I opened the door, not bothering to look through the keyhole, the monsters would not bother to knock—I was sure I could deal with anything else.

Gary stood at the base of the marble stairs, looking up at me in concerned confusion, though he seemed less surprised by the carnage than I would have expected, he barely gave the epic destruction of my front door a second glance. Mud caked his shoes, and his uniform was rain soaked. On the soggy ground beside him knelt a handcuffed prisoner. The prisoner was most likely nineteen or twenty, though he looked a lot younger. He had a dirty face, and skinny freckled limbs poking out of his mud splattered T-shirt. Beneath the cuffs, red rings stood out in harsh relief against his skin—the red rings told me he was a fighter, Gary was too kind to allow such a thing—they were self inflicted. His brown eyes were huge in his white face, they met my gaze and his expression turned defiant. Keeping eye contact, he spat on the ground.

"Witch!" he hissed. Gary smacked the back of his head—the kid pitched forward.

"Cara, thank god you're okay!" said Gary.

Which one? I thought and walked down the stairs. When I was in arms reach the boy growled and dove at me. Spit and bits of gravel flew from his mouth as he shouted. I waited, my face devoid of emotion, watching Gary wrestle him back to the ground. The headlights of the parked cruiser flashed twice, casting us in shadow while illuminating sheets of falling rain. Ryan Johnson got out of the car and slammed the driver's door, sauntered over and stepped on the kid's calf, the boy howled and fell still.

"You good, Saint?" asked Ryan, kicking a clump of wet mud off his boot.

"Fine." Gary wiped his hands on his pants and gave me an apologetic glance. "We came by earlier."

"I know, I heard you got here just in time. Thanks Gar, you always save the day. You too Ryan, thank you so much."

Ryan touched the brim of his Police cap casting a shadow over his full lips and dark skin. He moved to the prisoner's left, took his arm and lifted him to his feet. The thought of fighting back flashed in the boy's doe eyes, but he looked at the man who out weighed him by a hundred some pounds and reconsidered his strategy.

"You know we'd do anything for you Cara," said Ryan. "A man came by a few minutes after we got here…"

"Drake," Gary put in, sounding like the name left a bad taste in his mouth.

"Yeah that was it, he didn't give us a second name. He saw you walking to that graveyard and took off after you before we could say anything."

"He told us the wounded girl was his sister," said Gary. "We figured you knew him."

"I argued to let him go," Ryan cut in. "Gary thought we should shoot to kill."

I smiled. "I'm glad you didn't. He's a friend."

"I had to step over a few burning corpses to get to Lily," said Gary. I tried to search my mind for an explanation, it was unnecessary, however, he was still talking. "It's them," he grunted. "The Fairhaven Warlocks— points on originality for that one—" he told the prisoner, then turned back to me. "You would not believe the things we've seen in the last few days."

"Try me." I said, then I squared my shoulders, stretching out my hand. "Let's get this over with."

"Ain't nothing to get over," the boy hissed. "I'm a high priest, not telling you shit!"

"You won't have to," I said, pressing a fingernail to the silver chain hanging around his neck. "I am a witch." I took a deep breath over that hated word. "You know," I told him, conversationally. "That's the first time I said that out loud." I stepped closer, unafraid—for once. Still, I braced for the pain, I looked at Gary, then Ryan. "If I scream or fall, don't pull him away."

"Cara, I— " Gary started. I cut him off.

"I mean it. We are talking about children's lives, don't stop this no matter what happens. Even if I twitch, yell, or generally weird out. Promise me. Both of you. Promise me!"

They nodded, though neither said a word. My eyes went back to the kid. "What's your name?"

"I already told you, I ain't— "

"Telling me shit, yes, I remember. I guess I'll just have to find out for myself." I placed my palm on his chest. As always, pain bloomed in front of my eyes like an exotic, red flower. Instant and blinding. I gritted my teeth, rather proud of myself for not making a sound.

"Hi Trevor," I gasped. "It's not that nice to meet you." Hearing his name on my lips made his eyes liquify in panic. Ryan shook Trevor forcefully when he tried to pull away from my touch. The boy whimpered on the third shake, going limp in all his joints. I closed my eyes and remembered earlier tonight, during the fight in the library when I touched the gun and used my mind to push at the darkness. I had made the visions dissolve and the feelings retreat.

Now, when the pain came rushing at me, I tried to do it again. I imagined the pain leaving me, flowing out of my body, and going into Trevor. I knew it was working when Trevor started to scream. Long and loudly, the way I had wanted to scream my whole life, he screamed for all the years I had kept my own bottled up. He screamed until I wondered if I might kill him. Together we fell to our knees. My body shook uncontrollably—twitching in all directions like I was being electrocuted—I listened to my broken breaths, my hand on his heart, and Trevor stayed with me in the agony, sharing the pain, somehow lessening it as he did, until I could speak through the crashing waves.

Blood pounded in my ears, the visions came knocking, I braced myself again, then let them through my mental force field. "The knife is still in Rose's neck," I breathed. "I can see a sign: welcome to Falls Park, no littering. They're lighting torches, now she's burning. I can see the killer." I could hear myself struggling to breathe, but I pressed on. "His name is Mason Paul, he calls himself the Raven. Auh!" My free hand grabbed my stomach as a knifing pain took me there. "Rose's blood is on his hands and… singing, they're singing while she burns." My body arched, I could not hold back my own threadbare wail. "Singing. Oh…oh my gods! They're singing while she burns." I sang the words tricking through my mind, words I impossibly knew by heart. "Take us to the place that be, far across the golden sea. From the gates of Tartarus take us away. To live, to die again—in the mists of that fated day." Abruptly, the visions stopped, like an invisible hand had flipped a kill switch. My eyes snapped open and I saw the reason for my light show termination—Trevor lay beside me in a dead faint.

"What did you do to him?" asked Ryan. I thought he sounded impressed rather than afraid.

"I don't know." I rubbed the hand that did the touching, and cradled it against my chest like a wounded thing, it ached something fierce. "I've never done that before, well kinda. Once, ish. Trevor isn't that great of a guy, so it was pretty painful."

"Poor Trevor, I've only heard one other scream like that in my life," said Gary, fuming visibly, looking at me like he had never seen me. "From a man falling out of a building, and he was on fire." He took a step toward me, I gazed up to his dripping face. "Is that how it felt for you?" he asked. "That day by the lake when I held your hand? You cried, pushed me away…and… " his voice dropped to a low whisper. "Is that how it felt? Like falling from a burning building?"

"Yes," I admitted, wishing I could lie. "But, it was you Gar, so it wasn't that bad, not really. We are friends, and aunt Jane is right, you're pure good all the way to your toes." I stood up, my nightgown stuck to my legs and made a sucking sound when I pulled it away. "You have your killer's name. Go get him, and Gar… be safe." Gary looked like he might be sick, as if he had a hundred question for me, yet was unsure which to voice first. I made the decision easy for him. I turned and walked back to the shambles of my home.

I went in the kitchen and flicked on the light. It was worse than the hall. More glass made a path to the little white window over the sink. A cluster of chamomile flowers lay dying on the marble island and an arm still twitched in the center of the floor.

"Stupid thing." I kicked at it, then walked over to the kitchenware drawer and took out a pair of silver tongs. I used them to lift the arm and shove it down the garbage disposal. I flipped the switch on the wall and the little metal teeth in the disposal chomped. They made short work of the rotting bones. I waited till the crunching stopped and the gentle whirr returned. I placed the tongs in the sink, put the kettle on, wiped the mud off a barstool and sat down in the center of my ruined kitchen. I took it all in while my mind tried to assimilate the events of the last few hours. The zombies were not a figment of my imagination. That, at least was a certainty. Hanna was in the forest. Okay, maybe not all of her—maybe she was sitting over a cauldron somewhere, busy projecting her soul across an ocean, or drinking lamb's blood and chanting in old Latin—whatever the case, she had been with me, she had helped. That was another fact. I swam in the lake of souls and kissed the man of my dreams. Those were facts too.

I swung my leg absently until my sore toe stuck something solid. I dropped my head and peered under the island. The Book of Shadows lay on its side in a pile of muddy leaves.

On the stove the kettle whistled. I ignored it and picked up the book.

"How did you get back here?" The book did not answer—even though I half expected it to, it was however warm to the touch. I brushed the leaves off the cover and ran my fingers over the interlocked rings of our family symbol. With a *whiff* and a visible puff of air the book fell open. The page it opened to held a summoning spell—an incantation to bring a lost soul home. I lifted the tip of the page meaning to turn it. The rough paper broke free of my hold and the pages went wild. They shuffled back and forth like a dancing slinky. The kettle screamed and wind whistled through the kitchen. Hoots and howls fell off the pages and whirled around me. One page in particular rippled as a forked tongue licked over it. I let go of the book. It had actually burned me. It smacked down on the island. I could feel myself giving it the stink eye.

"Don't just sit there staring at it. Do something."

The voice startled me. Badly. I jumped, jerking a muscle in my neck. My back went ramrod straight and I spun around, my palms going all clammy.

"You," I whispered, simultaneously shocked and unsurprised. It was a weird feeling. Andi stood ten feet in front of me, her shiny hair looked dull, but her eyes were dark and alert, tragic in her white face.

"It doesn't work if you just stare at it," she told me.

"You're walking," I said, stating the obvious. "How? I saw the blood. Your chest? You were…"

"Stabbed? Yes I know. It's hard to kill an immortal." Andi tilted her head, giving me a moment to recover myself and reply to her extraordinary statement. When I did not, she continued. "Hard, but it can be done." She put one hand on her hip. "Don't give me that deer who has headlights look—surely you have put two and two together by now."

"Deer in headlights," I mumbled.

"What?" Andi's brows arched to her hairline.

"Nothing."

"I can help you," said Andi, I heard her trying to soften her voice. She took a step toward me. I backed up, vividly remembering the pain of her touch. She regarded me, her expression holding equal parts of hope and disdain.

"Why?" I asked, my stance and voice wary. "Why would you want to help me now?"

"Not just now. I wanted to help you remember long before I met you. We came to America for you. Why do you think I gave you that book? You think it was an accident? That's your story, yours and Drake's, and in a way I guess it's mine. I want to help because, even though my brother can be a villain, I love him." She took another step forward. I stepped back and bumped into the hard edge of the marble island.

"And you," Andi pointed a manicured nail at my heart. "You are a part of him, whether or not I like it. You will either be the final death of him, or you will save him. I am counting on the latter. Besides, you need that book. The Nori are after you, and you might not escape a second time."

The girl in my head shuddered, and I felt like crossing myself or throwing salt over my shoulder at the very least. Out loud I muttered, "fourth time."

Andi took another step. I had nowhere to go.

"Don't you want to remember? Aren't you curious? Thousands of souls repeat life, but very few get a chance to remember an old one. Don't you want to know who you are—really are?"

"Yes," I said. It was the truth. "And, no," that was true too. "I've been told, that thirteen days from the day I remember, I'll die. My repetitive nightmares went on for thirteen nights—there were thirteen priestesses in Aphrodite's temple, and there has always been a dark spook around the number thirteen. Call me crazy, but I see a scary pattern."

For a second Andi looked enraged, her lips twisted and the bloodshot stood out in the whites of her eyes. "It's a curse! A stupid curse. Maybe if you had been reborn centuries ago, it might have applied. Not in this century. Here in this time, it is just a stupid curse, and it doesn't matter now, as my mother would say the wheel is already spinning."

"Your mother?" I asked. "You mean Helen of Troy."

"Yes," said Andi. "Yes, that's what I mean. Do the spell, Cara. Remember my brother." She pointed to the Book of Shadows. "There are spells in there that can make a man fall so in love he will cut out his heart and eat it while it beats, and not a single one holds even a tenth of the power to the one cast on you and my brother. Aphrodite cast a love spell on you—unimaginable as that may sound, it's the truth. Her first love spell started a world war, it only got worse with time." Andi took another step and I froze. "Don't you want to remember the love of your life?"

"I don't know," I asked. "Do I?"

Her look drilled holes in me. "You are in another body, thousands of years later, he is a complete stranger to you, and the two of you *still* can't keep your hands off each other, and you—untouched in this life as you were in the last. Draken didn't even know you lived until you called him in your dreams. He heard you and came running. He heard you. All the way across the world, in this house, through all its wards and protections, he heard you. He is the other half of your soul."

Andi reached out to take my hand. It twitched away before I could stop myself, and she froze.

"Look," said Andi, and dropped her hand. "My brother's been searching for you for so many years, I lost count a millennium ago. You are all he wants. Once, many lifetimes ago, you loved him and then you died, a real death, a tragic one. We lived. Over the last few millennia, we have been so many different people, it didn't matter where we went or the company we kept. You have always been the love of all his lives."

I swallowed. Hard. "What happens to me if I remember this dead priestess? What happens to Cara?"

"You may change a little, that is inevitable. It will connect you to a larger portion of your soul. Arias was not my favorite person, but it was never her fault. It was what she represented that scared me. Then, she died and I thought it was over. Your soul was never meant to be reborn." Andi threw her hands in the air, shrieking out an exasperated sigh. "Gaia has a mind of her own and what's done is done. Since I don't see her lurking around, it is up to us to fix it."

"What? Seen who?" I asked, totally confused. "Gaia?"

"Yes, why? Have you?"

"Have I what? Seen Gaia?"

"Yes!"

"No!"

"Well, then?"

"Okay, Andi. Tell me what to do."

■   ■   ■

Andi was crazy, crazy like Alice enslaved to that upside down world, crazy like Snow White who thought she could have her prince, her life and the shiny apple. Okay by me—it was nice to have some company in the rabbit hole.

I studied the wrinkle in her brow as Andi stirred the cauldron. She mumbled words from the book and barely flinched when the potion bubbled up and splashed her soft hands.

"I need your blood," she said, her accent thickening over every word.

"Classic," I sighed. "Fine." I walked over to the knives and chose a cheese knife, with an inlaid pearl handle and a serrated edge. "Gotta say, not a fan of the bloodletting, in the top three worst necessities of spell casting, in my book."

"Yes," said Andi, sounding unconcerned by my plight. "I hate it too." Heat from the boiling pot rouged her face, and a few silvery blonde locks fell over her forehead. I held my hand out over the cauldron, hesitating.

"What?" she threw up one eyebrow. "It hurts less if you just do it."

"I know, it's only..." I turned to face her. She stood about half a head taller than me, and this close to her I had to tilt my head up to meet her eyes. "I have a million questions I want to ask you."

"Cut your hand. Drink the potion and you won't have to. You'll know it all."

Those last words, 'know it all', sounded so ominous it was almost comical. I leaned in closer to the shimmering potion and inhaled. It smelled like honey and rain, sea washed air, and a low winter fire. It smelt like lost memories.

Andi gave the knife in my hand a little nudge. "Blood, Cara. Do it now."

I lifted my hand; held it over the cauldron, then took the knife and pressed the sharp little blade against my palm. I cringed. Sucked in a breath and sliced, the cold metal opened the skin like hot butter, I ground my back teeth to keep in my gasp. My blood ran down the knife and a big drop splashed in the muddy liquid. The cauldron hissed.

"It's finished," she told me. When my blood had stopped sizzling, she went about quickly ladling a generous amount into a coffee mug. She pushed it into my hands. "Drink."

My eyes flew to her face. "All of it?"

"Yes, all of it. I am not positive I got the portions right. We need to make sure it works."

"You've never made this before?"

"No!" her tone was sharp, as if my question had offended her somehow. "I am not a witch! I know what any girl my age knew of flowers and herbs—more than the current world's collective knowledge granted—but I am not a witch. I was always rather terrible at it all."

"Wow, not inspiring a lot of faith here, Andi."

She waved her hand through the air, narrowly missing my face. "I'm sure it is passable."

"Yes! I love staking my life on passable."

Andi smiled. A real one that changed her expression from hard to stunning. I brought the cup to my lips and inhaled the stirring aroma, meeting Andi's eyes over the dewy rim of the mug.

If only I knew then what I know now. If only I knew what mayhem my little action would cause, had known that one sip would alter my life forever, one little choice would take so many lives. Hindsight is always 20/20, but in the present we are blind. The choice was mine, the action was mine, and the hands smeared in innocent blood are mine. Sometimes, I wonder if someone gave me the cup and choice again, knowing what I know, would I still drink it? I often fear the answer is yes.

I lifted the cup to my lips and took a gulp. It was delicious. I took another, then another. Like Snow White or Eve with their apples. Some part of me knew it was wrong, yet I could not stop.

I felt it instantly, that slow slide down my endless tunnel. The world spun in dizzying circles, I saw everything through a kaleidoscope of time and infinite space. Andi receded, the halo of her silver hair the vanishing point of my disappearing world. A face appeared in my colorful tunnel. Drake's face. But it was all wrong. A violent rage twisted the handsome lines of his lips. His pupils pulsed crimson.

"NO!" he roared in the voice of a madman. Strong hands gripped my upper arms and shook my dazed frame.

"Cara, look at me!" More roaring, like the swell of an angry ocean. It hardly mattered, the voice came from so far away and I was busy fading—floating. The grip tightened into bands of steel. It hurt and I whined a little, wanting the pain to stop.

"Andi, reverse it now!" the madman demanded.

"I can't." From the edge of the tunnel I heard her. "It's for the best," Andi told him. "You'll see. Please trust me."

"No." I whispered. Not knowing if they could hear me. Not caring. Drake blurred in and out of focus. The flames in his eyes looked real, they were a forest fire gone wild. I felt a rush of fury at him that added to my dizziness. "You should have told me!" I accused in a weakly fading voice. "How dare you? Have to remember. Have to know."

"No, Cara, you don't," he shook me. "Open your eyes, Cara. Andi, do something." He sounded desperate. Broken. I felt him fall to his knees, his arms encircled my waist and his breath left a ripple of warm chills on my skin.

"You should have told me," I whispered again.

"Androsia!" Drake was begging her now. "Please reverse it. I'll do anything. Whatever you want."

"Oh?" I heard Andi snap. Heard the sharp edges resurface. "Can you give him back to me? Can you go back in time and remove your blade from

Ares's heart?" The venom in her voice changed the colors of my tunnel. They turned menacing and I felt myself burning from the inside out as the spell did what the monsters, flames and darkness could not. It pulled me under. Drake caught my body before it hit the floor.

I was in a forest and Drake held my face between his hands. "Will you love and honor her?" A deep voice from somewhere asked. "I will," vowed Drake. He slid a circlet of gold onto my finger. It was the ring I had found in the forest, the amber-threaded band I had known was mine. A wolf howled and I stood on a snow-drenched mountain top. Through the wash of white flakes falling from the sky I saw two warriors locked in a vicious battle. One held a blade of fire, the other, a sword of ice and glass. They fought under a brilliant sun, battled in the cool light of the moon. Light split the world creating a supernova behind my closed eyes. In the next frightening moment there was nothing—only a blank interval void of time—as if what happened next would change everything. Then, the world fell away and I was everywhere, in every plant, animal and tree. I was in the waves, a speck in the wind, and a brilliant star in the sky. It connected me to it all, and all of it was one.

CHAPTER 16

SPARTA MARCH 13TH, 1202 BC

The flickering lights of a hundred torches bathed the room in a moving, golden hue. My eyes flew open and I jerked my arms. The metal cuffs on my wrists cut in my skin and slid over my fresh flowing blood. I heard myself hiss in pain. Consciousness came to me slowly, and I listened to my panting breaths. Blinking heavy eyelids I took in my surroundings. All around me men in black robes chanted. Their voices ran together and merged into a single, eerie sound.

I saw only Nori, skin peeling off their old cheeks in large chunks. When they sang their blackened lips pulled back, showing me yellowed teeth and rotting gums. Firelight flickered and changed them. Now they had fleshy cheeks, and cracked, purple lips. The chanting continued. I tried to move again, the cuffs grated against my bones, I filled my lungs, then coughed violently. When the dry, heaving cough choked itself out, my flailing calmed, and my limbs settled.

"The circle of the gods," I whispered. My lips moved, though it was not my voice. "Shadows and dust," I continued, and closed my eyes. "Nothing more than shadows and dust. The gods demand it," I chanted. "The gods demand it."

In my dreams the altar had been cold under the naked skin of my back. Now there was no discomfort. It was like I floated atop my body. I looked down at my feet in hazy confusion, gold dust painted my skin and nails, a sheer cloth covered my breasts and hips. *"I've fallen into the past,"* I whispered, and I was the voice in the mind.

"No, this is my present. My fate. My reality," I said out loud in the foreign, nearly unrecognizable voice, that was also mine. My new eyes flashed wildy around the space closing in on me. I was in the center of a circular, golden room. The groveling priests formed a semicircle from my feet to my waist. I watched them turn their backs on me and face the north of the room. On knocking knees they bowed as one, and reached their hands out in supplication, paying homage to… *her.*

The goddess who murdered me in my dreams.

Aphrodite stood on a golden podium bathed in the glow of a thousand stars. Her pale feet were bare, except for three toe rings wrapped in glittering chains, linking to a dark ruby anklet. One leg—long, and porcelain white—showed through a slit in her gown. My eyes moved to her face and I heard my broken gasp, my dreams had not done this goddess justice. Her was hair piled high atop her head, a few escaping curls tumbled down to her bare shoulders. A glittering cloth swathed her slender body, a strand of watered pearls dangled from her slim waist. Blue lights swirled from her eyes and her lips were red as Sleeping Beauty's rose.

A man stepped out from the shadows at her back. Eyes hazy and trance-like, he turned and walked to me. He was naked except for a cloth of gold around his waist. I saw instantly, that this world suited him; my eyes had to adjust to the dazzle of his skin—it reflected the firelight, golden and prismatic.

Drake. I felt my whole soul sag in relief.

"Come, Draken," the goddess purred, her red lips caressing the words. "Come and take my gift to you." Aphrodite threw a handful of petals in the air. Fluttering down, they settled into the imprints his footsteps left in the sand.

"*Asha Aveda,*" the goddess chanted. "*Asha aveda kavar.*"

A shadow loomed over me. It was him. It had always been him. I did not know if it was better this way, or the worst thing ever.

"Draken," I whispered.

"Arias," he breathed. I saw the same gold that covered me, painted his chest and hands. Reaching out he touched my face, ran his trembling finger over the edge of my cheekbone. I felt it. I was the girl in the mind, Arias the girl on the altar, yet somewhere Andi's magic slowly merged the two, and I felt his touch.

Draken buried his face in my neck. "Hades! Arias! You're alive."

I took another deep breath full of wine, dark night air and him. I knew I would die soon. It did not matter; I had feared this moment, now I wondered why? It did not matter because it would be with him—it was always him. At least that part of the ritual was true. Arias's fears had been meaningless. The legend did not lie. The love she felt for this man was very real.

"I prayed it would be you," I told him. "These last few days, I hoped...hoped..."

A hot, wild spark flashed in Draken's eyes, he leaned down until his mouth was a breath from mine. He slid his hand behind my neck and cupped the back of my head, his fingers caressing points of heat on my scalp. "I wanted to kiss your lips the second I saw them," he said. I think he just meant to barely touch his lips to mine, but the moment our mouths met it all changed. He lifted me to him and deeply kissed me. It was an incredible kiss, harsh and passionate, hotter than open flame. My head swam. I clutched his shoulders while his mouth moved over mine in drugging, unfamiliar patterns. I touched his face, lifted my hands and ran my fingers through his hair. He pulled away when we were both gasping for air, and rested his forehead against mine, just like he had done on the cold, muddy earth of Wynter haunt when he took Cara from the lake of souls, and kissed her for the first time. His harsh breaths ruffled the lashes resting on my cheeks.

"They said you didn't drink the venom," he was panting out each word. "Why?"

"I couldn't," I told him. "I wanted to be myself when this happened. I almost drank it, then I remembered Alora, and the truth they won't tell us."

"They who? The priests? The gods?"

"All of them—there is no euphoria in the poison, it's a death sentence." I dropped my voice. "It doesn't matter, I wanted to remember every second of you."

Unshed tears shone brilliantly in his eyes. "Arias, I swore I would not do this to you. The drug was in my wine. I didn't know until it was too late. Tell me what to do, Arias, I'll do anything. Tell me how to get us free of this."

"There is nothing we can do now," I told him softly. "We are under the spell of my goddess. You will literally go mad until you have me, or another woman, but," I looked around me, "considering where we are, I prefer it be me."

Draken groaned, his breath hot on my shoulder. "I can fight this, Arias. I will fight it."

I knew he would try. It was unnecessary. This moment was mine. What I had lived for, and all I would die for. What had come before and what would transpire centuries later did not matter. This fantasy here and now was mine.

"You can't fight it, Draken. It is a love spell made by the goddess of them, even if you could resist it they would kill me anyway."

"I will take us from this place," he rasped.

I brushed the dark hair out of his eyes, then placed a butterfly kiss on his cheek. "No, Draken. I was born for this. I am yours. Your Leisha. I have always been yours." The words I spoke belonged to Arias, yet I meant them with all my heart.

The priests continued their chanting, two of them stood up and threw incense in a flaming brazier. The flames spat out puffs of ocher smoke. A few of them stared at me, a kind of bored fascination lighting up their dull eyes, like they had seen this spectacle too many times, yet could not wait to witness another.

"We will shut them out," he said, and turned my face away from their pudgy grins. "Arias. I will make it beautiful for you."

The altar was large and made for this game. He climbed up beside me and saw my restraints. "I will stop the beating heart of every creature in his room," he growled, and reached up to snap the lock. The steel crumbled under his fingers like styrofoam, and the cuffs that held me fell to the ground. My hands, thus freed grabbed the shift covering my breast and hips, then ripped it away. Draken froze, I heard him swallow hard as he looked at me.

"Please," I whispered. "Please, I want you."

"Gods, you are so beautiful," he rasped, leaning down and kissing me like he could not help it, kissing me until I was dizzy. I could feel the heat emanating from his skin, proof of the drug burning through him. In his dazed eyes I saw colors dancing in the bestial shadows against the wall.

"I dreamed of this," I told him. *Yes, I have,* I whispered in the mind voice that was now my own. *Dreamed of this so many times.*

"This is just a dream," he said. "Just you and I alone, anywhere you want. The gods may be watching, but we don't care. The goddess Selene shields us in moonlight," he kissed my forehead. "You can hear the ocean breaking against the rocks, and you are not afraid."

I reached up and touched his face, the hard line of his jaw, the curves of his beautiful mouth. "I am in the sparkling center of my destiny, I am not afraid, I was born for you, here in this place or any other, I am yours."

Draken kissed me softly cutting off my words, he whispered her name. I wanted him to call me Cara, to speak my own name in this moment of all moments. Of course I could never ask, so I kissed him back, ran my fingers through his dark hair, and reveled in the fireflies floating through my body. "After this is finished," I whispered. "They will take me from you. Give me the venom. There will be no fighting them. The drug that grips you will enter its last phase, you will be dead to the world. Well, for a couple hours anyway. I want you to know," I cleared my throat—it was strange speaking her words and meaning them with my whole soul. "These last thirteen days have been the most beautiful of my life."

"Drug or no drug, they will not take you from me," said Draken, looking at me the way he looked at Cara when he swam with her in the lake, or held her in a haunted graveyard. "How could you imagine I would let someone take you from me now? I can't do this, Arias. When I say the word I want you to run. Don't stop running until you reach Condora. I will meet you there."

"I'll never make it, Draken," I said. "They will kill me. Many wards surround this room. Magic brought you here, only the absence of it will let you leave—we must finish this spell. I don't speak from fear, it is a simple fact. Besides," I traced the full curve of his bottom lip. "What are you going to do? Kill them all? No more talk of running. It is my life or theirs, either way someone dies."

"You think I care if these rotten old fools die? Arias, there is no comparison. Your life is sacred. They should never have been born."

"Draken," I sighed, loving him so much I thought it would burst out of me in words. "Perhaps I will die," I breathed. "Perhaps you will save me. Neither of us in this moment can say for sure. We *can* have this. I have wanted you my whole life, even before I saw your face. I've been yours since birth. Don't take this away from me. Not now. Not here. Take the power Athena will give you—become the god you are meant to be."

My words seemed to take him over his crumbling bridge of sanity, and I saw him submit to the persistent need hammering at the base of his skull. My hands fluttered nervously over his shoulders, his hair brushed my face as my head tossed unconsciously from side to side. He kissed my neck and moved lower, my gasp was a scream.

"I don't know what to do," I said. It was true, I—Cara—had never prepared for a moment like this. "I just..." I had no words. "I want...I need..." My stuttering dropped away when I felt his shoulders shake. I slapped his back. "Are you laughing at me? I'm being serious! I know I am just supposed to lie here and pretend I'm in love… I came here tonight meaning to give the performance of my life. I never expected to actually feel it." I dug my hands in his hair, his lips were hot on my stomach. "Now I want things…gods! I want so many things." I finished in a lame whisper, hardly able to believe the words I was saying.

Draken reached up and ran his finger over my lips. "You're babbling Arias," he said, and kissed me. Kissed me until I felt my skin glow. My fingers dug into his lower back, and he growled against my mouth. He was a creature of pure instinct now.

The muscles of his chest stood out against my hand, I felt the racing beat of his heart, watched his resolve crumble. His hand tangled in my hair and he lifted me up to him. "Are you sure?"

"Yes," I whispered. "Please."

Our eyes locked on his exhale, when he spoke, his voice was low and sincere. "Tonight we alter history, Arias. Tonight Actheron knows the woman in his arms, and he loves her with all his soul."

■   ■   ■

I came back to the world slowly, safe in the circle of his arms. Drake held me so close, as if he could pull me into the grains of his skin by sheer will alone. My chest heaved under my uneven breaths. Beneath my damp cheek the muscles of his right shoulder bulged, his skin was damp and warm. It felt like magic had replaced the blood in my veins, I closed my eyes and reveled in it. He had been mine for hours, my dark stranger, my exquisite god—wild and ravenous—I was his, and for a beautiful space in time—he had been mine. In the afterglow of this dazzling pleasure I knew I would love him for each remaining moment of this life, and every moment of any others.

I knew how this went. I finally remembered it all. Not because of the spell—it was just the vehicle that brought me back to this dark, beautiful place. If time was a whirl rather than a pathway, then what was now, had already been, and what could be, was already ours. Arias, and I just two parts of the same glittering soul. A soul we had joined to this man. Classic that I had to leave my current millennium to lose my virginity. I thought about sharing my observation with Lily, pictured her expression and smiled.

"What is it love?" asked Draken. Words slurring, and a sleepy fog clouding his eyes.

"What?" I purred.

"You smiled," he murmured. "I felt your lips move."

"You did not," I giggled, charmed. Arias loved that side of him—young and playful, eyes full of wild dreams—the side I had never seen. Memories of the past hours glittered across my vision. I saw images in the fine cloud of gold dust still shimmering around our bodies. Draken had tried to be gentle at first, I would have none of it. I wanted him so desperately, it was a fever in my blood. I touched him everywhere, when he finally settled his body over mine, I locked my legs around his waist, and I dug my hands in his hips.

"Do it," I told him. When he hesitated I saw my reflection in his eyes. I barely recognized myself. I was a thing driven wild, each movement fueled by my passionate delirium.

"No. I don't want to hurt you, Arias. It has to be perfect."

"There is no one in the world but us. It couldn't be more perfect." I dug my nails in his lower back. "Draken, now!"

He said my name and kissed me until I felt my veins ignite. Only a flash of pain and it was done. Then, he moved and I lost all sense of anything but him. I looked into his face when it happened, watched as the spell reached its pinnacle, and witnessed Athena blast him with the promised strength. Beams of light shot from his pores and tongues of flames exploded in his wide eyes. He gasped and buried his face in my neck.

"I feel like I would not need Pluto to fly," he panted in my ear. "I feel like…"

"A god," I said, cutting off his words with my lips, I arched my hips to meet his. "You feel like a god."

He was. My lost soul. My god.

"Are we alone?" asked Draken, his foggy voice bringing me back to the present.

"Yes. I don't know when they left. I don't even know how long we have been in this room. They will be back to take me, I remember, Alora…" my words broke off. I would not think of that horrible moment. I would not let Arias think of it. We would state the facts, no supposition, or sorrow. "Now I will drink the venom and go to the mists." I moved even closer, put my hand on his shoulder almost to assure myself he would not vanish. Perhaps, the venom and Arias's consequential death would break the spell and return me to my own time, perhaps not. Maybe I would just float away and it would all be over. I was not sure which option held the greater appeal.

"No, Arias." Draken tried to lift himself up on his arms, find a sitting position he could hold. His muscles spasmed, he gasped sharply, and fell back. "I should never have touched you in this cursed place," he hissed. I saw the effort it took him to open his eyes. I put my arm around his shoulders and tried to help him up. It was like a butterfly trying to assist a panther.

Draken swung his legs over the altar. "Now!" he rasped. "We have to leave now." He stood for a second on swaying legs, before he crashed down to the sandy floor and did not move. His even breaths ruffled the dark curls falling across the side of his face. I bent down and touched his pulse, it beat like a war drum, strong and steady under my fingers. Almost as if they had been waiting for him to fall, the priests filed back in the room. Hands crossed beneath ponderous bellies, and cowls pulled up to hide their faces, they marched in two straight lines reminding me of pallbearers at a funeral. My body tensed wanting to bolt—there was nowhere to run. I was here to relive my own death and it was time.

EPILOGUE: DEATH GOD

IF YOU DIE UNDER A SPELL...DO YOU WAKE IN A DREAM?

A priest grabbed my arm. I tried to shake him off. My right foot kicked him in the gut. I heard his satisfying *ooof* and took a second to smile at it, then a fist crashed into my face. The sound of flesh colliding echoed off the golden walls. Another fist came out of nowhere and struck my jaw. My head snapped back and my vision wavered. Draken's hand twitched and dug in the sand. I thought I saw him struggle to lift his head, but the movement was so small, when he did not move again I suspected it was my imagination. Sweaty hands clamped around my arms and dragged me away. I did not resist. They continued to pull me to the far side of the room and my body bumped against the uneven ground, while my heels cut grooves in the sand. When the priests felt there was enough distance between us, and the sleeping god, they stopped. Grunting and snorting, one of them lifted me into a kneeling position, another grabbed a handful of my loose hair and yanked my head back.

It would happen now. I watched the first golden drop of poison fall in slow motion. I felt the body I was in, surrender. My head fell back, my lips parted obediently, making a waft of musky air rush down my tired lungs. I clamped my mouth shut and shook my head. "No." I whispered, whether I spoke to myself or the poison-wielding priests, I could not be sure.

"Quiet now," said the hair puller. He tightened his grip, twisting my head back until I thought my neck might snap. A different priest grabbed my chin between his fat fingers and shoved a pudgy digit between my lips.

"Open, girl," he said.

"*NO!*" I threw my head back. The base of my skull smashed against the hair grabber's nose. I heard a resounding crunch. He fell, squealing in pain, taking a chunk of my hair. I barely felt it. My veins pumped hot adrenaline, flushing my mind with the soul-consuming desire to live. Another fist rushed at me, I saw it seconds before it connected to my cheek. I ducked, and the swing sailed harmlessly over my head.

"Draken!" I screamed. "Draken! Wake up!" A hot hand clamped over my mouth, cutting off my cries. I had no time to take my next breath before a sweat soaked priest tackled me to the ground.

"Hold her!" one of them growled, his vile breath coasted over my face. Hands grabbed at my legs, wrestling them into submission. I bucked and shouted denials, one of them caught my wrists, locking them firmly them above my head.

"Arias?" Draken called out, sounding drunk but conscious. I opened my mouth to scream his name. A hot stream of poison came rushing in. The venom coated my tongue in a sticky paste. I coughed and spat but it was too late. It cut a burning path down my throat, making it constrict. I swallowed hard. Coughed and swallowed again.

It was done.

It tasted horrible, shuddering in revolsion I lifted my head, easily finding the dark shape of Draken despite my hazy gaze. He was on his knees, his body swayed in looping circles, both hands pressed against the sides of his head as if trying to hold it in place. He blinked in dizzy confusion; I watched his eyes narrow as he tried to make sense of the spinning room, when they came to rest on me—his body went deathly still. I looked up to the sweaty faces of my killers and smiled—brilliantly. This was it, the fight scene, the piece of the trailer that made you watch the movie in the first place. I only hoped to live long enough to see my god kick all their asses. I did not need to have 'Blood and Shadows' open in front of me to know how this was going to play out. In Drake, I had seen first hand the wild streak of violence he kept carefully leashed; this was another place and a different time, there were no restraints here.

My eyes returned to the face of the priest who still held the empty bottle of poison in his hand. "You're all about to die," I told him softly.

Sweat puddled in the deep grooves cutting across his furrowed brow, big drops of it tangled in his sparse lashes and pooled in the red hollows of his beady eyes. He leaned closer, a sneer twisting his purple lips. "We are not the ones gulping down venom, child."

"No," I agreed. "You'll all still die before I do." The priest leaned back and spat in my face. It was hot and ran down my cheek in a long, goopy string, like a dying snail broken free of its shell.

I spluttered. "Oh my god, that was so disgusting—" he raised his hand to smack me. The hit never came. Draken caught the hand mid-air, lifted the priest off his sandaled feet, and hurled him across the room. His rotund body hit the base of my altar and made a crunching sound. He twitched, then all movement died.

The hands holding my wrists locked above my head shook, making my whole body tremble. Draken reached the priest in one stride, grabbed the front of his robes, swung the man full circle over his head, then smashed his face against the packed sands. Red blood, thick as mud spewed when the priest's face burst apart. The two priests holding my legs squealed. One let go, shuffled to his feet, and turned to run. Draken's hand shot out and into the man's retreating back. The priest wailed. Draken twisted his hand and ripped out the man's spine. There was a small *whoosh* followed by a sound like popping corn, and Draken dropped the strand of shattered vertebrae at his feet. Then he was on his knees and lifting me in his arms, cradling me against his chest. He touched my mouth and his fingers came away smeared in yellow venom.

"I drank the poison," my voice was the barest whisper of a breath. "I'm so sorry. I tried not to. I tried."

"No!" Draken's cry of denial broke against my lips, he kissed me deeply, like his kiss could take back the damage already done. "It will be alright, Arias," he pulled away from my mouth, kissed my forehead and my swelling cheek. "I won't let you die."

"It doesn't matter now," I said. "I got more from life than I ever expected. I meant what I said before—even if the ending never changed, I wouldn't trade the last thirteen days of my story for any other life in the world."

A tear ran down his cheek, I caught it on my fingertip.

"Don't, Draken," I said, rasping over the hot poison that scorched my throat. "Don't cry. I'll always stay near you, even in death."

Draken lay his head against my heart; his shoulders shook while I threaded my fingers through his hair, whispering how much I loved him. Some of the words belonged to Arias—some of them were mine. To our left, I heard the little patter of approaching feet. Draken lifted his head, his burning eyes found my few remaining assailants. He leaned in their direction and roared. One priest pulled a shot of bravery from a hidden, smelly place, he darted at us, a chunky chain swinging from his hands. Draken did not move or try to dodge the attack, he simply set me down, reached up and ripped out the man's jugular. A soft gurgle, a blood-drenched moan and the priest died.

I felt a rush of air on my face, and for a beautiful second, a swirl of twinkling blue lights engulfed me. Then, a figure formed in the center of the sparkles and turned beauty into terror. It was her, of course. My dreams already told me how this novel ended, the minions had failed, so the queen was here to take my heart.

Aphrodite moved with breathtaking speed. In seconds, I was back on my altar, the cold surface made chills rush over my naked skin. I fell back panting; eyes wide, staring in pure shock at the goddess hovering above me, a luscious smile curving her lips, a knife poised over her head. "He will not save you, you are mine," she said. I looked away from her and kept my eyes on Draken. He ran to me, but there was no chance. The goddess knew it and so did I. Aphrodite whispered in my ear.

"Asha avda, meshia envier
Karat me mortando,
Teresa dianda miyha Leisha encada."

"You will love him in the mists," she told me, and brought the blade down. I felt piercing pressure and a bright flare of pain, then I heard my ribs crack a second before her knife pierced my heart. I screamed his name. It was a scream tore from the depths of my soul. A scream of denial, pain, and a loss so terrible it would be felt for always. Up went another swirl of blinding sparkles and Aphrodite was gone. The only proof she had existed at all was the bone knife still vibrating in my chest.

I'm dying, I thought, realizing this in a strange distant sort of way. Not too terrible, kind of like falling into one of my visions or blacking out. Draken was beside me in an instant gathering me in his arms, crying denials, shouting his rage at the golden dome and the stars beyond. Screaming my name until blood vessels burst in the whites of his eyes. I used the last of my strength to lift my hand and touch his cheek, he turned and kissed my palm.

"I know you will say I haven't known you long enough," he rasped, tears making his voice thick. "I know you would tell me it's impossible, but there is nothing left for me if I lose you. It's not just a love spell, without you I will be a dead heart inside a living body," his voice broke. "I think you are here to save me. Please don't leave me. Please, Arias, look at me—don't leave."

    I wanted to tell him I loved him, to assure him I would never leave. Blood saturated my lungs, and just like in the dreams, all I can do is choke on my gulps of air. My heart in my eyes, I stared into his soul and took my last breath.

■ ■ ■

The sound of my dying breath went through Draken like a blunt dagger. A small drop of blood trickled down my chin, he kissed it away and held his breath, moving his mouth to mine. For a time, we stayed like that—lips touching, while my soul lifted from my body. I was like the aunts now—a ghostly spector—nothing to do but watch the sad tableau unfold.

    For days, he had told himself he would let no one take me from him. He wanted to scream out in denial at what had apparently been a hideous lie. The few living, left the room. Now, it was just him and his dead. The ones he had killed, for the one he had failed to save. None of it felt real. Shaking, barely able to keep his footing, he stood, my limp shell cradled in his arms.

    Draken walked, no direction in mind. He only knew he needed to take me from this place. Take me away like he should have done in the beginning, before the drug and the spell, before I melted in his arms and stole the last pieces of his heart. My face was pale in the waning firelight, lips slightly parted and painted ruby with my blood. The priest who had stolen his focus—right in that crucial moment—lay sprawled in front of the arched doorway. Light from the dying braziers and torches stuck into the cave walls, spilled through the entrance; pouring onto the priest's bald skull, illuminating the chain still clutched in his paw. Death twisted his neck, exposing the yellow folds of fat seeping from a gaping hole where his throat had once been. A split second distraction and he had lost me. All color had drained from his world when I died, now he saw only harsh shapes broken by slashes of black and white. Draken looked again at the body of the dead priest and wanted to kick it. Wanted to know if the body would explode when it hit the wall. I felt him, in my soul. I heard all the thoughts in his mind like they were my own. When he left the golden chamber my ghostly form trailed after my dead shell.

We stepped into the open night, movement in the air funneled through me and swayed my shifting body from side to side. Draken raised his head to the stars and let loose a screaming whistle, in seconds a braying came back at him through the foggy rain.

"PLUTO!" he shouted and ran to the Pegasus. My limp body dangling from his arms and my head flopping against his shoulder. Draken grabbed a fistful of mane and vaulted us onto the horse's back. The ebony monster breathed out a long whine of welcome and kicked his hooves against the ground. He could smell the blood on Draken's face and feel his fury, I knew Pluto sensed the rush of the kill. Over our heads an owl screamed.

"Fly, Pluto," Draken urged, digging his heels in Pluto's muscled stomach, and locking his free hand in the thick mane. "Give me all your speed. Fly like the wind."

The massive Pegasus spread his wings. Man and beast broke from the ground, their bodies moving together like a single unit. Draken cradled my face in one cold, rain soaked hand and lifted his head to shout at the thrashing sky. The sound of his rage so loud, I was sure somewhere beneath us the earth quaked.

"I will not accept her death," Draken told the stars and the gods hiding among them. "I will not lose this soul. Athena, I chose her. Do you hear me? I CHOSE HER!" His voice crested, reaching a volume that far surpassed any human capacity. "I am bastard son of the death god. Do you hear me Hades?! *I chose her! WILL NOT LET HER GO!"*

His voice faded away as we flew through the dark sky, I felt and saw it all. Somewhere in my mind I knew Drake had picked me off the floor of Wynter Manor and carried me to my room. He lay me in my bed thousands of miles and years away, and I found myself living simultaneously in two separate times, in both of them I was in his arms. Dead or alive, it was where I wanted to be. This was my destiny, if the past thirteen days had taught me anything it was that you can not run from destiny. Here in this time I was weak—taught to die—in my own time I had learned to survive. My head lying on his chest in both worlds, Arias and I whispered our thoughts, and *I* prayed some part of him could hear me.

"We are not just a pair of unlucky lovers anymore," I told him, I told the listening gods. "The world is different now and I am stronger, the old ways are nothing more than ancient dreams."

To be continued…

ABOUT THE AUTHOR

Author, dreamer and wild child extraordinaire: JP Roth is an American Novelist, and owner of Rothic comics, founded in 2012, through which she has produced and published five of her original series. JP Roth lives in Long Beach, CA with her beautiful family, and their adorable Bichon Frise.

Her days are spent writing fanciful stories, walking on the beach, and attending comic conventions across the globe. While JP Roth enjoys travelling to exotic locations, she admittedly prefers to stay home, wrapped in a soft fluffy blanket, drinking tea and penning her next novel.

NOTE FROM THE AUTHOR

Word-of-mouth is crucial for any author to succeed. If you enjoyed *Ancient Dreams*, please leave a review online—anywhere you are able. Even if it's just a sentence or two. It would make all the difference and would be very much appreciated.

    Thanks!
    JP

Thank you so much for checking out one of our
Young Adult Fantasy novels.

If you enjoy our book, please check out our recommended title for your next great read!

Manufactured Witches by Michelle Rene

2019 Maxy Awards "Runner-Up Young Adult"

"A masterfully woven story pulsing with the multi-colored heartbeat of magic and acceptance." Jesikah Sundin, multi-award-winning author of *The Biodome Chronicles*

View other Black Rose Writing titles at
www.blackrosewriting.com/books and use promo code
PRINT to receive a **20% discount** when purchasing.

Lightning Source UK Ltd.
Milton Keynes UK
UKHW011838200520
363522UK00001B/13